Little Girl Blue

Other novels by David Cray

Keeplock
Bad Lawyer

Little Girl Blue

DAVID CRAY

An Otto Penzler Book

———————

CARROLL & GRAF PUBLISHERS
NEW YORK

LITTLE GIRL BLUE

Carroll & Graf Publishers
An Imprint of Avalon Publishing Group Inc.
161 William St., 16th Floor
New York, NY 10038

Copyright © 2002 by David Cray

First Carroll & Graf edition 2002

Library of Congress Cataloging-in-Publication Data
is available.

ISBN: 0-7867-0943-X

Printed in the United States of America
Distributed by Publishers Group West

To the Reader:

Although my novel, *Little Girl Blue*, does not concern itself with terrorism, several pivotal chapters are set in lower Manhattan, blocks from where the towers of the World Trade Center once stood. Given the length of time between the writing (*Little Girl Blue* was completed in October 2000) and the publication of books, I'm sure my situation is far from unique. Nevertheless, I feel obliged to make a statement.

I love the city of my birth, the city in which I continue to live, every greedy, grimy, glorious inch of it; my sense of violation could not be more profound. Nor can I overstate the gratitude and respect I feel for the cops and the firefighters and the paramedics who gave their lives in those stairways. It is to these men and women, and to their wives and their daughters and their husbands and their sons, and to all the grieving families whose tears now flood our hearts, that I respectfully and humbly dedicate this book.

One final note. In the year 1835, a great fire swept through lower Manhattan. Driven by high winds, the fire raged for two full days. More than six hundred buildings were utterly destroyed, including the Merchant's Exchange. A year later, five hundred new buildings had risen from the ashes and the city was again marching north.

Keep the faith.

David Cray, September 20, 2001, New York City

1

WHEN LIEUTENANT JULIA BRENNAN pushed through a semicircle of uniformed cops to view the body for the first time, the words *Little Girl Blue* jumped into her mind as if they'd been crouching in her unconscious, patiently awaiting an opportunity to catch her unawares. She brought her gloved right hand to her mouth, though she hadn't spoken aloud, but was unable to withdraw the words, or even to stop thinking them, because the body was, indeed, the milky blue of the winter sky above Central Park. It was the body of a little girl as well, curled into a fetal position beneath the folded leaves of a wintering rhododendron.

"Ain't this a shame, loo? Ain't this a shame?"

Julia turned from the body to find Detective Albert Griffith standing alongside. He was shifting his weight from one foot to another, biting at the edge of his lower lip. Griffith was a deeply religious black man, had been, as he put it ". . . church-raised by my Auntie Bernice."

Julia looked back at the girl. Maybe eight or nine years old, she wore no clothes, not even shoes or socks, and her hair was matted with dried leaves and clods of dirt. The soles of her feet were also dirty. They appeared to be abraded, as if she'd walked or run some distance.

"You look around?" Julia asked.

"The ground's froze up. There's no trail. Nothin' obvious, anyway."

Julia sighed. "I was hoping for a dropped wallet," she admitted. When Griffith didn't respond, she quickly added, "They're gonna be screaming for blood. The brass, the mayor, the press, the public." A frigid gust of wind rattled the dry leaves of the rhododendrons and Julia instinctively hunched her shoulders. "Us, too," she added. "We're gonna need this one, too."

At five feet ten inches tall, Julia Brennan was able to look her subordinate in the eye. Griffith had been a part of C Squad, Manhattan North Homicide, for the five years she'd been its supervisor. There'd been some friction at first (whether more or less than would have been aroused by an equally young, equally ambitious male she couldn't be sure), but it had disappeared when C Squad's clearance rate, mediocre when she'd come on board, rose to compete with those of the top squads in the city.

"How you think she got here, Bert?" Julia asked.

Griffith caught his lower lip between his front teeth, then shrugged. "Could'a walked. Could'a been carried."

"But not driven."

"Uh-uh, not driven. Can't see it, lieutenant. Not unless there was two of 'em."

Julia nodded. Central Park's nearest east-west transverse road was almost a quarter-mile from where they stood, and Central Park Drive, which traced an irregular ellipse within the park, lay two hundred yards to the west, as did Fifth Avenue, the nearest city street. Because there was no legal parking on any of these roads, it was extremely unlikely that the perpetrator—if there was a perpetrator—left his vehicle unattended for the time it would take to carry the girl to where she now lay, then return.

"What about a car? Could she have jumped out of car, maybe coming down Fifth Avenue? What if she was snatched somewhere else, then escaped? If her abductor wasn't somebody she knew, he just might let her go."

Detective Frank Turro, Bert Griffith's partner, came up alongside them. "The ME's here," he announced. New to the squad, Turro was six months short of his third decade on the job. He'd been sent over from Queens Homicide after Julia arranged the transfer of C Squad's most notorious fuckup. From what little Julia had seen of him, Turro could be relied on to do what he was told but lacked initiative.

"Already?"

"What could I say, loo. Somebody must've got him motivated." Turro's breath whitened the air in little bursts. "Also, Chief Flannery's waitin' for you on Fifth Avenue. In his Lincoln."

Chief Linus Flannery was the Manhattan North Borough Commander, a man more at ease with a flow chart than an investigation.

"Is he alone?"

"He's with Clark."

"Great."

Linus Flannery's protégé, Harry Clark, was the Manhattan North Detective Commander. In theory, he reported only to the Chief of Detectives; in fact, he was a notorious sycophant who sucked up to any superior officer. Thus, if Flannery said, "Bring me a suspect in ten minutes," Clark would check his watch.

Assistant Medical Examiner Solomon Bucevski, a cigarette dangling from his lips, trundled up to stand alongside Frank Turro. Bucevski had only recently immigrated to the United States from Moscow, where crime had skyrocketed after the breakup of the old Soviet Union. Unimpressed with the virtues of democracy at the best of times, he stared at the corpse through narrowed eyes, then muttered, "Whoever does this, you must to kill him."

TEN MINUTES later, Chief Flannery echoed Bucevski's sentiments. "This scumbag oughta fry," he declared. "They oughta bring back crucifixion for this scumbag."

Julia's gaze lingered on Flannery's tiny mouth. Somewhere along the line, he'd learned to speak without exposing his teeth, as if protecting a toothache. She wanted to ask him if he'd been to the scene, maybe approached the victim, contaminated the search area, but ever mindful of the relationship between discretion and valor, kept her insubordinate tongue in check.

Harry Clark spoke up from the front seat of the Chief's midnight-blue Towncar. "We been to the scene," he announced, "We snuck a peek before you showed up."

"We were in the neighborhood," Flannery explained. "Coming from Mass at St. Pat's. We do it every month." He cleared his throat. "The Holy Name Society."

A rebuke. The Holy Name Society was the largest of the job's fraternal organizations, and though dominated by Irish cops, included Germans, Italians, and Hispanics in its membership. Julia was Irish, at least nominally Catholic, and a member of the Holy Name Society, but she neither attended prayer meetings nor made the monthly mass. Even for a climber like herself, the NYPD's fraternal societies were a bit too fraternal. There were the little digs at the monthly dinners, the offhand references to "femiNazis," the dirty jokes once the drinks began to flow. After a while, no matter how strong your stomach, how thick your skin, it got depressing.

"We can't be sure it's a homicide," Julia finally said, hoping to change the subject, maybe get to the point.

"You think she was takin' a walk?" Flannery's chortle quickly became a phlegmy cough. He lowered the window to his right and spat onto the sidewalk.

"We can't be sure," Julia insisted, "that we're looking at a homicide."

"And what," Clark asked, "leads you to that conclusion, lieutenant? Exactly what?"

"The fetal position. It looks to me as if she lay there for some time, trying to conserve body heat, and the soles of her feet are abraded. I think she might have walked into the park."

"It's January, for Christ's sake." Flannery glanced out the window as if the date was somehow in question. "It's gotta be what out there?"

"Ten degrees," Clark dutifully responded. "Fifteen at the outside."

"I mean, if she was only cold, why didn't she just walk out of the park and ask somebody for help?" When Julia replied with a shrug, he continued. "We want you to brief the reporters."

Clark laughed, "But we don't want you to tell them anything."

"Anything," Flannery corrected, "you don't *have* to tell them. Understand, lieutenant? We may have a formal press conference late this afternoon."

RELEASED, JULIA walked south on Fifth Avenue, from Seventy-sixth Street directly across from the crime scene to the Seventy-second Street transverse road running from Fifth Avenue to Central Park West. Then she retraced her steps and continued on to Seventy-ninth Street and another transverse. The townhouses and apartments on this section of Fifth Avenue, directly east of the park, were among the most expensive in the city. Not only did every apartment building have a doorman, most of them also had surveillance cameras mounted on the outer walls. The doormen would have to be questioned, the tapes viewed. If Griffith wasn't already on top of it, she'd bring him up to speed when he got back to the station house.

There was nothing more to do at the scene, but Julia lingered on Fifth Avenue as the words *Little Girl Blue* again forced their way into her thoughts. This time, however, she resolutely pushed the words away, telling herself to be a professional. Telling herself, You can't bring them back to life.

When Julia had first come on the job, nearly twelve years before, she'd believed that her sex would protect her from the most soul-deadening aspects of her profession. Now she understood that it was not possible to acknowledge even the smallest part of the misery that pervades a cop's workday. You either harden or find another line of work. That was why cops, though overwhelmingly Christian, have such contempt for bleeding hearts. If cops, including herself, were to allow the slightest tear in the armor that protects their own hearts, they would lose every drop of blood in an instant.

Inevitably, because she hadn't quit, Julia had toughened. Her husband, Sam Brennan, had been first to pick it up. "You look at me," he'd complained, "as if you were trying to make up your mind about something. You look like you're waiting for me to make a mistake."

Poor Sam. He'd married his high-school sweetheart, the compliant blonde who'd cheered his exploits, both on the athletic fields of Bayside High and in the back seat of his father's Cadillac; adjusting to the woman she'd become was beyond him. As for Julia, there was no going back for her either. Instead, in the years following her divorce, she'd advanced from sergeant to lieutenant, from patrol to detective. Only a week before, she'd been notified that she'd ranked twelfth on the captain's exam and was likely to be promoted within the next couple of years.

A celebratory dinner with the woman Julia had come to think of as her "rabbette," Deputy Chief Bea Shepherd, had followed the formal posting of the list. They'd met at the Hudson Cafe, then lingered for nearly two hours. As far as Julia could remember, at no point had they discussed the virtues of law enforcement or the historically low crime rate. Instead they gossiped about the job through cocktails, exchanging rumors and anecdotes, then moved on to their ex-husbands, their children, boyfriends past and present.

A SHARPLY spoken *"Damn you"* drew Julia's attention. A middle-aged man in a cashmere overcoat was shaking his fist at a retreating taxi. The man looked at Julia, his jaw thrust forward as if he expected her to offer some objection to his display, then strode beneath the canopy fronting an apartment building, through a glass door held open by a uniformed doorman, and into the lobby.

As the door closed, Julia became aware of her huddled shoulders. As a general rule weather was something you learned to ignore, but the cold was now reaching down into her chest. Her feet, even in fur-lined boots that rose almost to her knees, were cold enough to hurt. Still she lingered; still the words rose into her consciousness. *Little Girl Blue.*

There was a song, she remembered, called "Little Girl Blue," but it was a sad song about someone a lot older than ten, a love song. Plus, there was the nursery rhyme, Little *Boy* Blue, a very sad poem as well.

Julia stamped her feet. She'd been an ambitious cop long enough to know that high-profile crimes, the kind that make careers, are usually stolen away by even more ambitious superiors. She would have to fight to protect her interests and it was past time to get on with it. As if to confirm her judgement, a FOX-TV news van slid into the bus stop on the Central Park side of Fifth Avenue. A moment later, a CBS van followed. Julia didn't wait for the doors to open. She turned her back and quickly marched off toward Madison Avenue, her unmarked department Taurus, and her cell phone.

A T NINE o'clock on Sunday morning Julia started the Ford, turned on the heater, and settled down. As she waited for the engine to warm, she watched a man and a woman, trailed by a pair of young girls, march north along Madison Avenue. The family was dressed for church, the girls in hooded yellow parkas and patent leather shoes. The younger of the girls had a runny nose, which she wiped with the sleeve of her coat.

"That's disgusting, Annie," the older girl remarked.

Annie's mouth curled into a defiant grimace. "I don' know whatta do," she insisted.

"Can you spell *handkerchief*?"

"No."

Inside her Taurus, with the heater pushing warm air across her ankles, Julia made two phone calls. The first was to her mentor, Bea Shepherd. Bea listened patiently as Julia explained the situation, then asked, "What do you want here?"

"I want the case."

"There's only two ways you get to keep the case, Julia. You make an arrest within the next seventy-two hours, or your investigation goes nowhere. If it looks like the job's gonna be embarrassed, like the case *can't* be put away, Harry Clark will leave you to swing in the breeze. Count on it."

"I don't care, Bea. I want the job. If Clark decides to organize a task force, then I want a piece of the task force. What I don't want is to be cut out."

"Duly noted." Bea Shepherd's voice carried a wistful undertone. If Julia chose not to follow her advice, Bea Shepherd would not be held responsible when things turned out badly. "Anything else?"

"Don't get pissed off, Bea. I'm a detective, remember? I *asked* for the detectives."

"And I advised against that as well."

"True enough." Julia paused long enough to be sure Bea had nothing to add. Despite the negativity, Bea had a vested interest in Julia's remaining with the case. Julia would be Deputy Chief Shepherd's eyes and ears in an environment where knowledge and power were as intertwined as the bodies of copulating snakes. "There's something else," she said, pleased to note that her voice was steady. "I need to reach someone in Sex Crimes, maybe in the DA's office. Somebody I can talk to if I need help."

"Sex Crimes? What makes you think you're looking at a sex crime? Why couldn't she be emotionally disturbed, maybe retarded? Why couldn't she be running away from physical abuse? Why couldn't . . . By the way, Julia, do you have a name for this kid yet?"

"Little Girl Blue." Julia was sorry for the words almost before they'd left her mouth. Almost.

"That's good. That'll play alongside Son of Sam. The reporters will eat it up." Bea laughed into the phone, then said. "But you haven't answered my question."

"I don't know where she came from, Bea. And I don't know how she ended up in Central Park. I just want to be ready for anything."

Bea drew a breath, then sighed. "Julia, I have to leave. Keep me up to date."

J ULIA DUG Robert Reid's number from her phone book and quickly punched it into her cell phone. Reid, Julia's uncle, was the dean of New York reporters. His column, *My Town*, had been running in the *Daily News* longer than anyone cared to remember.

When Reid answered on the third ring, Julia said, "It's me, Uncle Bob."

"Julia," Reid replied without hesitation, "got something good for me?" After decades of near-legendary boozing, Reid's voice was little more than a hoarse rasp, despite his having cleaned up his act five years before.

"A body in Central Park near East Seventy-sixth Street. A child."

"White?"

Julia swallowed, then replied, "Yeah, she's white."

"She?"

"A little girl, maybe eight or nine."

"How'd she die?"

"Don't know yet."

"I'm not getting this."

"She's naked, Uncle Bob, and there's no sign of her clothing."

"Ah."

2

FATHER JEAN Lucienne turned to the congregation and spread his hands. *"Ite, missa est,"* he said. Go, the mass has ended.

Peter Foley, from his place in the choir loft, responded, *"Deo gratias,"* then rose to put on a gray car coat, a tweed cap, and a pair of lined leather gloves. Having long ago accepted the fact that his fellow parishioners were drawn as much to Holy Savior's clubby atmosphere as to the Latin rite it espoused, Foley usually forced himself to join the buzz of conversation that followed Sunday mass. But on this particular Sunday he had an appointment that left him no time for more than a nod and a smile as he snatched his briefcase, then made his way down the stairs and out onto East Eighty-first Street.

A moment later, after quickly shaking Father Lucienne's hand, Foley was heading west toward Central Park, covering the ground with long casual strides. At 41, he stood an inch-and-a-half above six feet and kept in shape by throwing himself whenever possible into the seemingly endless stream of pedestrians making their their way along the sidewalks of Manhattan. These hikes meant at least as much to Foley as the masses he attended several times each week, and there were moments when he felt himself pulled forward by the flow as if weightless, a twig on the surface of a river. Then he might walk for hours, from neighborhood to neighborhood, weaving around slower pedestrians until the solid ache in his legs drew him once again to the specifics of flesh and gravity. Until fatigue made sleep again possible.

On this occasion, however, with a destination in mind and barely enough time to get there, Foley was too preoccupied with his coming appointment to appreciate the joggers, the cyclists, and the in-line skaters who'd braved the cold to display their skills on Central Park's inner drive. He was unaware, too, of the bright winter sun, though he often came to the park in winter to escape the shadowed sidewalks. He thought only of Wallace Carpenter, and the investment he, Foley, had already made in the man. Now it was crunch time.

I T TO O K Foley forty-five minutes to cover the three miles between Holy Savior and the Paradise Diner on Tenth Avenue and Thirty-ninth Street. The Paradise was a typical New York coffeehouse: Formica tables, Naugahyde benches, an acoustical drop ceiling, water-stained in the corners. Beneath a plastic dome, a half-consumed peach pie leaked glutinous filling onto a greasy aluminum pie plate.

As Foley entered, a young woman bearing a stack of menus approached him. She wore a tight green skirt over lumpy hips and spoke in a distinctive Greek accent. Her face was very broad across the top, then narrowed to a tiny pointed jaw below which an incipient double chin swelled ever so slightly. "One for breakfast? There's room at the counter."

"I'm meeting someone."

The hostess tossed her hair before stepping around Foley to greet another party. Foley started for the the rear tables, then spotted Carpenter walking toward him.

"Let's take it to the street," Carpenter announced. He was a short, muscular man with a a sharp assertive nose that complimented his feisty manner. "It's too crowded in here."

Outside, Carpenter stared up at the flat cloudless sky as if searching for a message. He shoved his hands in his pockets, then, without looking at Foley, said, "Fucking cold."

"You want to go somewhere else?"

"Like where?"

"You have a car?"

"Yeah."

"We can talk in the car." Foley fixed Carpenter with a noncommittal gaze. "Or we can do it right here."

Wally Carpenter glanced at the briefcase dangling from Foley's right hand. "How much?" he asked.

"How much?" Foley let a touch of anger edge into his tone. "We've been through this, Wally. Too many times. I'm not interested in money."

Carpenter shifted on his feet, then chopped at the air between himself and Foley with the edge of his right hand. He seemed on the verge of a tantrum. "How do I know I can trust you? How do I know?"

"I come recommended. Just like you." Foley opened the briefcase, fished inside for a moment, then withdrew a snapshot and passed it over. The photo was of a young boy, nude except for a San Diego Padres baseball cap with a rounded brim. The boy had been posed with one hand on a cocked hip; his mouth was slightly open, his legs slightly apart. His blue eyes were so utterly without focus that he might have been blind.

Carpenter's eyes narrowed as he drew a sharp breath. It was lust, Foley knew, pure lust and not the cold wind that reddened the man's cheeks and ears. Lust was flooding Carpenter's entire being.

"Tell me what you wanna do here, Wally?"

Carpenter pulled the lapels of his overcoat across his throat. "How much tape you got?"

"Forty-five minutes." Foley smiled, then leaned down to tap the shorter man's chest. "And it's all hot. Every frame."

"Shit." Carpenter's head swiveled from side to side. The nearest pedestrian was two blocks away, but the line of cars pounding up Second Avenue was relentless. They were coming from the Lincoln Tunnel, making their way to the theater district for the Sunday matinees. To Foley, the various traffic sounds, the rise and fall of the engines, the squeal of brakes and the occasional tapped horn, the crunch of wheels dropping into potholes or clanging over metal construction plates, had the inevitability of surf, or of wind, as he imagined it, through a field of wheat.

"Did you drive over?" Carpenter asked, his tone wistful.

"I don't own a car."

"Then we better go to mine." He took a step, muttered, "Ah, shit," then took another, then another.

SIGHING, WALLACE Carpenter reached beneath the seat of his Lexus to retrieve a videotape wrapped in a Gristedes shopping bag. "Thirteen," he said. "Prepubescent girl. Not my bag,"

Foley exchanged tapes, then watched Carpenter settle into the Italian leather seat. "A bit on the ancient side for my taste," he said, "but no problem. I can always trade down. I got a guy takes the Bangkok tour every three months. This'll be right up his alley." He paused, then casually asked, "You ever do the tour?"

"I used to do Honduras, but I stopped about ten years ago. What I heard, them kids all got AIDS." Carpenter put his hand into the stream of air coming from the heater, then turned up the fan. "I got a wife, ya know, and two daughters."

Foley extended his legs until they reached the fire wall. He raised his eyes slightly and smiled. "What I think it's about," he explained, "for me, anyway, is innocence. That's why I don't do the tour. I mean, a pro is a pro, right? No matter how young she is." He went back into his briefcase, plucked a second photograph. "You ever see this one?"

Carpenter stared down at a photo of Peter Foley kneeling beside a young girl, perhaps ten years old. The girl's dark hair was braided on either side. Her lips were full, and spread in a wide grin; her eyes were clear and brown. "I don't know from girls," he said. "From girls, you got the wrong guy."

"I'd give anything to get her back. You ever see her, let me know."

"In life," Carpenter shot back, "you gotta take what you can get, then move on."

Foley was pleased to note the cynical tone, pleased again when Carpenter took a fat cigar from the glove compartment and lit it up. "There's somebody I want you to meet," Foley declared. "Later on, when you're more comfortable."

Carpenter put the car in gear, checked the rear-view mirror. "I gotta go," he said. "I promised to take the kids to the movies."

3

THE ICY wind cut Robert Reid to the bone. It cut through his down parka, through his tweed jacket, through the wool turtleneck and the long-sleeved silk undershirt he wore next to his skin. It numbed his cheekbones and the ridge of bone above his eyes; it curled his toes, shrank his penis, and left him wondering why he'd come to Central Park when he could have remained in his nice warm bed. He was a columnist after all, and not a reporter; he could pick and choose his stories.

Five years before, in quick succession, Robert Reid had lost his two great loves, Mary-Margaret, his wife of thirty-seven years, and single malt scotch. He'd lost them both and had overnight become a diabetic old man nursing a cirrhotic liver, a bad heart, and a prostate the size of a beach ball. He, Robert Reid, who'd once dived from a westside pier in the dead of winter, searching the polluted waters for a .45-caliber automatic rumored to have been tossed there by a killer.

Resigning himself, Reid hunched his shoulders and adjusted his scarf to cover the back of his neck. He'd been to the crime scene and glimpsed the small defenseless form lying in the dirt. The story would play, he was sure of it, a morality tale in there someplace no matter how she came to be in Central Park on a frigid winter morning in January.

A moment later, Reid watched his niece, Julia Brennan, emerge from the Seventy-sixth Street pedestrian entrance to the park, then beckon the knot of reporters (including himself) closer. As always, he was first impressed with her presence. Julia wasn't classically beautiful; her face was a bit too broad and a bit too long, her jaw a bit too assertive. But her narrow, full-lipped mouth was very sensual and her eyes, framed by sharply arched brows, were the impenetrable indigo of the eastern sky just after sunset. Angelic was the word that came to mind when he looked into those eyes, a concept belied not only by a confident physicality and an unflinching gaze, but also by lines of tension at the corners of her eyes and mouth.

Reid listened to Julia begin her prepared statement, then quickly tuned out. A quarter century before, when he'd stepped in to replace his brother, Paul, as her dad, he'd found Julia extremely tenderhearted, a kind child whose charity extended even to her father, a degenerate gambler and a drunk who came home to his family only when he was flat broke. Now there was something hard about his niece, hard and hardening.

The cops, of course, had contributed to the change. Pornography in her locker, obscene phone calls, and off-color remarks—the harassment had gone on for years, but Julia hadn't quit, hadn't to his knowledge even been discouraged. Instead, she'd risen through the ranks, effectively ending the nonsense, a success story with the last chapters still to be written. She'd paid a price, though, and there were times when she wore her isolation like body armor.

GOOD MORNING, everybody. I'm Lieutenant Julia Brennan, Manhattan North Homicide." She waited until the reporters dug out their notebooks and the video cameras were up and running, then continued. "At 7:58 this morning an anonymous caller to 911 reported discovering a body in Central Park. The first uniformed officers responded to the scene at eight-oh-six and the victim, a Caucasian female, a juvenile, was found at eight eighteen. She is presently unidentified and there are no suspects at this time."

For the next ten minutes, Julia fended off nearly every question. The investigation was in its earliest stages. The Crime Scene Unit was still gathering evidence. The Medical Examiner had yet to claim the body. Unidentified meant no identifying documents were found on or near the victim.

As the reporters began to drift away, Julia nodded to her uncle, then walked back to the crime scene where a pair of burly techs from the ME's office were approaching the victim. The older of the two, a short man with a noticeable limp, carried a green body bag large enough to hold an adult. His younger companion, who chewed gum incessantly, pushed a gurney along the footpath closest to the body. When they reached the victim, the younger man collapsed the gurney while his coworker unzipped the body bag. Nearly in unison, the cops working the scene stopped to watch as the girl was lifted and placed into the bag. Her skin, Julia noted, was uniformly purple on her left side and along her left thigh where it had rested against the frozen ground. It was purple on the left side of her face as well, but the color lightened as it crossed her chest and her back, from lavender to violet to a pale, robin's-egg blue.

As if drawing a curtain, the older tech zipped up the bag and the cops went back to work. Bert Griffith approached Julia, his brows drawn up high enough to wrinkle his forehead. "Are we havin' fun yet?" he asked.

"Tell me what we have here," Julia responded

Griffith shrugged. "We got matchbooks, crumpled tissues, candy wrappers, a frozen condom. Look like they been here since the ice age. We got no cause of death, no . . ."

"Bert," Julia interrupted, "you think she walked into the park?"

Always a cautious man, Griffith took his time with the question. His response, when he finally decided to answer, was predictably noncommittal. "Her feet were pretty torn up, loo. Guess she could'a."

Julia turned to face her detective. "We know she died where she was. The lividity was consistent."

"That's Bucevski's opinion."

"Which is also consistent with her having walked into the park."

"Can't deny it."

"So, except for her shoes and socks, was she dressed?"

Again, Griffith was caught off-guard. "You figurin' somebody walked her in barefoot, then stripped her and took her clothes away?" Griffith shook his head. "Why would the perp do that?"

"How do we know somebody walked her in? Maybe she walked in by herself. Maybe she ran into the park. Maybe whatever she was running away from was worse than Central Park on a January night."

"Say that again?"

Julia rubbed her hands together and looked up. The winter sun, hanging just above the highest branches of the trees to the east, caught her eye. She blinked defensively for a moment before turning to meet Griffith's steady gaze. "I've got a bad feeling here, Bert."

"You worry too much, loo. We put her face on the tube, little kid like this, somebody's gonna come forward. Especially if she was snatched, then jumped out of somebody's car."

"Ah, just what I was thinking. The more publicity the better. We'll get her face on the *Today Show,* and *Dateline,* maybe do *Larry King* and *Oprah.* That way, if we don't close the case, the entire country will know it."

Julia turned to find Griffith staring at her, his look frankly evaluating. He (and everybody else in C Squad) knew that she'd recently passed the captain's exam, that she was going places he'd never see, never even visit. "We gonna hold onto this one?" he asked. "We're not gonna give it up?"

"Bert, as far as I'm concerned, there's only two ways this job can work out. Either we break it, or it breaks us."

Though Albert Griffith had spent much of his professional life displaying what he thought of as a great stone face, a face carved from ebony, he broke into a broad, toothy smile at Julia's remark. "Then I guess we'll just have to put it away," he said. "Being that our careers are on the line."

4

IT WAS seven o'clock that evening when Julia finally sat down to a dinner of lemon chicken, steamed asparagus, and wild rice. The dinner had been prepared by Julia's thirteen-year-old daughter, Corrine, a freshman at Stuyvesant High School. Lately, where Julia was concerned, Corry had become almost motherly, as if her own weekday trek from their Woodside home in Queens to lower Manhattan left her with enough time to claim the household chores for herself. Julia found the protective gesture touching, but knew that her daughter was in a transitional stage, no longer a child yet not quite an adolescent. Soon the hormones would begin to flow and Corry would lose interest in cooking and cleaning and the other hundred-and-one chores that keep a household up and running. Lord knew, Julia had tired of them long ago.

They would have a talk, Julia decided as she sliced off an asparagus tip, a negotiation during which they would separate their responsibilities. In the meantime, the chicken was only a bit overdone, the sauce only slightly bland. The rice and the asparagus were perfect.

Robert Reid apparently thought so, too. He was reaching for the platter of rice, trying to control the tremor in his right hand. Julia suspected that he made this effort for her sake, in his own way as protective as Corry. There'd been a time in Julia's life when Uncle Bob and Aunt Mary-Margaret had been her only positive influence; when she'd thought of family, she'd thought only of them. That relationship had reversed after Mary-Margaret's cardiac arrest when Julia had become her Uncle Bob's only family by default. His brother, Paul, was ten years dead, and his sister-in-law, Julia's mother, now living in Phoenix, was far too self-centered to provide support for anyone but herself.

As they ate, Corry went on about the progress of the school play, to be staged for the first and only time in mid-April. Corry was working backstage with the costume manager, Alfonso Cahill, who'd gone nose to nose with student-director Harj Paranian on Friday afternoon. The kids were doing *Grease* this year, and Harj was insisting that the show be set in the present even though everybody else wanted to play it as the period piece it surely was.

"I thought Alfonso was gonna punch him out big time," Corry said. "For real."

Julia looked at her skinny daughter. All arms and legs, Corry had her father's large dark eyes, his strong nose as well. As an adult, her face would have the character that Julia felt her own lacked. "And where were you when this altercation took place? Far away, I hope."

"Please, Mom." Julia shook her head in disgust. "I mean, they're all juniors and seniors. Except for Harj, they don't even notice me."

"Are they blind?" Reid asked. "I was under the impression that Stuyvesant High School was for the gifted, not the visually challenged."

Corry blushed, then changed the subject. "What'd you bring for dessert?" she asked.

"An Italian cheesecake from Veniero's."

"No raspberry tarts?"

"Perhaps one or two."

After the briefest of pauses, Reid launched into a long anecdote about a shylock named Salvatore Marriano who took payment in salted herring from a destitute fishmonger named Bernard Boyle.

"And then," Reid said, his throaty voice barely a whisper, "Salvatore's troubles began."

Julia, who'd heard the story before, felt her attention wander back to her conversation with Bert Griffith. The Central Park homicide had been played up on the radio, while the cable news station, NY1, had aired live feeds from the scene and all three networks had run with the story on the evening news. If it was going to be easy, somebody would have come forward by now. But no one had, and before returning home Julia had assigned her best detective, Carlos Serrano, to review a stack of missing-person reports too large to contemplate.

Julia cut a piece of chicken and brought it to her mouth. Maybe the most curious development of the afternoon was Chief Flannery's decision not to hold a formal press conference. Harry Clark had relayed the news: "For now, we're gonna let 'em sit on your briefing."

Which meant, bottom line, that it was *her* face on the six o'clock, *her* voice on the radio. Her *ass* on the line.

I T ' S A natural," Robert Reid declared to Julia over mugs of decaf in the living room. Corry was in her bedroom, watching television, listening to music and doing homework, all at the same time. "A dead child in Central Park. Doesn't matter where it goes from there. It's party time for the media."

"What if she died from natural causes? Something like hypothermia?"

"You mean, if no crime was committed?" Reid leaned forward to retrieve his coffee cup. Though a Manhattanite to his bones, he felt entirely comfortable in Julia's little suburban house. A flat-roofed cube attached to an identical flat-roofed cube, the house, with its small rooms, small porch, and tiny back yard, embodied everything he ordinarily disliked about New York's outer boroughs. But Julia had filled those small rooms with color from the sofa's floral upholstery, to the art nouveau posters on the walls, to the blood-red carpet in Corry's bedroom. The department-store furniture, including the club chair on which he sat, was meant to be used, so unlike his Central Park West co-op where Mary-Margaret (after the sale of his first book, when the money began to flow) had demonstrated a previously unimagined propensity for the most delicate of antiques. The canopied four-poster they'd shared was so expensive he was afraid to fart.

"What I'm getting at," Julia announced, "is her identity. If the ME decides that she died of natural causes, we won't know if a crime has been committed until we establish her identity. We've released an artist's sketch to the media, but . . ."

"But?"

"But someone should have come forward by now."

Reid sipped at his coffee, then changed the subject. "If I've got this right, you're thinking that she walked, stark naked, into Central Park on the coldest night of the year? You're thinking she did this *voluntarily?*"

"The soles of her feet were abraded and there were pebbles of asphalt imbedded in the abrasions. If she didn't walk barefoot into the park, she walked barefoot somewhere else in the city before she was taken to the park."

Reid arched his back and wished for an aspirin. There were times when the ache in his kidneys was nearly constant. "Before we go any further, do you want me to run with this?"

"Right now, all I want to do is vent." She gathered the coffee cups, rose to her feet. Her uncle was giving her that worried look, his small sad eyes with their drooping lids projecting a concern for her welfare that she'd come to rely on. She stared down at him for a moment, try-ing not to think about how she'd get along if he wasn't there. These days he looked ravaged, as if he'd been on the planet way too long. His features were skewed, the right side of his mouth and his right eye noticeably raised; when he smiled, two lumps formed on his cheeks, like walnuts, and his lips virtually disappeared. "Lemme go refill these. Help yourself to the cheesecake."

When Julia returned, Reid cut a minuscule slice of cheesecake, forked a few crumbs into his mouth, and began to chew thoughtfully. "You really want this case?" he finally asked.

"I do."

"Well, there a problem for you. My highly placed sources within the New York Police Department tell me the glare of publicity is likely to provoke the creation of a special task force. If I was making book, I'd put the odds against your heading it at ten-to-one." Reid pulled himself to his feet. Unknown to Julia (Reid had never betrayed a source, not even to his wife), Chief Linus Flannery, Manhattan North Borough Commander, had long been one of his sources.

"Why don't you let me worry about holding onto the case." Julia took her uncle's parka from the closet and watched him shrug into it. His arms and chest were very thin, his shoulders bony, his once-black beard now a dingy gray. There was a time, she remembered, when he'd been a bear of a man, when he'd taken her on his lap and she'd fallen instantly under his spell. Never mind that her father hadn't been home in three weeks, that the rent hadn't been paid and the phone didn't work, or that her mother was blind, falling-down drunk. In Uncle Bob's arms, Julia felt protected. The stories he'd told her, of crooked politicians and bumbling cops, had charmed her as surely as any fairy-tale. "There is one other thing," she said as he settled a Russian fur hat over his wispy hair.

"And that would be?"

"I don't want the girl tucked into a cardboard box and buried on Hart's Island. I want her to have a funeral and a tombstone that doesn't say, 'JANE DOE/R.I.P.'"

Reid glanced at the small crescent-shaped scar above Julia's right eye. The scar had come from the tip of a mutt's boot less than a week after Julia graduated from the Academy. She'd been knocked to the ground and kicked in the head, but had clung fast to the mutt's leg until her partner came rushing up. Whereupon they'd clubbed the man senseless.

"Am I hearing right? Is the case personal for you?" He removed a fur-lined glove from his right pocket and began to fit it over his hand. "Surely not."

Julia blushed. "She was so little, and she looked so cold. Her skin was blue."

"Blue?"

"Pale blue, Uncle Bob. Like she was reflecting the sky."

5

JULIA WITNESSED the autopsy from beginning to end, from the initial examination of the girl's body, through her gutting, through the inspection, weighing, and sectioning of her internal organs. She heard the plop of each organ as it was dropped onto a hanging scale, heard the girl's scalp emit a wet sucking sound when it was pulled from the midline of the skull and draped over her face as if to prevent her witnessing this particular degradation, the removal of her brain.

Julia watched and heard, thinking it would have been better that she, Lieutenant Julia Brennan, not witness it either. But there she was, standing next to Detective Frank Turro, who had no choice in the matter, a few feet from Assistant Medical Examiner Solomon Bucevski, who wielded scalpel and saw and who also had no choice.

On the other hand, Julia Brennan might have been anywhere else, in her office, in the field, or even at home lingering over a cup of coffee and a burnt Pop Tart. The reason she'd given herself, her reason for coming, that she needed a cause of death and a finding of homicide as soon as possible, she now understood to be pure bullshit. There wasn't going to be a finding of homicide and the cause of the little girl's—*Little Girl Blue*, she might as well say it and get it over with—Little Girl Blue's death would only deepen the mystery. The news was going to get worse before it got better, if it ever got better.

Bucevski gathered the girl's internal organs and dropped them into a blue recycling bag. He placed the bag into the yawning cavity produced by their removal, then began to sew the cavity shut. Bucevski worked quickly, drawing the stitches tight, and the girl's body, what was left of it, rocked slightly from side to side, as if she was trying to rouse herself, to make some comment, to protest this last violation.

"Please to wait in my office," Bucevski said without turning. "And please to not smoke, detective. I am already in big trouble for this smoking in office."

Julia sat alone in Bucevski's office while Turro went out to the street for a cigarette. No doubt he believed her presence to indicate a lack of confidence. She hadn't, after all, looked over Bert Griffith's shoulder as he gathered video surveillance tapes and interviewed the doormen along 5th Avenue. Nor would she review the missing persons reports she'd assigned to Carlos Serrano, though she might order him to go through them again.

Well, she'd just have make it up to Frank Turro. Sometime in the future, assuming he didn't go into a sulk. If he decided to sulk, she'd take him off the case, let him chase somebody else's killer.

Bucevski and Turro came in together, Bucevski going to the chair behind his desk while Turro lounged against the door.

"Alright," Bucevski declared, "I get right down to my business." He swiveled the chair, folded a skinny leg over a bony knee, obviously enjoying himself and his authority. "Here is what we are knowing. Victim is a prepubescent Caucasian female, approximately ten years of old. Trauma to body as following: minor abrasions on chest, abdomen and upper thighs; abrasions containing solid matter including vegetable matter, probably grass, on the feet. All internal organs appear normal with no presence of disease or injury, but vagina and rectum exhibit scarring from previous trauma. Trauma appears to be caused by sexual intercourse, but no sperm is present." He stopped long enough to tug at the knot of his yellow tie, smiling at Turro and Julia in turn. "We cannot be stating cause or manner of death until serology results are coming from laboratory. Girl seems to have died from exposure to elements, but also might to have been been drugged or poisoned. Time of death may be any time on Saturday night. Cold weather makes it impossible to narrow further." He cleared his throat, then continued. "As you have seen, I have taken purple fibers from victim's hair. Examination under microscope is revealing these fibers are long, fine, and synthetic. From drapes perhaps, or bedspread."

Julia listened to the words bubble forth, Bucevski's accent so thick he might have been forcing the syllables around a ball of chewing gum. When he finally wound down, she posed a hypothetical question. "Let's suppose," she said to Bucevski, who lit a cigarette, then flashed Turro a triumphant smirk, "that the victim exited a warm place, a building to the east of Central Park, or even a vehicle. Let's say that she was running. How far could she have come? How long before the cold brought her down?"

"As long as girl continues to run, she maintains body temperature. If distance she can run is one mile, this is how far she is coming. If only one hundred meters, then one hundred meters."

Julia heard footsteps, at that moment, the slap of bare feet on concrete, the steps coming one after another, driven by fear—whap . . . whap . . . whap . . . whap . . . whap. Then the huff of strained breathing, a bellows sharply compressed, opening out, again compressed, the exhalations slightly preceding the footsteps—huh-uh . . . huh-uh . . . huh-uh.

"And when she couldn't run any more?" Turro asked. "What happened then?"

"Then her body temperature drops very fast . . ."

"How fast? We need some numbers, doc."

"If she has exhausted all reserves of energy, if she runs until she collapses, she would become unconscious in two or three minutes."

"Could she wake up again? After that?"

"No. After this, she will die."

DETECTIVE DAVID Lane approached Julia a few minutes after she entered her office. His nose and cheeks perpetually aflame, Lane was a burly, hard-drinking veteran who hated civilians nearly as much as he hated criminals. "I found the spot," he told her, "the spot where she came over the wall. It was obvious, lieutenant. The dirt was scraped away where she rubbed the wall with her chest, and there's an impression, too, of a naked foot with all five toes visible." He shook his head, loosing several flakes of dandruff which drifted from his hairline to his eyebrows. "Those jerks at Crime Scene, they couldn't find their asses with a handful of toilet paper."

That was the another thing about David Lane. He was crude to the very core of his being, a dinosaur who played the bad-cop as if born to the role. Meanwhile, he had more snitches on the street than the rest of the squad put together. David Lane, who closed cases.

"I called those assholes at Crime Scene and *made* them send out a team while I was there. Then, I *watched* them photograph the wall."

"Did you check the camera for film?"

"Lieutenant . . ."

"That's your problem, Lane. You're a fuckup."

Lane managed a smile. More than humorless, he viewed any attempt at humor as a personal affront, which is why Julia provoked him at every opportunity. "The kid jumped the wall," he continued, "maybe three blocks south of where she was found, and she was alone. Nobody followed her into the park."

"It's what we figured," Julia said, "and now we can prove it. Anything else?"

"I canvassed the doormen from Seventy-ninth down to Seventy-second Street, all the way to Lexington Avenue. Last night. Nobody saw nothin'."

"How far do you think she could have come without anyone seeing her? Say at two o'clock in the morning?"

"Fifth? Madison? Park?" Lane named the avenues east of Central Park. "That time of night, you don't see too many pedestrians. But there's always traffic. I don't see how she could have crossed any of those avenues and not been spotted."

"So you think she came from close by?"

"Not necessarily." Lane's smile, this time, was purely malicious, making sure she understood that he wasn't above a little provoking in his own right. "Let's say you're some scumbag of a sleazy cab driver, like from Beirut, and you're working the Upper East Side of the island of Manhattan in the wee hours of the morning. You see this naked kid run across the street, right in front of you, and despite the cultural differences, you know somethin's wrong. That's because it's fucking *freezing*. But you don't stop. Uh-uh. You don't call the police, tell 'em there a little girl runnin' naked on the street. You just keep on gettin' on. Pickin' 'em up, droppin' 'em off." Lane raised a triumphant finger. "Now, lieutenant, when you wake up the next day and find out the kid's dead—the kid you drove by, the kid you left to freeze—what's the chances, out of ten, you're gonna pick up the phone and admit it to the world?"

"Out of ten," Julia admitted, "none. Now do me a favor, tell Carlos I want to see him."

While she waited, Julia swiveled her chair around to face the grimy window. She kept her office as clean as possible, even whipping out a dust rag and a hand-vac from time to time, but she could do nothing about the peeling paint on the walls, or the city's refusal to accept the fact that glass was meant to be transparent. The outsides of the windows were nearly opaque with grime.

"Lieutenant?"

Turning back to find Carlos Serrano standing in the doorway, Julia quickly motioned him to a seat. Tall, slim, and very engaging, Serrano was her best detective, a master of details. That was why she'd assigned him the task of sorting through the missing persons files. The same task, given to David Lane, would stretch into the next millennium.

"What's the good news, detective? You making any progress?"

"Actually, it wasn't as bad we thought it was gonna be. After you eliminate by age, race, and gender, you don't have that many cases left. And the ones you do have mostly involve custody disputes and there's usually a photograph."

"So it's just a matter of going through the open files?"

"That's about it."

"And how many open files would that be?"

"Citywide? Maybe ten thousand."

Julia sighed. The job commanded a budget sufficient to employ forty thousand cops, but couldn't afford a computer system that would allow a restricted search of missing persons files. No shock, though. The job had been neglecting the detectives in favor of patrol for the last fifteen years. "Keep at it," she told Serrano. "It's a base we have to touch."

"Got it." Serrano started to rise, hesitated, then dropped back into the chair. In his forties, his face was well-lined and very strong, especially his nose and chin. "If ya don't mind, there's something . . ."

Julia smiled. "Fire away."

"What I heard, the ME ain't gonna call this a homicide."

"So what are we doin here? Is that the question?"

Serrano returned Julia's smile. "That's it, loo."

"The Medical Examiner's office has no opinion as to the cause or the manner of Jane Doe's death. And it won't have an opinion until the toxicology reports come back from the lab. We're lookin' at a few days."

As Serrano rose, Julia realized that she'd answered the wrong question. It was the one Serrano had asked, but not the one he'd wanted to ask. Like Griffith, Carlos was smart enough to realize that his lieutenant was on her way up. There was no reason for her to hold onto a case like this, a pure headache, a mystery. He wanted to know if the case was being forced down their throats, or if Lieutenant Julia Brennan would cut it loose at the earliest opportunity, or if—by far the least likely of all the possibilities—the case was personal, if she'd go to the wall.

"You see Bert Griffith," Julia said after a moment, "send him in."

Bert's face appeared in the doorway a moment later, fast enough for Julia to wonder if he'd been waiting outside, a kid summoned to the principal's office.

"Any luck with those surveillance tapes?" Julia asked.

Griffith shook his head. "Most have them have been recorded over so many times they're completely black. You can't even see shadows. We're viewing the rest of them, but it's slow going. The only good news is that the tapes are recorded six to one. One second of tape for every six seconds of real time. It's choppy as hell, but it cuts twelve hours of tape down to two."

"Any blocks completely uncovered?"

"Yeah, Seventy-eighth Street. If she came that way, we're not gonna know it." He crossed his legs and sipped from the coffee mug he'd carried into the office. "Something else, loo. For the last couple of hours I've been getting calls from all over the country. From law enforcement, and citizens, too. Seems they think our DOA might be some kid who disappeared six, seven, even eight years ago."

"How many so far?" Julia folded her arms across her chest. She should have anticipated this. To the parents of a child missing for that length of time, any resemblance between their little girl and the sketch released on the prior night, even hair color, would raise long-buried hopes and fears.

"Twenty-eight. With more to come."

"And any one of them could be our victim."

"Yeah, Little Girl Blue."

Though Griffith's expression didn't so much as flicker, Julia was instantly guilty. The *New York Post* had used the phrase to headline their front page: LITTLE GIRL BLUE. Running it over a grainy photo of the ME's techs hoisting a body bag onto a gurney. Bea Shepherd's work, no doubt.

"I'm watching the tapes with one eye," Bert continued after a moment, "taking these calls at the same time . . . I could use some help."

"I'll do what I can. In the meantime, tell the civilians to contact their local police departments. Be nice to them, but firm. Any calls you get from cops, you tell them if they want DNA samples or fingerprints, they should contact the Office of the Medical Examiner. Give them the number, then get them off the phone. We're talkin' about kids who've been missing for a long time."

"Gotcha," Griffith rose.

"Good. Is Frank Turro in the house?"

"No, he's still out canvassing." Though Bert Griffith's expression remained grave, his black eyes glowed momentarily as he delivered a parting comment. "Him and the two uniforms you gave him to help out."

6

JULIA SPENT the remainder of the morning and most of the afternoon at work in her office. The death of the little girl she'd begun to simply call Blue did not mean that everything else in C Squad's professional life had ground to a halt. There were ten cops under Julia's command and the cases of the four she'd detailed to cover the child's death had to be reassigned to the other six, each of whom bellyached about the additional workload. Julia absorbed their complaints, knowing they viewed their failure to be included in the Blue investigation as a slight, and she tried her best to smooth their ruffled feathers. Bottom line, though, it was tough shit on them. She was their supervisor, not their friend.

At two o'clock, as she was finishing an egg-salad sandwich and a bottle of Sprite delivered from a local deli, Julia received a phone call she'd been anticipating for some time. It was Harry Clark, Manhattan North Detective Commander, asking for an update. If she could spare the time.

Ever the dutiful civil servant, Julia carefully detailed what C Squad had done, what they were doing, and what they hoped to do, all the

while acutely aware of Clark's hidden message. The chain of command in the Detective Division normally ran from lieutenant, to captain, to deputy inspector, to inspector, to commander. By jumping
three intermediate levels, Clark was making the brass's interest abun-
dantly clear. Big Brother was watching her.

"What I'll do," Clark announced once she'd finished, "is assign a
couple of detectives from my office to expedite the fingerprint and
DNA requests. I'll assign them to the ME's office."

"You want to make identification a priority?"

Clark dismissed her with a snort. "I'm sorry, Lieutenant," he said,
"did I hear you wrong? Did you say you were making . . . progress?"

Julia let Clark hang up first, wondering as she returned to her
sandwich if this was the beginning of the end for C Squad. Even
assigned to the medical examiner and not to the investigation, Clark's
detectives might eventually form the nucleus of a task force. Well,
she had to call Bea Shepherd anyway. She would bring it up then, get
a feel for what was going on.

Ten minutes later Bert Griffith, a huge smile dominating his normally deadpan expression, poked his head through the door. "I got
her," he told Julia. "Little Girl Blue. I got her."

THE CAMERA had been angled to sweep the entranceway of a
twelve-story apartment building at 2 East 73rd Street. It was the merest luck that it also included a few yards of the sidewalk on the other
side of the street. Even so, the little girl who appeared in just a single
frame of the tape was no more than a white blur, a ghost. By contrast,
the two men (one of whom sported a doorman's uniform, complete
with gold epaulets) standing in front of 2 East 73rd Street were very
substantial. Especially when their heads swiveled to follow that blur,
that ghost, as it ran west toward Fifth Avenue. The time of day,
stamped on the tape, was 2:11 A.M.

Julia watched the tape six times, stopping its progress on occasion
to freeze a particular frame. When she was absolutely certain, she
turned to the detectives who'd assembled behind her. "Lane," she
said, "let's take a ride."

David Lane rose up like a bear released from a cage. He slapped his hands together, said, "Would ya believe I interviewed that prick of a doorman last night?" Lane riffled through his notebook for a moment. "Linus Dwyer, that's his name. I made nice to him and he bullshitted me every step of the way? You want me to kill him, just say the word."

"And to think," Julia declared as she led him out of the squad room, "that I only chose you for your restraint."

THEY FOUND Linus Dwyer in the basement of the Sherbourne, a cooperative apartment building at 2 East 73rd Street. He was playing gin rummy with the Sherbourne's super, both of them sipping at quart bottles of Miller Light. Dwyer rose as they entered, his mouth jerking as if he couldn't make up his mind whether to smile or cry. Lane's return was the worst possible news for him, and he knew it.

"You wanna talk here?" Julia asked, nodding to the super who remained in his chair. "Or you wanna go someplace private?"

Dwyer led them along a narrow hallway to the furnace room at the far end of the building. He moved stiffly, as if to prevent the extra thirty pounds between his chest and his groin from jiggling. "In here," he told them, his brogue thick enough to slice, "if ya won't be mindin'." He let the detectives pass, then closed the door before finally turning, his most professional smile firmly in place. "Now, what can I be doin' for ya?"

Lane glanced at Julia, noted her quick nod, then slammed his fist into Dwyer's very soft gut. The doorman fell to his knees, gasping for breath. He made no effort to fight back.

"You saw her." Julia squatted down so that her mouth was only a few inches from Dwyer's ear. "You saw her and didn't report it and now she'd dead. If life was fair, I'd get to kill you right where you are, then leave your body for the rats." She rose on the balls of her feet, until she was looking down her nose at Linus Dwyer. "You a citizen?" she asked.

Dwyer nodded his head. He was staring at the tips of Lane's well-scuffed brogans.

"Let's see your green card."

"Can I be gettin' up? I've water on the knees, ya see, and it hurts me to kneel."

"Why not?" Julia replied. "I didn't tell you to get down there in the first place."

Dwyer grunted as he hauled himself to his feet and fished for his wallet. He had a moon face and tiny blue eyes set very close together. "Here she be," he said as he offered his Resident Alien Identification Card. "All stamped and legal-like."

If Julia had cared to examine Dwyer's green card (which, in fact, was white) she would, indeed, have found the card "all stamped and legal-like," but she simply took it from Linus Dwyer, then let her hand drop to her side. By federal law, a resident alien could be deported upon conviction for the most minor of crimes.

"Alright," Julia said, her tone matter-of-fact, "let's hear the story. And don't lie to me. And don't leave anything out."

Dwyer's story, which he told without hesitation, was simple enough. He was outside, trying to get a cab for a man he knew as Dr. Gass. Dwyer was looking east, toward Madison Avenue, the only direction from which a cab might come on the one-way street. The girl appeared out of nowhere, as if she'd just materialized on the block, in full flight; she was past him before he could react. Later, Dr. Gass, who'd been facing west toward Central Park and only seen the girl's retreating back, had begged him to keep it quiet.

"She'll go home," he'd said, reinforcing his conviction with a fifty-dollar bill. "When she gets cold enough, she'll go home."

Dr. Gass, as it turned out, had good reason to pursue anonymity, which he couldn't get from 911 because 911 traced every incoming call. A married man, Gass had just come from the apartment of Vivian Krepp, one of several married men who visited her on a regular basis.

The only thing Dwyer failed to disclose, because he didn't know it, was Dr. Gass's home address, forcing Lane and Julia to detour upstairs and confront Vivian Krepp in her Swedish-modern lair on the ninth floor. Bosomy and even more blond than Julia, Vivian readily acknowledged the nature of her relationship with the good and gentle physician. He, along with four other men, each of whom believed themselves to be her one and only, paid the eighteen hundred a month rent on her sublet apartment.

"It's a living," she explained.

D R. L E O N A R D Gass was alone in his York Avenue condominium when Julia Brennan knocked on his door. Short and flabby, he wore what was left of his tightly curled, salt-and-pepper hair in a combover that began at the top of his left ear.

"My wife and daughter will be home any minute," he explained. "We need to do this in a hurry."

Smart cops that they were, David Lane and Julia Brennan understood that Dr. Gass's standing in the community precluded the possibility of a good shot in the face. It was one of those sad facts of cop life. You just couldn't smack wealthy white professionals, no matter how much they deserved it.

Fortunately, Julia's anger had already dissipated. She was there only to put Gass on the record, knowing that if he was facing west as Blue ran by he couldn't know where she came from. Julia already knew where she went.

"When I left," Gass explained, "I assumed Linus was going to report the . . . incident."

"Is that what he told you?"

"He has a telephone at his desk in the lobby."

"That's not an answer."

"Do I need a lawyer, detective?"

"Lawyers are for suspects, and you're not a suspect." Julia paused long enough to allow the message to settle, then asked, "Did you give Dwyer fifty dollars and ask him not to report the . . . *incident*?"

"Is that what he said?"

"That's what he said."

"Well, he's lying."

"I see." Julia glanced at David Lane's reddening face and moved slightly to the left, placing herself between Gass and Lane. "Tell me this, doctor. On Sunday morning, when you found out that a little girl's naked body had been discovered in Central Park, approximately three blocks from where you'd stood with Linus Dwyer, why didn't you pick up the phone and report what you observed?"

Gass stood silently for a moment, then shoved his hands into his pockets. "How did I know it was the same girl?" he countered. "It could've been anyone."

A few minutes later, as they were exiting the lobby of Gass's building, Lane waved the doorman away, then opened the door for Julia. "You got a mean streak," he told her, his tone admiring. "No doubt about it." When Julia failed to respond, he continued. "What you need is a nickname. How 'bout we call you Tiger? Tiger Brennan. Whatta ya think?"

"What I think, Detective Lane," she replied after a moment, "is that I'm your boss and if you get too familiar, I'm gonna bust your sorry ass all the way back to patrol."

7

THOUGH JULIA repaired her makeup and ran a brush through her hair, she didn't really expect to find any television reporters on the scene when Lane finally pulled to the curb. It was twenty after six, ten minutes from the completion of the local nightly news. Nevertheless she wanted to be ready, just in case, and this time she got lucky. Angelina Valero, a twenty-something who'd only recently come to New York from KRAM in California, had somehow convinced her CBS crew to hang around, also just in case.

Angelina's dark brows rose to form perfect little crescents above her pudding-brown eyes when she saw Julia. Her arm began to pinwheel. "Yo, team, wake up. Time to go to work." She ran her fingers through her hair, the gesture automatic, like a ballplayer tracing the sign of the cross before stepping up to the plate.

"You're not gonna do this?" Lane asked Julia as they watched the van's door open from the inside.

"What'd you think, detective, I was going to let them get away with it?"

Now Lane's eyes positively glittered. "And it's not like folks wouldn't find out eventually, right?"

"Right."

Julia was content to let it go at that, but she had an additional reason for disclosing the existence of her two witnesses. The press and the public, as they tore these men to pieces, would take its collective eye off C Squad, at least for the duration of the feeding frenzy. After all, nobody could say they weren't making progress.

"We've placed the child, alone, on East Seventy-third, between Fifth and Madison at 2:11 A.M.," she told Angelina Valero and several print reporters. "She was seen by two witnesses."

"Did those witnesses call 911?"

"They did not."

"Are you prepared to name them?"

"Not at this time." As all involved knew, the phrase meant: Check with your sources. "However, we feel there are other witnesses out there and we beg them to come forth *voluntarily*."

I N T H A T righteous note, Julia marched off to the squad room, where she found Bert Griffith and Frank Turro sharing a cup of coffee. Both appeared to be exhausted.

"Anything new?" she asked.

Turro shook his head. "Uh-uh."

"Then go home, get some sleep. I want you out knocking on doors early tomorrow morning, while the night-shift doormen are still on duty. Now that we know Blue was on the street at 2:11 we may be able to locate someone who was outside at the same time, maybe a cop passing by, or a pedestrian. It's supposed to snow hard tonight and you'll find people at home, which is all to the good."

When Turro sighed, Julia quickly added, "Frank, we don't put this one down in a few days, you know what's gonna happen."

"They'll take it away from us."

"And you know what they're gonna tell us? When they take it away? They're gonna tell us, 'Hey, you had your chance and you couldn't cut it. So sorry.'" She turned her attention to Bert Griffith. "I want you to re-work the surveillance tapes, Bert. Now that we have time of day, it shouldn't take all that long. Start with the tape closest to the Sherbourne, then move east toward Madison. If she's not on any of those tapes, then she must have come from a building on the block."

"Fine," Griffith responded, "but there's a little problem. As in the Indonesian Mission to the United Nations, which just happens to be located on Seventy-third between Fifth and Madison. As in diplomatic immunity, as in we can't touch them."

"And they refused to hand over their tape?"

"Not exactly, loo. They told me the system wasn't working."

"System?"

"The mission, it's in a townhouse near Madison Avenue. There's steel grates on the windows and the place is covered, front and rear, by four surveillance cameras."

JULIA TOOK that thought to Bea Shepherd, tracking her down by phone just as she and her current boyfriend, a cellist with the New York Philharmonic named Milos something-or-other, were about to set off for dinner. According to Bea, she and Milos were in the infatuation stage of their relationship, a stage she hoped to prolong indefinitely.

"You can go public with the embassy's refusal to cooperate," she told Julia, "and hope the political pressure will convince them to change their attitude, but you can't force the Indonesian Mission to hand over those tapes. If they claim the system was down, that's it"

"I think what I'll do," Julia replied, "is bank it."

"Bank it?"

"We found a couple of witnesses. That'll satisfy the press for now. Later on, we'll give 'em Indonesia. A whole country? I'm sure they'll be properly grateful." She took a moment to describe the sequence of events that led C Squad to Linus Dwyer and Dr. Gass, knowing full well that Bea would pass the information along, that come tomorrow morning, Gass and Dwyer would awaken to their fifteen minutes of fame.

"Something else," Julia finally said. "Clark's putting a couple of suits in the ME's office. To expedite requests for fingerprints and DNA samples. I get the feeling I'm about to be blindsided just when I'm starting to make progress. It'd be a real drag, Bea, if Clark took over at the last minute, not to mention cruel, unfair, and just another example of the male hierarchy putting a female police officer in her place."

Bea Shepherd laughed. "Attitude, girl, that's how we do it. That's how we survive. Now, I gotta run. Milos dropped a tab of Viagra a few minutes ago and we wanna have dinner before it kicks in."

"Trust me on this, Bea, after six months of celibacy, I'm sympathetic. But there's just one more thing. You remember my asking you to reach into Sex Crimes, find somebody willing to talk to me off the record? Well, I could use a little help here. A guide to put me on the right track. The way it is now, I feel out of my depth."

"I'm working on it," Bea announced, a note of exasperation, not to mention finality, in her voice. "Just as I intend to work on Milos an hour from now. Good night."

JULIA HUNG up, her eyes sweeping the room, then searching her desk for unattended tasks. In many ways, this was the hardest part of her day—getting ready to go home, to become a mother. It wasn't merely that she repressed her motherly instincts while she was at work, but that she buried them so deep she was never entirely sure they were still there, or that she could retrieve them.

She put her hands behind her head, leaned back, let her eyes close. Her thoughts returned to David Lane's comment after they'd finished with Gass. For the whole of her career, Julia Brennan had made an effort—mostly successful—to separate her work from her family. Personal was for Corry, and her Uncle Bob, and even her greedy, grasping mother. Personal did not extend to crime victims who were entitled to no more than respect, a bit of rote sympathy, and the punishment of those responsible for their pain. Her entire career affirmed that basic principle. Since making lieutenant, she'd rarely had contact with victims.

Well, the child had drawn her out, the sensational aspects of her discovery mandating that Julia Brennan pay close attention, that she come to Central Park on a freezing Sunday morning and see what Blue looked like, a little girl, naked and huddled up, fleeing a terror beyond Julia's imagining. Julia could hear the footsteps, the slap of the girl's bare feet on the cold sidewalk, the huff of her breathing, could see the plume of her breath as she rushed past the Sherbourne. Blue had run until she couldn't run any more, until she was exhausted and she had to stop, to lay down, to die.

How fast did the wind and the cold do their work? Thirty seconds? A minute? What did she feel in those last seconds? Fear? Relief? What did she think? Certainly not of rescue, because she'd sprinted past Gass and Dwyer, hadn't turned to them for help, believing in her heart that she could trust no one. That she was utterly alone.

The phone rang at that moment, and Julia, glad for the interruption, picked up. "Brennan," she said.

"I'm gonna try to make this clear, lieutenant." The voice belonged to Commander Clark, though he didn't identify himself. "In the future, you get any developments, I don't wanna hear about 'em on the fucking nightly news."

He hung up before she could reply, leaving her to consider the possibility that her strategy had backfired, that her impromptu news conference would result in her losing control of the case even sooner. Still, if she'd phoned Clark first, he might very well have nixed a press conference, or demanded that he be the one to give it.

The phone rang again and Julia picked up, figuring it was Clark back for a second round. Instead, she heard the voice of her daughter.

"Mom," Corry said, "do you have any idea when you're coming home? I was about to start cooking dinner, but I can wait a few minutes if you're getting ready to leave."

8

PETER FOLEY sat before the computer in his west-side apartment, scanning photos into the Mac, photos of children. His apartment was tiny, a single room with a micro-kitchen against one wall, a bed against another, a long workbench holding his computer equipment against a third. A battered Formica table, a single chair, and a row of gray metal filing cabinets occupied the fourth wall. The table was covered with files, thick and thin.

Foley's work was tedious, requiring little of his attention. He placed the photographs, one at a time, on the scanner's face, clicked twice, then waited for the two machines to do their work. Computers, he was certain, and their inevitable descendants, thinking robots, would one day relieve humans of the Biblical obligation to earn their daily bread by the sweat of their brows. Necessity would then vanish, consigning poor *Homo sapiens* to their own perverted devices.

Well, he needed those perversions, no doubt about it, to animate his own life. Without them, he would shrivel, diminish, atom by atom, like a puddle of city water beneath an August sun. Perversion kept him alive.

Once he finished scanning the photos into the computer, Foley used Adobe GoLive to set about arranging them in a series of thumbnail sheets, so that visitors could view fifteen children at a time, then expand whatever thumbnail excited them until it filled the monitor. Until it filled their imaginations.

Foley updated his website every month, religiously. The site's visitors lived mostly in fantasy, and their fantasies required periodic refueling, the need for that fuel as powerful as a junkie's need for a fix. That was why they risked everything—their families, their reputations, their freedom—by downloading the chicken porn Foley provided into their home computers.

He glanced at the clock. It was 4:08 P.M. Still plenty of time to finish up and make the six o'clock mass at Holy Savior. Foley returned to the computer and quickly encrypted the update before sending it off. Then he leaned back in the chair and closed his eyes for a moment. He'd always liked this part of it, imagining the data as they ripped (not in a stream, but in small pellets of information, little Pac Men tracing the maze, one behind the other) through wire and cable, always at the speed of light. Running beneath rivers and oceans, across mountains, through cities, overcoming every obstacle until they found the single computer, of all the millions of computers in the world, prepared to receive them. To decrypt the data, to follow instructions, to post the photos in a small corner of the computer that ran New York University.

They would uncover the site, of course, the computer security people at NYU, sooner or later. But if any government agency thought him worth pursuing it would have to trace the same route his upload had taken. From New York University, that route would lead, first to a computer in Moscow, then to a second computer, this one in São Paolo, Brazil. Then to a third, and a fourth. Each, in turn, though guaranteeing anonymity, might be persuaded to cooperate, but it would take a joint effort by the FBI and the State Department extending over several years to navigate the route that led to Peter Foley's front door. By that time, of course, he would be long gone. One way or the other.

9

THAT NIGHT, Julia left her Jeep Cherokee in the parking lot of a diner fronting Queens Boulevard. It was already snowing, and according to the forecasters it would snow until morning, blocking the narrower residential streets. At another time, Julia would have parked the Jeep in her own tiny driveway. She would have been glad of an excuse to spend the morning with Corry, waiting for the plow to come through, eating French toast smothered in real maple syrup from a can that'd been sitting in the cupboard for the last year. But this was not another time and Julia would leave for work (if not on time, because shifts and tours were meaningless now) within an hour of awakening. Bert Griffith would do the same, as would the rest of her detectives. It was just part of the job, the balancing of career and family, a problem for every cop. Which was why so many cops were divorced, about to be divorced, contemplating divorce. That's why so many cops were *estranged*.

Over another meticulously prepared dinner, Corry asked Julia about the case. "I mean, like," she declared, a forkful of salad poised a few inches from her lips, "Blue was just *abandoned*? Like there isn't *anybody* who wants her?"

Julia flinched at her daughter's casual use of the word Blue, as if that were the victim's actual name. She wondered if the whole city was calling her Blue, if she, Julia Brennan, had gotten what she wanted, a monkey's paw in the making.

"I guess she's our baby," Julia said, more to herself than Corry.

"You mean like when they find a dead baby in a dumpster?"

"Yes," Julia replied, "just like that. Only with a little more human emotion."

"I didn't mean . . ."

"It's all right, Corry." Julia cut into her lamb chop. "I never had that happen to me, finding an abandoned infant, but it happened to another cop I knew. This was in the Bronx, a few months after I came out of the Academy. The cop's name was John Richmond and he was a classmate. He found . . . yeah, it was a girl, and he found her on the the hood of his patrol car. She was wrapped in a pink blanket."

"Was she dead?"

"Yes, and John Richmond couldn't deal with it. He quit the job a couple of months later. If I remember, he had a little girl of his own."

Corry's mouth curled into an elaborate pout, an expression she'd only recently begun to display. Like her emerging breasts and rounded hips, the changes in Corry's life were coming to define her in Julia's eyes. At times, Corry seemed to be only about change, to have no fixed anything.

"How could somebody do that?" Corry finally asked.

"I don't know." It was the simple truth. Julia's need to protect her daughter had begun with Corry's birth and showed no sign of abatement. A month before, when Corry announced that an older boy in her school had made a crude sexual remark, Julia's first urge was to put her Glock to the jerk's head, explain the facts of *real* life. As in power grows out of the barrel of a gun. "They eventually found the birth mother. She was severely retarded and it was her own mother, the baby's grandmother, who dumped the baby. The grandmother told John that it was his fault the baby died. If he'd ordered his hamburger and fries to go, he would have gotten to the girl in time."

"Was she crazy?"

Perhaps a year before, having come to realize that if her daughter was to be open and confiding during her adolescence, she would have to reciprocate, Julia had begun to reveal a bit of her working life to Corry. "You gotta figure, daughter of mine, that a grandma who leaves her granddaughter on the hood of a car in the middle of winter. . . . Well, you gotta figure there's a glitch in her computer *somewhere*."

Two hours later, as Julia was undressing in her bedroom, Bea Shepherd took advantage of a postcoital interval to call. She'd been in touch with Sex Crimes in the DA's office and she had a contact for Julia, assuming Julia hadn't by now cracked the case. As the case was closer to cracking Julia, she gratefully accepted the name, Lily Han, and the phone number Bea offered, then hung up. A moment later, before she could slide into the oversized T-shirt and nylon running shorts she wore to bed, the phone rang again. It was Robert Reid, just checking in.

"Did you get the names of the witnesses?" Julia asked.

"I did," Reid announced, "from an anonymous source who outranks you by a considerable degree."

"Ah, I see." Julia knew that her uncle was hard-wired to the NYPD hierarchy. She also knew that Bea Shepherd was not one of his sources. That meant somebody else was leaking information. "Tell me, Uncle Bob, is an anonymous source anything like a confidential informant?"

"More like an unindicted co-conspirator."

Julia started to laugh, then caught a glimpse of her naked body in a full-length mirror hanging on the closet door. A sobering moment for an unmarried thirty-something whose last serious relationship was a distant memory. "I know you have something on your mind, Uncle Bob, or you wouldn't have called so late. C'mon, fess up. You'll feel much better afterwards."

It was Reid's turn to respond and he managed a less than heartfelt chuckle. "Do you plan to re-canvass the blocks around Seventy-third Street?" he asked.

"How'd you know?"

Reid ignored the question. "There are folks in that community," he told his niece, "who don't want you poking around."

"Right, and we call those folks the bad guys."

"Julia, not only is that whole neighborhood money, it's *old* money."

"And what's the old money saying?"

"The old money is saying there are reporters following your detective, knocking on doors, asking if someone in the building is a suspect. The old money says your detective is rude and overbearing."

Julia tried to imagine Frank Turro, the most laid-back detective in C Squad, browbeating some Fifth Avenue matron. It was like trying to imagine Mother Teresa abusing an invalid beggar. "Thanks for the warning, Uncle Bob."

"*De nada*, my niece. I'll speak to you soon."

Julia disconnected, consulted her phone book, then was again drawn to her reflection in the mirror. She knew she was attractive because she could see it in the flicking eyes and outright stares of her male colleagues, but on this night she was only aware of her flaws. She focused initially on three small folds just below her navel, a by-product of her pregnancy that'd defied many thousands of abdominal crunches in the thirteen years since Corry's birth. Her breasts had suffered as well, had remained swollen through her pregnancy and while she nursed her daughter, then failed to snap all the way back when her milk dried up. The weight bench hadn't helped, though she'd grown considerably stronger, and neither had a Nautilus when she'd switched to a private gym.

What you are, girlfriend, she finally told herself, is horny. You always hate yourself when you're horny and there's nobody around.

She sighed, then slid into her gym shorts and pulled the T-shirt over her head. Life, she reflected, would be so much easier if she dated cops.

A minute later, Frank Turro's sleepy, "Hello," had Julia muttering, "Hey, sorry I woke you, Frank."

Turro responded with the traditional, "That's okay, loo. What's up?"

"I want you to go right into the field tomorrow, without coming to the house. Call Serrano and take him with you. And be thorough, Frank, because the way it's shapin' up, we're not gonna get another shot."

10

WHEN JULIA awakened from her nightmare, she was sitting upright, her feet dangling over the edge of the bed. For just a moment, she imagined herself a child again, waking up to make breakfast for herself and her mother before heading out to school. She lost the dream in the process, and though she tried for a moment, she couldn't get it back. Then the LED display on the clock radio next to the bed flicked from 6:11 to 6:12, catching her attention. Time to get up, get going.

Drawn by the scrape of shovels, she crossed to the window and raised the shade far enough to look out. The snow had been lighter than predicted and New York City was up and running. Go Team Go. Meanwhile, she could have brought her Jeep home, left it in the driveway. Now she'd have to walk the eight blocks to Queens Boulevard.

A half-hour later, showered and dressed, she was sitting on a hassock, pulling on her boots, when she heard her daughter's voice.

"You leaving?" Still in pajamas, Corry was standing in the doorway to her bedroom.

"Gotta go," Julia said, instantly guilty.

"Drive carefully," her daughter responded.

THE CALL was waiting for her when she finally got into the house, after two hours of crawling around a string of fender-benders that climaxed in the closing of the lower level of the Fifty-ninth Street Bridge for nearly forty minutes. The call was from Commander Harry Clark, his second attempt to reach Julia that morning.

"We're getting complaints," he told her, "from the locals." There was no anger in his voice, none that Julia could detect, at least. If anything, he sounded weary.

"About what, commander?"

"About C Squad's . . . interaction with the citizenry. Your people are being a little rough. That's what they're saying. And they don't like the implications."

"The implications?"

"Yes, lieutenant, the implication that one or more of them saw the child and didn't call the police, and the implication that one or more of them, the males anyway, is a pedophile."

"Right, I understand what you're gettin' at." Julia decided to go with her best defense, before the hint of impatience she'd detected in Clark's tone exploded into outright hostility. "But, see, now that we've put the victim's face out there and nobody's come forward, our only real hope is to work backwards. We know the victim was on Seventy-third Street, moving from east to west, at eleven minutes past two. If we can find someone, say, who was on Madison between Seventy-second and Seventy-third at 2:10 and didn't see her, we can work by process of elimination. I'm not saying we're gonna put her in a particular building, but I think we can narrow it down to a couple of blocks."

"You're talking about a thousand apartments. What will you do, turn the neighborhood over, see what falls out, hope it isn't the mayor's phone number?"

Clark gave off a tiny contemptuous snort as he finished. Unsurprised, Julia fielded his volley and slammed it back across the net. "Well, sir," she said, "I'm open to suggestions, but like I said, nobody's come forward and we have no physical evidence. Bottom line, I don't see another way to go."

Julia willed herself not to speak first. In essence, she'd just threatened her superior officer. She'd told him that withdrawing her field detectives would shut down the case, and that she was not prepared to do so unless ordered. If he instructed her to back off, the ultimate responsibility, given the number of leaks already out there and the identity of Julia's uncle, would fall on his head.

The challenge was dangerous for two reasons. First, and most obvious, Clark might decide to award the job to somebody a little more cooperative. Second, Julia had passed the captain's exam and would probably be promoted within the next year or two. But captain was as far as civil-service examinations could take her. All the higher ranks, from deputy inspector through chief, were strictly by appointment. Thus, making an enemy of the Manhattan North Detective Commander wasn't exactly in her best interests.

"What you did with the witnesses," Clark finally said, not only changing the subject, but neatly reversing the position he'd taken on the previous day, "it worked out all right. The reporters are tearing them to pieces." He laughed. "Imagine waking up one day to find you're living on a little island surrounded by sharks. You step outside your door, you get eaten."

Julia listened to him chortle for a few seconds, then said, "I thought we could take some heat off the job, put it on the bad guys. And they were definitely bad guys."

"Now, now, lieutenant, as police officers you know we're not allowed to punish."

Julia couldn't believe her ears. Clark was joking with her. Next thing, he'd offer to take her out for drinks. "No, sir," she replied, "but we *are* commanded to seek justice."

"Good, good." He cleared his throat. "Now, are you gonna put a team in the field today?"

"They're already out there."

"They have cell phones?"

"Yes."

"Call them, tell them to take it very easy, but to do what they have

to do. That's for today only, lieutenant. They don't go *back* out unless
I okay it first. Understand?"

"Yes, sir," Julia quickly replied. "I'll tell them to put on the kid
gloves."

B Y T H E time Julia entered the office of Assistant District Attorney
Lily Han, who'd been running the DA's Sex Crimes Unit for the past
ten years, one more piece of the puzzle had fallen into place. Serology
tests on fluids taken from the victim indicated the presence of
Demerol, a synthetic opiate, at the time of her death. The level,
Solomon Bucevski had been quick to report, did not contribute to
her death, the cause of which he now declared to be exposure.

"We should have met sooner," Han said, extending her hand. She
was a tall, slender Korean, with a round face, perfect almond eyes,
and a broad telegenic smile. In some ways at the very nexus of a bur-
geoning old-girls' network, Han was rumored to be in the running for
the DA's job when Robert Morgenthau finally died. There was no
longer any hope that he'd retire.

"We should've," Julia replied as she sat down. "I don't know why
we haven't."

They chatted about Bea Shepherd for a few minutes, exchanging
anecdotes. "The indomitable Bea Shepherd," Han called her at one
point, whereupon Julia nodded solemnly before intoning, "Amen to
that." Then, abruptly, Han settled back and crossed her legs. "Bea
explained your situation to me," she said, her tone all business now.
"For the record, I'm offering my sympathies."

"It's a little early for that," Julia replied.

Han ran a polished fingernail over the surface of her desk. "I'm
going to speak to you now as a prosecutor. As if you'd discovered
where Blue came from, then brought me the case. First, if the cause
of death is exposure to the elements, then you'll have to prove that
somebody dumped her on the street before we'd look at a charge of
deliberate murder."

As she had with Harry Clark, Julia put forth her best case. "A little
girl ran naked into the freezing cold. If somebody living with her had

reported the incident, we'd have had fifty cops out looking for her. Maybe she would've survived, maybe not, but either way it sounds like depraved indifference to human life. Or criminally negligent homicide. Or something equally heinous."

Despite Julia's impassioned tone, Han was unimpressed. "Tell me, detective, was anybody home when she left? If so, did that individual, or individuals, know she was gone? If so, when did they know? At the time she left? Or several hours later? It's nearly impossible to address these questions without witnesses."

"Like the other children in the apartment?"

"They'll do for starters."

Julia relaxed. Han wasn't giving up. She was suggesting a very reasonable course of action while at the same time requesting that Julia not embarrass the DA's office by presenting a weak case, then demanding a vigorous prosecution. "I keep thinking," she said, "that there might be other children involved. It's eating at me, you know? And the only way I can put it to rest is to find out where Blue came from. I feel like I have to do at least that much."

There was no arguing with that sentiment and Han didn't try. "I have someone," she announced, "who might be able to help you. This is an officer who's been working undercover for the last four years. He tracks pedophiles, gathers evidence, then turns the cases over to our investigators. He never testifies. His name is never revealed on any document. From the defendant's point of view, he doesn't exist." Han flashed a broad smile. "In some ways, he doesn't exist for us either. He basically does what he wants to do exactly when he wants to do it. Once, when I tried to rein him in, he pretty much told me to go fuck myself."

"Nice."

"Well, he works with the feds, too, on out-of-city cases, which means that he has options. Without doubt, he'd turn in his badge if he was assigned to other duties."

"Sounds like he's committed. Not to mention obsessed."

"He's obsessed all right, and for good reason. Four years ago, his only child, his daughter, vanished. Patti was six years old, in preschool, and somehow she failed to make it from her classroom to his wife, who was waiting outside. Then, two years later, his wife cut her wrists in the bathtub while he was on his way home from work. She was dead when he walked in the door."

"And the child was never found?"

"Not a trace," Han said. "My guess, for what it's worth, is that looking for her is what he's all about."

Julia thought it over for a moment, then asked, "What makes you think he'll work with me?"

"I don't really know if he'll *work* with you, but I spoke to him and he said he'd *talk* to you. His exact words were, 'Send her over, let's see how far she wants to go.'"

"Great." Julia's small mouth twisted into a sardonic smile. "I think I'm about ready to accept those sympathies you offered earlier. You sure this guy can help me?"

"All I can say for certain is that he's the only police officer in New York who really knows the pedophile scene. Just don't let him manipulate you. You'll think you understand him, you'll even think you're controlling him, but he'll be the one running the show. The man has his own agenda." Han slid her chair back and stood. "Anyway, if you decide to meet him, he'll be in a bar on First Avenue at six this afternoon. His name, by the way, is Peter Foley."

11

B Y T H E time Julia left C Squad's headquarters late that afternoon, the temperature had risen into the high forties and the previous night's snow had been reduced to salt-saturated puddles collected above blocked storm drains at a hundred thousand intersections. In an effort to preserve her boots, Julia leaped across these puddles, following a mass of pedestrians who hesitated briefly before launching themselves forward, like penguins at the margin of ice and sea. The sun had been down for more than an hour, but Third Avenue was brightly illuminated as stores of every kind, especially restaurants, four and five to a block, vied to attract the attention of a returning workforce. The neighborhood supermarkets would do the lion's share of their weekday business in the next two hours.

Julia found her Jeep where she'd parked it that morning, in a no-parking zone on Seventy-sixth Street near York Avenue. She looked around for a ticket, but her Restricted Parking Permit, displayed on the dash, had gotten her through another day. Every cop in the NYPD, all forty thousand, had one of these permits. A very generous perk in a city where garage space began at $350 dollars a month, and one for which Julia was properly grateful because it allowed her to forgo a nasty commute that would otherwise involve two subways.

The Jeep started on the first pull and Julia quickly headed north on York Avenue, toward Seventy-ninth Street and an entrance to FDR Drive. The traffic was heavy, though not abnormally so, and she was glad of the slow pace. An hour earlier, Bert Griffith had summoned her to the squad room for a little show-and-tell. He'd seemed very much the proud little boy as he'd stood before a map studded with pushpins and declared, without a trace of irony, that the Jane Doe, better known as Little Girl Blue, had emerged from a building on Seventy-third Street between Madison Avenue and the Sherbourne.

The pushpins represented various citizens—two cops stopped for a meal break on Madison Avenue, a doorman who'd come out for a smoke, a pair of lovers making their way home after a night at the clubs, an attorney for AT&T who'd slaved into the wee hours putting the finishing touches on a very complex contract with the Republic of China. What they had in common was that they were on the street at the time Blue made her run, and that they hadn't seen her.

There were nine pins in all, covering Madison and Park Avenues from Seventy-second to Seventy-fourth Streets between two o'clock and 2:25 in the morning. "True," Griffith had told Julia, "the times aren't exact and the victim might have slipped through, but then there's this."

Smiling the faintest of smiles, he'd pulled a remote control from his shirt pocket, pointed it at a small TV, and pressed a button before drawing his arms across this chest. On the other side of the room a videotape, already cued up, displayed a nearly static landscape: a sidewalk, a row of parked cars, an empty road, another row of parked cars, another sidewalk. Despite the poor lighting on the residential block, the picture quality was exceptionally good, the time-and-date stamp in the lower left hand corner easily discerned. It read 2:05 A.M. when the tape began to roll, and 2:20 A.M. when Griffith finally shut the VCR down. A few cars had passed in the fifteen minute interval, but no pedestrians.

"The camera's set up on the corner, loo," Frank Turro declared when Griffith shut down the VCR. "You can't walk—or run—up Seventy-third Street from Madison Avenue without going past it."

Impressed, Julia had taken a moment to congratulate her detectives. Then Turro, at a nod from Griffith, took down the map from the bulletin board to reveal a hand-drawn chart beneath. "These are the buildings between the Sherbourne and Madison," he'd announced. "Four apartment houses, two on either side of Seventy-third, six townhouses on the south side, with the Indonesian Mission to the UN on the north. Three of the townhouses are occupied by single families, the others are divided into duplex apartments. The bad news is that we've been to every one of those buildings, including the mission, and we showed the victim's picture to anybody we could find. What they're sayin', one and all, is they've never laid eyes on her."

"Do you believe them?"

"Yeah, loo, gut instinct, I do."

Julia had accepted Turro's judgement gracefully, though it was obvious enough that Blue was known to the occupants of at least one dwelling, the one she'd fled.

JULIA EASED the Jeep onto FDR Drive and began the southward crawl toward the lower part of Manhattan and her meeting with Peter Foley. In the distance, the Fifty-ninth Street Bridge with its Erector-set superstructure cut a bright swatch over a slick black East River. Julia was trying not to think too hard about Peter Foley and his miseries, nor about the wisdom of putting someone who'd been through what he'd been through on the streets with virtually no supervision. True, as Lily Han was quick to explain, Foley had begun investigating pedophiles while off-duty, bringing forth cases unknown to his superiors. It was only after it became clear that he intended to persist that he'd been reassigned to the Sex Crimes Unit.

But Peter Foley's determination wasn't at issue. He could have been ordered to stop, then brought up on charges if he failed to comply. From there, he might have been pushed into therapy or released with a three-quarters disability pension if all else failed. Instead, the job was using him for its own purposes, a devil's bargain.

There's a question, Julia decided as she parked the Jeep on Tenth Street, that begs to be answered here. A very simple question: What's in it for the devil?

Julia exchanged her Restricted Parking Permit for an ON OFFI-
CIAL POLICE BUSINESS placard, then locked the Jeep and strode
off toward First Avenue. Her movements were strong and confident,
the unconscious body language of a cop who'd walked a beat in some
of the toughest neighborhoods in a very tough city. Her Glock 9-mm
rested at the bottom of a leather bag, a tote, which hung from her left
shoulder. Again quite unconsciously, she held the purse against her
body with her elbow, protecting what was hers.

THE TWELFTH Street Tavern was that rarest of commodities in
gentrified Manhattan, a neighborhood bar: liquor bottles on glass
shelves before a well-worn mirror, an oak bar scarred with graffiti, a
bench fronted by round wooden tables opposite the bar. Two small
neon signs graced a front window nearly as dirty as the one in Julia's
office. The first, surmounted by a yellow harp, read, *Guinness*. The
second, in blood-red script, read *Budweiser*.

All in all, Julia decided as the door swung shut behind her, the
Twelfth Street Tavern was not a place you came to meet your soul-
mate, or even for a one-night stand. With a single exception, everybody seemed to know everybody else in the crowded room. The
exception was Peter Foley, who was sitting at a table by the front door
and who rose as she entered, then waved.

"Hi," he said. "Glad you could make it."

Suppressing a rueful smile, Julia extended her hand. Somehow,
she'd expected to find Foley unkempt and haggard, with dark, soulful
eyes and a haunted expression, a character out of a Russian novel. In
fact, he was startlingly attractive, a man in his mid-forties with a head
of nicely barbered hair and clear blue eyes that betrayed a hint of
amusement, as if he'd been counting on her reaction. Above a cleft
chin, his mouth was thin, but not unkind; his smile appeared genuine.

"I recognized you right away," he told her, "from your news conferences."

A recrimination? Julia couldn't be sure, but she recalled Lily Han's
admonition. Foley had an agenda of his own and could not be
trusted.

"It's a little loud in here," she said, "for a private conversation."

"What? Can't hear ya." His grin expanded as he put a hand to his ear. "That was a joke," he explained.

"A very old joke."

"And a bad one, too. Just let me settle the tab and we'll be on our way."

12

I COME here for the collegial atmosphere," Foley explained. "It's a great place." He failed to add that he, himself, did not participate in that collegiality, or that he spoke only to the bartender and limited even that conversation to the ordering of a single draft beer. Instead, he opened the door and waved Julia through. As she went by, the odor of the cologne she'd put on that morning drifted into his nostrils. The scent was too faint to be identified, which made it all the more enticing. Years had passed since he'd been on the street with an attractive woman by his side.

"Watch this," he said as a changing traffic light brought them to a halt at the corner of First Avenue and Tenth Street. Across the way, an elderly woman bearing a pair of well-stuffed shopping bags paused briefly, then (just as the DON'T WALK sign turned steady red) launched herself into traffic. An instant later, their movements so perfectly synchronized they might have been produced by computer animation, each of the drivers in the line of cars extending toward Second Avenue slammed the palm of his hand against the horn button on the steering wheel. The old lady seemed unaffected by the resulting din; her expression didn't change as she shuffled toward Foley and Julia, nor did she hurry. It wasn't until she came alongside Julia that she looked up and said, very clearly, "Fuck 'em in the ass."

"God, I love this town." Foley's smile was effortless. As a detective, he'd always played the good cop, and the joke, between him and his partner, was that he was too pretty to inspire fear. "Are you hungry at all?"

"I don't really have time for a meal." Julia returned Foley's smile.

"Well, a snack then. There's a Thai restaurant on the next block that's on the verge of going under. It's always empty."

"That wouldn't be a comment on the quality of their food, would it?"

"You think?"

"I do."

Foley felt his heart race. She was flirting . . . But no, flirting was way too strong. Playing was better. She was playing with him. "Well, how 'bout a walk-and-talk?" he asked. "*A la* the Dapper Don, Big John Gotti himself. Because I don't think we'll find another empty restaurant."

Julia nodded agreement, then jumped directly to the matter at hand, leading Foley to wonder if he'd offended her in some way. She told him about narrowing down Blue's place of origin to a single block, about two days of canvassing with no tangible results. "Is it possible," she concluded, "that the victim never left the apartment? Could she have been a prisoner?"

"A slave, more likely," Foley replied. "Probably Romanian, though she might have been purchased in Bosnia or Kosovo, or even parts of Russia."

"Purchased?"

Foley frowned, the gesture not too obviously theatrical, or so he hoped. "Children are bought and sold every day. What makes your Little Girl Blue unusual is that she's Caucasian. Not too many kids on the market in Europe. She must've been a real find." He allowed his frown to broaden into a knowing smile. "And, please, lieutenant, do yourself a favor and put Indonesia out of your mind. There's no way a nation would put its reputation on the line by running a brothel out of its mission to the United Nations. It just ain't happening."

Julia said nothing for a moment, thinking it over, taking her time. They were drifting east along Ninth Street and they parted momentarily in order to pass a young girl walking an overweight Labrador retriever. As they came back together, Julia said, "Why don't you just tell me what you think, detective? From the beginning, and minus the theatrics."

"All right." Though his tone was faintly reproachful, Foley was thrilled with Julia's assertion of rank. She'd probably been told that he was unreliable, if not actually unstable, and she was trying to get control of the situation. "Look, if you don't mind, I'm going to call you Julia. And I'd like you to call me Peter. I know it sounds paranoid, but I don't want anyone to know I'm a cop. So . . ."

"Fine."

Just the one word, and the implicit command: get on with it. Foley repressed a smile. "For most of the nineteenth century, in New York City, the age of consent was ten years old. There were brothels that specialized in children, male and female, and children who walked the streets. If these children were caught having sex with fully adult males, the kids would be arrested and prosecuted for the crime of prostitution. And this went on for almost a hundred years." Foley looked into Julia's eyes, found their apparent calm nearly convincing. Nearly. "Believe it or not," he continued with a smile, "there's a real, actual point here and it has to do with supply and demand. For a hundred years, the rape of little children was deemed a consensual act. I think that pretty much proves that there's always been a demand, a demand that still exists, and we all know that when there's a demand, especially a demand backed up by money, a supply won't be long in coming. In this country, today, on the low end, children are pimped by their parents, biological or foster. On the high end, on the Upper East Side within a block of Central Park, a small number of very rich men find their customers by word of mouth. It's all very discreet and very expensive."

"Why don't the kids just run away?"

"I think you know the answer to that question."

"They're afraid."

"Put yourself in their position. Your parents have sold you to strangers. You've been taken to another country and confined to a small apartment where you're forced to have very painful sex with adult men. You've been severely punished, even tortured, for the slightest act of rebellion. Tell me, Julia, was she on drugs? Your little girl?"

"Demerol."

"The final link in the chain that binds. Addict the child, then withdraw the drug for a few days, let 'em know what it feels like. Another thing you might want to consider. In countries like Thailand, Haiti, and the Philippines, child prostitution is pretty much out in the open. The cops look the other way because they're getting a payoff, and if the children try to run they're quickly returned to their pimps. Now, it's possible that your victim spent some time in a foreign brothel before she came here. Maybe she was sold out of a brothel, then smuggled into this country, say in the trunk of a car entering from Canada. If that was the case, she would have trusted nobody, certainly not two adults, one of them wearing a uniform. Nor would she have appreciated the difference between a police officer and a doorman."

Foley stopped speaking long enough to allow a scrawny man pedaling an ancient Schwinn bicycle to pass by. A tape player dangling from the bike's handlebars blared a saucy mix of Caribbean and jazz rhythms, and the man was singing as he came. *"Ay, mama, que pasa? Ay, mama, que pasa?"*

Julia looked after the man as he wove around the pedestrian traffic, then she and Foley walked on, maintaining an edgy silence that Julia finally broke as they approached Fourteenth Street and Avenue A.

"We've got fibers," she told Foley, "purple fibers from the victim's hair that we're hoping to match if we find where she came from." When he didn't respond immediately, she added, "The lecture was very nice, and I'm sure it was accurate, but it doesn't help much."

"I was only answering your question."

"I know."

Foley was tempted to offer Julia his arm, though he knew she wouldn't take it. Later on, perhaps, but not now. His voice toughened as he broke the silence. "I've known there was a brothel on the Upper

East Side for months, but I haven't been able to find it. I can't seem to convince my source to open up."

"And why is that?"

"Because up till now I've been asking nicely."

Julia took a couple of steps, then dipped into her bag in search of her cell phone. "Gimme a minute here," she said. "I'm gonna call my daughter, tell her I won't be home for dinner."

13

"TED GOODMAN here."

"Ted, it's Pete Foley."

"Who?"

"Pete Foley."

"Oh, yes, right. It's good to hear from you, Pete."

"Yeah, you too. Say, Ted, I gotta see ya."

"Sure, just give me a time and place."

"I need to see you now."

"Now?"

"Ted, it's real bad. I gotta see you right away. Like, this minute."

"This minute? You know, you're a nice guy and all, but for the life of me, I can't see any reason why I should drop everything and come rushing over. I barely know you."

"That's good, Ted, what you're doin', and I don't blame you for tryin', but I gotta see you, like this minute."

When the line went dead, Peter Foley looked across the seat at Julia Brennan. She was sitting behind the wheel, staring at the cell phone's speaker. "You should have made your point right away," she said.

"Now, where," Foley replied as he punched the redial button, "is the fun in that?"

As Julia was about to reply, Theodore Goodman's voice emerged from the speaker. "Goodman."

"It's me again."

"Foley, goddamn it, what do I have to do? Call my lawyer?"

"I'm right downstairs, Ted. I'm parked in front of the building. I'm sitting next to a cop, a detective. She's tellin' me if you don't come down, she's gonna come up."

"Bullshit."

Foley winked at Julia. "Like I already said, I don't blame you in the least. I know this has gotta be hard to take, what with no warning and all. But we're sittin' right out front, in a gray Jeep. You don't believe me, call down to the doorman, let him take a look. Bottom line, though, you don't come voluntarily, a couple of minutes from now Detective Brennan's gonna be poundin' on your door."

Foley nodded to a smiling Julia who opened the Jeep's door, hesitated, then slammed it shut.

"You with me, Ted?" Foley asked.

"Yeah, yeah. Alright. I'm coming down."

WHEN THEODORE Goodman slid into the back seat and shut the door, Julia flicked the switch that controlled the Jeep's door locks. The resulting thud as the locks slid home was painfully audible and Goodman's eyelids flicked shut as if anticipating a blow. When they re-opened, Peter and Julia had shifted around so that their backs were against the Jeep's front doors and they were staring at him.

Goodman looked from Foley to Julia. In the Jeep's shadowy interior, her dark blue eyes appeared black. "May I see some identification?" he asked.

Julia offered her gold shield and her department ID, allowed him a brief inspection, then returned it to her purse. "You can call me Detective Brennan." Her eyes narrowed slightly as she acknowledged a growing awareness. Goodman was terrified, the threat of exposure so awful he couldn't look beyond it to jail, trial, or prison. A short, compact man in his mid-thirties, Goodman wore a high-end cashmere overcoat which he nervously unbuttoned to reveal an equally expensive suit. His hair was dark and retreating from the front; his appearance was ordinary except for a fleshy mouth and a dense, five o'clock shadow that emphasized a pale complexion, now almost ghostly with fear.

"I told her everything," Foley said. "I had to."

Goodman mouth curled into a pout. "The only reason I came down," he announced. "is to inform you that I won't speak to the police without a lawyer present."

"Ted, listen to me." Foley's eyes turned down. "I told her about the . . . you know, the *material* I e-mailed to your computer. I told her about the videotape I gave you. I *showed* her the videotape you gave me. You can't get out of it. You gotta tell."

"Detective Brennan," Goodman said, turning to Julia, "are you formally denying my right to counsel?"

"You still don't get it, do you?" Foley asked. "She's not a vice cop, Ted. She doesn't give a flying fuck if you look at pictures of little girls when you jerk off. She's from *homicide*. She's here about Little Girl Blue." Foley's voice dropped to a near whisper. "If you remember, the last time I saw you a couple of months ago, you told me that you went to this . . . this chicken ranch and that you had a really great time. You said, 'She was flat as a board, Pete, just the way I like 'em.' You also told me, right before you left, there were other girls in the apartment and they were working on the Upper East Side, close to Central Park. Well, Central Park is where they found the kid and that's why Detective Brennan's here. She wants the address."

Goodman slipped a bit, at least in Julia's eyes, when he failed to renew his request for an attorney. Foley had offered the very beginnings of a deal, of a way out, and Goodman was thinking it over.

"I had to tell her," Foley insisted. He raised his arms, tossing away the coat which covered them, to reveal the handcuffs encircling his wrists. "There was nothing I could do, Ted. She had me by the balls."

"Detective Brennan," Goodman said, having apparently regrouped, "am I under arrest?"

"Ted," Julia responded, "you've been spending too much time in front of the boob tube. You've lost your hold on reality."

"I don't know what that means, but if I'm not under arrest, I'm leaving."

Julia smiled. Goodman had finally figured it out. He should never have come downstairs. He should have stayed right where he was and destroyed the evidence. "No, Teddy, you're not. You're not leaving."

"This is kidnapping. You know that?"

"Uh-oh. Now you've committed a serious crime."

"And what's that?"

"Contempt of cop. In fact, if you were twenty or thirty million dollars poorer, I'd haul your ass down under the Williamsburg Bridge and smack the shit out of you." Julia sighed. "I can't do that, of course, because you're a respectable upstanding American. But what I can do—and what I *will* do—is drag your miserable ass into the precinct and lock you in a holding cell while I use Foley's testimony to secure a search warrant. Then I'll go back to your home and seize your computer, your videotapes, and any other material which could by any stretch of the imagination be deemed obscene. If there's nothing in your home, nothing incriminating, you've got nothing to worry about. If, on the other hand, I find even one naughty picture, you'll be placed under arrest, taken into custody, and subjected to a public arraignment, at which time you'll be offered bail. Until that arraignment, no lawyer can help you. It's just gonna be short-eyes Teddy Goodman and the boys on Rikers Island, many of whom, interestingly enough, were sexually molested as children."

Julia looked over at Foley, guessed that he was enjoying her performance as much as she'd enjoyed his, then returned her attention to Goodman. He would cave; there was no doubt in her mind, and no mercy in her heart. "You know what a perp walk is, Teddy? When they lead the perp out of the precinct and all the reporters are waiting? You ever see one of those on the nightly news? Well, when that happens, you're gonna pull your coat over your head and turn your face away, just like the mutt you are, but it won't make any difference. By tomorrow morning, when we release your mug shot, you'll be as famous as those two scumbags who saw the girl and didn't pick up the phone. An entire city will hate your guts."

They were parked on Sixty-eighth Street, halfway between Madison and Park Avenues, before a ten-story, pre-war apartment building. It was still early, just eight o'clock, and there were pedestrians on the sidewalks and traffic in the street. Nevertheless, to Julia, as she maintained an intensifying silence, the interior of the Jeep seemed as isolated as a tomb.

"What . . ." The first word, when Goodman finally got it out, emerged from the back of his throat, thick and phlegmy.

"Keep going," Julia said.

"What do you want me to do?"

"Tell me the address."

"And that's it?"

"No, that's not *it*. But *it* isn't the point, right? The point is what you get in return for your cooperation." Julia hesitated long enough to flash a dazzling smile. "What I can do, Teddy, is keep your name off any official document. That's what you get in return for your complete and absolutely honest cooperation. That, and that alone. Now, give me the address."

"How do I know . . . Oh, *fuck*." Goodman pounded his fist into his thigh. For a moment it looked to Julia as if he was going to start crying, but then he pulled himself together. "How do I know I can trust you?"

Julia responded by turning away, then starting the Jeep.

"No, wait."

She put the Jeep into reverse and released the hand brake.

"For God's sake . . ."

Goodman's whole body shook as the Jeep rolled back, then forward, leaving Julia—who watched him closely in the rear view mirror—to wonder if he'd given even an instant's consideration to the terror inspired in the children he'd raped. The thought of letting him off the hook, even temporarily, was so repugnant she almost hoped that he wouldn't respond, that he'd take his lawyer and his punishment.

"It's on Seventy-third Street."

"I already know that."

"The Clapham, 42 East 73rd, apartment 9A."

Julia eased the Jeep back into the parking space, much to the chagrin of another driver, double-parked to her rear and waiting for the spot. She waved the driver around, then patiently endured a string of epithets before turning back to Goodman.

"You were there? Inside the apartment?"

"Do I have to . . ."

"Just answer the questions, Teddy. And whatever you do, don't lie."

"Yes, I was there."

"And someone offered to provide an underage female for sexual purposes in exchange for money?"

"Yes."

"And did you have sex with that underage female?"

"Yes."

"And was that underage female . . ."

"No, she wasn't. I swear it. But I saw her there. The one they're calling Little Girl Blue."

Julia took a deep breath. She'd won, but it didn't feel like any victory she'd enjoyed in the past. In lieu of elation, she felt soiled, in need of a bath she wouldn't get to for many hours.

"Here's what's gonna happen," she told Theodore Goodman. "First, we go to the office of Assistant District Attorney Lily Han, where you submit to a deposition under oath. Based on the information you supply, Ms. Han will write up an application for a warrant to search apartment 9A, then take you before a judge, where you will repeat the information, again under oath. In return—if you perform well and honestly—you'll be registered as a confidential informant and the search warrant sealed. Do you understand what I just told you?"

"Yes, I understand."

Julia turned to Foley, her eyes locking on his. For a moment she thought she saw something, something lurking beneath the surface, a challenge. But then his features softened.

"Did I do good?" he asked. "Did I give ya what ya wanted?"

"Yeah." She unlocked the handcuffs and dropped them to the gray carpeting on the floor. "You can take off."

Foley opened the door. "I'm sorry, Ted," he announced, "for what I did. But it was me or you, and you got the money. You can afford the hit."

14

I T WAS nearly ten o'clock when Lily Han took a thoroughly debriefed Theodore Goodman before Judge Andrea Marmelstein, leaving Julia to assemble the troops. She called Carlos Serrano first, then David Lane, Bert Griffith, and Frank Turro, telling each the same story. On her own, she'd developed a confidential informant who'd revealed the apartment from which Little Girl Blue had fled three days before. A resulting search warrant had already been drawn up and was about to be signed. C Squad would serve that warrant, hopefully by midnight.

"You're invited to the party," she explained, "but if you can't make it, I'll understand."

It was an offer that could not be refused, and ninety minutes later, five detectives strong, C Squad piled into a pair of identical Crown Vics and headed out. In the rear of the second car, Julia was trying to put a brake on her adrenal glands. Foley had flatly declared, "If you're thinking rescue, Julia, think again. Not only have the kids already been moved out, there's a good chance the adults have flown as well."

The adults, as described by Goodman, were a fortyish couple, Bud and Sarah Mandrake. "The girls," Goodman explained, "call them Uncle Bud and Aunt Sarah. In case they have to go to the doctor or something."

Well, there were still the purple fibers combed from Blue's hair. If they could be matched to fibers in the apartment, C Squad would have a place to start. It was next to impossible to live in New York for any length of time without leaving a paper trail. Unless the Mandrakes had been very thorough, C Squad would find them, and grill them, and hopefully, break them.

It began to rain when the two Fords entered Seventy-third Street from Madison Avenue, a cold winter rain that chilled as thoroughly as the most bitter wind. As they double-parked in front of the Clapham, Julia reminded herself that she hadn't phoned Commander Harry Clark, hadn't given him the opportunity to yank the rug out from under C Squad, or even to share in the glory. Sooner, rather than later, there would be hell to pay.

The doorman, whose name tag read "Aurelio," came out to stand beneath a tan canopy that stretched to the edge of the sidewalk. A tall slender Latino, he apparently knew a cop—or five cops—when he saw them. "Officers," he said, looking from one to another, "what can I do for you?"

"We have a search warrant for apartment 9A," Julia announced.

"The Mandrakes? Haven't seen them for a few days."

Julia shrugged off her disappointment. "What happened? They move out?"

Aurelio walked behind the mahogany counter that concealed his small desk and consulted a looseleaf binder. "Uh-uh. Nobody's moved out this month."

"Well, what can you tell me about them?" Before he could answer, she quickly added, "I appreciate your cooperation. Believe me."

Aurelio scratched a silky black mustache as he framed his response. "What could I say? They're, you know, forty-five, fifty, fifty-five. Very quiet, like everybody else in the building. Dress nice, act polite."

"They live alone?"

The doorman's face brightened. "That's something," he said, jerking a thumb toward the ceiling. "The ladies in here, you can't picture 'em pushin' vacuum cleaners, dustin' the antiques. Mostly, they have live-in housekeepers. But the Mandrakes, now they don't even use day help. And Joe, the eight-to-four man, told me they order tons of groceries. He says the goodies are delivered two shopping carts at a time. From the Gristedes on Third Avenue."

Julia willed herself not to glance at Frank Turro who, despite his diligence, had been asking the wrong questions. "Are they owners? The Mandrakes?"

"Nope. They lease. The owner's living in Australia." He smiled. "Should I call, see if the Mandrakes are home?"

"Not unless you want to be arrested." Julia tempered the statement with a smile of her own. "Any chance you have access to keys for the apartment? Otherwise, if nobody answers, we'll have to take down the door."

"Matty's got 'em," Aurelio said. "He's the super."

"Is Matty around?"

"He has an apartment in the basement. You want me to call him?"

"That's alright. I'll send somebody down."

Frank Turro peeled away without being asked, just as a middle-aged couple exited a taxi and began to walk toward the door. As the doorman stepped away, Julia put her hand on his arm. "They have any questions, you send them to me."

A moment later, Julia was showing her identification to Mr. and Mrs. Kenneth Schuyler. That was the way the husband had introduced them: "My name is Kenneth Schuyler and this is my wife." The wife sported a sable coat. The black pearls in her drop earrings were the size of grapes. "Would you tell us what's going on here?"

"We're on police business, sir." Having anticipated this moment, Julia reminded herself to be as nice as possible.

"Lieutenant . . . Brennan?"

"Brennan, that's right, sir."

"Lieutenant Brennan, as president of the cooperative board, I feel I have a right to know what's going on in my building."

Mrs. Schuyler offered her opinion before Julia could reply. "Oh, for heaven's sake, Kenneth, she's just doing her job."

"She's standing in the lobby, Margaret. I doubt very much . . ."

The elevator door opened at that moment to reveal Frank Turro and a small compact man bearing a large key ring. "Got 'em, loo," Turro declared.

"Sir," Julia said, her voice now firm, "what floor do you live on?" She could feel her heart slide into another, decidedly higher, gear.

"We're in the penthouse," Margaret Schuyler replied.

"Thank you." Julia turned to Lane, Griffith, and Serrano. Serrano was smiling softly. Lane was trying not to smirk. Griffith's expression, as usual, revealed nothing. "Let's go," she said, marching off.

When they were inside the elevator, she looked back at the Schuylers. "For your own safety," she explained as the doors closed, "I'm going to have to insist that you stay off the ninth floor. For your own safety, sir."

The tension rose with the elevator. Julia could smell it in the enclosed space, sharp and musty, a conflicting reek of fear and testosterone. Nobody, not even C Squad, had believed they'd get this far, especially Commander Harry Clark, who was ready to let Julia Brennan swing. Well, the sacrificial lamb had slaughtered the lion and she was damned if she was going to share the carcass.

"Frank and Carlo, I want you to trail off, handle the nosy neighbors. *Politely*. Bert, you take the far side of the door. Remember, we have no reason to anticipate armed resistance. These are not people we can push around. David, you stay with the super. If the unlikely happens and things go wrong, I want you to get him out of the way."

The elevator doors opened as if in response to the chorus of *Yeah, loo; right, loo; got it, loo*, that followed. Apartment 9A, one of three apartments on the floor, was directly ahead of them, at the end of a long hallway.

Silent now, they marched down the corridor, their footsteps muffled by the dense carpeting, past a succession of worn tapestries depicting a royal marriage and an ensuing feast. As Julia took up a position just to the side of the door, she removed her Glock from her shoulder bag and held it at her side.

"Ready?"

She took their collective failure to respond as an affirmative and rang the bell, holding it down for several seconds. Then she pounded on the door with the heel of her hand. The door was solid oak, heavy enough to hurt, and the thud of her fist against it seemed to her almost reluctant, as if she'd changed her mind at the last minute.

From behind, she heard a door open, then Carlos Serrano's soothing voice. "Police business, ma'am. Please go back inside your apartment."

Julia pressed down on the bell, held it longer this time, pressed it again, then finally placed her ear to the door. Nothing, not even a radio. She felt her heart sink. Foley had been right. The Mandrakes had begun to clean up right after Blue's flight. They were long gone and there would be no dramatic rescue. The other children, the children Blue had left behind, were somewhere else, perhaps already working.

"Unlock it," she told the super.

Matty stepped up to the door, keys in hand, then tried the knob. When it turned freely, his hand popped off as though burned. "It's open," he said, backing away.

"You ready, Bert?" Julia asked.

"Past ready."

Julia gave the door a hard shove and watched it roll away, perfectly balanced on its well-oiled hinges. She started when it slammed into the wall, but kept her eyes on the scene before her. She was looking across a small foyer, through a much larger living room, into a formal dining room perhaps fifty feet away, looking first for motion, for the presence of another living thing. It was only when she'd determined that there was no other living thing in view that her mind focused on the dead things, the pair of severed heads staring back at her from the dining-room table. The heads were male and female, and streaked with dry blood. Blood matted their hair, their eyebrows; blood clumped in the corners of eyes propped open with toothpicks. Their mouths were turned up at the corners, their lips held apart, again by toothpicks, to reveal obscenely white teeth.

15

FOR A long moment Julia didn't move, didn't breathe; her thoughts tumbled through her mind like clothes in a hot dryer, a sock here, a blouse there, now briefly visible, now vanished. From somewhere in the apartment a phone began to ring. As it continued, Julia somehow found herself imagining one of the heads turning to the other with a smile, "I'll get that, dear."

The image was just cop-cynical enough to stay put for a few seconds, to be the springboard to a semblance of control. It allowed her to narrow her focus, to hear, for instance, Bert Griffith's half-whispered, "Fuck, fuck, fuck."

Toughen up, she told herself, as she had so many times in the past. And whatever you do, don't play the dumb blonde.

"David, put the super on the elevator, send him home. Frank and Carlos, you come up here."

Her voice was firmer than she'd expected, firm enough to bring immediate compliance. She felt Serrano and Turro behind her, the warmth of their bodies, the whisper of Turro's breath on the back of her neck. Apparently as shocked as herself, neither spoke. Not so

David Lane. The super disposed of, he walked up to the doorway, looked into the apartment, and said, "What, nobody's gonna introduce me?"

Julia appreciated the comment and understood its necessity, which echoed her own. Now they would have to move.

"There has to be a lot of blood," she announced, "somewhere inside that apartment." The dining room, as much as she could see of it, was immaculate. "We step in the blood, we'll be executed. Understood? The whole world's gonna be looking over our shoulders." When nobody responded, she continued. "David, you have gloves in that bag?"

"Yup."

"Put on a pair, give a pair to Bert. I want you to go through the apartment, make sure there's nobody else inside."

"Got it, loo. And I promise not to play in the gore."

"Just make it quick. Carlos, you get on the horn, call it in. Let's get the show started."

Four minutes later, Griffith and Lane returned. Just a bit out of breath, Griffith's eyes were wide. "No other vics," he told the waiting detectives as he and Lane came out into the corridor.

"What about . . ." Julia gestured toward the dining room. "What about the rest of them?"

"In the kitchen," Lane replied. "The blood-soaked kitchen we were very careful not to step into."

Julia ignored the sarcasm. "I'm going inside. Give me a pair of gloves." She waited for Lane to locate the gloves and hand them over, then addressed C Squad, offering a semi-apology. "I'll be in there for five minutes, ten the most. After that, it's your investigation. Bert, you come with me."

She stepped into the foyer without waiting for Griffith's assenting grunt. The small carpeted room was bare except for a gleaming chest of drawers bearing a lamp with an elaborate cut-glass shade. Julia's first thought was that she was looking at a Tiffany lamp and a Chippendale chest, an irrelevancy she quickly dismissed in favor of a more pertinent question. Who owned the furniture, the Mandrakes or the co-op's conveniently absent owner?

"Bert, the guy who owns the co-op, you think he's getting a payoff?"

"Don't know, loo, but the man is without doubt on my must-phone list."

"Yeah, well, if he doesn't wanna come back from Australia there's no way to make him. My guess is that you'll be talking to his lawyer before long."

The living room, except for a Steinway grand piano in one corner, was all leather, glass, and metal. Julia glanced around, noted the abstract paintings on the walls, the crystal vase resting on a glass pedestal between the windows. The fireplace on the northern wall was generous; its black marble surround was shot with mica, and a walnut mantle bore a gilt clock the size of a small television set. What she didn't see was any sign of a struggle. The room was spotless.

She continued on into the dining room, trying hard to ignore the reek of violent death, of urine and feces and the very beginnings of decomposition. She told herself to look, to look and see. The entire scene was obviously (and elaborately) staged. It was created for the benefit of the viewer. It was created for her.

Julia glanced to her right, through open double doors, at the decapitated body of a woman resting on a marble-topped counter in the kitchen. The woman wore a blue sleeveless dress and matching shoes with three-inch heels. From the waist up, the blood-soaked fabric of her dress was stiff and stood away from her sides, as though overly starched. Her body, in full rigor, was stiff as well. She'd been dead for anywhere between ten and forty-eight hours.

Julia released her clenched diaphragm, took a breath. The air had the bitter taste of a half-rotted peanut and she could only hope there was oxygen in it somewhere.

"The other body," Griffith said, "it's off to the right, on a table."

"Laid out the same?"

"Pretty much."

"What about the cutting board and the cleaver?"

"Say again, loo?"

"Where her head should be. The butcher-block cutting board. And you see that cleaver on top of the board? That's quality, Bert. The thing gleams right through the blood."

"What's the point?"

"The point is not to dull the blade. You slam the cleaver into that marble counter a couple of times, it'd be useless."

Griffith's responding, "Uh-huh," made clear the fact that he still didn't get the point.

"I just mean it's a nice touch. Like keeping the dining room clean. Now how do you think he did that? How did he decapitate his victims, then get their heads from the kitchen to the dining-room table without leaving a trail of blood?"

"He did it very carefully is what I think." Griffith was shifting his weight from side to side, anxious, maybe, to be rid of his supervisor. "Either that or he cleaned up real good."

"Yeah," Julia agreed, "but the point you mentioned is that he was in control from beginning to end. He knew exactly what he was doing."

"Which is what?"

Instead of answering, Julia finally turned to the display on the dining-room table, half expecting to see, in the eyes of the victims, the agony of their deaths. But the victims' eyes, blue and brown, respectively, were flat and blank. They didn't reveal surprise or terror; they just looked dead. Slowly, Julia circled the table until she found the small entry wounds, one in the back of each skull. It was perfect, she decided, absolutely perfect. Just like the silver platters on which the heads rested. The platters were filled to the brim with coagulated blood, a gluey paste without which the killer's trophies would have toppled over long ago.

Julia re-traced her path until she was again standing next to Bert Griffith. He was bent over, staring down at a passport lying open on the table. The child they'd been calling Little Girl Blue stared back, a small kid with dark unruly hair and widely spaced features evenly distributed on a broad face. Her expression was grave, as if impressed with the importance of the moment.

"Anja Dascalescu," Bert said, stumbling over the last name.

"What?"

"That's her name, loo. See, over here. Anja Dascalesau. And her country of origin: Romania." He straightened up, and met Julia's eye. "It's good," he said. "We gave her a name."

"Not *we*, Bert. Whoever killed the Mandrakes and set this up gave her a name. *We* were just along for the ride."

Before she left the apartment, Julia, at Bert's insistence, visited one more room. Though small, the front room had a huge, heart-shaped bed virtually covered with small purple throw pillows.

"Over here, loo. Check this out."

Julia crossed the room to stand beside Bert Griffith at an immaculately clean window that offered an angled view, between heavy curtains, of Central Park. "How many hours?" Griffith asked. "How many hours you think she stood here, looking out, before she made her move?"

"Long enough, Bert." Julia let the curtain drop. "Long enough to know exactly what she was getting into. Long enough not to care."

16

PETER FOLEY stood at the corner of Broadway and Fifty-second Street, looking south into the heart of Times Square. He was wearing a lined microfiber trench coat, a duster, that fell nearly to his ankles, and a broad-brimmed wool Stetson so tightly woven it shed the rain as though made of rubber. Foley was particularly fond of the outfit and the vaguely romantic cowboy image it evoked. The boots were wrong, though. Insulated Gore-Tex ankle-highs with thick Vibram soles, they kept his feet dry and ate up the miles even as they diluted the fantasy.

Foley's destination was a small shop on Seventh Avenue near Thirty-ninth Street. As he'd come from downtown, from Waverly Place in the West Village, he might have approached the shop directly. Instead, he'd detoured to Eighth Avenue, then walked all the way to Fifty-second Street before coming back to Broadway and his favorite view of Times Square. He was looking down a gentle slope, into the brazen forest of neon signs lining both sides of Broadway and Seventh Avenue where the two converged at Forty-fifth Street.

Rain-smeared, the words and images blended one into the other, as if the whole had been designed by a single artist, a surrealist to be sure.

Like most New Yorkers, Foley had a clear memory of Times Square before the renewal project that had begun under Mayor Ed Koch, then proceeded relentlessly, clearing out most of the peep shows and X-rated bookstores, most of the prostitutes, most of the drug dealers, most of the grifters, and most of the muggers. Corporate America had moved into the vacuum: Virgin Records and Warner Brothers, the World Wrestling Federation and ESPN, Planet Hollywood, The Olive Garden, ABC, MTV, and the NASDAQ Market Site. Drawing tourists by the millions, from every country in the world.

It was a disconcerting change for a legion of embittered old-timers who somehow failed to understand, as Foley understood, that nothing at all had changed. Times Square remained the same old whore she'd always been. Yes, she'd had her tits lifted and her butt lipo'd, and she'd put on a hell of a fancy outfit, no doubt about it. But the whole area was a rip-off. The stores displayed shoddy merchandise bearing various logos hyping more shoddy merchandise, a gigantic cross-promotion supported by hundred of millions of advertising dollars. The food in the theme restaurants, as if determined to maintain the ambiance, was badly prepared, overpriced, and served in the tackiest of surroundings by surly waiters who spent their inebriated off-time proclaiming their eternal hatred of tourists. It was Brantley, Missouri, comes to the Big Apple, the dead-zero center of the consumer culture, American Gothic for the new millennium.

And all the while, just a few blocks to the west and south, the whores, the druggies, and the muggers awaited their turn. Sensing, perhaps, the impermanence of all that hype, seeing right through all that glitter, instinctively appreciating the difference between glitter and gold.

On that note, a satisfied Foley began to march south. It was eleven o'clock, the rain had picked up, and the sidewalks were virtually deserted. Within a few hours, if the temperature continued to drop, the roads would be streaked with ice and the taxis and trucks, the professional drivers, would shut down, leaving the city to the cops and the paramedics.

At Forty-third Street, Foley stopped again, just for a moment. The light was so intense here it seemed to penetrate his skin; he could almost hear the colors. For a moment, he imagined himself part of the show, a statue with its eyes perpetually raised . . . in awe? In homage? Or was it only, *Gee, folks, we're in Times Square?*

As Foley started off again, a figure approached from Forty-second Street, a man holding an enormous pink umbrella. The man advanced with determined strides, his gaze riveted to the sidewalk, the tip of the umbrella's staves even with Foley's eyes. For just an instant, Foley was tempted to play against character, to slap the umbrella out of his way, see what the jerk would do. Instead, he dodged to the side, then continued on. Interaction was not his game.

T H E F A T man seated behind the cash register at Pleasure World grimaced when Foley entered the store. "You're late," he said.

Foley removed his hat and shook the rain off. "Sorry. The weather. You know."

"Bein' late, it's disrespectful. I hadda keep the fuckin' store open after everybody else went home." The man's name was Alfred DeBennedetto and his problem was that he fancied himself a *mafioso*, a made guy, when he was just a clerk selling jerk-off tapes and stroke books to horny men. Alfred DeBennedetto, who lived all by his lonesome in a studio apartment in Flatbush.

"Fred, I'm sorry. I am. I'm really sorry. I was in Queens and the F train was running late. There was nothing I could do."

DeBennedetto hauled himself up, doing a kind of bench-press off the counter, and grunted his acceptance of Foley's apology. Then he locked the front door and led Foley into a back room. Once inside, Foley opened his coat to reveal a plastic shopping bag tied over his shoulder. The bag contained three videotapes, which he passed to DeBennedetto. The tapes had been copied from evidence that'd come into Foley's possession two weeks before. Foley routinely copied tapes and photos, using the copies to trade for still more evidence. On this occasion, however, Foley accepted a handful of fifty-dollar bills, stuffing them into a pocket.

"I hope I don't gotta tell you," DeBennedetto said, "what'll happen if these tapes come up bogus."

"Have I ever failed to produce?"

"It don't matter, kid. In my line of business, every time is the first time."

Repressing an urge to laugh out loud, Foley re-buttoned his duster, slapped his cowboy hat on his head, and exited Pleasure World. He walked directly north, to Forty-fifth Street, then turned east. As he entered the block, a car parked fifty yards away flashed its headlights several times. A moment later Foley was sitting in the back seat, looking into the amused black eyes of FBI Special Agent Raymond Lear.

"This a go?" Lear asked.

"I don't know. You tell me."

Though Lear's hand, bearing a thin manila file, came off the front seat, he did not offer the file to Peter Foley, not even when Foley removed the tape recorder and DeBennedetto's money, then held them up for Lear's inspection.

As Foley settled back to await further developments, he read the name typed onto an aquamarine identifying tag: ANJA DAS-CALESCU. "What now?" he asked. "Fun and games?"

Lear's hair, like his eyes, was jet black. Combed straight away from his forehead and lacquer-stiff with hair spray, it didn't so much as quiver when he shook his head in disgust. "The shit's hit the fan, Foley. It's all over the little tube. Two bodies up on Seventy-third Street. The kid . . . what do they call her?" He laughed. "Little Girl Blue. Yeah, they found Little Girl Blue's passport with her photo and her real name on it. Anja Dascalescu."

Foley shrugged. He'd caught the news as it flashed across the face of the *New York Times* building. It wasn't what he'd wanted, but there was nothing to be done about it. He would have to count on Ray Lear's ambition. DeBennedetto was the last piece of a year-long federal investigation into the distribution of child pornography. The feds had pursued it from the opposite end, targeting customers who'd ordered the material from an offshore website. Though they'd subsequently traced the website to a mobbed-up crew working out of Bensonhurst, the hard evidence necessary to make arrests had eluded them. That is, until Lily Han introduced Lear to Peter Foley and he showed them how to work the other end of the conspiracy.

"You wanna give me an explanation?" Lear finally asked.

"Not especially."

Lear put the file back on the seat, turned away from Foley, and folded his arms across his chest. His problem (as Foley knew) was that if he waited more than a few minutes, Alfred DeBennedetto would be gone, along with the tapes. "I can't give you the file," he finally said. "I can't take a chance."

"You think I killed them?"

"I think you're the craziest human being I know, or ever want to know."

"That's not an answer."

"Look, you can read the file in the car, even make a few notes, but you can't take it with you."

Relieved, Foley managed a grim smile before exchanging the tapes and money for the file. A moment later, as Lear used the radios to instruct his waiting troops, Foley went to work, jotting down names, addresses, dates, phone numbers. The documents he examined had been copied from an Immigration and Naturalization Service file. They pertained to the adoption of a Romanian citizen named Anja Dascalescu by an American couple living in New York City. The name of the couple was Norton, not Mandrake, and the question Foley asked himself was how Anja had passed from the Nortons to the Mandrakes without anyone noticing.

"You're gonna have to come out." Lear turned on the car's defroster and a rush of hot air washed over the fogged windshield. "There's no remaining anonymous. Not anymore."

"Turn DeBennedetto," Foley replied. "Then you won't need me."

"Your name's in the warrant."

"Redact it." Foley continued to write, only the tiniest portion of his attention given over to Lear.

"No. I want you on the witness stand, as a New York City police officer. I want to seal every crack. We're going to be in a federal court. We can't finesse your existence. One way of another, you're going to testify."

Foley closed his notebook and passed the file back to Lear. "But what," he asked, "if I did it? What if I killed those two people? Don't you think a murder conviction would negatively impact my testimony? Credibilitywise?"

I T WAS a quarter past two o'clock when Foley turned off the light next to his bed and buried his face in the pillow. He drifted off almost immediately, spiraling down to a vague fantasy which quickly expanded into a sharp-edged, full-color dream. He was on vacation, in Maine, with his wife, Kirstin, and his daughter, Patti. It was his and Kirstin's fifth anniversary.

Foley was sitting on a blanket, watching Kirstin as she shepherded four-year-old Patti, who was exploring the rock-studded beach. Overhead, a few puffy clouds drifted across an intensely blue sky, a sky bled of all impurities, a sky that hadn't been seen in New York City for two hundred years. From off in the distance, Patti's excited voice announced some precious discovery that required his immediate attention: "Daddy, daddy, daddy."

"Not now," Foley replied as he lay back on the gaily striped blanket. "Daddy's tired now."

But Patti continued to insist, repeating the same three words, over and over, until they became purely elemental, a complement to the calling gulls, to the rush of wind through the pine forest just a few yards behind him. Still, overwhelmed by a sudden, inexplicable lethargy, he did not respond.

Then it was night and it was raining and he was on his feet, panicked. He heard Patti call, heard the spatter of rain on the ocean, the harsh slap of waves breaking on the sand, the hoot of an owl in the forest. There was no moon in the sky above him, no stars, not even clouds; the beach, a swatch of black velvet that might have been inches from his eyes, lacked all depth. Nevertheless he staggered forward, toward the sound of his daughter's voice.

Daddy, daddy, daddy.

Foley awakened to find himself seated at the edge of his bed. The rain had changed to sleet; it rattled against the window, the noise primal and threatening. Foley listened for a moment, then glanced at the LED readout on his alarm clock. It was exactly 3 A.M., but he didn't consider returning to sleep. Instead, he rose and wandered off into the kitchen where he brewed a pot of coffee, poured himself a cup, then took it to his computer, the big Gateway and not the Mac. There was much to do and little time in which to do it. First he would find the Nortons, then Christopher Inman, the INS officer who passed on the adoption. Hopefully, by mid-morning, he would know enough to decide his next move.

As he waited for the Gateway to boot up, Foley opened a desk drawer and removed a photo, the same photo he'd shown Wallace Carpenter a few days before. Foley was in the photo, kneeling alongside a little girl whose arm encircled his neck. But it wasn't Patti Foley in the photograph, not the Patti he remembered, the six-year-old who would never grow up. It was Patti at ten, a computer-aged Patti who might or might not exist, a Patti he would never know. Unless he found her.

17

DRIVEN BY a prostate-compromised bladder, Robert Reid hauled himself out of bed, pulled on the flannel robe thoughtfully provided by his niece, and set off for the bathroom. As it was barely seven A.M. and he'd only gotten to sleep a few hours before, he stumbled from Julia Brennan's guest bedroom in a forgivable fog, nearly running over Julia who was standing in the hallway outside her daughter's room.

"Couldn't sleep," Julia explained. "You?"

"A message from . . ." Reid's voice rumbled up from his chest, a fair impression of James Earl Jones. "*It* who must be obeyed."

"It?"

"My prostate, dear. Now, if you'll excuse me."

Julia shifted, allowing her uncle to pass. "I'll put up some coffee."

"Great," Reid answered, though he'd been looking forward to several additional hours of sleep. Well, comforting his niece was the reason he'd come back to her home after the press conference given by Manhattan North Detective Commander Harold Clark. Though Clark had acknowledged C Squad's efforts, Julia's name hadn't been mentioned. Nor had she been present on the dais. She'd lingered, instead, at the back of the room, just another *schmucko* detective in a wrinkled suit.

The coffee was bubbling down into a carafe when Reid walked into the kitchen. A small glass of orange juice rested on the table before his chair. He drank the juice gratefully, then settled back to study his niece. They'd driven from Clark's press conference in separate cars, arriving at Julia's to find Corry still awake. Her presence had forced a delay of the heart-to-heart he and Julia were about to have.

"He was really pissed off," Julia said.

"Clark?"

"Yeah, and Borough Commander Flannery. They worked me over before the press conference."

"How bad?"

"About as bad as I deserved. I didn't notify Clark before we served the warrant." She was standing with her back to Reid, reaching into the cupboard for a pair of coffee mugs. "Clark expressly ordered me not to do anything major without letting him know. When he confronted me, I couldn't deny it. Flannery didn't say a word, but I could read the message in his eyes. He was disappointed. I'd been advertised as a team player, and I turned out to be just another hotdog."

Reid was about to reply when Julia spun to face him. By all rights, he decided, especially with no makeup, she should appear haggard, defeated. Because she *was* a team player, had realized from her first days in the Academy that she couldn't hope to advance unless she merged her own interests with the interests of the job. There was no way she would have deviated from that understanding unless powerfully motivated. Meanwhile, Julia's eyes were clear, her forehead placid. If anything, she seemed perplexed.

"I put out that bullshit name," she announced. "Little Girl Blue. I thought it up and I put it out there. It wasn't right."

"I don't get it."

Julia shook her head, jammed a hand into her hip. "She deserved a real name, not a *Daily News* headline."

"I hear you, Julia." Reid scratched his beard. "But I'm having trouble understanding why calling Harry Clark would have prevented the child's name from coming to the surface."

"I had to do it on my own." Julia waved him off. "It was like he was stealing my collar. No, not like that. I take it back." She hesitated, looking for the right words, then continued. "Look, Clark didn't deserve to be there. He and Flannery, all along they were betting C Squad would come up empty. He even told me that we'd offended the civilians with our little investigation and we should back off. I couldn't let him in at the last minute. He just didn't deserve it."

Reid nodded, though he didn't believe a word of what she was saying. That sort of principle was utterly irrelevant to a career-minded cop, to a heretofore single-minded woman who'd been a single-minded little girl. He and Mary-Margaret had been prepared—no, *expecting*—to take responsibility for their niece after Paulie deserted his family. Lord knew, Julia's mother, addicted as she was to equal measures of self-pity and alcohol, hadn't been up to the task. But Julia had risen to the occasion, somehow putting meals on the table, groceries in the cupboard, somehow getting herself off to school every morning. Robert Reid could not recall ever coming over to find the apartment dirty; Julia even rinsed the vodka bottles. At age eight, at age nine, ten, eleven, twelve . . . until the day of her marriage. Always responsible, always in control.

"So, where do matters stand right now?" he finally asked.

"I'm on vacation." She filled the two mugs, carried one to Reid, then returned to the kitchen counter.

"In January? You're on vacation in January?"

"In January, with Corry in school. Nice, right?" Julia opened the refrigerator, removed a carton of eggs and a pound of bacon. "They want to keep me away from the reporters."

"If I remember, Clark thanked C Squad, then announced he was organizing a special task force to investigate the murders. Doesn't that effectively isolate you?"

"You think it's overkill, do ya?" Julia shook hear head, her tone now flat. "The way it looks right this minute, I can forget the detectives. I'm not going anywhere in the division unless Clark retires." She began to arrange slices of bacon in a large flying pan, carefully overlapping the slices. Watching, Reid thought it was easier for her to speak of her humiliation while she busied herself with mundane tasks, while her back was turned. "You had to see it, Uncle Bob. In that apartment. You had to be there. Games upon games." She shifted the pan to a burner on the stove, twisted a knob, adjusted the flame. "The Mandrakes were prostituting the girls for between one and two thousand dollars a trick. We know because we found their books. They were also videotaping the sex, then selling the tapes to a New Jersey outfit, Patterson Distributing. We found a bunch of tapes in the Mandrakes' bedroom."

"What about blackmail? They weren't blackmailing the johns? With those videos?" He pushed himself up, the sharp tug in his lower back so familiar he almost welcomed it, and crossed the kitchen to refill his coffee mug. "Hard to believe."

"Blackmail is definitely a possibility, but there was no client list, Uncle Bob. And trust me, we looked very carefully."

"Did they have a computer."

"No computer. Sales to Patterson Distributing, customer visits, the records were kept in an old-fashioned ledger. There were entries for the cost of groceries, for the rent, but nothing to indicate they were blackmailing the johns."

"And nothing to indicate what happened to the other girls, either?" Regaining his seat, Reid carefully modulated his tone as he approached the heart of the conversation. If she didn't want to talk about it, he'd back off, wait for a better time.

"Nope." Julia took a package of English muffins from the cupboard, then a cookie sheet from a cabinet beneath the window. She carried these to the kitchen table and sat across from her uncle. "When you saw me this morning? Standing by Corry's door? I've been having nightmares, of Corry gone. I wake up and I know it's stupid, but I have to check on her. I can't stop myself." She tore open the package of muffins without taking her eyes away from Reid's. "I think of Corry going to school, that long subway ride into lower Manhattan. I think that sometimes she comes home late, after a rehearsal or a basketball game. Anything can happen . . ."

From upstairs, they heard a door close, then Corry's feet on the stairs, a flurry of thuds as she skipped her way down that brought the conversation to a halt. Reid turned to the door an instant before

Corry's face appeared. She was as close as he would get to a grand-child, this girl tilting on the cusp of womanhood. He loved her dearly, and he, too, worried about her.

"You made bacon," Corry exclaimed as she charged into the room. "God, it's like we're getting *normal* again."

18

NINETY MINUTES later, with Corry and Robert Reid gone, Julia took advantage of her imposed leisure and went back to bed. She slept soundly, and without dreaming, for two hours. When she awakened she found herself thinking, not of Corry, but of Peter Foley. She'd snitched, of course, exposing the roles played by Lily Han, Peter Foley, and Theodore Goodman in response to Harry Clark's imperious, "Spill it, Brennan."

Lily Han was a prosecutor. Peter Foley was a cop. Theodore Goodman was a registered informant. They could not be left out of the progression that led to the Clapham Apartments on East Seventy-third Street. But Julia had made no mention of Bea Shepherd. Nor had she revealed the disappearance of Foley's child or the suicide of Foley's wife. On the spur of the moment, goaded by Harry Clark's attitude, she'd kept those little details to herself.

Pulling on a white terry-cloth robe, Julia strolled into the bathroom and started water running in the tub. She added capfuls of bath oil and bubble bath as the tub filled, a pure indulgence on a weekday morning. Well, she would make up for it, maybe clean the oven, a

chore she'd been putting off for several weeks. And she'd get a laundry going, too, wash the comforters on the beds; she'd been intending
to clean them for longer than she cared to remember.

These practical concerns simply vanished when Julia lowered herself into the tub. The water was as hot as she could stand, and it only
took a moment for the heat to radiate to her bones. Her nostrils filled
with moisture and sweat beaded her face as every muscle in her body
relaxed. She closed her eyes, drew in the scent of jasmine, leaned
back against a folded towel on the lip of the tub. Maybe, she mused,
she'd call a hotel up in Lake Placid, take Corry skiing over the weekend. Monday was Martin Luther King's Birthday and the schools
were closed. Or maybe she'd call Mr. Raymond Singer, her former
lover. True, on their last date she'd threatened to shoot him if he
didn't cease ogling a certain waitress's nicely rounded posterior. But
that was four months ago. Most likely, he was over it by now. Most
likely, he'd made peace with his offended male dignity.

Foley's image flickered into Julia's consciousness, wavered momentarily, then jumped into clear focus, an excessively handsome man,
his nose and chin strong, his forehead as well. His hair was just a
shade lighter than auburn, a color so unusual if Julia had seen it on a
woman she'd have assumed that it came out of a bottle. But there was
something else, more elusive, in addition to Foley's good looks, an air
of playful self-confidence. Foley in charge. Foley in control.

What Julia had witnessed in the Mandrakes' apartment, the grisly
humor included, may have been the work of a psychotic; she would
leave that question to the expert witnesses. But Julia had examined
enough crime scenes, enough dead bodies, to be certain the Mandrakes' killer had not only been in control, he'd gone out of his way
to communicate that control.

An hour later, dried and dressed, Julia gathered up the laundry
basket and headed off for the washer and dryer in the basement.
Each comforter would have to be washed separately, and they would
take forever to dry. Best to get things started. It was only as she
reached for the light switch at the head of cellar stairs that she for-
mulated a very simple (and now obvious) truth. If she were still in

charge of the investigation, C Squad would be all over Peter Foley. Gut instinct, he fit the profile.

JUST BEFORE lunch, Julia picked up the phone and dialed Bea Shepherd's office number, another unpleasant task she'd been putting off. She got Bea's secretary and was put on hold for several minutes, feeling exactly like a schoolgirl summoned to the principal's office. Worse, like a schoolgirl turning herself in.

"Julia?"

"Bea?"

"I heard all about it."

"I assumed that."

"Clark was right."

"Agreed."

"Flannery was right."

"Also agreed."

"You challenged them. You had to be put in your place. I would have done exactly the same thing."

"Bea, do you think you could ask me how I'm feeling?"

"Not until I finish chewing you out. Remember, I recommended you to Clark. Your screwup reflects on me, especially when that screwup is the result, not of a simple mistake, an error of judgment, but of a swollen ego."

"Is that it?"

"Yes. Tell me how you're feeling."

Julia smiled, thinking now that Bea had supplied her with a motivation for her failure to notify Clark, she would not have to explain herself. Just as well, because she could still hear the bumbling attempts she'd made to rationalize her behavior to her uncle. It'd felt like she was guessing.

"I'm doing better than I would have figured, Bea. Now that I've given up all hope of a career in the Detective Division."

"Please, spare me the drama. Flannery likes you."

"This I don't believe."

"Flannery was a detective when you were in junior high school, Julia. You don't think he appreciates the fact that you found Little Girl . . . sorry, Anja Dascalescu? Because I'm telling you that if you'd called Flannery before you entered that apartment, he'd be pinning a medal on your chest."

"C'mon, Bea. Flannery's an ass-kissing jerk and we both know it. If I'd called him first, he'd most likely be pinning the medal on his *own* chest."

"So what if he did? Every ranking officer in the detective division, including the Chief of Detectives, would have known the truth. And these are the people who count. Not the reporters, not the public. I've explained this a thousand times."

Julia said nothing for a moment, wishing only for the conversation to end. She felt demeaned, though not surprised, by her mentor's patronizing attitude. In the last analysis, Julia Brennan was a supplicant, a beggar at the table, and humiliation was just another cost of doing business with the big boys. Eventually, if she was good, the roles would reverse; she would become the rabbi, the dispenser of blessings. That was the whole, rather pathetic point.

"What's my move here?" she finally asked. "What do I do?"

"You stay home for the next two weeks, enjoy your vacation. Then you go back to your desk, do your job, cash your paycheck, keep your head down. And don't worry about Harry Clark. He's got arthritis in his back and he'll be out in a year. He's not a player."

B Y LATE afternoon, the oven clean, the comforters returned to their respective beds, Julia was sitting before the trash pail in the kitchen peeling potatoes when the doorbell rang. Her heart jumped into her throat, the sound of the bell as penetrating as the ratchet of a shell into a shotgun. This is the way they do it—this is the way she'd done it—when they notify the unsuspecting relatives.

She tossed a half-peeled potato into a pot of cold water, washed her hands, walked into the living room, still unable to shake her fear.

"Who's there?"

"David Lane."

Feeling more than a little foolish, Julia opened the door. Lane was holding his hat in his hands, a stained fedora that would have looked just fine on last year's scarecrow. The only man in C Squad appointed to the new task force, Lane had been up more than thirty-six hours and his beefy, middle-aged face showed every minute of it.

"I'm gonna make this simple," he said. "A certain scumbag paper pusher who goes by the name of Inspector Edward Thurlow ordered me to come to your home and ask you if you're screwing Peter Foley?"

"Are you serious?" Julia looked into Lane's eyes, found shame instead of the amusement she'd expected.

"This guy, Peter Foley," Lane continued, his gaze dropping to his feet, "we can't find him."

"Say that again?"

"He's not livin' at the address in his file, hasn't lived there for a couple of years. The Post Office forwards his mail to a drop on Ninth Avenue. He picks up there every couple of weeks."

"Lily Han must know how to get in touch with him. She set up our meeting."

"Han's got a phone number that reaches an electronic answering service in the Bronx, Van Cortlandt Messaging. Foley pays for the service with money orders."

"And the service doesn't have an address for him? No phone number?"

"Nope."

Julia took a moment to collect her thoughts, then asked, "So what's this have to do with me?"

"Well, loo, this Foley, he's a good-looking guy, right? So the inspector's thinking, what with you not being married and all, maybe nature took its course and you know where to find him. I told the inspector that you never date cops, but he wasn't impressed. 'Let's just cover that base, detective,' is what he said. I wanted to fuckin' strangle the jerk."

"I see." Julia fought to contain her amusement. Old boys, she thought, not unlike old dogs, just can't be taught new tricks. What she liked best about Lane was that he didn't pretend to be something he wasn't. "Tell me, Lane, is Foley a suspect?"

"A suspect? Loo, he's a cop. I mean, Thurlow is real unhappy with Detective Foley and he left a message on Foley's service: Report forthwith or pay the price. But that doesn't make him a suspect. Thurlow wants Foley's help, just like you did." Lane ran his fingers through his thinning hair, then abruptly changed the subject. "You wanna hear a good joke? They put me behind a desk. I keep the case files in order, answer phones, relay information to the grownups. I'm a goddamned clerk."

"You handle every scrap of paper and you speak to everybody?" Julia waited for Lane's nod, then continued. "So you wouldn't mind telling me what's happening."

Lane smiled for the first time. "I divulge the details of a crime under investigation, my career, anybody finds out, it's in the crapper. Like, what's in it for me?"

"How about a beer?"

"A neat scotch'd go down better."

"You got it, Lane, now open up. You've been properly bribed."

But Lane waited until he'd downed his Black Label, smacked his lips and heaved a combustible sigh. Then he belched softly before turning watery eyes to Julia. "Know somethin', loo? It's better you're out of it. Crime Scene lifted about ten thousand prints, and we're gonna check 'em out, but you'd have to be a complete asshole to even hope the perp who set up that scene left his fingerprints on a lamp." He shifted in his seat, his eyes now glowing softly. "You remember the videotapes? The ones we found in the apartment? Well, Thurlow figures they were being used to blackmail the johns, one of whom took offense and chopped his tormentors' heads off. I mean, a grown man who rapes children, it's obvious he could do anything."

Lane held out the shot glass for a refill. "My last one," he said as Julia poured, "word of honor." He drank, then settled back. "Thing about it, loo, the company that got those tapes, Patterson Marketing, we tracked it to an empty storage garage in New Jersey. Guy who rented it paid cash. So what happened to the other kids, that's a pretty much a dead end for now."

"Then it's the johns or nothing?"

"Yeah. Thurlow's thinking we should take out warrants, put their mugs on the tube, but . . ."

"But," Julia finished Lane's thought, "Commander Clark, he's scared that one of 'em will turn out to be the mayor's father."

"Now you got the big picture." Lane rose to his feet, jammed his hat onto his head. "I got a hungry pit bull in Howard Beach needs my attention, loo, so I'm gonna get on my way." He paused long enough to look Julia in the eye. "You need anything, though, you got my home number. Don't hesitate."

"I'm on vacation," Julia returned as she led him to the door. "And by the way, you were right, a hundred percent right."

"About what?"

Julia opened the door, let the cold breeze wash over her face. "About my getting the better of the deal. Because the way it looks to me, you're going nowhere in a hurry."

19

J ULIA DIDN'T dream that night. She didn't have to dream. Even as she slipped beneath her freshly laundered comforter, dropped her head to the the pillow, her thoughts flipped, like a card dealt from the bottom of the deck, to the worst day in her life. Turned to that day and stayed there.

She is ten years old and quite skilled in the art of what she calls The Happy Family. Her own family, of course, is anything but happy, her father a drunk and gone, her mother a drunk and still present, at least physically. But that doesn't really matter. The point is to create an illusion solid enough to fool outsiders, the nuns at school, Father Blair, the social worker who pays monthly visits to their apartment.

They are on welfare, the Reid family, and Julia knows the social worker, Mr. Trentino, has the power to put her into foster care. She knows this because that's what he told her mother and her mother didn't argue. Mr. Trentino is a sour man, so thin Julia can see the bones in his Adam's apple when he swallows. He has an olive complexion and talks real slow, as if trying to communicate to people who don't speak English very well. One time he brought another social

worker with him, Mrs. Novak, who took Julia into the bedroom and
made her undress. "Does your mother ever hit you?" Mrs. Novak
asked. "Do you get enough to eat?" Then, finally, the bottom line:
"Have you ever seen your mother passed out on the floor?"

It's early evening and Mr. Trentino is coming on the following
morning. Lillian Reid is seated in front of a flickering black-and-
white television. She is watching the nightly news and sipping occasionally at a pint of Gilbey's gin, which she keeps in the pocket of her
bathrobe. She wears her plaid bathrobe over a slip and she is having a
good day, which means that Julia will be able to rouse her in the morning, convince her to take a shower, put on a clean dress, have a cup of
coffee, eat breakfast. Convince her to maintain the illusion for Mr.
Trentino. At this moment, Julia has no other aim or desire in her life.

At ten o'clock, just as Julia is beginning the process of getting her
mother to bed, the doorbell rings. It's her father, Paulie, come home
after an absence of seven months, bearing a quart of whiskey in a
brown paper bag.

Julia stands in the doorway, ten years old, sixty-five pounds, and
tells her father to leave them alone. He brushes her aside as if she
isn't there, as if he doesn't even know who she is.

They drink hard, the reunited lovers, until the bottle is empty.
Then they fight, a knockdown, bare-fisted donnybrook that ends with
the cops at the door and the little apartment in shambles. Lillian Reid
has a black eye and a split lip, but the cops merely send Paulie on his
way, then retire to their patrol car.

Somehow Julia does it. She drags her mother to her bed, yanking
at her hair when she threatens to pass out in the hallway, then sweeps
up the broken glass, mops the spills, straightens the upended furniture. She props a broken end table on a book, opens the windows,
refills a bookcase, vacuums the faded brown carpeting, propelled by a
bone-deep fear so pervasive it seems as solid as the walls that surround her.

At seven o'clock on the following morning, bearing three aspirin
tablets and a glass of water, Julia awakens Lillian, who immediately
begins to curse her husband, her life, her daughter. Julia waits
patiently for her mother to wind down, then offers the aspirin which

her mother smacks away. Julia retrieves the tablets, proffers them again, then again.

Mr. Trentino arrives at nine-thirty. He is in a rush, and if he notices Lillian Reid's makeup-camouflaged eye, her swollen lip, he keeps it to himself. He fills out papers, then leaves without addressing Julia. She has survived. Now it is only a matter of convincing her mother to write a note excusing her absence from school before Lillian is too drunk to hold the pen.

"You're a good girl," Julia's mother declares after her second drink of the morning. Tears stream from her eyes. "I don't deserve you."

THE INEXPLICABLE part, Julia decided, as she pounded the pillow, tried in vain to straighten the bedding, was that she hadn't called her uncle and aunt, hadn't asked them for help. How could she have believed they wouldn't have protected her? How could she not have known, as she knows now, that Robert and Mary-Margaret Reid would have made Julia Reid their own child before handing her over to Mr. Trentino and the City of New York? But she hadn't known, no more than Anja Dascalescu had known that any life but the one she lived was possible.

Again, Julia heard the slap of bare feet running on cold concrete. In the dark, with her eyes closed, she saw the plume of the girl's breath, turned faintly yellow by the streetlights, saw the two men on the other side of the street, their bewildered expressions as Anja flew by. They watched open-mouthed, scarcely believing their own eyes. How can this be? How can this be?

Eventually, a little after two o'clock, Julia managed to fall asleep. She woke up four hours later when Corry knocked on the door and, all innocence, asked, "Mom? Are you gonna be up for breakfast? Because I have to leave early today."

JULIA SPENT the rest of the post-breakfast morning engrossed in a mammoth history of New York entitled *Gotham*, a Christmas gift from her uncle. At noon, she bundled up and headed off to

Woodhaven Boulevard where she had lunch in a small Chinese restaurant, the Silver Dragon, then picked up a loaf of seeded bread at an Italian deli.

She was home by two, still a bit restless, when the phone rang. It was her uncle, Robert Reid. "Julia, I just received an e-mail. Anonymous." His breathing was rapid and shallow, the words emerging in little bursts. "I have to read it to you."

Half-amused, Julia responded, "Read away."

"All right." Reid drew a breath, then began. " 'I served up the Mandrakes' heads on silver platters. Now I present another tasty dish. On Fifth Street, in Long Island City, in the (alas) abandoned Empire Steel warehouse, in the sub-basement. Take a photographer, don't call the police, don't be a fool."

Julia felt her heart jump into another gear. The silver platters had not been included in Harry Clark's press conference, a detail held back in order to validate any future confessions, such as the one Robert Reid had just recited.

"Is it signed?"

"Yes. Destroyer and Destroyed."

"Say that again?"

"Destroyer and Destroyed."

"Okay, I get it. What about a return address? There must be a return address."

"The return address is cyberfree@heavenlyfire.com. I visited the site. It's in Hong Kong."

"Damn, what an ego," Julia said, following the train of her own thoughts. "What a clever little boy he is."

"Pardon?"

"Just a thought, Uncle Bob. Did you notify the task force?"

"I just got the thing a minute ago."

"And you called me first?"

"Yes. In case you want to come with me."

A moment of choice, a crossroads for Julia Brennan. If Robert Reid took a camera crew out to the warehouse, they would contaminate the crime scene irrevocably, assuming there was a crime scene to be contaminated. The smart move here was to insist that her uncle notify the task force, maybe call Harry Clark directly. She, herself, now that he'd phoned her first, had an obligation to . . . Julia tossed her hair and smiled, imagining herself warning Clark, Clark beating the reporters to the scene. Instant redemption.

"Julia, this is the biggest story of my career. Potentially. And I have to ask you about the silver platters. Are they details from the crime scene? Do you know what they mean? Off the record?"

"Yeah, Uncle Bob, they are. And that's why I'm not going with you." She gave him a moment to think it over. "I'm on vacation, remember? And this call? It never happened."

"So, if I get another one of these you don't want to hear from me?"

Her bluff having been thoroughly called, Julia beat a hasty retreat. "I didn't say that, Uncle Bob. Of course, I want to know everything. I just don't want anybody to know that I know."

Two hours later, Julia locked the front door of her house and headed off to the Twelfth Street Tavern in search of Peter Foley.

20

I THINK what it is," Peter Foley told Julia Brennan as they sat in Julia's gray Cherokee, sipping at styrofoam containers of bitter coffee, "is that I had a happy childhood. Too happy. I wasn't prepared, you know, for what happened to Kirstin and Patti." Foley's tone was matter-of-fact, betraying nothing of the joy he'd felt when Julia walked into the Twelfth Street Tavern. His heart had jumped in his chest at her appearance, as if trying to force its way between his ribs, as if trying to escape his body. "My folks really got along, even though my old man was a cop and had to do rotating tours, and my mom worked at an insurance agency. I mean, they weren't around all that much, but I always felt safe."

Foley paused, but Julia didn't respond, didn't so much as look at him. She hadn't responded to his warm greeting, either, when she walked into the bar. Instead, every inch the superior officer, she'd crooked a finger, said, "C'mon, Foley, let's have a little talk."

"I was only thirty," Foley continued, "when my mom died, and thirty-five when my father had a cardiac arrest. I'm not saying I wasn't affected, that I didn't grieve, but what I felt, it cleaned me out.

And I still had my own family, of course. My wife was a rock. She was there every minute."

He broke off again, but Julia still refused to so much as glance in his direction. Instead, as though speaking to someone outside the driver's side window, she said, "Come tomorrow, you're going to report to Lily Han, swear that you filled out a change of address form and handed it over to the Duty Sergeant when you moved. You're going to appear contrite, demonstrate submission, convince the bosses that you won't do it again. That way you'll most likely get off with a reprimand and a notation in your file."

It was Foley's turn to extend the silence as he tried not to smile. Thinking if it wasn't for Julia Brennan he'd already be an ex-cop, that he'd planned all along to quit. Carrying a badge had become more of a hindrance than a help.

"Anja's dead," he finally told Julia. "Anja Dascalescu is dead and so are her pimps and you'll never know what she was thinking. She might have been retarded, or emotionally disturbed. Maybe that's why her parents got rid of her in the first place. Because she wasn't perfect."

Julia shrugged, apparently at ease with the change of subject. "I'm just trying to find my focus," she announced, "while covering my ass at the same time."

"Does that mean you don't know why you're here?"

"Why I'm here with you?"

"Either way."

"Well, as it turns out, I know exactly why I dragged you away from the Twelfth Street Tavern. You were right, by the way, about Anja. There's nothing we can do for her, and if she'd been living in that apartment alone I'd be home now having dinner."

"Ah, you're after the other children and you don't trust the task force. I should have known."

"The task force, they're thinking blackmail."

Foley shook his head. "A setup like that, it's got a realistic lifetime of six months. The blackmail wouldn't start until the Mandrakes had already moved out. What would be the point? At two thousand dollars a trick, they were making plenty of money."

"A detail," Julia returned, "that you shouldn't know."

Foley folded his hands across his chest and tilted his head to the left. "Hey, lieutenant," he said, "Let's make a deal. I show you mine, you show me yours."

I'VE GOT the details of Anja's immigration case file," Foley said once his offer was accepted. "She was adopted in Romania by an American couple. Not the Mandrakes. The couple, Joe and Carla Norton, have vanished, likewise for the INS worker, Christopher Inman, who passed off on the adoption."

"And that's it?" Julia asked when it became clear that Foley was waiting for her response. "Now I've seen everything you have?"

"Not everything, but I may be down to my thong."

"Leather, I assume."

"Sequined, actually."

Julia unwrapped a buttered corn muffin and nibbled at the edge, knowing full well that no matter how careful, she'd end up with a lapful of crumbs. "So now it's my turn?"

"That's right."

As she retrieved her cell phone, punched in David Lane's cell phone number with her free hand, Julia's attention shifted to her daughter. Despite the divorce, Julia had fought hard to give Corry a stable life. Everything's okay was the message conveyed by the little house in its proper middle-class neighborhood, Julia's conservative wardrobe, the steady paycheck she brought home, even her personal ambition. The last thing pre-adolescent Corry needed, after thirteen years of sanity, was her mother partnered with a psycho like Peter Foley.

Lane did most of the talking in the one-sided conversation that followed. Julia took a few notes, thanked him profusely, then hung up. "More homicides," she told Foley. "Mandrake-related."

Foley's gaze, as he turned it on Julia, was mild. "How so?" he asked.

"Well, it seems a newspaper columnist, Robert Reid, who just happens to be my uncle, received an anonymous e-mail directing him to a currently unoccupied warehouse in Queens. Because the e-mail contained details that could only be known to the Mandrakes' killer, and also because Uncle Bob is curious by nature, he went out to the warehouse, where he discovered three bodies hanging from a light fixture in the basement. Two of the bodies were badly decomposed, but the third was in good shape. It belongs to a man named Theodore Goodman. You remember him, don't you?"

Foley ignored the question. "And that's what you're showing? That you're inside the task force, that you'll keep me . . . *us* informed? I stripped down to my thong, Julia. You took off your earrings. I don't think that's fair."

Julia shrugged, smiled. "Would you believe that's the best I can do?" she asked.

"No."

"And why is that."

"That's because there are too many other issues."

"Like?"

"You've been a cop for twelve years, Julia, and in that time you've obtained a master's degree in Criminal Justice, advanced to the rank of detective-lieutenant, and aced the captain's exam. Very nice, like your starter home in Queens, and your new car, and your thirteen-year-old daughter attending Stuyvesant High School, one of the best schools in New York City." Foley tapped the Jeep's dashboard. "It's a good life you've got, a very good life. I oughta know, because I used to have it."

He paused long enough to finish his coffee, to enjoy Julia's accusing, "You've been in my case file."

"The mutts we're going after, they won't be like Teddy Goodman, or even like the Mandrakes. The INS worker who okayed Anja's entry into the States? He's the director of the adoption section, a career bureaucrat, or so I'm told, and he oversees several thousand foreign adoptions every year. How much trouble would it be to rubber-stamp five, six, maybe even ten applications?"

"Not much," Julia admitted.

"How many tricks, at two grand per, do you think three girls could turn in six months? How much revenue would the sale of the videotapes generate? How much from the follow-up blackmail operation?" Foley crossed his legs, feeling very comfortable. "More to the point," he continued, "how much risk would the investors be willing to take for that kind of return? How far will they go to protect their investment?"

"You think I'm scared? What kind of sexist bullshit is that?"

"Hear me out. If we were dealing with a bunch of Teddy Goodmans, it'd be easy. You saw how scared he was. But that's not the case, at least not the way I see it. I think we're up against professionals and our questions are gonna have to be firmly put. Are you ready for that? Because me, if I have a stopping point, I haven't found it."

"You done now?"

Foley reminded himself that no matter what they did together, good fight or not, Julia would bust him if she thought he was involved in the killings. In fact, he had to admit, he wouldn't be surprised if that was among the reasons she'd come to the Twelfth Street Tavern. It was a big problem for him, this contradiction, the good Julia, the wicked Julia. But it was also part of the attraction, imagining what she'd be like cut free of the chain of command.

"Yes, I'm done."

It was again time for Julia to nibble, to sip, to pause long enough to ease the tightness in her chest, to let her adrenals settle down. Foley was an impossible read, even when she knew he was lying. She had to accept the fact, and not let him get beneath her skin. "You want a commitment? That's what this is all about? You want me to tell you I won't back off, no matter what the consequences?"

"Something like that."

Julia rummaged through her bag for a moment, then brought out a spiral notebook. She flipped through the pages, the gesture as theatrical as she could make it. Finally, she nodded before looking up at Foley. "The way I've got it, Foley, your loving mother died when you were two years old, and your faithful father married and divorced three times in the next fifteen years. You graduated from Holy Cross High School and spent a year at the University of Arizona on an athletic scholarship. Then you joined the cops after an injury capped your dreams of glory."

"You've been through my service record." He smiled, opening laugh lines at the corners of his eyes. "I should have expected it."

But he had, Julia suddenly realized. He'd expected her to check him out, and wanted to confirm his judgement. Thus, he'd baited the hook with a few lies, and she'd bitten hard, and now he knew. Score one for Peter Foley. At least he hadn't underestimated her.

"You know what I think, Foley? I think we're both still dressed. I think we haven't even unbuttoned our coats. I think we need to sleep on this conversation and start again tomorrow morning. After you've cleaned up your problems with the New York Police Department."

21

ROBERT REID dialed his niece's telephone number for the third time in two hours. He was in his Central Park West apartment, using an antique phone, the base, receiver and mouthpiece carved from ivory. The phone weighed a ton, but conveyed the human voice with a clarity his cellular didn't approach.

"Hello."

"Ah, Julia, I've been trying to reach you for hours."

"I was on the road and I had my phone turned off. Sorry."

As Reid could hear nothing in Julia's tone that even vaguely resembled repentance, he abandoned the guilt trip and got right down to business. "We found three men . . ."

"I know, Uncle Bob. I know what the crime scene looked like. I checked with a friend on the task force about an hour ago."

"And that's it? You have nothing to say? Julia, it's the first big New York crime story of the twenty-first century."

"The very *new* twenty-first century."

Reid carried the telephone to a cane-back chair, sat down, heard the chair creak in response. Though a mere reproduction of an eighteenth-century original manufactured in Ipswich, Massachusetts, the chair had cost more than his first six months' salary as a cub reporter.

He took a breath, calmed himself, finally asked, "How are you, Julia?"

"I'll be better when Corry gets home."

"When is she due?"

"In about a half-hour. She's rehearsing tonight."

"Isn't it a little too early to worry?"

"You're assuming the worry stops and starts. In fact, these days, it's always there, like a pilot light on a stove. You crank the dial . . . *WHOMP*."

Reid hesitated, hearing something beyond Julia's flippancy, an uncertainty foreign to him. He'd seen her angry many times, seen her sad as well, and of course he knew her kindness firsthand. But not uncertainty, that was novel.

"Uncle Bob, you still there?"

"I am." He cleared his throat. "It was horrible, Julia. Two of the bodies were decayed to the bone and the other one's face was covered with rat bites. The rat turds crunched when you walked across the room, like rice at a wedding."

"You walked onto the crime scene?"

"Only far enough to take photos. Then we backed away."

"I'm sure that made Inspector Thurlow feel much better."

"Actually, he was pretty upset. He reminded me of my civic duty to report crimes to the police and my liability under the penal code for shirking that duty. I told him there was nothing in the e-mail I received to indicate that a crime had been committed, that my constitutional rights as a journalist trumped his police powers, and that if he arrested me it would put the book I intended to write on the bestseller list."

Reid brightened when Julia laughed, wondering what she'd say if he told her that he worried as much about her as she did about Corry. His worry, of course, ran along a different line. Reid wasn't afraid that his niece would be kidnapped or assaulted. No, what he feared was that Julia had so tightly controlled every aspect of her life for so long that she'd fly off like a skyrocket if she let go. "The good inspector, he never stopped smiling. Do you know him?"

"Never met the guy."

"Well, he's somebody's yes-man. Greasy is the word that come to mind. Good for me, bad for the task force."

"Ya know, Uncle Bob, the more I think on it, the luckier I feel about what happened. The task force isn't going anywhere and the blame's gonna fall on somebody else. Praise the Lord."

"Can I quote you on that?"

"Only if you want to destroy what's left of my once-promising career."

"Perish the thought. But, look, I did call you for a reason. Thurlow, before he left, told me he thought we could work together in the future. Even gave me his card. I suggested that he encourage my cooperation by telling me if Theodore Goodman, now dangling at the end of a rope, was somehow connected to Anja Dascalescu. He told me he'd think it over."

"How'd you know? The name, I mean."

"Goodman's driver's license, bearing his photo, was lying on a workbench. Face-up."

Julia muttered, "Alright," then hesitated long enough to arrange her thoughts. When she spoke again, her tone was all business. "Uncle Bob, what I tell you now, I don't want you to print it until you confirm it from another source."

"No problem."

"And when you do confirm, *if* you confirm, I want you to attribute the information to multiple police sources."

Reid was encouraged by Julia's caution, by her reversion to a Julia with whom he was both more comfortable and more familiar. "Scout's honor," he said. "Now cough it up."

"Theodore Goodman was the confidential informant who led us to the Mandrakes' apartment. He was a client, Uncle Bob, a chicken hawk. He liked to fuck little kids."

22

FOR JULIA Brennan, who sat near the end of a pew at the back of Holy Savior Roman Catholic Church at 8:30 on the following morning, it was a first. Though Catholic-school educated, she had never before heard a Latin mass, and she was struck by the beauty of the language and an eerie sense that she'd stepped out of time, as if the rite were being performed in a museum, or as a theater piece. Peter Foley's presence thirty feet above her head, in the choir loft, did nothing to dispel the illusion. He'd invited her to meet him here, assuring her that by then he'd have cleared up his problems with the job, that he'd be ready to get down to business.

"I'd skip the mass," he'd explained, noting her surprise. "I don't want you to get the impression that I'm a fanatic or anything. But I sing in the choir and the team's counting on me. You know, you don't have to come. If you're not there, what I'll do is call you right after."

Another lie? Another dare? With Peter Foley, you were never sure.

The priest bent down over the chalice, then chanted, *"Hoc est enim Corpus meum."* He held that position for a moment, his back to the congregation, his fingers steepled in adoration, until the altar boy rang the bell. Then the priest elevated the Host, raising it high enough for all to see. *"Simili modo postquam . . ."*

Julia recognized the first part, *For this is My body*, but the rest of it eluded her. There was a time in her life when she was familiar with the Ordinary of the mass, when she'd followed along in her Sunday missal. But that was twenty years ago, more than enough time to forget.

Julia did not take Communion, one of the few in the church to refrain. She sat back, instead, thoroughly bemused. Foley the choir boy. Foley the cop. Foley trading batches of chicken porn with Theodore Goodman and all the others. Lily Han's warning had badly understated the reality. Foley had a dozen agendas, each pointed, as far as Julia could see, toward the same end. He wanted to maintain his equilibrium, not to mention his sanity, while he . . . Well, that part of it, Foley's ultimate goal, was still a mystery, one for which Julia was suddenly, and surprisingly, grateful.

The choir began to sing, a chant of some kind, the voices without harmony, rising and falling, neither ancient nor modern. Though she'd never heard him sing, Julia tried to pick out Foley's voice, imagining him for some reason a tenor. But the voices were so thoroughly blended, matching each other note for note, that she could barely distinguish among them. Finally, she gave up, allowing the music to sweep through her, a perfect complement to the little church, the Latin mass, to Foley himself.

After the mass ended, Julia waited for Foley at the rear of the church, next to a small table bearing tracts, some theological, some offering advice on how to live a good Catholic life. She pulled one from the rack, glanced at it, put it back. Foley was coming down a narrow flight of stairs, smiling broadly, happily, as if he'd hoped for nothing more in life than her appearance.

Outside, he introduced her to the priest, Father Lucienne, then to a dozen parishioners. As she shook hands and exchanged glances, Julia read a single message in the quick smiles of Foley's friends. They were hoping she was the one, that Foley had finally overcome the tragedy that set him apart and found himself a good woman.

"You ready?"

Julia took Foley's arm. "I am," she said, leading him down the street.

"Where shall we go?"

"Well, what I thought, being as you've straightened out your problems with your superiors and your residence is no longer a secret, we'd go to your apartment." She looked up at him and winked. "You still wearing that sequined thong."

Foley shook his head. "I switched over to latex this morning. You know, for the itch."

NOTHING FANCY," Foley said as he flipped a switch on the wall to light a ceiling fixture. "But it's home sweet home to me."

A dump, Julia thought as she scanned Foley's studio apartment. A clean dump, but still a dump. And pathetic, too, in spite of Foley's apparent ease.

She took in the equipment arranged along the room's outer wall. Two desktop computers, a Mac and a Gateway, a pair of notebooks, peripherals galore. More bait, but this time she wasn't biting. There would be nothing incriminating on the hard drives, or on the floppies, or anywhere else. Foley's little dump was a box of Cracker Jack without a prize at the bottom. That's why he was willing, almost eager, to bring her here.

"So." Foley leaned against the counter in front of the Gateway studiously, yet impressively, nonchalant. "Welcome to the neighborhood."

"It's the perfect spot for you," Julia responded. "A perfect non-fit."

They'd parked the car well east of Foley's apartment, on Grand Street near East Broadway, then walked into what had once been the heart of a predominantly German neighborhood, Kleindeutschland, a neighborhood that had given way toward the end of the nineteenth century to the Lower East Side, home to millions of Jewish and Italian immigrants. A hundred years later, Grand Street was still Jewish on its eastern end but west of Ludlow Street the signs above the storefront businesses were virtually all in Chinese. This was not the Chinatown south of Canal Street, with its curio stores and restaurants catering primarily to Europeans. Here, the faces on the crowded streets were almost universally Asian, customers and vendors alike, everybody hustling, out to make a buck in the big city. The scene was vibrant, the sidewalks crowded with pedestrians, the streets choked with trucks and cars. Double-parked vans, loading and unloading, blocked traffic. Fishmongers and their customers shouted over the din of the horns. Short, stocky men, bandanas tied across their foreheads, pushed hand trucks loaded with boxed produce through the crowds.

Foley had remained silent as he led Julia into the heart of the community, giving her plenty of time to absorb the bottom line. This was a world in which he could live as an outsider, where people minded their own business as a matter of reflex, where Peter Foley's business would have been unfathomable in any event.

"I've been in touch with the task force," Julia announced as Foley spooned coffee into a lined filter basket. "There's talk of passing the Anja Dascalescu part of the investigation to the feebs and there's a new strategy in place. The johns are gonna have their moment in the sun."

She didn't raise the question of Foley's status within the NYPD. Lane had been quite specific on that score, telling Julia that Inspector Thurlow had received an early morning call from Chief Flannery, then emerged from his office to announce that the task force had no further interest in Peter Foley, that Foley possessed no information relevant to their investigation. Had Lily Han spoken to Flannery? Or had the word come down from the almighty feds? Lane hadn't known, hadn't cared. With the help of a civilian computer tech, he'd created individual photos of the johns. The photos were scheduled for release at a press conference headed by Commander Harry Clark in time for the nightly news, after which all hell would break loose. Lane was looking forward to the explosion.

"What about the children?" Foley asked. "Why not release photos of the children?"

"The children are being written off," Julia replied. "Or maybe handed over to the feds. Either way, the NYPD wants no part of a long-term investigation. The press is clamoring for immediate results."

Foley noted Julia's bitter smile, the accusation behind it. Would he feed the results of their own little investigation to his federal connections? Without doubt, her smile said, they'd already approached him. What she couldn't know, however, was that he'd kissed off Special Agent Raymond Lear after exchanging several boxes of evidence for a very thin, very disappointing file.

"The INS worker who processed Anja's adoption," Foley said, "Christopher Inman, he's dead. In a Baltimore motel, garrotted, most likely a professional hit. The couple who officially adopted Anja, Joseph and Carla Norton, they're missing."

"Joseph and Carla . . . Like Uncle Bud and Aunt Sarah."

"Very much like Bud and Sarah. The Nortons rarely had less than five foster children living in their home. Kids arrived and left all the time."

"So the odd slave wouldn't attract all that much attention."

"Better yet. The Nortons' home is in Bayside, in a big-bucks neighborhood two blocks from Crocheron Park. Far from applauding the Nortons' efforts, the locals have been trying to get them out for a long time." Foley jammed his hands into his pockets. "I found six newspaper stories, spread out over three years, mostly in local papers. The Crocheron Civic Association never attacks the children directly. No, what upsets Bayside's finest are the relatives coming to visit, all those unwed mothers trudging from the Norton home to the bus stop six blocks away."

Julia crossed to the counter next to the sink and poured two cups of coffee as Foley took sugar and milk from the refrigerator. "I was up again last night," she announced, "thinking." She lifted the container of milk, took what she hoped was a surreptitious sniff before adding a dollop to her coffee. "I kept asking myself why an INS administrator would risk his career and his family to bring those kids into the country? How much money would you have to pay him to put his entire life in jeopardy? Because he had to figure, sooner or later, one of those kids was gonna get loose and blow the scam. Meanwhile, the paper trail leads right back to his desk."

Foley sipped at his coffee, but said nothing. His and Julia's minds had run along the same path, and he was curious to know how far she'd taken it.

"Those videos we recovered at the Mandrakes, we both felt they'd be used for blackmail, sooner or later. But what if the Nortons and Christopher Inman were being blackmailed? I remember Teddy Goodman, how scared he was, and I know if Teddy was an INS executive, he would've signed off on those adoptions. And if he was already a foster parent, like Joe Norton, he would have played the part of adoptive parent without a second thought. He'd have done anything to avoid exposure."

Julia stopped, took a breath, wondering if Foley's smile was mocking. "The Mandrakes are dead and my friend on the task force is telling me their phone records don't show a single person-to-person contact. It's possible they used a cellular to make appointments, but if so, it wasn't in their apartment or listed in their name. And the bills weren't sent to their address, either."

"So it's a dead end on the Mandrakes?"

"Unless you can tell me something I don't know." As Julia carried her coffee mug to the sink, it occurred to her that Foley's life was as carefully layered as the individuals they sought. "Inman was expendable, likewise the Nortons. The Mandrakes lived their lives prepared to move at any minute. I think we're looking at a mob crew."

"The dreaded Mafia?"

"No, from eastern Europe most likely, Russia, Yugoslavia, Romania, Bulgaria. Anja came from Romania, and the other children, the children on those videos, were all Caucasian." Julia stopped abruptly as a stereo started up somewhere in the building, a salsa played at ear-splitting volume. As if on cue, a pair of cockroaches darted from behind the sink, paused momentarily, antennae dancing, then streaked across the wall before finally disappearing behind a cabinet.

"We're in complete agreement," Foley announced, "but I think you left something out."

"Which is?"

"The possibility that whoever killed the Mandrakes took their cell phone, their client list, and whatever else he—or *they*—wanted."

"Why is it," Julia asked, "that I feel like I'm fighting a war on two fronts?" She continued before Foley could respond, then wished she'd waited long enough to find out if he intended to respond.

"Look, you're the one with the files, and you're the one calling the shots. At least for the present."

Foley's face brightened. "In that case," he told her, "it's off to the Nortons'."

"The Nortons, if you remember, will not be at home to receive us. They've gone missing."

"So much the better, Julia. Now we'll have a chance to look around without the bother of getting a search warrant. All those messy details, all that probable cause . . . you have no idea how much I've come to hate the charade."

23

MILES FROM the nearest subway, the decidedly upscale community of Bayside in eastern Queens County was affluent enough to notice (and, more importantly, to report) the presence of strangers. So Julia and Foley reasoned on the long ride out, and so, by necessity, they stopped first at the 112th Precinct to announce themselves and their intention to canvass the area immediately surrounding the Nortons' residence. The sergeant at the front desk, a thin nervous man who chewed at his lower lip throughout the conversation, eventually radioed the sector car assigned to the area surrounding Crocheron Park, informing a bored patrol officer that two suits from Manhattan North Homicide would be working the neighborhood and should not be arrested or shot under any circumstances.

Satisfied, they drove from the precinct to the Nortons' residence, a sprawling, three-story brick home on a bluff overlooking Little Neck Bay. Four times the size of Julia's little house, it was impressive enough to draw a whistle.

"Whaddaya think it's worth?" she asked Foley as they stepped from the Jeep. Above their heads, a swollen milky sun cast a nearly colorless light from behind a layer of smooth high clouds. The temperature was in the mid-thirties, neither hot nor cold for January, and there was no wind.

"Between the oversize lot and the view, I'd say a million and a half." Foley closed the door, waited for Julia to come up beside him on the sidewalk. "Credit where credit is due, lieutenant. It's hard to imagine the Nortons motivated by money."

The house was surrounded by a tall stockade fence that came within six feet of the curb. Even on tiptoe Julia could see only the upper windows. They were shut tight and nothing moved behind them. After a moment, she pressed her eye to a small gap between two fence posts, found a sandbox and a swing set. The swing set was bright red and looked to be freshly painted.

"You ready?" she finally asked Foley.

"After you, lieutenant."

Foley watched Julia ring the bell at the front gate, thinking that she was only one quality short of being a great detective. She wasn't ruthless, not yet, anyway. Nevertheless, reporting in to the local precinct was her idea, and her strategy was twofold. If the Nortons didn't answer, he and Julia would canvass the neighborhood, not just making their presence and their status known, but in the process learning which houses were empty. Later, when (or *if*; he still wasn't certain she'd go through with it) they jumped the fence, their actions would excite no undue concern. Even if they were observed, nobody calls the cops on the cops.

A few seconds later Julia rang a second time, then a third. Finally, she tried the handle, noting that the gate was secured with a deadbolt lock, not a simple latch. When the handle failed to turn, she looked at Foley and said, "Well, time for Plan B."

They began with the closest home, knocking on the door, ringing the bell. The only response was the frenzied barking of a very large dog. As Bayside was burglary heaven, Foley wasn't surprised. Property had to be protected and a dog was as good as any alarm.

The second home was also unoccupied. Good news indeed, as its northern face and the Norton's fence were separated only by a narrow flagstone path which was itself screened by a tall hedge in the front yard. Foley nodded to Julia, received a smile in return; both knew opportunity when they saw it.

They split up, then, Foley taking the north, and Julia the south side of the block. They kept it simple, asked a few general questions, then skipped to the chase: "Do you know where the Nortons might have gone?" Nobody did, but one young woman, flanked by twin toddlers, volunteered a relevant piece of information to Julia.

"The welfare took those kids outta there."

"How do you know?"

"I saw the van pick 'em up. Monday morning." Her hands dropped to the shoulders of her children. "Me and the twins, we're walkin' the dog, minding our own business, when Joe Norton leads the kids out. Six of them, in a line, the oldest couldn't have been more than seven or eight. When the van drove away, Joe said, 'Well, I guess you got what you wanted.'"

"Did you respond?"

"Nah. I mean, I gotta admit, I wasn't one of Joe Norton's supporters, but this was really pitiful. The kids were black and Spanish, and they were carrying their possessions in garbage bags. It was like they were being led off to prison." She shrugged her shoulders, riffled her boys' hair. "You'd expect they'd be crying, but they had on these stone faces, looking straight ahead, and you had to know they'd been through it before. They were little veterans."

Julia's own face remained expressionless as she made a note from time to time, nodded her head in the right places. Anja's murder had become public knowledge on Sunday morning. A day later, the Nortons had dumped the foster kids and taken off for parts unknown. Hopefully, they'd moved fast enough. Hopefully, they weren't already dead. Hopefully, in their haste, they'd left something behind to indicate where they'd gone to ground.

Julia was already waiting as Foley smiled his last smile, offering his final thank-yous to an elderly man who claimed not to know of the Nortons' existence. Then, together, while Julia revealed the fate of the Norton foster children, they headed back down the block, covering

perhaps a hundred yards before an NYPD cruiser pulled up alongside. The driver, young and cute enough to cuddle, rolled down his
window.

"Lieutenant Brennan?" The boy's voice was deep and manly, his
tone businesslike, but he did make one essential mistake. He addressed Peter Foley instead of Julia Brennan. Thus, when Julia replied
to his query, the color rose in his round, nearly beardless cheeks until
they were the deep red of a slightly overripe tomato.

"Sorry, ma'am . . . I mean, lieutenant. Sorry, lieutenant."

Foley watched Julia lean into the window, watched the kid squirm
away. She was hamming it up for his, Peter Foley's, benefit. Treating
him as an equal though his rank, technically, was no higher than that
of the patrol officer she was effortlessly intimidating.

"What can I do for you, Officer . . . O'Donnell?"

"I just thought I'd come by and offer my help, lieutenant." His
voice had risen a full octave and seemed to originate in the back of his
throat. "You know, if you needed anything."

"Like what?"

"Like . . . anything."

"What do you know about the Nortons?"

"They the ones with the foster kids?"

"Yeah."

To his credit, O'Donnell sat up straight while he composed a
response. "Thing is," he finally said, "those kids, they never played
on the streets. There are plenty of other children on the block, you
see 'em after school with their skateboards and their bikes. But those
kids who stayed with the Nortons, they were kept behind that fence."

Foley found himself unprepared for the young cop's observation.
Ordinarily, he didn't allow himself to think about the children and
what they experienced. There was no point to it. Chicken hawks were
like murderers, or burglars, or thieves. They went on forever.

But this time he actually saw the children as they'd been described,
marching in a straight line, eyes front, little soldiers of pain. Off to
the next circle of hell.

"Great," As Julia backed away from the car, she glanced at Foley and rolled her eyes. "Just what I wanted to hear." She tapped the roof of the car, took another step back. "We need you, officer, we'll call you."

After that, Foley had only to follow Julia Brennan down the block, around a thick hedge, and along the flagstone path running parallel to the Nortons' fence. To watch her pull off her coat, toss it into the neighboring yard, then vault the fence before he could offer a boost.

"You coming, Foley?" she called back. "Or are you having second thoughts?"

24

FOLEY'S EYES jumped to the recessed front door, then from one window to the next. He proceeded systematically, stopping for a few seconds at each window, including those in the single-story addition at the rear. There were no lights behind the curtains, blinds, or drapes, and no sign of an alarm, which did not surprise him. With five kids living in the rarely empty house, it would present a highly uninviting target to any burglar who valued his liberty.

Satisfied, he walked over to the front gate. The lock was set high in the fence, out of reach of younger children. He twisted the latch and the bolt withdrew with a little snap. Now he and Julia would be able to claim they'd found the gate unlocked, then approached the door as they'd approach the door of any dwelling. Now they could claim it was only when the bell went unanswered that they circled the property in search of the minors they knew to live in the house. Fear of foul play uppermost in their minds.

Julia rang the bell once, just to make it look good, then followed Foley around the side of the house. Though her pulse was zipping along and her senses were on full alert, she felt comfortable, as though she'd been doing this all her life.

They walked the full length of the house, then circled around the back, to a small, double-hung window overlooking the bay. The homes on either side did not extend this far and there was no one to see when Foley stooped to gather up a rock the size of his palm. One of a series forming the border of the narrow garden, the upper half of the rock had been painted white and it looked to Julia like a gigantic vanilla cone as Foley raised it to shoulder height then crashed it into the window's upper pane.

The rock landed on the floor inside with a solid thud. It was, Julia decided, the last link in an improbable chain of events designed to establish, of all things, probable cause. Their fear for the safety of the children justified a walk around the house. That same fear, once they discovered evidence of a forced entry, justified a cursory search of the residence. The saddest part was that it would play in a courtroom, but no experienced cop, including Commander Henry Clark and Inspector Edward Thurlow, would believe it for a second.

But that's my story, Julia thought as she pinned her badge to her coat, then followed Foley through the window. That's my story and I'm stickin' to it. Poor and pitiful as it may be.

Julia stepped down from the windowsill to find herself standing between two pairs of unmade bunk beds set against opposite walls of a bedroom. The drawers of a narrow chest positioned next to an open door were scattered over the wall-to-wall carpeting, as were a dozen wire hangers from the empty closet. The Nortons had been moving fast when they packed the kids up. Had they already received a phone call from their sponsors? Or had all parties realized, the minute Anja vanished, that the game was up, that losses would inevitably be cut?

Foley and Julia covered the first floor quickly, glancing into rooms, looking for a home office which they finally discovered on the second floor at the front of the house. Here, too, they found evidence of a hasty retreat. The floor was virtually covered with the scattered contents of a two-drawer filing cabinet.

"I'll get the computer." Foley removed a utility tool from a case on his belt, extracted a screwdriver, and went to work on a Gateway computer resting on a particleboard workstation. Quickly, while Julia sifted through the paperwork, he pulled the casing, set it to the side, then carefully extracted the computer's hard drive, a green circuit board striped with gold wire. "If they made a mistake," he told Julia as he laid the hard drive on the desk, "it's in here."

"You don't think they deleted the files?"

"That's what I'm hoping." He unbuttoned his coat removed a small padded envelope from his front pocket, finally pulled a second hard drive, which he held up for Julia's inspection before installing it in the Gateway. "Now if the feds seize the computer," he said as he replaced the casing, "they won't know it's been touched."

"What did you mean," Julia asked without looking up, "about hoping the files were deleted?" She was scanning the documents on the floor, Medicaid forms and correspondence with one or another city, state or federal agency: welfare, home care, children's services, food stamps, disability. The Nortons had led busy lives trying to satisfy the city's many bureaucracies. One letter, addressed to an Assistant Deputy Commissioner named Mauritano, began, *This is the fourth time I have written to you on this matter. . . .*

"Deleting a file," Foley said, "does not erase the file." He pulled a drawer out, closed it, then pulled out another. "It remains where it was written until the space is needed for something else. There are programs that overwrite the files with zeros, effectively erasing the data, but I'm hoping the Nortons didn't know about them, or didn't have one available."

"That's assuming they deleted the files in the first place."

Foley began to rummage through the wastebasket. "If the files haven't been deleted, then there's nothing on them to help us. You find anything interesting?"

"Forms," Julia replied. "Government forms dating back to 1992, all carefully filled out. Tell ya, Foley, I wish my detectives were as thorough. I spend half my time demanding they do the paperwork over." She laughed shrugged her shoulders, settling down. "What I don't find, on the other hand, are phone bills, mortgage receipts, bank statements, brokerage statements . . . It's like I'm searching a government office."

They lapsed into silence then, a silence extending until their stay could no longer, by any stretch of the imagination, be termed a cursory search for the missing children. No matter that they'd found nothing of value beyond the hard drive, they had to get out.

WITH JULIA in the lead, they were halfway through the kitchen when they heard the sound for the first time. Foley initially thought he was listening to the rush of wind in a chimney, but even through the curtain-covered windows he could see that the day was perfectly calm. Julia first thought it the creak of a floorboard, then the mewing of a cat in a closet. Her head swiveled as she tried to gauge direction.

They stood there for nearly a minute, the two of them, before they heard the noise again. Julia was prepared this time, and she followed the sound to a door off to their right. The door gave way to a flight of stairs leading into the basement. Though Julia had opened the door a few minutes earlier, neither she nor Foley had gone down.

"That's a cat, right?" She looked over at Foley to find that he'd drawn his weapon, a 9-mm Browning. Without hesitation, she followed suit. "Talk to me, Foley? What are you hearing?"

Foley didn't respond. His eyes were riveted to the cellar door when the motor of a large refrigerator suddenly kicked on with a soft, yet clearly perceptible squeak. A moment later a bird began to call from the shrubbery just outside the window to Julia's left, an intermittent chirping insistent enough to draw her attention. From below, she heard the steady rumble of the furnace.

For a moment Julia tried to make it work, the refrigerator, the bird, the furnace. She told herself the sound that had stopped her in her tracks was one of these, or one of a hundred natural sounds made by a home as it settled.

It was a decent argument, but one Julia found unconvincing. After more than a decade on the job, her cop instincts quickly dismissed each rationalization. That sound, that faint mewing she'd heard a moment before was wrong, a square peg jammed into a round hole. She could not make it fit.

"We're gonna check out the basement," she told Foley. "You'll notice that being your superior officer, I didn't pose that as question."

Resigned, Foley smiled. Though the sound hadn't repeated, the hair at the back of his neck was still standing on end. "Lemme go first, lieutenant," he finally said, crossing the room to open the cellar door. "Lemme take the bullet for you."

THOUGH BOTH cops tried to keep their weight as close to the wall as possible, the simple planks that made up the cellar stairs creaked at every step. The sound was so loud and distinctive that Foley simply gave up a third of the way from the bottom, taking the last four steps in a single jump. He landed with his weapon raised, Julia following an instant later. She quickly moved off to Foley's left, putting some distance between them as she swept the room. There was no movement of any kind, save for the heave of her chest, and the odd sound they'd heard in the kitchen did not repeat.

The element of surprise now irreparably lost, Julia decided to play it by the book. You always announced your presence and your authority. Otherwise, if you got your ass blown away, your killer would claim self-defense.

"Police. Is anybody down here?" She was staring at a closed door in the center of a roughly finished wall maybe twenty feet away. To her left, the rush of the furnace was augmented by a slight rattle somewhere in its sheet-metal housing. The laundry was to her right, a washer and a dryer, a cast iron sink, a Formica-topped counter piled with wrinkled sheets. "Police," she repeated. "Is anybody down here?"

The furnace continued to roar, its housing to rattle. Beyond that, the only sound Julia detected was her own shallow breathing. She crossed the room to crouch next to the door. The sheetrock wall offered little protection beyond concealment and there was no point to offering a larger target than necessary. Ten feet away, she watched Foley drop to one knee, pin the sights of his Browning on the door, finally nod.

Julia reached for the knob, spun it, pushed the door open, then jerked her hand back to her side as what appeared to be a ball of knitting wool flew through the open door, dashed across the room to the stairway, then leaped onto the fourth step before stopping long enough to become a gray Persian cat.

"Jesus Christ," Foley muttered. The animal, which was now preening its tail, had passed within a foot of his face.

"I was right. It was a cat."

Without warning, as if her initial terror had suddenly turned around to reveal its hidden face, Julia was seized by a powerful urge to laugh.

"Tell me something," Foley said. "Why are we both still sighting in on the poor cat?"

"I don't know about you, but I wanna be ready." Julia lowered the barrel of her weapon. "In case it goes for its wallet." She giggled once, then twice, then heard the sound again. Heard it and knew absolutely that it was the muffled cry of a young child, coming from somewhere deeper in the basement, from the other side of the house.

Julia went through the doorway first, stepping quickly to her right. The room, about as large as the one she'd left, was crowded with department-store racks holding children's clothing on wire hangers. Perhaps four feet high, the racks had been pushed to one side, creating a corridor down the center of the room. The corridor led to another door, this one with a lock above the knob. There was no key in the keyhole.

"Announce your presence," Julia said to Foley. "Let whoever's in there know I'm not alone."

"Police. Come out of there."

Nothing. Not a sound.

"Police," Julia shouted. "Is anybody in there?"

Nothing, then a whimper, then another.

"This is the pits," Foley muttered.

Julia nodded agreement. The clothing racks had been pushed close to the walls on either side of the room and might conceal a dozen bad guys. No matter how much she wanted to dash along that corridor and burst through the door at the other end, they had to clear this room first. They could not risk being ambushed from behind.

"Call it in to the locals, Foley," she said, her voice surprisingly calm in her own ears. "Request backup."

She waited until she heard Foley's cell phone chirp, then dropped to her knees and swept all four walls. She didn't find any telltale legs, but a rack against the opposite wall had boxes piled beneath it, blocking her view. Slowly, remaining close to the wall, she began to circle the room in an effort to come upon the rack from the side. From behind, she heard Foley identify himself to a 911 operator, then ask to be connected to the 112th Precinct. From in front, the crying of the child on the other side of the wall suddenly became continuous, a thin choking wail, arousing all Julia's protective instincts, inspiring a nearly overwhelming rage. It was only with a great effort that she continued on course, one step at a time, eyes moving in little jerks until she came up against the front wall and saw that the space behind the rack was empty.

As Foley walked up beside her, Julia peered into a small gap between the door and the frame. The bolt on the lock had been thrown.

"Done," Foley whispered. "The cavalry's on the way."

Julia turned slightly, kept her voice as low as Foley's. "Take it down," she said, pointing to the door.

"You don't want to wait for backup?"

"Nope." She could feel Foley's breath against the side of her face. "No more announcements, either. You take it down. I'll go in first. Let's do it."

"Right."

The lock was a Medeco, of fairly good quality, and would have resisted a great deal of abuse before giving way. The door frame, on the other hand, was constructed of cheap pine. It splintered under Foley's heel, allowing the door to trace a half-circle on its hinges before crashing into the wall. An instant later, Julia was inside, tracing her own half-circle, trying to see everything at once, the cots, the small black refrigerator, the closed door on the other side of the room, the four children huddled together, round-eyed faces seeming as pale as the rumpled white sheets on the cots. One of the children, the youngest and smallest, her face already streaked with tears, began to sob.

Again Julia had to struggle with an impulse to rush to the children, gather them in her arms, tell them it was all right now, they'd be protected at last. Instead, she held her position, the barrel of her Glock raised slightly, her finger on the trigger. Her head swiveled, very slowly, away from the closed door on the far side of the room, to the right and the left, patiently, until she found the little piece that was out of place.

"Get the kids out of here," she told Foley. "Get them upstairs."

"Julia. . . ."

"The key, Foley. It's still in the lock. In the wrong *side* of the lock."

Foley glanced at the door behind them, muttered, "Yeah, I should have caught it." If the key was on the inside of the lock, it had been used not to contain the children but to keep Peter Foley and Julia Brennan out.

Julia dropped to one knee, then trained her weapon on the closed door at the far end of the room, her anger focused at last. Though her gaze didn't waver, she was aware of Foley as he asked the children to follow him, and of an answering wail that sprang from all four throats.

"We're the police," Foley said. "It's okay. We're going to take care of you. Just come outside with me."

He took a step toward them and they backed into the wall, clinging to each other, almost a single organism. A dark-haired girl raised a hand, palm out. Her eyes began to blink rapidly, as if expecting a blow, then she shouted something, her voice betraying utter panic. An instant later, the door at the back of the room flew open and Julia found herself transported to a place beyond calm or terror. She recorded the figure of an adult male, the revolver in his left hand, her right index finger as it squeezed the trigger, the Glock jumping in her hands, a lacy red spray from the back of the man's skull. What she didn't record, not until she looked down to find the Glock's slide open and no bullet in the chamber, was that she'd fired her weapon sixteen times in just over five seconds.

25

WHAT A spot for the bosses," Julia told Robert Reid and Corry. It was nine o'clock in the evening and they were gathered around the kitchen table. "News vans backed up for two blocks. Children sold into slavery. Children rescued from slavery. The bad guy dispatched without further injury. Where do you go with that?"

Julia was running on and on, and she knew it, knew also that she'd dropped the reins somewhere along the line and was just along for the ride. She could still hear the roar of gunfire, incredibly loud in that confined space, and the screams of the children. She could still see Peter Foley, squatting next to the corpse, rummaging through the man's pockets, calm and methodical, in a vain search for identification.

"I'll tell ya where they went," she continued. "They went to a place called hero cops. I knew that was where they'd end up when Internal Affairs accepted my statement without running me through an interrogation. The bosses didn't want anything on the record to impugn my integrity. Which is not to say they were happy. I went from IAB to Chief Linus Flannery, Commander Harry Clark, and Inspector Edward Thurlow."

"Out of the frying pan," Corry said.

"Yes, but I'm sure the fire wasn't all that hot." Robert Reid stroked his beard. He could see the stress building in Julia, as he'd seen it before in the the bulging eyes and rapid-fire speech of other cops who'd killed in the line of duty. "I should know because I sat through the longest press conference in the history of the New York Police Department. The mayor, the commissioner, Flannery, Clark, even Lily Han from Sex Crimes in the DA's office. They each had something to say, and each found a moment to praise the work of their crack detective, Julia Brennan."

"Way to go, Mom." Corry used her finger to ease the last bit of a raspberry tart onto a fork. "You said you were gonna find them, and you did."

Julia looked down at her untouched dessert, at what must have been her sixtieth cup of coffee. "The kids were told that we'd come to kill them," she said. "That's why they didn't respond when we announced ourselves. The man I shot, they called him *Uyak* Juso. *Uyak* means uncle in Serbo-Croatian."

"You mean," Corry asked, glancing at Robert Reid, "they, like, *loved* him?"

"I mean they believed the police were there to murder them." Julia sighed, shook her head. In response to a reporter's question, Lily Han had announced that the kids were already receiving therapy, and that they'd need therapy for a long time to come. "Thurlow and Clark, they were really pissed off, but I think Flannery thought it was all very funny. They'd dumped me because they couldn't control me and now I was a hero and Clark was a jerk. Somehow, that made Flannery happy. When Clark told me I was being appointed to head the task force's day-to-day operations, Flannery chortled."

"Chortled?" Reid was smiling now.

"He made this wet sound in the back of his throat. Like he was trying to chuckle and gargle at the same time." Julia pushed her raspberry tart over to Corry's side of the table. Her brain seemed to be running at half speed, yet she felt as if she'd never sleep again. "Clark and Thurlow took off a few minutes later, but Flannery stuck around long enough to lecture me on the chain of command. He told me, straight out, that this was my last chance to get my act together. 'You remember that Sicilian business,' he said, 'about revenge being a dish best served cold? Well, your promotion to captain depends, to a certain extent, on your conduct as a police officer. Likewise for that gold shield.'"

"A potent threat," Reid observed.

"I had a vision of myself commanding a squad of property clerks, shunned by all who matter, put in my place. I think that's why they kept me away from the press conference. And that's why Thurlow's still running the overall investigation. In the end, the bosses always rule."

Eventually they took the conversation into the living room, eventually Corry went to her bedroom to do some homework. By that time it was eleven o'clock and they turned their attention to the local news. Though Julia's name was mentioned twice, her likeness did not appear on the little screen. At 11:30, as Jay Leno began his monologue, Julia re-approached the moment in which she'd taken a life.

"If I hadn't been kneeling down, I wouldn't be talking to you now."

Reid dropped his head, resigned. He did not want even to imagine Julia's life threatened, much less hear the details from her own lips. "Go on," he said.

"When he came out of the bathroom—that's what it was, a bathroom. I thought it was a closet at first, but . . ." Julia ran her fingers through her hair. "Anyway, he came out and he fired once. The bullet went over my head and through two walls before it hit the foundation on the other end of the basement. If I'd been standing up, it would've gone right through me. But the funny thing is that I didn't even know he'd fired at me until later. I just saw the gun and went on automatic pilot. When it was all over, I thought I'd fired maybe two or three times, but my Glock was empty." She rubbed her eyes, then resettled herself in the chair. "Here's the amazing part. It seemed like everything was going in slow motion, that I was absorbing every single detail, like I was a camera, you know, getting it down permanently and forever. But I didn't have any idea what was happening, Uncle Bob. And I have to admit, it really bothers me."

Reid started to say, You must have done something right, you killed the man. But then he thought better of it. "Look, Julia, something that's been bothering me. A lot of cops, they kill someone, take time off to . . . to adjust. Don't you think . . ."

Julia closed her eyes for a moment. Her uncle was right, of course. The smart move here was to take an administrative leave, keep a low profile until Little Girl Blue was last week's bad news, maybe even repair a few bridges along the way.

"I'm in the middle of an investigation," she finally said. "When it's all over, I'll see how I feel."

FIFTEEN MINUTES later, Julia rose from her chair. "I have a lot to do," she announced. "I have to get some rest." Her voice, in her own ears, had a toneless, almost languid quality.

"Do you mind if I stay over?" In fact, Reid did not intend to leave until he was certain his niece would be all right.

"The bed's made," Julia said as she started up the stairs. "I'm gonna have to be out of here early, so if you want breakfast . . ." She left it at that as she climbed to the second floor, made a stop in the bathroom to remove her makeup, then came back along the hallway to her bedroom. Inside, she sat on the edge of the bed, began to unbutton her blouse, finally let her hand drop into her lap. She was aware of her things, her possessions, around her, the mission furniture, a teak jewelry box given to her by her uncle on her sixteenth birthday, the overflowing hamper in the corner. A shield-back side chair, its velvet seat a particularly brazen gold, rested next to the dresser. The chair, or so the story went, had been carried to the New World from Ireland by her great-great-grandfather in 1871. Though Robert Reid insisted it was mass manufactured and remarkable only for its age, the chair was (by default, there being nothing else) the family treasure.

From the hall, Julia heard Corry advise her great-uncle to change the pillowcase. "I've been meaning to dust the room," she explained. "but I can't seem to get around to it."

"Sloth," Reid declared. "One of the seven deadly sins. As for the pillow, I'll turn it over. It can't be dusty on both sides."

Julia listened to the closing of Corry's and her uncle's bedroom doors, then lay back on her bed. She closed her eyes and was instantly transported back to the Nortons' basement, the scene movie-sharp, as vivid as a dream. She saw life and death, a man who breathed, whose heart pumped blood, reduced to carrion. It would take an autopsy to determine how many times he'd been hit, but his torso, when the paramedics cut his shirt away, had been riddled with entrance wounds.

Impatiently, Julia turned her head, as she'd finally turned away from *Uyak* Juso to confront the terrified children, to feel their terror wash across her body, a hot wind blowing over the desert of their lives. She'd imagined them, at that moment, to be infants again, newborns with the same possibilities, the same hopes, the same capacity for love and wonder and awe as any other child. Now she saw it again, what had been taken from these children, and she wondered exactly what therapeutic strategy could restore their innocence.

She began to cry then, a sudden onrush of tears that overwhelmed her defenses, that quickly escalated into a sob, then another, and then she was gone, returned to an essential loneliness she had not acknowledged for many, many years.

When she came back to herself she was sitting up, with Corry on her left, Robert Reid on her right, each with an arm about her shoulders. Her first instinct was to pull away, to re-establish her independence, but she knew the attempt would prove futile. This was her family, her comfort. This is what was denied Anja Dascalescu, and the other children, and truth be told, Peter Foley as well.

26

PETER FOLEY stood in front of a greengrocer's shop on the corner of Thirty-third Street and First Avenue, sipping at a container of hot chocolate, inhaling the commingled odors of lilies, carnations, and roses. The sky above was cloudy, the temperature close to forty degrees, and the grocer had put his stock of flowers outside his store, hoping to attract passersby. Foley had no special interest in the shopkeeper's wares, but he watched an elderly woman sort through a white bucket filled with sunflowers. The woman examined each stalk, picking them up one at a time, squinting through her bifocals until finally satisfied. Then she straightened with a noticeable effort and became aware of Foley's scrutiny.

"I buy summer flowers in the winter, and winter flowers in the summer." She gave her bouquet a little shake. "Only a fool would do otherwise."

She smiled, then made her way inside to pay for her bit of August sun. Foley watched her uncertain progress for a moment, then turned his attention back to the Little Kitty Day Care Center. There was a time, months stretching into years, when he'd come to this spot nearly every day. As if his mere presence would draw Patti through that front door, a skinny, freckle-faced girl in perpetual motion, her braids flying about her face as she skipped down the stairs to the sidewalk.

The story, the way it had come from the other children, and from Nancy Abbot, their teacher, was consistent. Each child had been assigned a partner whose hand they were to hold whenever the class was on the move. Patti's partner, Eva Eisenstein, was also her best friend.

At the close of the school day on the afternoon Patti disappeared, Nancy Abbot had gathered the children, going so far as to count heads before leading them from the day room where they'd been playing a few moments before. Patti and Eva were at the back of the class, holding hands, when Patti suddenly realized that she'd forgotten a finger painting destined for the refrigerator door. She'd let go of Eva's hand, then dashed back to the playroom while Nancy Abbot led the children on.

Outside, when asked where Patti was by Nancy Abbot and an already concerned Kirstin Foley, Eva had initially broken into tears. How could she tell on her best friend? Eva's mother, Miriam Eisenstein had been quick to reassure her six-year-old daughter. Nothing bad, she'd explained, would happen to either of the two girls. This one time it was okay.

Eva finally did tell, after the loss of a precious moment, and Kirstin Foley had gone into the school, half-expecting to find Patti flying down the hall. But Patti hadn't been in the hall, or in the playroom, or anywhere else.

Kirstin's search, though frantic, had been thorough. Every room, every closet, working from the front of the school to the back, where she found a self-locking fire door slightly ajar.

The detectives uncovered the rest. The fire door's lock had been malfunctioning for a week. Even when pulled tight, the lock released at odd moments, sounding an alarm, a buzzer, which could be heard throughout the school. Rebecca Morone, owner of Little Kitty Day Care, had called a locksmith two days after the initial malfunction and made an appointment to have the door repaired, but the locksmith hadn't shown up. In the meantime, until she could find a moment to consult the Yellow Pages, to find someone more professional, Rebecca had disconnected the alarm. Its buzz, she'd finally admitted, upset the children.

Foley finished his hot chocolate and tossed the container into a wire basket thoughtfully supplied by the city. He was wearing a navy peacoat, a knit cap that hugged his skull, and stiff blue jeans. He called it his sailor-home-from-the-sea outfit.

There was a time in Foley's life, again months stretching into years, when he'd played out the sequence leading to Patti's disappearance a dozen times a day, adding or subtracting a single detail. His favorite had the locksmith keeping the appointment, fixing the door, ending the threat. But there were others as well: Rebecca not disconnecting the alarm; Patti calling out: "Mrs. Abbot, I forgot my drawing. I have to go back."

It was only after many, many repetitions, hundreds, thousands perhaps, that Foley had added a little fillip to the story. In this version, the monster is hunted, cornered, and destroyed before reaching the Little Kitty Day Care Center.

As FOLEY walked north toward Holy Savior Church, already late for choir practice, his thoughts turned to Julia Brennan. Though he never broke stride, he saw her directly in front of him, her face a little too soft, her eyes a little too hard, a lioness in repose.

After the shootout, a pair of IAB investigators had worked on him for three hours without mentioning the hard drive he'd taken from the Nortons' computer. Julia had apparently stuck to her story, a final gift, as he'd stuck to his. They'd rung the bell, circled the house in search of the foster children, discovered a broken window, finally gone inside to look around. A moment later, while they were still getting their bearings, they'd heard a noise from below that might have been a weeping child, then immediately called for backup.

Eventually he'd been released by the headhunters, told to go home and stay there. He'd looked for Julia on his way out, but she was nowhere to be found and he hadn't heard from her since.

As Foley turned away and continued walking north, passing

beneath one of the 59th Street Bridge's great stone arches, his thoughts drifted to the shooting on the prior afternoon. He remembered placing himself between the opening closet door and the children, Julia Brennan stitching the gunman's torso, the little squirts of blood moving up the man's chest, to his throat, finally to his head before he collapsed.

He, himself, had not been afraid, fear as far in his past as the hope that Patti Foley would finally emerge from the Little Kitty Day Care Center. But fear was apparent in Julia's flared nostrils, her saucer-wide eyes. Still, she hadn't flinched, not for a moment, just knelt there on the concrete floor, her weapon gripped in both hands, and taken care of business.

The image of Julia Brennan, warrior, continued to occupy Foley's attention as he approached Holy Savior Church, climbed the steps, pulled open the massive wooden door, only now he felt that image accompanied by an emotion so long suppressed that it took him a moment to realize exactly what it was. Then, as he dipped his fingers into the holy water font, he laughed long and loud, amazed that he, Peter Foley, after all that had happened to him, after all he'd done, could still be lonely.

T WO HOURS later, Foley left Holy Savior, hailing a cab in lieu of his usual walk. He was anxious to get back to his apartment and his work. Every file in the hard drive he'd taken from the Nortons' computer had been systematically deleted but not erased. Retrieving them had not been difficult, a matter of two hours using a commercially available utility program. The problem was that the file names did not describe the contents. Instead, files were indicated by the letter A, followed by three numbers: A001, A002, A003, etc. Without a key, each of the 258 listed files would have to be individually examined. The process would take many hours, but he was a patient man.

Back in his apartment, Foley went first to the refrigerator in search of lunch, noticing as he pulled the door open that the red light on his telephone answering machine was winking lewdly. He took a container of cottage cheese and pineapple from the refrigerator, grabbed a spoon, finally pressed the machine's play button. The tape rewound swiftly, then Lily Han's voice poured from the tiny speaker, requesting that he call as soon as possible.

More amused then annoyed (after all, he could have surrendered his badge and gun, told the bosses to go fuck themselves), Foley dialed Han's number and was put through without delay.

"I called you," Han told him, "to say good-bye."

Foley's first thought was that he was about to be suspended in anticipation of a hearing on departmental charges. "You wouldn't want to represent me?" he asked.

"I'm more likely to prosecute you than defend you, Peter. But don't worry, you've become quite the golden boy. In fact, your immediate transfer to Manhattan North Homicide, specifically to C Squad, was conveyed to me by the Chief of Detectives. You're to report forthwith to Lieutenant Julia Brennan. Go get 'em, tough guy."

27

AT EIGHT o'clock on the following morning, as Julia Brennan entered the 19th Precinct on East Eighty-fourth Street, home to Manhattan North Homicide, the acrid stench of urine rose up to greet her. She found the odor familiar enough to raise her spirits. The Phantom Pisser had struck again.

The Phantom Pisser had first left his calling card in the wee hours of the morning on August twenty-first of the prior year. In the intervening months, every two weeks or so, he'd come back to mark his turf. The betting in the house was that P. P. was actually a cop, but that was only the police affirming their own authority. No civilian, so the reasoning went, would have the balls (or the bladder) to so affront the power that flows naturally from the end of a night stick.

"Hey, lieutenant, welcome back."

Julia smiled at the sergeant manning the reception desk, a bony hairbag named Floone who'd been six months from retirement for the last decade. "What's new and exciting?" she asked.

"You." Floone turned back to a painfully young patrol officer and the two handcuffed teenagers standing before his desk. "Now, Officer

Prager," he said patiently, "we got a little chargin' problem here. You say that you were walkin by, minding your own business, when these miscreant teenagers made snorting noises which you naturally associated with a certain barnyard animal. Supposing yourself the target of these rude noises, you took offense, which I can understand, but what I'm asking you here, for the third time, is what you're gonna charge 'em with? Makin' pig noises without a license?" Floone shook his head. "There's somethin' you should understand, Officer Prager, these little white boys, where they live they got more servants than I got ex-wives."

Julia took the steps leading to the squad room housing Manhattan North Homicide. Though she'd barely slept, she felt suddenly energized. She was back at work now and work had always comforted her, work had always been the great escape.

Except for Carlos Serrano and David Lane, the squad room was deserted when Julia presented herself. Serrano looked up, then broke into applause, Lane following a moment later. Julia appreciated the gesture, even as she noted a decidedly circumspect bottom line in their measuring stares. She'd humiliated the task force detectives by finding the children on her own. That was okay, said detectives (except for David Lane) being outsiders. The question was whether she'd do the same to the detectives of C Squad.

"Serrano." Knowing their suspicions were anything but unfounded, Julia kept her manner businesslike, "I want you to stay close. I'm gonna need you to gather the troops."

She poured herself a mug of coffee, took it into her office and made three telephone calls, one after the other. First, she called the Childrens' Services Administration, where she ran down the caseworker handling the foster children removed from the Nortons' Bayside home and informed her of the strong possibility that one or more of the children had been molested.

The second call followed immediately and went to Lily Han. "The men who appear on those videos," Julia declared after an exchange of greetings, "are no longer homicide suspects. I want to pass them on to Sex Crimes."

"Anything to help out," Lily Han replied.

Both knew that Sex Crimes had been offered a gift. The videotape evidence was irrefutable and photos of the men had been splashed all over the media. More than likely, they were already consulting their attorneys.

The third call was placed to Commander Harry Clark, who (perhaps because Julia had jumped a link in the chain of command named Edward Thurlow) kept her on hold for nearly fifteen minutes.

"Already?" he asked without preamble when he finally came on the line. "It's not even ten o'clock."

"I want to disband the task force," Julia replied. "The children have been found. We're dealing with a straight homicide now."

"Five homicides," Clark pointed out.

"Five homicides, one perp."

"You sure of that?"

Julia backed up. "Maybe two perps acting together. But it's still a problem best handled by a tightly knit homicide squad, not a bunch of jerks from burglary or narcotics who already hate my guts for showing them up."

Clark had worked Homicide for twelve years before his promotion to Manhattan North Detective Commander. Thus Julia was not surprised when his next question cut to the chase.

"You think you can nail this down?"

"Yeah, I do. Probably be some more bodies first, though."

"See, that's it. You're talkin' about a serial killer here. We handle it as a routine homicide, the media's gonna want to know why."

Prepared for the observation, Julia responded without hesitation. "Throw us a few patrol officers to run errands, and a civilian computer tech. Anybody asks, we're a task force."

"Huh," Clark grunted in reply. Julia could almost hear his thoughts as they spun through his head. "How do you know the . . . the Mandrakes weren't killed by whoever took those kids to Bayside?"

"Because the perp went out of his way to tell me. That's what the business with the heads was all about. So I wouldn't make a mistake."

"A challenge, then?"

"Exactly."

"And the motive?"

"Revenge."

"You think this was a kid they molested?"

"I think this was someone who believes he can resolve his emotional problems by killing pedophiles."

"Then tell me, how did he target the vics? How did he find them?"

The million-dollar question, which Julia Brennan was not prepared to answer. "Ask me again in a week, Commander. Right now, I couldn't really say."

"Alright, anything else."

"Yes, the detective who worked with me, Peter . . ."

"I know who he is."

"Yes, well I'd like to have him transferred to C Squad."

"Why, is he a suspect?"

Julia nodded in admiration. Again, the question had gone right to the heart of the matter. "I wouldn't say that, sir, but I think it's a really bad idea to leave him out there by himself."

I T W A S near noon when Julia realized that not only hadn't Bea Shepherd called, she, Julia, hadn't considered reaching out to her mentor. Despite knowing that it was she, as the offender, who was obligated to make the first move. Another break with her past, with more to come. She'd moved into a realm she'd avoided for her entire career, and she would move further before this business was over. Taking Peter Foley into the task force virtually guaranteed the result.

Think like a cop, she told herself. You've got victims and perpetrators and the rest of it is bullshit. Play to your strengths.

Good administrator that she was, Julia's greatest strength was organization, and she made it her goal not only to be up to date by the end of the day but also to have assigned tasks to each of her detectives. To that end, she called in the members of the original task force, accepted the relevant paperwork, finally took an oral report on their individual activities. By late afternoon, she had, she felt, a grasp of the details.

Every entrance to the building where the Mandrakes lived had been covered by surveillance cameras. The newly installed system produced very clear tapes that had led the task force exactly nowhere. The murders had occured on a Monday night between 10 P.M. and 1 A.M., and the traffic in-and-out of the Clapham had been light. A few residents, a few deliveries, a few visitors. All had been interviewed and none were suspects.

When she found the time, Julia decided, she would go back over the witness statements, make sure the interviews were conducted in an aggressive manner. She would examine each of the entrances to the Clapham and the windows on the first floor as well. The cameras were recording a second of tape for every four seconds of real time. Maybe it was possible to slip between exposures, Maybe one of the windows leading into the basement work areas had been jimmied. And there was also the possibility that the killer had entered the Clapham at an earlier time and hidden in the building or held the Mandrakes hostage for an extended period of time.

In the meantime, there was plenty to do. The medical examiner had determined that each of the victims, including those in the warehouse, had been killed by a single gunshot wound to the back of the head. The hangings and beheadings were postmortem. The murder weapon, according to the forensics tech who examined the single intact slug and the various fragments recovered at autopsy, was a .22-caliber pistol. The good news was that if the murder weapon were recovered, a ballistics comparison could be made.

The children taken from the Nortons' home had been interviewed by a psychiatric social worker who'd then relayed information deemed relevant to the task force. As each child told the same story, the facts were not in dispute. On the night of Anja's disappearance, they'd been taken from the Mandrakes' apartment to the Norton home by Joseph Norton, then locked in the basement room. Unaware of the Nortons' vanishing act, they'd passed the week eating the junk food thoughtfully left for them and drinking from the tap in the bathroom. All the while growing more and more panicked. Eventually *Uyak* Juso, who'd accompanied two of the children (the others, like Anja, were Romanian) on the trip from Bosnia to the United States, had come to get them. They did not know where they were to be taken.

All attempts to identify *Uyak* Juso, who spoke unaccented Serbo-Croatian, had proven fruitless. His fingerprints had been run through the Automated Fingerprint Identification System maintained by the FBI with no matches emerging, while a close examination of his clothing had revealed only that his garments were mass-produced and well worn. He might have been anyone from anywhere.

Also unidentified, the decomposed victims found in the warehouse with Teddy Goodman were resting in the morgue on First Avenue. That meant a return to the missing persons files for some lucky detective.

Taken altogether it came to a whole lot of nothing, and that included a personal attempt by Inspector Thurlow to obtain the cooperation of Truman Drayer, owner of the apartment leased to Bud and Sarah Mandrake for fifteen hundred dollars per month, less than half the market rate. Now living in Australia, Drayer insisted that he knew nothing of the Mandrakes' activities, legal or illegal, and wasn't planning to return to the United States any time soon. So sorry.

But Julia, as she sat behind a desk littered with reports from a half-dozen agencies, was not discouraged. To the contrary, she was certain that C Squad would find this serial killer and drag him before the bar of justice. She'd always liked that phrase, bar of justice; it had a hallowed ring to it, a time-honored dignity.

Laughing, Julia swiveled to face the single grimy window in her office. Talk about an oxymoron. New York City justice was many things (sometimes it was even just), but it was never dignified. Never.

She let her thoughts run to Peter Foley who waited in the squad room outside. Her crew was in there as well, Serrano, Lane, Griffith, and Turro. Hopefully, the children were making nice. Not that she cared all that much. No, Julia Brennan was going to collar a serial killer. And she was going to find the individuals who sold those children into slavery as well. Maybe show them just how inflexible the bar of justice could be.

28

JULIA WAS in the squad room, just about to address her attentive troops, when the telephone in her office began to ring. She was tempted to let it go, but there was always the chance that one of her bosses, Clark or Thurlow, was on the other end of the line. Wanting to jerk the leash.

"Brennan here."

"Lieutenant Brennan, this is Detective-Sergeant Erwin Bromowitz. Manhattan South Homicide. I think we got one of yours here, one of your johns, or a dead ringer for him. Man named Claude Renker, lives in the West Village. We found him last night in a community garden on East Third Street between A and B at ten o'clock. Been dead about two hours."

"Lemme guess, detective, a gunshot wound to the back of the head?"

"Right, plus his throat was slashed to the bone."

"Postmortem?"

"Naturally."

"Was he robbed?"

"Found him with five hundred dollars and a half-ounce of powder cocaine in his coat pocket. Gotta figure him for a buyer, lieutenant. The townhouse the guy owned is on the market for three and a half mil."

Julia could feel the collective eyes of C Squad drilling into the back of her head through the open doorway to her office. "How far you get on the investigation?"

"Well, first thing, we did a tight canvass of the block, hopin' somebody heard somethin', maybe looked out the window. No such luck. Lotta trees in that garden, lotta shrubs, and the vic was all the way in the back. Plus, it's not a neighborhood where people come forward to aid the police." Bromowitz paused long enough to draw a quick breath, then continued. "I talked to the wife personally and you can put her out of your mind. She broke down so bad they hadda take her to the hospital. Look, you want the case, I could leave the paperwork with the duty sergeant, but I gotta go. There's a stiff waitin' for me down in Tribeca."

"Two more things, sergeant. You say the vic was concealed in the back of this garden. How'd you find him? You get a tip?"

"Call from a pay phone on Fourteenth and A. Told us just where to look."

"And the bullet that killed him, was it intact?"

"Nope. Cut through the vic's brain, then flattened against his forehead. Sorry to disappoint."

Julia hung up a moment later, then returned to the squad room. As she explained the content of the call, she watched Peter Foley, who had a rather neat alibi. At the time of the murder, he was being raked over the coals by the Internal Affairs Bureau of the New York Police Department. She wondered if he imagined this turn of events amounted to a free pass. His interested expression, lips compressed, chin up, blue eyes tightly focused, didn't so much as flicker when she stated the time of death.

"Alright," she said after giving her detectives a chance to think it over, "talk to me, gentlemen. Start with the discovery of Anja Dascalescu's body. What do we have here?"

She let them go back and forth for nearly fifteen minutes, until they finally reached a consensus in line with her own analysis. Then she gave out their assignments. As she went along, she realized that she'd never felt more in command, never more certain of her abilities and her authority.

"Lane," she began, "I want you drive down to Manhattan South, pick up the paperwork on the Renker homicide. Then I want you to go over to the morgue and make sure that Renker is one of the men on those videotapes. I don't care if you have to show the tapes to his grandmother. If Manhattan South has it wrong, we need to know."

"That it?"

"No. I want you to review all the paperwork on the warehouse vics. If the task force missed something, we need to know that, too." Julia leaned back against the edge of a desk as she turned to Frank Turro. "Turro, I want you to call 911, get the tape on the Renker tip sent over. If they can't deliver in forty-eight hours, pick it up yourself. Then you've got missing persons duty. The unidentified warehouse victims were killed somewhere between eight and twelve months ago. Take the basics, height and weight, and go to work."

"Never a dull moment, loo."

"Griffith," Julia ignored the grousing comment, "I want you to find Joseph and Carla Norton. Check with the neighbors, go over the paperwork removed from the house. We know they were okay when they left, neighbors saw them drive off and they were alone. Let's root 'em out before the feds do."

Griffith's demur was reasonable. "I thought we agreed," he said, "that we're looking for a single perp, in his twenties, with a grudge against pedophiles. I don't see how Joe and Carla Norton fit that profile. Seems more likely they'll turn up victims."

"I understand," Julia replied. "But the INS agent who handled the adoptions, Christopher Inman, was killed in Baltimore, so there's another player out there somewhere. Maybe that player also did the Mandrakes, then tricked up the crime scene. We can't ignore the possibility, not knowing Joe Norton was in the Mandrakes' apartment shortly before they were killed. Look, Bert," Julia used Griffith's first name deliberately. In light of the fact that she was lying through her teeth, it was the least she could do. "Just stay on it for a couple of days, make that good-faith effort. I promise not to get fixated."

Julia turned to Carlos Serrano, her best detective. His deep brown

eyes seemed faintly amused. But then, most likely, they were all
amused by her newfound intensity. That was okay. As long as they did
as they were told.

"You worked organized crime, right?" Julia asked. She knew the
answer, that Serrano had spent four years with the Organized Crime
Control Bureau, but she wanted everybody else to know it as well.

"Four years."

"You still have friends there?"

Serrano's generous mouth widened into a full grin. "With my
charm, loo, I make friends wherever I go."

"What I'm looking for here is some sort of an overview of Yugosla-
vian gangs, possibly with ties to the sex trade. Serbian, Croatian,
Bosnian, whatever's out there. The shooter who came out of that
closet was a professional. He's gotta be mobbed up."

"Sure, I can definitely do that. What else you have in mind?"

"This one's a little trickier. There's probably a dozen crime-victim
support groups in New York. It's possible that our actor visited them,
looking for a way to let the anger out. Take the e-mail he sent to
Robert Reid and ask around." Julia ran a finger across her forehead,
shifted an errant strand of hair away from her eyes. "Better use all
your Latin charm here, Carlos, because you'll be an outsider and people are gonna be reluctant to open up."

"Maybe I can invent myself a little crime-victim background, talk
about the abuse I been hidin' all these years."

"Really, I didn't know. And thank you for sharing."

Julia's feeble attempt at humor broke the tension and the detectives
began to stir, ignoring Foley who looked up at Julia, his gaze mildly
curious. Julia met his eyes, but did not return his smile. She thought
of herself as a hard woman, but she wasn't hard enough for that.

"Serrano," she said without turning away from Peter Foley, "in my
office. I need to talk to you."

W HEN YOU check out those support groups," Julia told Serrano
once the door closed behind them, "I want you to do it in person, no
telephones."

Serrano stroked his mustache. He had a very sweet manner that concealed a deeply engrained macho attitude. Whenever faced with a specific assignment, he inevitably found something to criticize. "Ya know, I didn't wanna say anything out there, but this business with the support groups, it's not goin' nowhere. Think about it, loo. All I got to offer is angry and male and mid-twenties. I need something more specific."

"Well how about this, Carlos." Julia sat behind her desk, crossed her legs, listened for a moment to the patter of rain on the window. It was going to be a miserable night, and a long one, too. Corry was spending the weekend with her father, and Julia had no reason to be home at any specific time. "I want you to take a photo of Peter Foley and show it around. Find out if anybody's seen him, if he's got any special friends." She noted her detective's surprise with a good deal of satisfaction and wondered if Foley would be equally surprised. "I've got a civilian computer tech coming over, a woman named Olga Pavan. I want you to go online with her, check out any crime victim website with a chat room. You've seen the e-mail, look for someone with the same attitude. And while you're at it, have Pavan work on the e-mail's return address, heavenlyfire.com."

Serrano thought it over briefly, then said, his tone completely professional now, "You think Foley put someone up to killing the Mandrakes and the warehouse vics?"

"How'd our boy target his victims, Carlos? I'm talking about the Mandrakes and Teddy Goodman. How'd he find them if he didn't have somebody to point the way?" She leaned forward, unaware that her mouth had turned down, that the expression on her face was somewhere between a sneer and a snarl. "How do we even know the man who killed the Mandrakes also killed the warehouse victims? The Mandrakes' killer was having a good time, but the warehouse killer was all business. The similarity is that they were each shot with a small-caliber handgun, but there's no forensic evidence proving they were killed with the same weapon. Look, Carlos, I know I'm fishing here, but we've got unlimited overtime and I want to cast as many lines as possible. In any event, whatever you hear about Peter Foley, you report it to me and nobody else. There's no reason to let the bosses know what we're doing, not until we have something solid."

Julia pinned her detective with a speculative stare. Commander Clark had reinstated C Squad much too quickly. That meant he probably had a rat on the inside, someone to keep him up to date. She could only hope it wasn't Serrano.

"What I'm gonna do," he said, his brown eyes seeming perfectly innocent to Julia, "is get the computer tech started, then run over to organized crime. Tomorrow morning I'll put in a call to the social workers, see if I can get a list of victims' support groups."

"Alright, Carlos, as long as we're in sync." Julia's tone softened. Serrano would be up most of the night, as would the rest of C Squad, herself included. "Remember," she said, "unlimited overtime. Now you can replace that leaky washing machine your wife is always complaining about."

PETER FOLEY was sitting at a desk, fiddling with a Palm Pilot, when Julia re-entered the squad room. He did not look up, and she waited patiently until Serrano was gone before speaking.

"You have a prior engagement, detective?" Except for the two of them, the squad room was now empty.

"I just consulted my social calendar," Foley explained, "and it turns out I'm free this evening."

"Then I guess it's your lucky night."

"How so?"

"Because we're gonna go to your place right now and have us a little threesome. Just you and me and the Nortons' hard drive. From what I hear, it doesn't get any better than that."

29

THOUGH IT was after seven o'clock, Julia Brennan drove downtown through extremely heavy traffic. The rain had slowed to a driz-
zle, but the vehicles ahead were throwing up a mix of gasoline, oil,
antifreeze, and New York City mud that coated the windshield
evenly, a greasy film made worse by the wipers. Unsure of the last
time she'd filled the reservoir, Julia was using the Jeep's washer fluid
sparingly. Thus, as she drove, she leaned forward, little by little, until
she was hunched over the wheel, peering between the streaks. It was
only then that Foley decided to break the silence.

"There's a problem," Foley declared as they entered an underpass
running beneath the United Nations complex, "with the hard drive."
He gave it a second, then explained that while the files on the Nortons' drive were intact, the names given to them provided no clue to
their contents. Thus he and Julia would have to retrieve and examine
each file in the hope they'd come upon some sort of address book, or
maybe a cache of deleted e-mail, or even a diary. Anything to point
them in the right direction.

"It seems that one of the Nortons," Foley continued, "or maybe

both of them, was a game nut. I've already recovered a couple of
dozen computer games and I guarantee there are more to come. Also,
every document we found in their office was scanned into the hard
drive. There are files upon files. Every document, every piece of correspondence, a separate file for each agency."

"How big?" Julia interrupted.

Foley smiled. "I'm afraid to ask what you mean by that."

"I mean how big is the hard drive?"

"Ah, I see. Thirty gigabytes."

"Giga means billion, right?"

"Exactly."

"That's big."

"Yeah," Foley agreed, "gigantic."

Suddenly they were both laughing, the sound explosive in the con-
fines of the Jeep, yet at the same time purely intimate, a signal, as
Foley read it. As if a third party, watching, had rendered a judgment
from which there was no appeal.

"You think there were other children?" Julia asked. "Brought over
from Europe."

"We won't know until we find the right person to ask."

"But there should be, right? The professional way it was set up,
using the Mandrakes and the Nortons for cover. That kind of organization, it's bound to have its grubby fingers in more than one pie."

Foley nodded. "You remember the file I showed you? Anja Dascalescu's file?"

"Sure."

"Well, I didn't put my finger on it until last night, but something's
missing. There's no adoption agency listed on the visa application.
What's the chance Joe Norton navigated the Romanian bureaucracy
on his own? And how long would it take him for each child? Six
months? Ten months? Meanwhile, we know the Nortons were foster
parents for years and nobody we spoke to in that neighborhood said
anything about them going off to Europe for months at a time."

A hundred yards ahead, Julia saw a yellow cab parked in the right
lane. Its hood was up and its red emergency blinkers splashed across
the Jeep's greasy windshield. The driver was standing outside the

vehicle, a Sikh whose rain-soaked turban drooped over his ears. Julia flipped the turn signal and edged to the left. From behind, a horn blared ferociously.

I S   T H A T   her?" Julia asked, even though the small photo displayed on the Gateway monitor was clearly labeled, Patricia Foley.

"That's her." Foley's tone betrayed no more than mild curiosity. Julia had gone directly to the computer, typed a simple request into Yahoo's search engine: *missing children + photographs*. Then, aided by a DSL line that transmitted huge chunks of information, she'd chosen a site maintained by the federal government where she'd found Patti Foley's photo. "It's computer-aged, though. She was much younger when the original was taken."

Julia continued to stare at the smiling little girl, and Foley continued to watch her closely. He was certain that she was feeling very sorry for him, imagining a grief he'd shed a month after his wife's suicide, a skin he did not intend to re-grow. If he wished to, he decided, he could bring her to her feet, bury his mouth in hers, that she would not refuse him, that it would be a mercy fuck for the ages.

But he didn't do it. He restrained himself because he wanted her at her hardest, with her instincts on full alert. Nothing less would do.

Thus he'd waited for hours, until after they discovered a cache of photographs so obscene Julia's fair complexion faded to porcelain white before she spun away. Until after they discovered a spread sheet in which the Nortons had recorded their financial lives, and a phone-address book that meticulously listed e-mail addresses. Until after Julia made a reassuring phone call to her daughter, then took a phone call from her highly excited uncle who'd received an e-mail from somebody claiming credit for the Renker killing. Until after he, Foley, set the alarm he'd installed that morning, watching Julia as she regarded the key pad on the wall, a smile playing faintly on her lips, the fact that he'd only installed the alarm after his address became known to the job inescapable. Only then did he draw her close and kiss her.

She came to him eagerly, her body closing on his, her mouth demanding, as if she would swallow him whole. Seared, he pulled away far enough to look into her eyes, to see all that he expected to see, yet know she'd revealed absolutely nothing, that he couldn't even be sure whether he'd done the seducing or been seduced. In the brief moment before her fingers began to unbutton his shirt and her lips and tongue found his throat, he asked himself who was taking the risk here, who was crossing lines now? Then he was gone.

30

C ELL PHONE in hand, Julia sat on the closed lid of the john in Peter Foley's tiny bathroom, watching him through the open door as he slept. He was lying on his side, facing her, and the bedding had fallen back to reveal his broad flat chest and the twisting musculature of his abdomen. A hunk, to be sure, a man-toy who might turn on you at any moment, become that psychopath out of every woman's blackest nightmare.

Still, regret was the furthest thing from Julia's mind, though she hadn't decided to fuck (that was the word for it, she had to admit, there just wasn't any other) Peter Foley until after he set the alarm. That was when she remembered that the alarm was off when they entered the apartment, that Foley wasn't locking the bad guys out, he was locking them both inside, as if the question of whether or not she'd spend the night had already been addressed. Another challenge, to be sure, one she'd accepted without hesitation, her body on fire. They'd battled to an unacknowledged draw, falling back onto a sweat-drenched sheet with the full knowledge that nothing was settled, nothing at all.

It was a first, nevertheless, the first time in her life that she'd been to bed with a man she could not even imagine as a suitable mate. True, her imagination had been wrong every time so far, her definition of the word suitable on occasion reeking of desperation. But not even a crack-addicted New York street psychotic would be fool enough to mistake Peter Foley for a long-term proposition. No, it was easier to imagine herself ushering him to a holding cell than standing by his side while a priest led them through the marriage vows. In Latin, of course.

So it was definitely a first, the impulsive one-night stand she'd missed as an adolescent when she'd clung to poor Sam Brennan like a starfish to an oyster. Though at times she'd honestly believed she loved Sam, love was beside the point. Having a boyfriend who would eventually become a husband was just one more responsibility to be faced unflinchingly.

Foley rolled onto his stomach and turned his head to the wall, yanking Julia back into the present. It was six o'clock in the morning and Julia wanted to reach Carlos Serrano before he left home. In fact, she caught his sleepy-voiced wife, who pulled him out of the shower. Nevertheless, when he finally picked up the receiver, his voice was cheery enough.

"Morning, loo, what's up?"

"There's been an e-mail claiming credit for the Renker homicide."

"Sent to Robert Reid?"

"Right. I had him fax it to my office. I want you to check it out, compare it to the first one."

"You know, loo, we've got a sergeant down at the big house who does profiling. Myself, I think we've already done the profiling part. It's the suspect part we're havin' trouble with. But if you wanna give it a shot . . ."

"Actually, my goal is to keep the investigation in the house. But why don't you try to arrange something informal, a look at the evidence, a quick response, no paperwork. And tell him it's gotta be right now. A week from Thursday is not gonna help us. If he can't offer a snap judgment, don't let him see the evidence. And don't leave copies under any circumstances."

"Got it."

As she rang off, Julia looked over at Foley. She couldn't see his face, didn't know if his eyes were open or closed. She didn't care all that much, either. They were past the point where it mattered.

TELL ME what you did," Julia asked Peter Foley an hour later. She was again seated on the closed lid of the toilet, watching Foley through a pale-blue shower curtain as he soaped his chest. She might have been in there with him, but the shower was much too small for romance.

"When?"

"Yesterday, when *Uyak* Juso came out of the closet." She shook her head. "*Uyak*. What a joke. I keep hearing this little voice in my head, telling me that Juso was a human being. You know, he was born just like anybody else, just like Anja and the others. But I can't make myself believe it. He's dead and I couldn't care less." She sighed. "Anyway, tell me what you did while I was killing *Uyak* Juso."

"I dropped down in front of the kids."

"You wanted to shield them?"

"Exactly. I remembered, when I saw the gun, that the best way to preserve innocent life was to eliminate the threat. That's the way we're trained. But I didn't want to draw the shooter's attention and I hesitated for a second. By then it was all over."

Julia rose and left the bathroom as Foley emerged from the shower, retreating a few feet into the other room before turning to face him. "I could have been killed in that second."

Foley laughed. "The poor bastard never had a chance." He wrapped a towel around his waist, then opened the medicine chest in search of his razor and a can of shaving cream. "You know he dropped the gun right away, don't you? With the first shot? His hand jerked like he was having a seizure and the gun went flying."

But Julia couldn't remember the gun falling to the concrete floor, bouncing away. She knew only that it was found against a wall twelve feet from the body. "I fucked up," she said. "I'm lucky I'm alive." She watched Foley spread a layer of foam across his face, pronounced his attitude noncommittal. "In a situation like that, you don't lose your cool and you have a big advantage. Meantime, I thought I pulled the trigger maybe three or four times when I actually emptied the magazine and I can't remember a single detail after the door opened. I can't remember what the shooter was wearing, what he looked like. I can't remember seeing the gun drop."

It wasn't the full truth. There was one little detail Julia remembered only too well, the back of *Uyak* Juso's head as it flew into the room behind him.

"According to the ME," Foley said, "you hit the mutt thirteen times. Hard to believe it was just a matter of chance."

Julia refused to be mollified. She would do better in the future, that was the main thing; she would fall back on her training, insufficient though it may have been. Next time out, the man who tried to kill her might not be standing in the open three feet away. Next time, she might have to be more than lucky. She might have to be competent.

"We set?" she finally asked, retreating to a shelf covered with printouts. After the sex, they'd gone back to work, discovering a cache of letters, another of deleted e-mails. Though each had to be pulled up and examined, most of what they found was routine correspondence, and included letters and e-mail addressed to various civil servants involved in the foster-care program. But there were nearly two dozen between Joe Norton and a woman named Elizabeth Nicolson. Elizabeth was Joe's younger sister, a widow of independent means who lived in Hackettstown, New Jersey, with a perpetually sick parrot named Troy. The Nortons spent their rare vacations with Lizzie Nicolson, while Lizzie was present in the Nortons' Bayside home on every major holiday.

"No." Foley slid the razor down over his chin, raising his head, peering into the mirror along the length of his nose. "No, we're not set. There's something I want to show you first."

31

THE TOPIC of the day in the chat room at little_love.com was HOME SCHOOLING: OPPORTUNITY OR TRAP? Despite the relatively early hour, the spirited discussion among the pedophiles in the room was solidly grounded in the practical.

A chatter who called himself Brahmin wanted to know if schooling your children at home would draw undue attention unless you were affiliated with some religious group.

Zorro advised Brahmin to affiliate.

Papi declared that home schooling was a fundamental right, and would not result in unannounced visits by child-welfare workers. As long as the children performed at grade level, he continued, school boards were happy to forgo the cost of educating the little tykes.

Scholar interrupted to add that home schooling was a useful tool in fostering a sense of us (meaning the child or children with whom he was currently having sex) and them (meaning everyone and everything else in the known universe). The more isolation, he urged, the better. REMEMBER! OUR ENEMIES SURROUND US!

Zorro returned to moderate the tone, urging Brahmin to visit a website maintained by a prominent Pentecostal church in Alabama. Said website, he explained, offered a very detailed, step-by-step guide to successful home schooling.

I DON'T believe what I'm seeing," Julia couldn't take her eyes off the screen. "They're right out in the open. How do they get away with it?"

"A matter of priorities," Foley replied, "allocation of resources, that sort of thing."

"You don't think we take child molesting seriously enough?"

"Like you said, it's right out in the open. These men can be tracked down. I'm not saying we can eliminate pedophilia, but if there was enough money available, we could make it a lot harder for pedophiles to network. Do you know about private chat rooms?"

Julia shook her head. "This is the first time I've been in a chat room of any kind."

"Okay, you can invite anybody in a public chat room to have a one-on-one chat by double-clicking on their name. In theory, privacy is guaranteed."

"But in reality . . ."

"In reality, if it's your own website, you can do just about anything you want."

Foley clicked, not on an individual's name, but on a menu option labeled PRIVATE CHAT. A window appeared, asking for his password, which he dutifully entered. A second window appeared an instant later, listing the identities of all private chatters. Foley selected a name at random, clicked twice, then settled back.

The chat Foley chose was between Poobear and Plato. Though on a different topic and a good deal more specific, it was every bit as practical as the chatters' collective response to the home-schooling question.

Some six years before, Poobear had hired a live-in housekeeper, an undocumented alien named Dolores Ibarra who'd fled Nicaragua in the aftermath of its brutal civil war. He did this, not out of the goodness of his heart, but because Dolores Ibarra had no friends and only one relative in the United States. That relative was her nine-year-old daughter, Blanca.

Within a month, Poobear and Blanca were lovers. A year later, when Dolores figured it out, she did nothing to risk the food on her table, the clothes on her back, or the roof over her head.

Three years of paradise, of joy, of trips to Disney World, Great Adventures, of little presents, of birthday cakes and Christmas trees. Poobear was madly in love with Blanca, as Blanca (he insisted) was madly in love with him. Still, it was an affair destined to end in tragedy as Blanca, at thirteen, entered puberty, as her innocence gradually faded.

I'm not a hard guy, Poobear insisted, but for Christ's sake, the fuckin' bitch is hairy as a goat.

As further evidence of his bleeding heart, Poobear explained, he'd put up with her teenage bullshit for three years, put up with her pimple-faced boyfriends and her stubbly armpits. But now it was time for her to go. Preferably, before she opened her mouth and told someone.

Plato took that moment to break into Poobear's pitiful monologue. He knew, he declared, certain people in San Francisco and Los Angeles who specialized in legal teens. These connections were prepared to handle any resistance from Blanca, but what about the mother? Would the mother go along?

JULIA TORE her eyes from the screen. Foley was watching her intently.

"This is your website?" Her voice was so soft, she might have been asking the question of herself.

"Yes."

"And you have photographs, that people can see?"

"You have to be a member to browse the galleries."

"A member?"

"You have to give us a verifiable e-mail address. In most cases, that's enough to get me a name, a home address, and a telephone number."

Julia stood up, crossed the room, then turned on the ball of her foot to face Foley. "You can't sell someone contraband, then arrest them for possession of that contraband. It's entrapment."

"I'm not *selling* pornography, I'm giving it away. But I don't use the website to make cases. I use the website to find chicken hawks. I lure them in with lust, then . . . My cybername, by the way, is Goober."

Foley spun to face the computer. "Watch." He brought them back to the open chat room, typed a command, then sent it out over the DSL connection. An instant later, a single line appeared: <GOOBER'S IN THE ROOM.>

Plato: Yo, Goober.

Scholar: Bring on the trumpets. Raise a fanfare.

Papi: <Whaaasssssuuuuuuuuuuuuuuuup>

Zorro: GooBER, GooBER, GooBER.

I T   T O O K only a few seconds for Foley to exit the room and the site. "Enough is enough," he said, turning away without shutting the computer down.

Julia crossed her legs, leaned forward to lay her elbows on the shelf holding the computer. "Okay, so you meet them on the Internet. Then what?"

"If they live reasonably close to New York, I arrange an exchange of pornography. Video mostly." Foley drummed his fingers on the table, a quick rat-tat-tat. "Quality video is very hard to come by."

"And what do you do with the . . . the contraband they give you?"

"I copy it, then pass the originals on. Some to Lily Han, some to the feds. Still photographs get posted on my website."

"And that brings in more suspects."

"Exactly."

Julia leaned back in the chair. She inclined her head slightly, keeping Foley in her peripheral vision. "These videos, you watch them, right? From beginning to end. I mean, you wouldn't be able to judge their quality without looking at them."

"Yeah, I look at them."

"Even after what happened with your daughter. With Patti?"

Foley winced, despite himself, thinking he should have seen it coming. Not that the blow was fatal. No, for a number of years he'd felt as he imagined a surgeon would feel, cutting away the same cancer that had killed his own child years before. Flinching was not an option.

Suddenly, Foley experienced a surge of vulnerability, the emotion so foreign he took a moment to put a name to it.

"I used you," he finally said. "When Lily Han called me, I was looking for a way to get to the Mandrakes without Goodman finding out I was a cop. You've seen what happens on the internet. If Goodman found out I was cop, Goober would have been exposed at the speed of light. That's all it would take, Julia, a few keystrokes and I'd have to start all over. Remember, I was sure the other children, if there were other children, were already gone, so it just wasn't worth the exposure. Then you came along and it all fell into place."

"Did you realize you'd be a suspect?"

Foley laughed. "Very nice, but I didn't know the Mandrakes were dead until after the raid. However, once I learned the facts, yes, I was pretty certain Julia Brennan would consider me a suspect."

"And that's why you used me to establish an alibi?"

"That question implies that I had advance knowledge of Claude Renker's murder."

"Did you?" Julia rose, crossed the room to the apartment's single window, stared out at the tenement across the street. As ratty as any of its neighbors, its first floor and fire escape were painted a pure red while the upper stories were lemon yellow. A hand-painted sign on the front door carried the legend "American Society of Bhuddist Studies."

"I'm not going to help you find him," Foley said to Julia's back. "I'll promise you this, though. He's spinning out of control, taking risks. Most likely, within the next couple of weeks, he'll either blow himself away or be collared at the scene."

Julia filed the last bit away for later reference. "You could help? You could help, but you're refusing?"

"Listen to me, Julia. The Mandrakes, Teddy Goodman, Claude Renker, when I hear they're dead it makes me feel happy."

"You're a cop."

Foley sighed. "I have a badge, but I'm not cop. I stopped being a cop a long time ago. I'll never be a cop again. I never *want* to be a cop again." He walked across the room, laid his hands on Julia's shoulders. "If you remember, you came looking for me at the Twelfth Street Tavern when you could have kissed me off. Do you think I planned that as well?"

"The fisherman baits the hook, drops the hook in the water. Sometimes the fish are biting, sometimes they're not." Julia continued to stare out the window. Her eyes were raised, now, to the roof where a trio of elderly Asian women were doing *tai chi*. "Do you know who he is?" she asked. "Are you helping him?"

"The better question is how he found the Mandrakes."

"Yes, how did he find them without your help?"

"You'll have him within a couple of days if you answer that question."

"Positively or negatively?"

Gently, Foley turned Julia until they faced each other. "That first time, when you came through the door and I was sitting there, nursing a beer, wondering if you'd show up, I . . ." He stopped, looking for the right word, finally gave up. "I admire everything about you. Your intelligence, your determination, even your command presence. There's a fire in you that warms my bones."

Julia laid her head against Foley's chest, noting that he was already hard. Just as well because she, herself, truth be told, was already wet. Stepping back, she slid his belt free of the buckle, pulled his shirt free of his trousers. "Just one question, Foley," she said, "before we get carried away. When I have my fourth orgasm, do I get to call you Goober?"

32

PETER FOLEY'S responding laugh was still echoing in the small room when someone pounded hard on the door, creating a second echo that chased Foley's laughter from corner to corner, as if trying to affect a capture. Startled, Julia looked at her lover who winked as he re-buckled his belt, then called out, his voice steady: "Who is it?"

"Special Agent Raymond Lear."

"Ray, you should have called ahead." Foley glanced at the bulge in his trousers. "I'm busy right now."

"I've got a search warrant for your apartment, Pete. You don't open the door, we're gonna have to force an entry."

Julia held up a finger, said, "Slide the warrant under the door."

"Who's that?"

"Lieutenant Julia Brennan, NYPD."

The door was so thin and so poorly manufactured that it simply popped free when a pry bar was inserted in the frame above the lock and given a hard twist. As Julia watched the door swing toward her, an entirely unexpected thought entered her mind. Three days before, she'd killed a man. She'd killed a man and she could do it again. For just a moment, she allowed herself to feel dangerous, to project that danger at Special Agent Raymond Lear who had yet to more than glance in her direction. Followed by four agents, all male, Lear strutted to the center of Foley's little apartment. His dark eyes swept the room until they fixed on the winking red light above the key pad next to the doorway.

"What's this?"

"It's my alarm. You broke the contact when you forced the door."

"You wanna shut it down?"

"I don't think so."

Foley's computer, the Gateway, began to chatter at that moment, an insectlike noise that commanded instant attention. Lear's mouth opened in disbelief as he raced across the room, his arms extended. The chattering ceased just as he reached the computer.

"You . . ."

Lear could not find the words and Julia, watching him as she'd watch an unattended suspect in an interrogation room, shook her head in wonder. The man had a full head of stiff black hair that looked as though it had been extruded from little molds hidden beneath his scalp. Finally, unable to contain herself, she laughed out loud.

"What?" Lear demanded, finally turning his attention to Julia. "What do *you* have to say?"

Julia grabbed her purse, settled the strap on her shoulder. "I want you to know," she said, "that I don't despise you because you exploited Peter Foley for everything you could get, then turned on him, or even because you're a feeb asshole. No, the reason I wouldn't piss in your mouth if your heart was on fire is because you were stupid enough to believe that you'd recover evidence by coming through that door."

It was a good speech, or so Julia thought until Special Agent Lear surprised her with a jibe of his own. "Tell me something, lieutenant," he asked, "have you ever put your hormones aside long enough to entertain the possibility, the mere *possibility*, that your boyfriend's sob story is just his way of disguising the fact that he likes to hump little girls?"

I SET it up," Foley explained over breakfast in a coffee shop on Varick Street a few blocks from the Holland Tunnel, "the way the Nortons should have done it. When the alarm tripped, the computer sent a command to the first uplink, an internet server in Auckland. The first uplink forwarded the same command to the second, then zeroed itself out. The second uplink . . ." He smiled, glanced at his watch. "Within an hour, little_love.com, along with all links to and from, will cease to exist."

"And what about all the other data you collected on pedophiles?"

"Stored on diskettes, locked in a safe place. Agent Lear has everything he's going to get."

They were waiting for Detectives Griffith and Turro to arrive, armed with warrants naming Joe and Carla Norton as material witnesses in a conspiracy to prostitute Anja Dascalescu and the other children. Julia had understood that securing the warrants would be time-consuming when she'd asked Lily Han to draw them up, but they were essential in case the Nortons refused to leave their New Jersey refuge. Assuming they were there at all.

In fact, Julia reminded herself, the Nortons could be anywhere in the world, literally; they need not be holed up with Joe Norton's sister, Elizabeth Nicolson, in Hackettstown. Still, using credit-card numbers recovered from the Nortons' hard drive, Foley had somehow accessed records showing a pair of recent purchases, both at a mall in Rockaway Township, New Jersey. They were the only credit-card purchases made by the Nortons in the last week.

It was enough, Julia decided as she buttered a slice of whole-wheat toast, to justify a two-hour drive into central New Jersey, especially when the only alternative was to rely on the locals.

"I knew your apartment was a dead end the first time I walked in the door." Julia bit into her toast, chewed for a moment, swallowed, finally sipped at her coffee. "You're smart and you had a long time to think about it. But tell me one thing. Did you know Lear would try to bust you?"

"Him or Julia Brennan," Foley declared. "One or the other."

AN HOUR later, they were exiting the Holland Tunnel in a pair of unmarked Fords, Turro and Foley in the lead car, Bert Griffith and Julia trailing behind. The hope was that the Nortons would agree to return to New York, the alternative being a county jail while they fought extradition. Separating them on the return trip would be essential.

As Julia's driver, Griffith had the task of reporting C Squad's progress over the past twenty-four hours. The problem was that he was sulking. He'd been assigned the task of finding the Nortons, then shut out. Now he felt like a chump.

Julia let it ride for a few minutes, enduring her detective's mono-syllabic responses, then decided to confront the issue head-on. "I know you're pissed off," she said.

"About what?" Griffith stared straight ahead, his face composed, as usual.

"About my finding the Nortons without you." When Griffith didn't reply, Julia offered the only excuse she had. "What I did, Bert, if anybody found out, it would be the end of my career." She thought of the Nortons' hard drive, seized without search warrant, and Foley's perusal of the Nortons' credit reports. "At the very least."

"That bad, huh?"

"I don't have a moment's regret. We're gonna get the scumbags who brought Anja to this country and we're gonna find any other kids who're still out there."

"The ends justify the means? That how it goes?"

"Yeah," Julia replied without hesitation. "These particular ends justify these particular means. For me, not you. Now do me a favor, tell me what's going on."

"Joe Norton," Griffith said after a moment. "He's got two pistol permits, nine millimeter automatics, a Browning and a Colt. He belongs to a gun club in Belmont, so you gotta figure he knows how to use 'em."

A potential problem down the line. Julia would prefer to approach the Nortons casually, without attracting the attention of the locals. But if Joe Norton was armed, standard operating procedure called for him to be taken down hard.

"What else?"

"David Lane bullied Claude Renker's brother into watching one of the videotapes. Renker was definitely a client of the Nortons. About what we expected." Griffith eased the Ford around a gray eighteen-wheeler hauling a load of municipal waste. Even in January, the stench of rotting garbage was strong enough permeate the Ford's interior. "Turro thinks we might have more vics out there."

"He thinks there's another dump?" Julia had assigned Turro to the missing persons reports, hoping to identify the decomposed victims found with Teddy Goodman.

"Men walkin' away from their families? You know, there's plenty of that goin' on, always has been. But Frank's sayin' he found a dozen men reported missing in the last year who fit the vic profile."

"Which is?"

"White, between thirty-five and fifty, with money."

Though Julia couldn't remember creating this particular profile, she knew that Frank Turro was C Squad's least intuitive detective, and the least likely to exaggerate.

"Carlos was busy all morning and most of last night," Griffith said. "The guy's got the energy of a squirrel. He never stops."

Julia nodded. Serrano hoped to make detective, first grade, within the next few years, a rank claimed by fewer than three hundred detectives at any given moment. "What's he got to say?"

Griffith smiled for the first time. "Believe it or not, he called Hong Kong and checked out that website, heavenlyfire. The good news is that it's government-sponsored. The bad news is that the government is Red China."

"And they're not cooperating?"

"Afraid not."

"Well, it's like we already figured," Julia said, almost to herself, "Our killer's a smart boy. He's smart and he likes to rub it in our faces."

"That's what the profiler said."

"Pardon?"

"Serrano took you at your word, when you told him to make it casual. He took this profiler, a sergeant named Ross, out to a cop bar and they got drunk together while they discussed the case. Ross claims it's a no-brainer."

"He offer the perp's address?"

"Nope, but he thinks all the homicides, the warehouse vics, the

Mandrakes, Claude Renker, he thinks they were committed by the same man. Somebody who's been molested as a child, which we already figured out by ourselves."

Though surprised, Julia merely signaled for Griffith to continue.

"Ross thinks our boy's been at it for a long time, that there's other bodies someplace. The way the story goes, he had to work himself up to the Mandrakes. To that level of staging."

"What about the way they were shot in the back of the head? All that gore, it came after the fact, like he didn't want them to suffer."

"That what I thought, loo. That what I been thinkin' all along. But Ross, he says the perp was afraid of the vics, that these chicken hawks were powerful figures and he couldn't control them without a gun."

"So he kills them first, then tortures them?"

"He wants to humiliate them, shrink them down to his size, make them safe. But he doesn't have the *cojones* to do it while they're still alive."

Griffith eased off the gas. Absorbed in the conversation, he'd gotten too close to Foley and Turro in the lead car. Sitting beside him, Julia fiddled with the buckle on her seat belt. As she continued to question Griffith, she found herself wishing she cared as much about the killings as the men she'd assigned to investigate them. Maybe that would come later, maybe after she finally put Little Girl Blue to rest.

"Anything else?"

"Yeah, our actor is sliding over the edge, at least according to Ross. Decompensating is the shrink word for the process. It means he's losing control, taking risks." Griffith tapped the wheel, turned slightly to look at Julia. "Makes sense when you think about it. He left those videos where we'd find 'em, so he had to know we were also looking for Claude Renker. The same with the Mandrakes. He only beat us to the Mandrakes by twenty-four hours."

Julia looked out at the broad swatch of grass at the edge of the road, the forest beyond. There were patches of snow on the ground here, deeper snow beneath a stand of pines. Above the trees, the cloudless sky to the north was a deep, flat blue and had the texture of paint in a bucket. Or so Julia mused, as she recalled Foley describing the killer's psyche. Something about spinning out of control, taking risks. Then a prediction: ". . . he'll either blow himself away or be collared at the scene."

It was all very fine, this decompensating killer afraid of his victims, but it didn't answer the essential question. How did he find the Mandrakes before she did? You could explain everything but that.

Maybe it's even possible, Julia told herself as she turned to stare through the windshield at the back of Peter Foley's head, that Foley murdered Claude Renker. Maybe there's some way to fake time of death, to establish that ironclad alibi. She'd have to look into it. Meanwhile, Foley was chattering away, his head bobbing, hands flying, having the time of his life.

And she? Well, she had to admit as she pushed the soles of her boots into the mat covering the fire wall, then flexed her back, she wasn't doing too bad herself, a dangerous woman at last.

"One other thing," Griffith said, "from Ross."

"Ross," Julia muttered, "I think I'm already sick of hearing his name."

"Me, too, lieutenant. But for what it's worth, Ross thinks the perp knows the end is coming and he wants to go out with a bang."

33

ROBERT REID glanced at his reflection in the mirror on the other side of the bar and told himself, not for the first time, to calm the hell down. He told himself that he was an old man, a sick man, a wrecked man. He told himself it'd been so long since he'd done any serious investigative reporting that he wouldn't know a lead if it popped out of a bottle. For years now, he'd been using his contacts—and not just in the NYPD, but in virtually every agency of city government—to create columns that appeared to work the cutting edge. But field work? Burning shoe leather? Coaxing the truth out of a lying general public?

Well, it had been a long time and now here he was in the Golden Harp on Bedford Avenue in Brooklyn, feeding Irish whiskey to an Italian doorman named Basilio Donatelli.

"So what else you wanna know?" Donatelli was perfectly at ease. It was Monday, his day off, and he was in his usual haunt, settled down to an afternoon of serious drinking. Donatelli had a long narrow face that echoed a long, decidedly hooked nose. The crown of his scalp was smooth and shiny and red.

They were sitting in a booth at the back of the bar, photos of the Mandrakes' clients spread out before them. Donatelli had identified all but one of the photos and even knew the names of several. Or the names they'd given him when he'd called upstairs to announce their arrivals. Reid did not expect anything to come of this line of inquiry. Not only had the cops already covered the territory, but the johns, accompanied by their lawyers, were now surrendering. Within hours, they would be out on bail.

Not so for the dozens of pedophiles snatched off the street by an army of federal agents under the leadership of Special Agent Raymond Lear. Those arrests had begun in the early morning hours and were expected to continue into the night. Somehow, despite the Times Square cleanup and the thirty-seven million tourists, New York had become Sin City once again. Way to go, New York.

"I'm looking for a face that's not here. Somebody who visited the Mandrakes a couple of times a month."

"I don' know. Mandrake, he say he's some kinda consultant. He say he gives advice on how to invest. Thassa why so many people, they come to see him."

"But there were others," Reid persisted, "besides the men in these photos?"

Donatelli took the photos up, one by one, examining them closely. "People, they come and go. Could be anybody. Grocery man, laundry man, UPS. Me, I open the door, I close the door. Goo' mornin', sir. Affaternoon, ma'am. Grin like Pinocchio when Gepetto pulla strings." He glared at Reid, eyes bulging, thick brows rising to the center of a low forehead. "I no looka too hard at people. They don' like it."

"What about that day? The day the Mandrakes were killed. Did they have any visitors?" Reid waved at the photos. "Any of these?"

"The cops ask me thissa question, you know how many time? You know how many time I tell 'em, 'No, nobody come here?' " Donatelli rolled his eyes, his expression passing from indignation to exasperation in the space of an eyeblink. "Maybe somebody sneak in through the service entrance. When I'm onna john."

"You don't have a video camera on the service entrance?"

"Alla tapes, they go to the cops. What happens then, I don' know."

Reid laid his palms on the table, knowing the cops had been all over those tapes and they'd been worthless. Still, he now had enough for a story. Bud Mandrake had posed as a financial adviser; the johns had posed as clients, visiting only during the day or early evening, and only two or three on any given day. It was a good scam and it would suffice for tomorrow's edition. Meanwhile, he would tap his contacts in the FBI and the AG's office, probe for a connection between their investigation and Julia's. It was something she'd want to know, assuming she didn't know already. Julia had been one step ahead of Robert Reid for quite a while now, and her lead was increasing.

Reid had twice attempted to contact Julia, only to find her cell phone off. The second time, he'd left a message asking her to call, that he had information of interest to her.

It was that information that had Reid's journalistic antennae twitching. Unknown to his niece, he'd sent an e-mail to the killer, addressing it to cyberfree@heavenlyfire.com. In Reid's opinion, Julia had given scant attention to the killer's e-mails. He didn't know of her preoccupation with the adoption scam that brought Anja Dascalescu into the country, or with Sergeant Ross's profile, or with Peter Foley. But he had a strong hunch that the man responsible for six homicides, and perhaps more, was within reach. It was just that he, Reid, was missing something, a piece of the puzzle already on the table. Or so his reporter's intuition insisted.

There was one point that especially excited him. Everyone, it seemed, from the experts trotted out on the nightly news to Julia Brennan, believed that Destroyer and Destroyed, as he signed his e-mails, had been molested as a child. But if that was so, and his molester had been a gay male, why were all identified victims heterosexual? Something wrong there, without a doubt. And if he'd been molested by a woman, a slight possibility, his choice of victims was even stranger.

The killer had made that clear in his reply to Reid's e-mail which had pleaded with him to surrender, going so far as to offer Reid's services to mediate the time and place.

David overcame Goliath and went on to become the King of the Israelites. My Goliaths are legion. They battle from within and without. You've missed it all, scribbler, but I shall make myself clear very soon. Catch me if you can.

Destroyer and Destroyed

Robert Reid settled up with the barmaid and headed for the streets. At the door, he paused to draw a deep breath, to pull the smell of beer and booze to the very bottom of his lungs. There was a time in his life when the bars of New York . . .

Enough, he told himself. Take your sniff and make an exit. Corry'll be a-waitin'.

Earlier that morning, Corry had gone from her father's home in Staten Island directly to Stuyvesant High School, a ferry ride away. She would be coming back to Queens in a few hours. For some years, ever since Corry had graduated from day care to latchkey child, Reid had made it his business, on nights when Julia came home late, to have dinner with Corry as often as possible. Occasionally they had a heart-to-heart talk, but most of the time Reid worked with Julia's computer and the cellular he now carried, while Corry did her homework or prepared dinner. The talks were nice, when they happened spontaneously, but the point was that Corry not come home to an empty house.

34

JULIA LET Bert Griffith do the honors, another concession to his hurt feelings. They were parked at the open end of a cul-de-sac lined with single-family homes. Though not identical, the homes were all colonials, two stories with an attic above and an attached garage. Set on generous, well-groomed lots, they were overshadowed by hardwood trees planted decades before. Elizabeth Nicolson's house, fourth in from the corner, was fronted by a wraparound porch that left the first floor, or what Julia could see of it, in deep shadow.

Griffith accepted the phone without hesitation and quickly proved up to the task. When a man answered on the second ring, he said, "Hey, Joe, it's Bert. Bert Griffith."

"Bert?"

"Yeah, Detective Bert Griffith, NYPD. How ya doin' today?"

"I don't . . ."

"Joe, before you hang up, listen for a minute. I'm in New York, remember?" Griffith hesitated briefly. "What I wanna do is make a date for you to come in for an interview. Or, we could go to you. Either way, there are some matters we gotta clear up."

"How do I know you're who you say you are?"

"Gimme a break, Joe. The game is over. It was good while it lasted, true, but if you don't wanna go the way of Chris Inman, you gotta come to us. For Christ's sake, there's no way around it. Who else is gonna protect you?"

Julia was looking out the window as she listened to her detective, staring across a snow-covered field at the January sun as it dropped below the trees. The clouds above, elongated and compact as cigars, were pure gold along their outer edges. A rare sight for a city girl, and one she drank in gratefully before signaling to Griffith.

"Joe," Griffith said, "wait a minute. I'm gonna put my boss on the line."

"Mr. Norton?" Julia asked.

"What?"

"This is Lieutenant Julia Brennan, Mr. Norton. Can I speak to you for a minute?"

"You have no jurisdiction in New Jersey." Joe Norton's voice rose at the end of his statement, rose into a howl of anguish that forced Julia to move the phone away from her ear. She'd heard it all before, of course, and knew full well that even the most committed psychopath was able to feel his own pain. Even if he couldn't feel anybody else's.

"Right now," she said, ignoring the outburst, "we only want you as a material witness. That means you won't have to go through the booking process and you won't be housed with the general population. It also means your lawyer will have maximum leverage to cut a deal somewhere down the line. You following this?"

"The other one said you just wanted an interview. Now you say you want to lock me up. Why should I believe anything you say?"

"Because if you don't, we'll ask New Jersey to make an arrest. And if you run, we'll put your name and face on the little tube, maybe ask *America's Most Wanted* for help. You wanna find out what it feels like to have thirty or forty million people looking for you? You really want that for you and your wife? The reporters will descend on your sister in packs. Looking for blood, anybody's blood."

Julia let it go there. If he bit, she'd tell him they were parked at the end of the block, ready to rock and roll. If he didn't, they'd settle down to wait, hope he'd make a run for it. If neither event came to pass. they'd have to call in the locals, let the State of New Jersey take the Nortons into custody, do it by the book.

A moment later, the line went dead.

THEY SAT for three-quarters of an hour, until it was completely dark, Bert and Julia in the front car, Foley and Turro directly behind, communicating from time to time by two-way radio. Julia could see Foley through the rearview mirror. Apparently talked out, he was staring through the windshield, guarding his energies. One thing about cops: they all knew how to wait.

Still, there was a limit and Julia reached hers just as a half-moon rose above the house at the end of the block. She signaled Foley and Turro to join them, waited until they made their way to the back seat of the Ford, then announced a decision she knew would be unpopular.

"Bert, Frank, I want you to scare up the locals. Take the warrants, get as much backup as you can." She didn't bother to explain the obvious. Joe Norton had a pair of gun permits and no weapons were found in his Bayside home.

Though each hesitated, Griffith and Turro left without protesting. Julia had chosen Foley over them, again. She, of course, as the ranking officer, could not leave a scene complicated by severe jurisdictional problems. In theory, Joe Norton could pack up his car, drive on by, heave a finger as he passed. The right to stop and detain had been surrendered midway through the Holland Tunnel.

"I'll go a sawbuck," Foley said.

Julia watched the second Ford's taillights disappear as Griffith turned left, toward the center of town. "What?"

"The traditional bid for someone's thoughts is a penny. I'm just tryin' to show how much I value what you think."

"Pay up." Julia extended a raised palm.

Foley laughed, fished out a ten-dollar bill, watched Julia stuff it into her purse. "You have great presence," he told her, quite sincerely. "You own the space around you."

"I thought we were talking about *my* thoughts?"

"*Mea culpa.*"

Julia cleared her throat. "The Nortons are the key. If we can't turn them, we can't get past them to the . . . I guess the word here is . . ." She flicked a stray hair out of her face. "Ya know, I don't think there is a word for someone who uses an adoption service to smuggle children into a country for the purpose of prostitution."

"Pimp is good enough."

"Yeah, well we need the little pimp, Joe Norton, to get to the big pimps. If New Jersey takes him and he lawyers up while awaiting extradition, we'll have to cut a deal with said lawyer. Now, usually, I can live with that, the extra time and all the bullshit, because I'm a patient type. But what if the big pimps are Bosnian? Or Romanian? Or Serbian? What if they hold foreign passports?" She tapped Foley on the shoulder. "The big pimps might be on a plane right now. I could live with that, too. But if the big pimps are holding firm, if they're waiting to see what happens and they split when Joe Norton's arrest becomes public knowledge . . ."

"That would be tough," Foley admitted.

Julia slapped the steering wheel. "Give me Joe Norton for ten minutes, and I'll break him. The wife, too. They really don't have any other way to go."

"You wanna force the issue?" Foley, who'd given up hope when Griffith and Turro drove off, was now grinning from ear to ear.

"I don't know." Julia turned away. "Most cops, they go through a career, they're maybe involved in one or two shooting incidents. I lost my virginity four days ago and I'm not due for another decade. Besides which, we knock the door down, we could be arrested for burglary."

Outside, with the coming of night, a rising wind clattered through the branches of the trees. It was every bit as cold as on the morning Anja Dascalescu's body was discovered, and Julia, watching and listening, found her thoughts returning to Central Park. The words *Little Girl Blue* had jumped into her mind as though placed there by a witch, a spell that had carried her to the wilds of New Jersey where she had no business and no authority. By all rights she ought to have turned the investigation over to the feds after finding the Nortons gone from their Bayside home. But she couldn't; the images were still too close, Anja Dascalescu on the autopsy table, four terrified little girls huddled in a corner. There was no walking away from them.

"You know what they're gonna do?" Julia asked. "The feds, what they're gonna do to your apartment?"

Foley scratched at the stubble of beard on his chin. "I'm not worried about it."

"You have someplace to go?"

"Yeah."

Foley's response was abrupt and Julia might have let it hang there. Instead, she persisted. "Did you know they wouldn't arrest you?"

"That's the last thing they want." Foley turned his head to meet her gaze. "I made a deal with Lear. I traded evidence I'd collected for the files on Anja Dascalescu and Christopher Inman. If the feds aren't making arrests even as we speak, they'll be making them within the next few days."

"So, why the raid?"

"Lear wants me to testify in open court, to reveal my Goober identity to the world. That's why I'm not worried about him actually arresting me. If he arrests me, I'm just another pedophile cutting a deal. No, Lear wants to pressure me, but . . ." He grinned. "The hard drive in the Mac? I filled it with celebrity photos, starting with Edwin Booth and working forward. It'll take a week to go through them."

They again lapsed into silence, looking out through the windshield at a narrow, wind-whipped cedar bent back on itself as if trying to attach crown to roots. Down the road, a loose garbage can rolled across the street and into a neighbor's driveway. Smoke rising from a half-dozen chimneys streamed downwind.

"Bucolic, right?" Julia waved her hand at the scene before them. "All the fine folks tucked inside their homes. Fires in the fireplace, dinner on the stove, mommy and the kids waiting for dad to come home? You gotta like it."

"Personally, I prefer Chinatown."

Julia tugged the steering wheel, all the way to the right, then to the left, finally coming back to center. The engine was running, the heater blowing a stream of hot air across her feet. "You see out there, behind the houses, there's nothing but woods. Somebody hops through a back window, runs into the trees, they might come out in Pennsylvania. So what I want you to do is drive up in front, pop the siren a couple of times, then call Norton. Tell him I sent you to pick him up. If he bites, key the radio a few times and I'll come running."

"Running from where?"

"From the woods, Pete. In my Davy Crockett hat and my buckskins."

Foley opened the glove compartment, hauled out a pair of binoculars. "You wanna peek in the windows," he said, "you're gonna need these."

On impulse, Julia leaned over to kiss Foley's mouth, just a touch, really, then pulled away to open the door. "When I get in place, I'll key the radio, Meantime, watch your ass." She paused to adjust the bulletproof vest beneath her coat before adding the obvious: "Sitting in front like that, you'll be an easy target."

35

I T TOOK Julia almost ten minutes to get back into the tree line fifty yards behind Elizabeth Nicolson's home, then another two minutes to settle into a small open space between three fir trees. She chose these particular trees because their branches swept almost to the ground and offered protection from the worst of the gusting wind. Julia's cheeks were on fire, her fingertips and toes already growing numb. Nevertheless, resisting an impulse to jam her gloved hands into her pockets, she brought the binoculars to her eyes and aimed them across the snow-covered back yard.

There were eight windows, all lighted, in the back of the house, four on each of the two stories, and a door leading into the kitchen. Julia began on the second floor, sweeping from right to left. The curtains drawn across the windows were translucent and there were no shadows behind them. From the second floor, she moved down the side of the house and reversed course, discovering a long white couch beneath the raised blinds of the window closest to the garage. The middle-aged man sitting at the end of the couch was extremely thin.

The inflamed wattle running from his jaw to the base of his throat would have been appropriate to an aroused tom turkey.

Julia recognized Joe Norton, whose photo she'd viewed in his Bayside home. The photo, in a silver frame, had been one of a half-dozen neatly arranged on a baby grand piano in the living room. The piano, she remembered, was highly polished, and the upholstered furniture was spotless as well. It was a sure bet the foster kids never entered the room.

Continuing on, Julia found two women seated at a kitchen table on the other side of the house. The younger of the women appeared to be in her mid-forties. A blonde, she'd woven her hair into thick braids, then arranged the braids along the side of her head. The other woman, Carla Norton, was a good deal older. Her thinning gray hair was brushed away from her scalp to create what amounted to a nimbus, a floating aura that jiggled slightly as she bent to her work.

The women were cutting string beans into thirds, dropping them into a colander, and they wore identical grim expressions. As well they should, especially Carla Norton, who at the very least had tolerated her beloved's eccentricities. Julia smiled to herself, wondering if Carla was preparing a Nazi Germany defense. Don't blame me. I didn't know. I'm a victim, too.

Julia dug into her pocket and keyed the radio, signaling Foley to move into place. Then she swung the binoculars back to the living room windows and instantly realized her mistake. This time, Joe Norton was not alone. There were two men with him. Standing with their backs to the window, they were large men, and much younger than Joe Norton.

Julia felt the beginnings of a panic with which she was very familiar. Her heart rate accelerated and her breathing became instantly shallow and more rapid. She seemed to be looking through a tunnel, as if the small area revealed by the binoculars contained everything of significance in the known universe. Nevertheless, a stray thought managed to reach her consciousness. Anja and the others, when they were taken from their parents, were little girls, and presumably without sexual experience. Somebody had to break them in. Somebody had to teach them to please. Somebody had to make them ready for the day when their virginity was auctioned off.

Early on, Julia had begun thinking of Joe Norton as the victim of a blackmail plot; though a pedophile and deserving of no sympathy, he had, or so the theory went, been pressured into his role in the adoption scam. She now realized that she'd been completely wrong. Joe Norton had been a willing participant from the beginning. He proved it by rising from the couch and shouting into the faces of the two younger men, who recoiled as though struck.

Julia let the binoculars fall as she again reached for the radio. Foley had to be warned away. Norton was already in a rage and there was no telling what he'd do if confronted. Better to wait for the locals, for a show of force powerful enough to drive Joe Norton's hopeless situation home. Her hand was inside the pocket of her coat, fumbling for the radio's send button, when she heard, from the far side of the house, the whoop of a police siren. Once, then again. Then again.

FOLEY WATCHED Julia pick her way along the icy sidewalk. Her gait, so in contrast to her usual confident stride, was tentative as she tipped to the right, then to the left, arms extended for balance. The spectacle brought a smile to Foley's lips. He was, he knew, half in love with Julia Brennan, amazing because he hadn't once been tempted to seek a relationship in the years following Kirstin's suicide. New York being a city of single women and he being an attractive man, there'd been opportunity galore, and he was not so utterly preoccupied that he failed to recognize the essential female invitation when it was offered. But he hadn't taken the next step, not even in the early days when loneliness gnawed at his heart, implacable and persistent as a beetle attacking the trunk of a tree.

A moment later, Julia stepped into the woods and Foley returned his attention to the Nicolson home. Without thinking all that much about it, he'd more or less accepted her assessment of Joe and Carla Norton. They were in their early sixties and not likely to resist, especially as he didn't plan to leave the car unless invited inside.

Nevertheless, reflexively, Foley decided to cruise past the Nicolson home, then turn around so the driver's side of the car faced away from the house. He would also block the driveway in order to prevent a panic flight. New York traffic being what it was, Foley had never participated in a high-speed chase and didn't intend to start now.

Still, Foley reflected, for him it was a time of new beginnings. A month before, he'd sublet a furnished studio apartment on West 106th Street, cutting an all-cash, sub-rosa deal that generated no paper trail. The agreement was for six months while the current renter, Malcolm Freemantle, toured Europe.

And after that? Foley asked himself. After that, exactly what? Well, he wouldn't be a cop any more. Lear's raid was sure to generate an investigation by Internal Affairs and he, Foley, would turn in his badge before submitting to an interrogation. But that was as far ahead as he could see. Despite the prevailing belief that he was as premeditated as a politician at a televised debate, most of the time Foley felt himself drawn forward by an irresistible force into a future even darker than his present. If such could be imagined.

The words fate and karma presented themselves for Foley's consideration. To a Roman Catholic, of course, those words were near heretical, obscenities to be avoided at all cost. The doctrine of free will was a central tenet of Catholic thought and always had been. You were in charge. You were the boss. And the blame, therefore, was yours.

Foley opened his coat, loosened his gun in its holster, let his eyes sweep the street ahead of him. It was his secret pride that he'd never sought a chemical solution to his problems. Not in drugs or alcohol, or in the antidepressants currently in vogue. Maybe that was the free-will part. Peter Foley had welcomed his obsession, pretending it had been there all along, a demon waiting for the planets to align before claiming his soul.

As if emerging from a dream, Foley began to laugh. In addition to everything else, somewhere along the line he'd begun taking himself much too seriously, a fundamental error for a leaf in a hurricane.

He let his thoughts return to Julia Brennan, imagined her fighting her way through snowdrifts in her city boots and her city coat. Perhaps, if all went well, he'd give her the ultimate gift, the serial killer whose apprehension would greatly advance her career. First things first, of course, though he felt in no way bound by his earlier refusal to help. Besides, the solution to the problem was simple enough, the facts already out there. Once Julia was finished with this phase of her investigation, once the Nortons were arrested and their co-conspirators unmasked, she'd most likely figure it out for herself.

In the meantime, he'd have to content himself with Julia's apparent rejection of Raymond Lear's parting accusation. Lear, of course, could have no idea what viewing the photos and videos had cost Peter Foley, no idea how easy it was to imagine Patti . . .

Peter Foley doesn't go there, Peter Foley reminded himself. Never, never, never.

The radio chirped, at that moment, three times in quick succession. Foley settled himself, drew a breath, then put the Ford in gear. A few minutes later, he was parked across Elizabeth Nicolson's driveway, reaching for the cell phone, when the first gunshots rang out.

36

A S T H E first shots echoed through the trees, Julia, much to her surprise, immediately calmed down. Her pulse slowed until she was no
longer aware of her beating heart; her mind slowed as well, even as her
focus narrowed still further. She did not have to force herself to recall
her Academy training, or the resolve she'd formed back in Peter
Foley's apartment to learn from her mistakes. These items flitted
through her mind like a feather duster across a table top, but they
were in no way responsible for the cold determination that took
charge as if her common self was no more than an annoying child that
needed to be protected from its own stupidity. They were shooting at
her partner. They were shooting at Peter Foley. Those bad, bad boys.

She let the binoculars drop into the snow, drew her weapon from
her purse, lined up the automatic's front and rear sights with the
back of the man closest to the window. Then she corrected for a brisk
wind blowing from right to left, and for the effect of gravity, before
gently drawing down on the trigger.

The 9-mm hollow-point round expanded properly, mushrooming
as it impacted the upper left quadrant of the man's back without

fragmenting. It entered just beneath his scapula, dug a two-inch channel through his heart, then somehow managed to worm its way between his ribs before exiting his body. The man did not fly forward, or spin aroun, nor was he thrust into the air. Instead, as if the puppeteer holding his strings had quit without giving notice, he crumpled and died.

Though the sharp crack of the bullet as it accelerated past the sound barrier seemed, to Julia, instantly swallowed by the relentless moan of the wind, it was powerful enough to stir the snow-covered branches of the evergreens above her head. The mini-avalanche that followed began in the upper branches, tumbled down like water along the channels of a mountain stream, came to rest finally on Julia Brennan's head and shoulders. She jerked once, in surprise, then calmly wiped the surface of her weapon with her free hand. When she looked up, Norton and his companion had vanished.

An instant later, while Julia was still trying to get her bearings, the rear door of the house flew open and the second of Norton's companions crossed a tiny porch, descended two steps and marched into the back yard. The man's long blond hair appeared silver in the moonlight and his face was drained of all color. In his left hand, he carried a large-bore revolver, his finger through the trigger guard, barrel pointing straight up.

Julia watched his halting progress through snow that rose to midcalf until he was too far from the house to return. Then without moving anything but her lips, she shouted. "Police, drop your weapon."

But the man did not drop his weapon, at least not immediately. He spun in Julia's general direction, slipped in the snow, his right leg flying high enough to shame a Radio City Rockette, and fell over backwards. Somehow, he managed to hang onto the revolver until his head crashed through the snow and into the frozen dirt beneath. Then he let go as his left arm, following his body, swept up and back, the gun tracing a short arc before disappearing beneath the snow.

Julia crossed the yard as quickly as the snow allowed. In her peripheral vision, she registered shadows behind an upstairs window. There was nothing, she knew, to be done about them, not at this point, but they couldn't be discounted, either. The moon was too bright, her vulnerable flesh only too exposed.

The man sat up as Julia approached. He seemed to be in control, a professional who understood that power and strength are relative and she was the one holding the gun. Nevertheless, Julia took no chances. She stopped six feet away, then said, her voice steady, "You don't roll over on your stomach right now, I'm gonna shoot you through the head."

"No kill." The man obeyed, extending his arms to either side before adding, "I have rights."

Julia dropped her knee to the center of his back and cuffed him. Then she got up and yanked him to his feet, carefully positioned him between the Nicolson home and her fragile flesh. Bulletproof vest or not, she was perfectly willing to let her prisoner take the first round.

FOLEY WAS leaning across the front seat when the first shots broke out the Ford's rear window. Instinctively, he flattened himself on the seat as a second volley tore through the window above his head and a round, or a fragment, smashed into his vest above his right kidney. The pain was so intense that for a moment he thought he might lose consciousness. A curtain of pure black, darker than the sub-basement of a tenement he'd once searched with a dying flashlight, slid from the periphery toward the center of his vision. It was only the pain, finally, that kept him awake, pain that aroused a fear so great that he reached for his back, forcing his hand beneath his vest, expecting to encounter a cascade of blood.

But the vest had done its work, which meant that he'd live to see another sunrise if he managed to get out of the car without being shot again. This time, say, between the eyes. The problem was that he was stretched across the seat with his arms and his head closest to the house from which the bad guys were shooting. The other door, the one that offered safety and protection, could not be reached, at least not by his hand, unless he sat up and reversed position. Not a good idea, not if he didn't want a bullet doing to his brain what other bullets had done to the shattered glass heaped on his coat.

A single shot rang out as he considered the problem, this one from the back of the house. His first thought was, Julia to the rescue. Instantly followed by, Maybe not. Maybe Julia under fire. Propelled by a surge of adrenaline, Foley kicked at the rear door. He was hoping to trigger the latch with his toe or his heel, but succeeded only in jamming his ankle beneath the armrest. He cursed softly, then louder, finally settled down long enough to work up a plan of action that would at least get him out of the car. He pulled his knees into his chest, forced his right leg over the edge of the seat, seeking purchase against the fire wall, then raised his torso slightly as he fumbled for the latch with his right hand.

Okay, he said to himself, the word seeming hollow, a prayer more than a judgment. Nevertheless, he repeated himself, this time with even greater emphasis: Okay. Then he shoved the door open and dove, headfirst, from the car.

T ALK TO me," Julia said. She was standing behind the man she'd captured, holding his jacket with her left hand, pulling backwards. The automatic in her right hand was pressed against the back of his skull. "Talk to me," she repeated.

"I demand lawyer. You understand this?" His accent was thick, *this* emerging as *ziss*.

Julia twisted the barrel of her weapon into his scalp. Her tone of voice seemed to her as cold as the wind swirling around them. "Talk to me. Tell me your name." Above them, a silhouette half-hidden by curtains suddenly became darker. Somebody was standing by the window.

"I give up. I am under arrest. I am not making any troubles. You cannot allow for me to freeze." A little spume of saliva jumped from his mouth as he completed his thoughts, landing on the lapel of his jacket. He'd run into the cold without putting on a coat and he was now paying for it.

"What's that I hear in your voice? Confusion? Terror?" She hesitated for the space of a heartbeat. "Tell me your name. Start with that. Your name."

"You are crazy bitch." He made it into one word, crazybitch, as if that was the way Julia had introduced herself.

"You don't tell your name, Ivan, I'll keep you out here until your balls turn to ice."

"Nevin Gorovic. You are now satisfied?" His eyes jerked up as the curtains in the window were pulled aside and the window raised.

"Julia, don't shoot me."

Though the self-identified Nevin Gorovic shivered from head to toe at the sound of Peter's Foley's voice, Julia herself did no more than glance in his direction. He was standing next to the house and there was blood on his forehead, running down between his eyes.

"You shot?" she asked.

Foley touched the wound, then smiled. "Gravity and concrete. When I exited my vehicle, I landed on my head." His expression turned grave. "Look, I think it might be for the best if you come over to the house. You're a bit exposed where you are."

"That right?"

"You know it is."

Julia held her ground. "This man calls himself Nevin Gorovic. He says he wants a lawyer. Somehow, that doesn't work for me."

"It's not supposed to work. That's why they make you do it. Now, please . . ."

"Hey, Pete, weren't you the guy who told me you were *glad* about the killings?"

Foley took a moment to compose his reply. When he finally spoke, his voice was just loud enough to be heard above the wind. "The fact that I don't care about some lunatic out there capping chicken hawks doesn't mean that I would kill a chicken hawk, or play any part in getting one killed."

It was the first time Peter Foley had formally denied all involvement in the killings and for a moment Julia fell silent. Finely honed in the course of a thousand interrogations, her instincts told her he was being truthful.

"Let's go," she told Nevin Gorovic without taking her weapon from the back of his head. "Nice and easy."

As they began to move, Joe Norton, wattle and all, leaned out of the second-floor window. The stainless-steel revolver in his hand caught the moonlight and held it long enough for Julia to push Gorovic to one side and fire a round in Norton's general direction. She did not aim her weapon, or hold it two-handed; there was only enough time for a snap shot as likely to hit the moon as Joe Norton. Nevertheless, Norton ducked back through the window and vanished.

"Where," she asked as she walked toward the house, "is Annie Oakley when you need her?"

"I hate to be the one to tell you this," Foley returned easily, "but Annie Oakley is up in heaven. With Buffalo Bill."

37

JULIA WALKED past Foley, who was holding onto their prisoner, to the closest window. She took a quick peek inside, then jerked her head away as a voice, a female voice from behind her screamed, "What are you doing to poor Elizabeth? I'm going to call the police."

Though Julia couldn't imagine why the the police hadn't already been called, she shouted, "We *are* the police. Please go to the far side of your home. You're not safe where you're standing."

"How do I know you're the police?" the voice persisted

"Well," Foley responded, holding up his shield, "there's this. And you also might wanna consider that if we were the bad guys, we'd most likely have reacted more aggressively to your intrusion."

Smiling, Julia moved to the other side of the window and took another peek. She was looking over the body of the man she'd shot, over the gun still in his hand, through the living and dining rooms doors into the kitchen where Elizabeth Nicolson sat, crying into a dish towel.

"Pete," Julia said as Nicolson's neighbor, having apparently gotten Foley's message, slammed her window closed, "Take Mr. Gorovic up to the corner, wait for the locals, give them a heads-up on the situation in the house. They just drive up and park, somebody's liable to get shot."

Foley shook his head in wonder. "And what are you gonna do, Lieutenant, play hero? You gonna do a Pickett's charge on the bad guys?"

Julia was tempted to baldly state the fact that it was none of his business. Instead, she shrugged her shoulders. "I'll watch the house, make sure nobody escapes. And look, while you're waiting, you might want to examine the prisoner's identification and talk to him a little bit. See if he'll listen to reason."

Though Foley wanted to further complain that Julia was establishing a pattern by ordering him about whenever they faced a crisis, he simply led his prisoner away. This was not the time and place to remind her that he didn't give a damn for her rank, or for his own badge, either. The locals had to be warned and if he didn't do it, it wouldn't get done. Julia Brennan wasn't going anywhere.

"You try to run away from me," he told Gorovic as they crossed the neighboring yard. "I'll kill you, handcuffs or not."

"First crazy woman, now crazy man. Everybody wants to kill Nevin Gorovic."

Foley left it at that until they reached the corner. Then he searched Gorovic for weapons, eventually settling for the man's wallet. Though he was hoping the locals were close at hand, when he listened for sirens he heard only the whistle of the wind across the utility lines above his head.

"Are you the one who shot me?" he asked. The pain in his left kidney had settled into a bearable, though relentless, throb.

"I am freezing," Gorovic responded. "You are making police brutality on me."

Calmly, deliberately, Foley slammed his fist into his prisoner's unprotected stomach. "I asked you," he said as Gorovic dropped to his knees, "if you were the one who shot me?"

"I am not shoot anyone."

"See?" Foley hauled Gorovic to his feet. "That wasn't so hard, was it?" He went back to Gorovic's wallet, using the light from a street lamp to examine the various credit cards, debit cards, and business cards inside.

"Hey, whatta we have here?" Foley dangled a business card before his prisoner's eyes. "*Pancevski and Markovic. International Adoptions*. You work for them, Nevin? You on the books?"

"I want lawyer."

Foley shook his head. "Ordinarily," he explained, his voice weary, "I'd be the first to applaud that move. That's because, ordinarily, it'd be the right way to go. First get the lawyer, then cut the deal. The problem, Nevin, is that all those bad boys at Pancevski and Markovic, they're gonna rabbit back to their ancestral homelands as soon as they find out what happened here. And old Joe Norton, well you can see he's gone looney."

"Joe is crazy man," Gorovic admitted. "He cannot take pressure."

"Not like you, right? Tell me where you grew up."

"In Sarajevo."

"Exactly my point. Joe Norton, he came up soft and now he can't live with the disgrace. If he doesn't get shot, he's gonna cap himself. You know where that leaves you, right?" Foley fished out Gorovic's driver's license, checked the DOB. "Lemme put this in practical terms. First, there's no walking away from this. You're gonna do serious time. But that doesn't mean there's no difference between fifteen years and three consecutive life terms. You're twenty-eight, yes?"

"Yes,"

"Well, I'm forty-three, which means that if you had to do the full fifteen, you'd be my age when you got out. Now look at me, Nevin. I'm not an old man. I'm not falling apart. My dick still gets hard. So ask yourself, when they finally open those prison gates do you wanna be my age, or Joe Norton's?"

"You are only city detective. How you are going to do this deal?"

"Good question. Shows you're using your head. But we're right back to the original problem. By the time you get a lawyer to negotiate an ironclad deal in return for your cooperation and testimony, there won't be anyone to testify against. On the other hand, if you name your bosses right now, tell me how you brought the girls over to this country, the NYPD, represented by yours truly, will arrest the bad guys before the night is over. That puts them in jail where I promise you they will stay. Tell me, are you the boss? Are you running the show at . . ." He glanced at the business card, cleared his throat, then looked up, eyes all innocence. "Pancevski and Markovic?"

"Hah, these peoples, they are Serbs." Gorovic spit the word out. His blue eyes in the moonlight were so pale Foley couldn't separate them from the surrounding whites.

"And you're not?"

"I am Bosnian."

"So much the better." From far away, a mere sharpening of the wind's oscillating hiss, Foley recognized, finally, the cry of approaching sirens. "You hear that?" he asked. "You hear the sirens? They belong to the local police. *New Jersey* police. Once they take you into custody, I'll be out of it, so you gotta make a decision. I know it's hard, asking you to trust a cop after what you been through. But sometimes fate puts a choice right in front of your face and you *have* to pick the direction you want your life to take. Nevin, this is definitely one of those times."

38

JULIA WAITED a few minutes, until Foley was out of sight, then made her way to the kitchen door through which Nevin Gorovic had fled. There was a window in the door's upper half, divided into four small panes, and Julia approached without hesitation. Still at the kitchen table, still clutching her dish towel, Elizabeth Nicolson glanced up when Julia's face appeared in the window. Nicolson's own face was round, plump, and noticeably reddened. Her brown eyes were reddened as well, her makeup streaked by tears.

Julia flashed a reassuring smile as she displayed her badge, then turned the door's handle and walked inside. She'd been counting on nobody having relocked it after Gorovic took off.

"Hi. How are you tonight?" With her left hand, Julia tucked her badge away. She was holding her automatic in her right hand and her eyes swept the rooms within her view as she pushed the door closed with the heel of her boot. Then, after taking a moment to enjoy the sudden warmth, she introduced herself. "I'm Lieutenant Brennan. Are you Mrs. Nicolson?"

"I am." Elizabeth Nicolson's mouth curled up beneath her rather flat nose, a bulldog expression that Julia was unable to interpret.

"Do you know why I'm here?"

"I'm sure I don't."

"Do you know why those other men were here?"

The question took Elizabeth by surprise. Her expression softened as her eyes dropped to the towel in her hands, but she did not respond.

"Do you know why they shot at my partner when he drove up?" Julia persisted. "Do you know why they had guns in the first place? Do you know what's going on here, Elizabeth Nicolson?"

Elizabeth responded without looking up. "I got a call from Joe last week. He said he needed to stay with me for a while, but he wouldn't tell me why." One of her braids had come loose and now hung by the side of her face. She flicked it away impatiently. "Joe and Carla arrived on Monday. The others came on Wednesday. They've been coming back every day since then. I complained to Joe, but you can't tell him anything. He's always been a bully."

"Did he molest you when you were a little girl?"

For just an instant, Elizabeth Nicolson's face collapsed. Then she drew herself erect and raised her eyes to stare at the wall in front of her. "That's what this is about?"

"In a general sense."

"Well, my brother ran upstairs after Mr. Grebo was shot. He forced his wife to go with him."

"She's a hostage?"

"He forced her up the stairs." Nicolson somehow managed to shake and nod her head at the same time. "Joe's room is at the end of the hall, but I don't know if that's where they went."

Julia approached Elizabeth Nicolson from behind, then dropped a hand to the older woman's shoulder. "I need you to stand up, Mrs. Nicolson. I'm going to have to handcuff you."

"What?"

Though Nicolson made no move to escape, Julia tightened her grip. "It's not that I don't believe you, or that I don't think you're a victim in all this, but I can't leave my back exposed. C'mon, get up."

When Julia lifted, Elizabeth followed, her movements near robotic as she tried to assimilate what was now happening to her. A moment later, she was handcuffed to the handle on the oven. Not the most secure spot, but Julia was in a hurry and didn't have time to drag the woman, even assuming she'd cooperate, from room to room in search of a better one.

"I've called for backup," Julia explained, "and when it arrives, you'll be let go. Until then . . . Well, like I already said, I'm sorry."

Julia shrugged off her coat and crossed the living room swiftly, only to pause at the foot of the stairs to collect her thoughts. What, she asked herself, do I hope to accomplish here? Norton's surrender? That would be all for the best, though there isn't much chance of that, not in the few minutes until the locals arrive.

On the other hand, there was the possibility, if she fanned the flames of his rage, that he'd make some sort of an admission that would lead her to the next rung on the ladder. There was also the possibility, rather more likely, that if she pushed his buttons, he'd turn his anger on his wife, Carla, or on Julia Brennan. And there was another potential outcome as well, one that could not be ignored. Given his age and the evidence against him, Joe Norton would spend the rest of his life in jail, an elderly middle-class short-eyes, prey to each and every prison predator.

Would he decide that death was the preferable alternative? Would he take his wife with him? Or would he find himself unable to turn the gun on himself or his beloved? Would he decide the only way out was to die at the hands of a police officer? "Suicide by cop" was a time-honored tradition among hostage-takers.

Julia left it there as she climbed to a landing two steps from the top where the stairway made an abrupt left turn. Time to focus now. In front of her, a finely wrought gilt mirror on the wall blocking the western end of the corridor provided a view of the hallway, past a series of open doors, to a closed door at the very end. The presence of the mirror was the first break, as far as Julia was concerned, that she'd gotten all day.

"Yo," she shouted without exposing the merest inch of her flesh, "Joe Norton. It's Lieutenant Brennan. We spoke on the phone."

A fusillade of gunshots, fired through the door, shattered the mirror into small fragments. "Don't try to come in here." The voice, a man's, was thin, barely carrying the length of the hall.

"Trust me on this, Joe, I'm staying right where I am." Julia brushed glass from her shoulders, shook out her hair. "You okay in there?"

Norton's responding laughter was pitched at the edge of madness. "How about your wife? Is Carla okay?"

"She will be as long as you stay where your are."

"But she's alright?"

After a long hesitation, a woman's voice declared, "I'm not hurt. Please don't try to come in here."

"Why does everybody think I'm about to storm the gates?" Julia asked. "Joe's the one running this show. It's all up to him."

As if to prove her point, Julia lapsed into one of those pregnant silences beloved of cop interrogators. Her major goal had already been accomplished. Joe Norton was too old to climb out the window, even with the porch roof so conveniently close. He was trapped, and when the truth finally sank in he'd make his move.

The silence continued for several minutes, until Norton's frail voice again traveled the length of the hallway. "You told me you were in New York," he accused.

"I lied. But, you know, I'm a cop. What'd you expect?"

"You said you just wanted to talk."

"Joe, who started shooting when we drove up to the house, you or me?"

Another, briefer silence, then, "You weren't in the car. There was only one cop in the car and he was a man."

"I was around the back. Watching the door."

Norton laughed again, a choppy cackle that ended in a phlegmy cough. "You're all fucking liars," he called.

Julia shook her head, though nobody was there to see.

"Uh-uh, Joey, we've already established that fact. What you need to think about now is what's gonna happen next. I mean, how many times have you read about somebody or other taking a hostage, or even a group of hostages? A hundred? Two hundred? How many times you read about someone getting away? Even if we gave you a plane, which won't happen, no country will accept you. Not one country in the whole world."

Julia stopped abruptly. She knew nothing of hostage negotiations, how these things were supposed to work. Maybe stressing the hopeless nature of Joe Norton's predicament would drive him to commit some desperate act for which she would hold herself responsible. Not a happy thought.

God, she told herself, not for the first time, how I'd like to have this jerk alone in a basement somewhere.

"But that," she shouted, "does not—and I emphasize the *not*—mean you can't help yourself by cooperating. Remember, you haven't killed anybody."

"No, that's true. Although I tried my best, I didn't kill anybody. Say, when would this cooperation begin? Should I just pour my heart out right this minute? Or should I wait for a larger audience?"

"Well, first thing, I haven't informed you of your right to avoid self-incrimination, which means everything we say is off the record. Second, if you want, I could probably get a lawyer down here. Just give me a name."

Norton responded with another choppy laugh. No doubt about it, the man was enjoying himself. "Hey, Brennan, you wanna hear something funny? There's nothing hotter on this planet than a ten-year-old virgin if you treat her right. I'm talking about on *fire*, Brennan. They love it."

Surprised by the change in Norton's tone, Julia recalled Elizabeth Nicolson declaring that her brother had always been a bully. Then she flashed to Foley's little tour of his website. What was it Poobear had said of the seventeen-year-old girl he wanted to be rid of? Ah, yes, Julia remembered, the child, according to Poobear, was hairy as a goat.

"Hey, Brennan, you have a daughter?"

Beneath Norton's voice, like an accompanying cello, Julia heard Carla Norton begin to sob.

"No, I don't," Julia returned, careful to maintain her bantering tone. "I don't have children. I'm a dyke."

"Really?"

"Really."

"Well, we could have had some fun together, me and you. Old Carla, here, was a bit too inhibited. Knew how to keep her mouth shut, though. I'll give her that."

"Christ, Joe, it sounds like you've been at it for a long time."

"I was one of the lucky ones, Brennan. I found my vocation early."

"Then you must've thought you'd died and gone to heaven when you stumbled on the adoption scam. Innocent young girls, straight from the farm, never knew anything but their families. I'll bet you don't find 'em like that in Thailand."

"Or anywhere else. It was a miracle. I can still see them, at night when I try to go to sleep. Especially the one they call Little Girl Blue. What a beauty. Those doe eyes looking up at me. A mouth that was made to be kissed. I tell ya, Brennan, it brings a tear to my eye."

Outside, the rise and fall of onrushing police sirens was now clearly audible, the potential for an imminent crisis rising with each decibel. What do I do, Julia asked herself, if shots are fired from within the bedroom. What do I do if Norton comes out? How do I protect the hostage and still protect myself? One thing sure, I can't just wait for the situation to unfold.

"What I said about the lawyer," she called as she mulled the various possibilities, "it's not a joke. You get a lawyer down here, let him negotiate a protective custody arrangement, see where the evidence leads. Because what you're doing now, you're overreacting, just like you did when my partner drove up to the house."

"Brennan," Norton finally said, "you're a damn good liar. I have to admit it. But you and I, we both know what's gonna happen when those kids start talking about how they're emotionally scarred for life and they'll never be able to trust anybody ever again. Who's gonna want to hear the truth? That they *begged* for it. That they couldn't get enough."

Julia thought of Anja Dascalescu as she'd appeared on that Sunday morning, naked and alone, in Central Park. Did Joe Norton really believe what he was saying? Or was he simply regurgitating the party line? Again, she remembered Poobear's description: Hairy as a goat.

The police sirens, now loud enough to overwhelm the howl of the wind, were no longer advancing. One by one, as Julia nursed her rage, they shut down. Then, a moment later, the radio in her pocket clicked twice.

"What about the money?" she asked Norton as she keyed the radio three times in response. "I mean, you put it all together, the girls in New York and the others, we're talkin' about serious revenue. Were you getting a piece of that?"

"You think I'm a pimp?"

Julia nodded to herself. Norton hadn't denied the existence of "the others." There was more to be done. She thought of Foley and his prisoner. Maybe Nevin Gorovic had turned. She couldn't be sure, but she could hope.

"I'm just asking, Joe."

Another laugh. "Well, your comment about the money is right on the money. Which I ran out of some time ago. Not that filthy lucre was my primary object."

"Maybe not, but bringing those children into the United States, that had to be a lot of work to set up."

"It wasn't all that hard. Remember, as a foster dad, I knew how to manipulate bureaucracies."

"Manipulating is one thing. Having your own man on the inside, Christopher Inman, that's something else. But tell me, does it hurt to know your partners are gonna get away clean? While your little life, one way or the other, is over and done with?"

"Oh, psychology now. How pitiful. Say, are your feet flat, too? Are you the traditional dumb flatfoot? Because it seems to me that if I were to reveal the names of the . . . ah, yes, the *higher ups*, that lawyer you promised won't be of much use."

"That's not entirely true, Joe. A lawyer can still get you into protective custody. As for the other part, look at what we have here. We have a dead body in the living room, shots fired at cops, a hostage situation, and pedophilia leading back to Little Girl Blue. Once the news gets out, your partners, they're gonna take off for Bosnia or Serbia or wherever they're from. That leaves you holding a very large bag." Julia thought about Foley, wondered if he'd run the same line

on Nevin Gorovic. Given the time pressure, it was the only line available. "Moving fast is your only hope, Joe."

"Hope? Forget hope. Right from the outset I knew that one of
those kids would eventually escape. Sooner or later, it had to happen.
Hey, I'm an old man. but I'm still a player, and I intend to play this
particular game to the very end."

"That was then, this is . . ."

The squeak of a revolving doorknob, followed by the creak of an
opening door, shut Julia down in mid-sentence. She was looking at
the wreckage of the mirror, at a long triangular shard. In it she could
see, as if from a great distance, a pair of figures emerge from the bedroom, a woman in front, a man following. Julia could not make out
the man's features, but she could see the gun in his hand. He was
pointing it, not at his wife, but along the hallway. In search, apparently, of Julia Brennan's head.

"Where are you, Lieutenant Brennan?" Joe Norton called as he
and his wife inched forward. His arm was around her chest, pinning
her close. "I think it's time we became better acquainted."

Julia backed down the stairs, then crossed the living and dining
rooms into the kitchen. Pausing long enough to gather her coat, she
opened and slammed the back door as Elizabeth Nicolson watched
silently, her eyes now dry, her gaze speculative.

"Up to you, Elizabeth," Julia whispered as she took a position
alongside a breakfast bar cut into the wall between the kitchen and
the dining room. Assuming a two-handed grip, she brought her
weapon to her chest, pointed the barrel at the ceiling, then fought to
slow her breathing. With her back to the wall, she told herself, you
can spin, aim, fire through the opening in less than a second. Norton
will release his wife on the steps or somewhere in the living room.
And Elizabeth is definitely going to help you. Even if . . .

"Brennan?"

Julia looked across the room at Elizabeth Nicolson. The woman's
eyes were blazing as she returned Julia's gaze. Norton was coming
down the stairs. It was decision time for all concerned.

"Brennan?"

"She's gone." Elizabeth's voice was little more than a rasp. Nostrils flared, she closed her mouth, swallowed, turned her head to look out through the kitchen door.

"What are you saying?"

"I'm saying she went out the back way, Joe. She could be anywhere."

"Bad for me," Norton replied, "and for you, too."

"Are you going to kill me, Joe? What you've already done to me isn't enough? You want my life as well?"

Norton didn't bother to reply. Instead, he ordered his wife to close the window blinds.

Julia listened to the rattle of the blinds as they came down, trying to locate her enemy. The breakfast bar would afford an almost unobstructed view of the dining room, but there was a wall between the dining and living rooms. If she wanted to retain the element of surprise, she would have to wait for Norton to come to her. And he would come, of course. Ever practical, he would want his two hostages together and Elizabeth was still cuffed to the oven.

"Get in here, Lizzie," Norton called, as if to prove Julia's point.

"I can't."

"Don't give me a hard time. For once in your miserable life, just do what I say."

"I'm handcuffed to the stove, Joe." Elizabeth's voice was so drained of emotion it might have come from a computerized phone menu. "I'm not going anywhere unless somebody takes this thing apart."

"That bitch. That fucking bitch."

Julia smiled at the epithet, smiled again as the blinds in the dining room were lowered, then drawn shut. Norton would be in the dining room now, keeping an eye on things. She could turn, get off three or four rounds before he responded. No warning need be given, not after he'd fired on the police, not after he'd taken hostages.

"Alright, ladies," Norton said, "here's what's going to happen. Carla, you're going to go into the kitchen, find a screwdriver, unscrew the handle, bring Lizzie to me. If you try to run out the door, I'll kill you. If Lizzie's not in here in five minutes, I'll kill you. Understand?"

Julia drew a breath, rehearsed the sequence in her mind: extend the weapon, turn, locate the target, aim, squeeze. It was funny, all

those police documentaries with doors flying off the hinges, cops
screaming contradictory orders at the tops of their lungs, all those
adrenal glands spurting into all those veins. Stupid, stupid, stupid.
Cold was the way to go, cold, calm, purposeful. This wasn't a barroom
brawl; this was a problem to be solved by simple mechanics. Extend
the weapon, turn, locate the target, aim, squeeze. As easy as that.

She waited only until Carla Norton's foot extended beyond the
doorway, then she dropped the barrel of her automatic and spun to
face the dining room. Joe Norton was standing against the wall ten
feet away. He was holding his weapon at his side and she might have
given him a chance if her mind, less disciplined than she wanted to
admit, hadn't chosen that moment to offer the image of Anja Dascalescu as she'd appeared just before the medical examiner began to
sew her up.

*Those doe eyes looking up at me. A mouth that was made to be
kissed. Hairy as a goat. They loved it.*

39

ROBERT REID parked his car in the closest available parking space, two hundred yards from Julia Brennan's home. He threw the transmission into park reached for the key only to check himself at the last second. Then, smiling, he switched the heater fan to its highest setting and let his weight drop back against the butter-soft leather covering the seat. The January wind outside was strong enough to rock his Mercedes on its springs.

Corry was not yet home. The light in its fixture next to the front door was lit, and there was a light in the kitchen as well, but the rest of the house was dark. Though well after sunset, it was still a few minutes short of five o'clock. Corry usually didn't return from school until close to six.

Reid shifted his feet to allow the stream of air from the heater to sweep beneath the cuffs of his trousers, his thoughts turning to Destroyer and Destroyed. In the preceding hours, Reid had convinced himself that the man he'd come to call D&D had another dumping ground somewhere. That opinion had been confirmed after Reid cashed a series of markers in order to obtain a five-minute phone interview with Sergeant Aaron Ross, the profiler who'd studied the crime-scene evidence. Ross was of the opinion that D&D had been in the killing business for years.

A second e-mail, fired off to cyberfree@heavenlyfire, which put the question directly, had drawn a terse reply: *Dig deeper, hack.*

"The actor in this case," Ross had explained, "is torn between a certain knowledge of his eventual capture, and a certain knowledge that he's some kind of superman who cannot be caught. Now you and I, we think it's impossible to consciously maintain both positions, because we know they can't both be true. But our man, he does believe both at the same time and it's driving him to take risks. It's driving him crazy."

Reid slapped the steering wheel with the palm of his hand, once, then again. Destroyer and Destroyed. The abused child, destroyed by a predatory adult, now become a destroyer of predatory adults. Except it was backwards. It should be Destroyed and Destroyer, destroyed first. But could you expect a psychopath, torn apart by contradictory impulses, to be consistent? Maybe he'd typed the first thing that came into his head. Maybe he hadn't given it ten seconds of thought.

Dig deeper.

Assume, Reid told himself as he checked the rearview mirror for a glimpse of Corry walking up the block, that all communications from D&D were written by the superman part of his personality. What would a superman's boast to make things clear very soon mean in real terms? What did he mean by the command to dig deeper? And why do his Goliaths battle from within and without?

Suddenly, a few small pieces of the puzzle came together. Dig deeper was meant literally. Somewhere in that Queens warehouse, in a lower sub-basement, or literally beneath the foundation, there were more bodies. The Empire Steel warehouse, eight stories tall, occupied a full square block of Long Island City. Had the cops searched every inch of its hundreds of thousands of square feet? There was no electricity in the building and the basements were as dark as caves. If the earliest victims, taken when D&D was still perfecting his game, hadn't been displayed, if D&D, still cautious, had concealed the bodies . . .

Reid shut down the Mercedes, then carefully attached a steering wheel lock before getting out. He paused only for a moment, to set a car alarm so loud the manufacturer guaranteed that exposure for more than sixty seconds would liquefy a thief's brain. Then he headed off to Julia's, fumbling for the house key as he hurried along the sidewalk and up the two steps to the front door.

The key jammed in the slot momentarily and Reid had to jiggle it up and down before the cylinder finally turned. As he stepped across the threshold and closed the door behind him, he made a mental note to buy a tube of graphite and lubricate the mechanism before it froze up altogether. Vaguely, he remembered formulating the same resolve on multiple occasions. That was one of the pleasures, he decided, of growing old. Given enough time, you forgot that you forgot.

He flipped on the light in the small foyer and began to shrug out of his coat when he he suddenly realized that it was very cold in the house. There was a draft blowing through the rooms as well, distinct enough to notice as it washed over his exposed face and hands. Instinctively, as his pulse began to accelerate, he turned his head from side to side, tracking the source of the breeze, an open window somewhere, or an open door.

"Shit," Reid muttered. "Shit, shit, shit."

He walked into the living room and flicked the wall switch, lighting a halogen torchiere in a far corner. The room was reassuringly empty. It's funny, Reid told himself, as he took a few tentative steps toward the kitchen, the closer I get to the abyss, the more fearful I become. There was a time when I would have gone from room to room, hoping there was a burglar still inside the house.

Reid stepped into the kitchen, glanced at the secured windows and back door, then backed away. The problem was on the second floor, a judgment confirmed when he crossed to the foot of the stairs and felt the draft strengthen. He laid his hand on the banister, lifted his right foot to the first step, then shook his head. The smart move here, without doubt, was to return to the kitchen, call the police and let the professionals check it out. More than likely his timidity would draw a condescending smile from the responding officers, but that was easier endured than searching the house, room by room, on his own. His chest was already squeezing down, his throat as well. If he kept this up . . .

Reid was halfway to the kitchen when he was shaken by a conviction that emerged from nowhere to literally buckle his knees.

You've missed it all, scribbler, but I shall make myself clear very soon.

"Corry?" Suddenly desperate, he turned back, mounted the stairs, pulling himself up by the banister. "Corry, you there?" The only answer, the slap of a blowing window shade in Corry's room at the end of the short hallway, propelled him beyond any rationality. He ignored a rapidly intensifying pain that radiated from his chest across his left shoulder and down along his arm. He ignored, too, the possibility that Corry, in a moment of adolescent carelessness, had simply left the window open and that Julia had been too busy or too distracted to notice. He ignored everything except his own terror. Not Corry. Please, please, not Corry.

"Corry."

Reid's voice was no more than a whisper, forced from lungs that refused to contract as he stopped in the doorway of her room to catch his breath. The window beyond the bed was wide open, but there was no sign of a struggle. Corry's stuffed dog, Wally, a companion since infancy, lay on his back, paws raised in play, head against the pillow. A collection of perfume bottles on a glass-topped vanity was undisturbed, as were the carefully piled notebooks on Corry's desk and a wastebasket piled beyond its rim with discarded computer printouts.

Relief flooded Reid's body, a drug every bit as powerful as the Demerol they'd fed him after his heart attack, or the rivers of good booze he'd poured into his gut for decades. He shuffled across the room, closed and locked the window, then sat for a moment on the edge of the bed. He would be all right, he told himself as the bands across his chest tightened, millimeter by millimeter, he would be all right if he could just get to a phone.

Reid tried to draw a breath but could manage only a trickle of air, a reversed whisper that didn't come near filling his lungs. He looked for Corry's phone, the panic rising in his chest nearly as intense as the pain, but the handset for the cordless phone was not in its cradle. Nor, when he swept the room, was it conveniently lying on the night table or bureau. Finally, he slid off the bed, dropped to his knees, and crawled into the hallway. The effort took all of his concentration, since no part of him, not even his head, was willing to work on its own. He had to instruct his right hand to slide along the carpet, his left knee to follow; if his attention wandered, even for a moment, he came to halt. Thus, he was completely unaware of the man following behind him, and unaware, too, when, as he came to the head of the stairs, the man gave a little shove that sent him tumbling down.

40

J ULIA DID everything right. She fired four times in rapid succession, burying each round in a tight pattern to the left of Joe Norton's sternum, then stopped when the gun fell from his hand and he slid to the carpet. Her weapon still at the ready, she stepped forward, retrieved Norton's automatic, checked for a pulse, only to find that Norton had achieved his final wish. He'd played the game to the very end.

As Julia reached for the radio, Foley's voice, emotion-filled for once, poured from the tiny speaker: *Brennan. Brennan. For Christ's sake.*

"Brennan here," she responded, her chest tight, voice much thinner than she would have expected. "The scene is under control, Pete. Send in the cavalry."

She needn't have bothered. A dozen New Jersey State Troopers crashed through the door even before she returned the radio to her pocket. Absurdly, they surrounded Elizabeth Nicolson and Carla Norton, leaving Julia, the only woman holding a gun, to her own devices. True, her badge was displayed on her chest, but a badge can belong to anyone. It was not an error, Julia decided, that she would have made.

A moment later, Foley's head appeared in the doorway on the other side of the kitchen. He glanced around, nodded to Julia, said, "The other one, Gorovic, he turned. I've got the name of the adoption agency that brought the children into the country."

"Great."

Julia walked over to the kitchen table, sat down, laid her weapon on the table top. Her legs, relieved of the burden of her weight, began to tremble, her hands as well. Nevertheless, she retrieved her cellular and managed to punch in Commander Harry Clark's number at the big house. It was now six o'clock.

She got through first to the lieutenant who guarded Clark's time, a big-bellied vet named Brittman, then was put on hold. As she waited, a middle-aged trooper sporting a pair of stars on either shoulder approached her. The man's right ear was noticeably larger than his left, lending him a goofy aspect despite the stern expression. The spider veins running along his cheeks and over his nose didn't help either.

"Lieutenant," he said without introducing himself.

"I'm reporting to my superior." Julia offered an explanation she knew the man would accept. The New Jersey Troopers were reputed to have great respect for the chain of command. "The women, by the way. . . ." She swept her hand in a wide semicircle. "I have no reason to believe that either played a part in the shooting."

"Clark here."

Julia held up a finger, then began to speak rapidly. Clark listened without comment, willing, apparently, to absorb the facts while he pondered his next move. "I don't have all the details yet," she finished, "but there are others involved, foreign nationals who have every reason to flee as soon as they learn what happened here."

To his credit, Commander Clark made his command decision quickly. "I'm coming out," he told her, "by helicopter. Anything you need before I arrive, route it through Brittman."

"It won't be me, sir." Julia looked down at her trembling knees, thinking so much for the dangerous-woman persona. She'd never felt weaker in her life. "I need some time, administrative leave if at all possible, medical leave if that's the only option. But I have to stop, sort things out. If I don't . . . Anyway, I'm putting Bert Griffith in charge. It's better that way anyhow. The locals'll have me tied up for hours, but Griffith wasn't near the scene when the shooting started."

When Clark spoke, after a brief pause, his voice was gentle, even kind. Julia would never have expected it of him. "I shot somebody once, put the mope in a wheelchair for life. My partner wanted to go out and celebrate, buy me drinks 'til I dropped, but I turned him down. Instead, I went up to St. Mary's and spoke to a priest I knew. It made a big difference. Now, let me talk to whoever's in charge."

Julia folded her hands, in part to hide, if not still, their trembling. She laid them on the table, waited patiently until the trooper, who identified himself to Clark as Colonel Thaddeus Harman, finished his conversation. Then she immediately dialed her home number. "I have to call my daughter," she explained, "tell her I'll be late."

Instead of Corry, Julia listened to her own voice request the favor of a message. How insipid I sound, she thought, like one of those incompetent jerks who think they're in complete control when they've never done anything right in their entire lives.

"Corry," she said, after a sharp prompting beep, "I'm in New Jersey. I'm okay. I'll be home as soon as I can. Love you."

For a minute, Julia considered leaving the cellular on, just in case her daughter needed to get in touch, deciding finally that she wouldn't have time for a reassuring conversation, not until she was debriefed by the locals and by her own superiors. As soon as things cleared up, though, she'd retrieve her messages, make another attempt to reach Corry. Meanwhile, she was unavailable.

When Julia looked up, Colonel Harman had vanished. She glanced into the dining room, saw Foley seated across from a trooper who'd laid his Smokey Bear hat on the table beside him. She noted Foley's relaxed shoulders, the amused smile on his face, and felt a quick surge of affection. When she'd ordered him away from the scene to warn the locals, he hadn't simply obeyed. Not Peter Foley who believed the chain of command to be at best an inconvenience. The local cops had to be warned. Somebody had to to watch the house. If he hadn't believed in her, he'd never have marched off, Nevin Gorovic in tow. If she hadn't believed in him, she'd have interrogated Gorovic herself.

All right, she told herself, back to business. The girl and the guy don't get together until the end of the movie.

"Bert Griffith," she called. "You out there?"

Griffith emerged from the living room a moment later. He made a wide circle, edging through a knot of cops and paramedics gathered around Joe Norton's body, then stepped into the kitchen.

"You need me, loo?"

"I'm putting you in charge."

"In charge of what, exactly? We don't have jurisdiction here."

"I know that, Bert. Which means somebody from our side of the Hudson is gonna have to sit up and beg for information. Right now, I don't have it in me."

Griffith's expression softened. "It's okay," he said, "you did good here."

It took Julia a moment to come up with a snappy response, *And the world's a better place for it, right?* By that time Griffith had gone a-begging and Peter Foley was sitting next to her, enfolding her hands in his. The trembling in her fingers instantly ceased, though her knees continued to bounce up and down as though she were in the final hundred yards of a bicycle race.

"I thought they were ripping you apart in there," Julia said.

"Maybe that's what they had in mind, but I told them I wouldn't be giving a statement until Commander Harry Clark, my lord and master, arrived at the scene."

"You worried about something?"

"Not especially."

"Then why the delay?"

"Because I've been a cop too long to believe that innocence will protect me. Maybe the honcho trooper out there, Colonel Harman, has a hard-on for New Yorkers in general and New York cops in particular. Maybe there's a sheriff in the background who's running for re-election. Maybe one of the ladies, Carla Norton or Elizabeth Nicolson, is claiming that we drove up to the house, guns blazing. Why should I take a chance?"

Julia looked down at Foley's hand, large enough to cover her own. "This killing thing," she said, "it's starting to get to me. I swear to Christ, I don't know who I'm going to be from one minute to the next."

COMMANDER HARRY Clark hit the Norton home like a thunderbolt, descending onto the lawn at the back of the house as though he'd come to claim it. He advanced on Colonel Thaddeus Harman, one hand extended, cashmere overcoat flowing behind, wingtips agleam. All in the same motion, he shook the Colonel's hand, laid an arm across his shoulder, led him out into the back yard.

"Please, please, do me this favor, a one-on-one, just to bring you up to date on what's already gone down. Trust me, this is big, Colonel. Big, fat, and juicy."

When they returned a few minutes later, both men were smiling.

Julia watched from a great distance, unconcerned, as if she were sitting on a park bench alongside a dog run, watching the puppies at play. Clark and Harman parted a moment later, Clark taking a seat at the kitchen table. He was still smiling.

"Just the facts, ma'am," he said to Julia.

"I was the one who interrogated Nevin Gorovic, sir," Foley responded. He moved slightly to his right, away from Julia, drawing Clark's attention.

Again, Julia played the part of observer, a field scientist watching two primates interact, the role so entirely natural she could imagine it continuing forever. Foley offered up a series of names and Clark wrote them down. Foley offered several addresses and Clark wrote them down. When they were done, Clark phoned Chief Linus Flannery who presumably wrote everything down.

"All right," Clark said as he hung up the phone and returned it to a tooled leather case on his belt, "lemme bring you up to snuff, lieutenant. First, all day today, and even as we speak, the feebs have been out busting chicken hawks. They're billing the operation as the largest ever conducted." He leaned a little closer. "The rat bastards didn't give us so much as a crumb. They cut us out altogether, but now they want a piece of our action. Ain't that a dog? And we're gonna give it to 'em. First, because we're talkin' about interstate, and maybe international jurisdictions, and the feebs are the only ones who can work all sides of the fence. Second, the Justice Department and the FBI have agreed to let Flannery stand on the platform when they do the press conference. They won't let him speak, but they'll say something about a joint investigation."

The federal busts caught Julia off guard. If Clark's information was accurate, Foley had taken nearly a hundred pedophiles out of circulation. Though Agent Lear had known that when he showed up at Foley's apartment, search warrant in hand, it hadn't stopped him. But neither Foley's, nor Lear's, efforts were the most interesting part of Clark's little discourse. No, the deal between the NYPD and the FBI could not have been negotiated on the spur of the moment, which meant that her earlier guess, that Clark had a snitch inside C Squad, had been correct. It was enough, she decided, to renew a girl's faith in herself.

"Are you ready for me, commander?" she asked as her knees finally came to rest.

41

C LARK SWIVELED his head all the way to the right, then all the way to the left, the dramatic gesture tempered by a sly smile. Nevertheless, his voice, when he spoke, was barely above a whisper. "You sent your detectives to fetch help before you approached the suspect's home, right?"

"Yes," Julia replied.

He turned to Foley, "When you drove up, detective, you were fired upon before you exited your vehicle and you took a round in your vest, correct?"

"I did."

"What I hear, that really hurts."

Foley looked over at Julia for a moment, noted the shocked expression, was glad to see it. He knew Clark was leading him through a series of facts Clark wanted to find in Peter Foley's written statement. He knew, also, that Clark didn't really care if they were true or not.

"Correct again," Foley said. "Without doubt, I'll be pissing blood by morning."

Apparently satisfied with Foley's response, Clark shifted again to

Julia. "And you, lieutenant, you shot both of these men in order to preserve innocent life." He gestured to the dining room and Joe Norton's body which had yet to be moved, and to the living room beyond. "You know, it's obvious to me, Julia, that you're shaken up by the experience. As anybody would expect."

"I am, sir."

"In fact, you've already requested leave."

"I have."

"Then it's settled. I'm sending both of you back to New York for medical treatment. You can work out your statements on route. Just give me fifteen minutes to nose around."

Foley watched Clark walk back to Colonel Harman, who was standing just outside the kitchen, then turned to Julia. His back, except when he pressed directly on his right kidney, had stopped hurting. "Our savior," he announced. "Commander Harry Clark."

"One of the good guys," Julia replied. "Give me a minute. I'm going to call my daughter." She reached into her pocket, removed the police radio, looked down at it as if for the first time. Then she laid the unit on the table and returned to her pocket in search of her cellular. "I know I'm part of the internet generation," she told Foley, "but I'm starting to get very sick of electronic devices."

Julia punched the on button, prepared to dial her home number, when the phone began to ring. Startled, she flinched, her eyes momentarily closing as she drew back.

"You okay?"

She looked at Foley and smiled. Though her fingers and knees were again at her command, she was as weary as ever.

"Hello."

"Mom, Uncle Bob had a heart attack. Where have you been?"

As scornful of mere flesh as any bullet, Corry's words cut through Julia's chest to settle at the center of her heart, a solid painful weight that anchored her to the chair. Before she could summon even the flimsiest defense, tears welled up in her eyes.

"He's not . . ."

"No, but he hit his head on the stairs when he fell. He's unconscious. I wish you'd come home." Corry's voice edged into a wail. She wanted to be a little girl again, which couldn't happen until she had a mother, on scene, to protect her. "I found him when I got home from school, Mom. It was so horrible."

"Is that where you are? Home? Are calling me from home?"

"Mom, please. I'm at Woodhaven Medical Center. Uncle Bob's in the cardiac care unit."

Julia took a breath, took another, ran her fingers through her hair. She knew she had to pull herself together, despite her exhaustion, but it wasn't coming easy. "Is there a doctor close to where you're standing?"

Corry didn't reply directly, though Julia heard her shout: "You have to talk to my mother. She's a cop. In the police department. A *lieutenant.*"

A moment later, a male voice, clearly amused, said, "Hello, I'm Doctor Ryan. What can I do for you?"

Julia got into it without wasting time. She introduced herself, then said, "I'm Robert Reid's closet relative and I'm stuck in New Jersey, on police business. If you can tell me what happened to him and what I can expect in the immediate future, I'd be very grateful."

"We don't have the blood work back yet, but we believe your uncle had a mild-to-moderate heart attack. He also, apparently, fell down the stairs and struck his head. We've done X-rays, and there are no fractures and no signs of intracranial bleeding. Right now, he's breathing on his own; his neurological signs are good, too. Of course, he's at risk of a second heart attack, given his history, but at present he's stable."

"Anything else I need to know?"

"Not that I can think of."

"Well, thanks for your time. Can you put my daughter back on?"

"Mom?"

"It's all right, honey. Tell me, did you hear what the doctor said? Just now?"

"He was, like, standing right next to me."

"Okay, so you know that Uncle Bob's doing well, right?"

"But he could have another heart attack."

Julia was tempted to say, So could I and so could you; it's only odds were talking about here. Instead, she modulated her tone. "Uncle Bob had no fractures and the heart attack was mild. Didn't you hear the doctor say that?"

"He said mild-to-moderate."

Julia nodded to herself. If Corry wanted to be assertive . . . well, studied annoyance was far better, and far easier to handle, then juvenile terror. Especially when Julia herself was scared enough for the both of them.

"I'll concede that point," she said. "Now, look, I'm in New Jersey, about two hours away. I want you to remain at the hospital until I get there. Is that alright?"

"Mom?" Corry stretched the word out, adding a syllable. "Do you think I'd leave Uncle Bob *alone?*"

Julia took the guilt like the good mother she was, thinking guilt came with the territory, that if there was a guilt-free way to raise a child, she hadn't heard of it. "Did the cops show up?" she asked. "At the house?"

"They got there before the ambulance."

"Did they do CPR?"

"No, Uncle Bob was breathing."

"Good. That's a very good sign. You didn't, by any chance, get the officer's name?"

An exasperated, and very theatrical sigh poured into Julia's ear. "Oh, puh-*leeze.*"

"Does that mean you did?"

"Officer Hijuelos, at the 104th Precinct. He said you could reach him through a sergeant named Evans."

Julia nodded to herself as she wrote the names down. Corry had been responsible, despite everything. Just like her mother would have when she was Corry's age. "I'll be leaving here in a few minutes, honey, and I'll be coming directly to the hospital. Call me if you need me."

"Does that mean, like, you won't turn off the phone? This time?"

42

FOLEY LISTENED to Julia's conversation with her daughter, then with the doctor, catching the drift from her end of the dialogue. He watched her face initially collapse, fear rush into her eyes with the unreasoning force of an avalanche. He remembered his own fear then, the terrible fear that invaded his heart after Patti's disappearance. He'd carried the terror for days, then weeks, then months, until it slowly, slowly receded, along with its complement, hope. Along with, truth be told, every other emotion.

Unspeaking, he watched Julia summon Harry Clark, demand to be taken back to New York without further delay. "I gotta go now," was the way she put it, "my uncle's in the hospital and my little girl is all alone."

Who could say no to that? Certainly not Harry Clark who, ever resourceful, assigned Sergeant Moe Jacoby from Legal Affairs to drive them. "Maybe," he said as he bid Julia good-bye, "if you're up to it, you and Foley can work on your statements. That way, you won't have to be bothered later on."

It wasn't until Foley was inside the Ford used by Turro and Griffith to summon the locals that he finally stumbled upon the truth. The fear he now felt had nothing to do with the past.

He watched Julia call the 104th Precinct, ask for a sergeant named Evans, get put through, finally, to patrol officer Hector Hijuelos. Then, making no effort to conceal his intentions, he leaned against her as he listened, only to feel her weight drop onto his chest as if her muscles lacked the strength to support her bones.

"Lieutenant, this is Officer Hijuelos. I responded to the 911 at your house. Me and my partner. How is your uncle doing?"

"He's holding his own," she responded, the curt statement belied by a weary tone. "Tell me, did you take a look around?"

"With your daughter's permission, yeah, I checked the house. Mr. Reid had a pretty severe scalp wound and he wasn't conscious when we pulled up. He could have been hit and there could have been an intruder in the home. I mean, I didn't wanna . . ."

The prolonged silence that followed led Foley to guess that Hijuelos wouldn't proceed without Julia's benediction. Julia must have sensed it as well, because she broke the silence by saying, "Well, I'm glad you did. Tell me what you found."

"Mr. Reid was on the staircase, up against the banister about three-quarters of the way down. He had a profusely bleeding scalp wound and his pulse was weak, but steady. Like I already said, he wasn't conscious. He didn't appear to be in pain, either, so I decided not to move him."

Another pause, another pat. "Good, good," Julia said. "Let the paramedics handle it."

"Yeah, anyway, first thing, I asked your daughter if the front door was locked when she came in and she told me it was. Then I checked the back door and the dead bolt was thrown, which you can't do from outside without a key. The window next to the door, though, it wasn't locked. Closed, but unlocked."

"Was the lock jimmied?"

"No sign."

"Alright, go on."

"Upstairs, all the windows were locked and I didn't see any sign that the rooms had been tossed, but there was an indentation on the blanket in your daughter's room. That blanket, it's down-filled and it's real thick, so it takes a good impression. Mr. Reid must have gone in there for some reason, then decided to come back downstairs."

Julia sighed, the gesture so extended it might have been the theatrical exhalation of an antebellum debutante. "We open that kitchen window almost every night when we're cooking. I usually remember to lock it, but Corry sometimes forgets."

"Okay, so it's probably nothing. But the thing is, lieutenant, and I don't mean to be mindin' your business, you need better locks on those windows. They got slim-jims now that can open the locks you got without leaving a mark. And that tree in the back yard, the limbs come right up to your daughter's bedroom window. You might wanna trim that tree."

"Good night, Officer Hijuelos," Julia replied without a trace of irony, "and thank you for being thorough."

As Julia closed her eyes and settled against his chest, Foley let his arm slide around her shoulder, not really caring what Sergeant Jacoby made of their embrace. One thing sure, he and Julia, listening to the same conversation, had come to radically different conclusions. Easily jimmied locks? An impression on the bedspread in the room of someone who wasn't home? Tree limbs offering access to that same room? The window in the kitchen led to the back yard, and offered an efficient avenue of escape, say in case you'd just knocked some poor old man down the stairs.

Foley wondered, idly, how many times Corry Brennan had been observed in her bedroom. She's a little old, of course, for her stalker, but not impossibly ancient, and her value as a prize would override his reluctance in any event. Julia Brennan is his main pursuer, a name he's read in the papers, a face he's watched on television, a New York hero. No surprise that he'd decide to show her the error of her ways, the false premise underlying her position. Even if she finds him, even if she takes his life, he will make sure that she never forgets him. He will take something from her which cannot be replaced.

Foley stared over Julia's head, through the window on the opposite side of the car, at a snowy meadow. In the distance, a tilting barn

loomed on the horizon. They were up on the interstate now, Jacoby
driving with the usual cop contempt for the speed limit.

"Say," Jacoby called without turning around, "you think we could
talk about your statement, lieutenant? You up to it?" His tone was
familiar, as if it was understood between him and Julia Brennan that
his law degree cancelled any distinction based on rank.

"Sure, why not?"

Again Foley listened, Julia's matter-of-fact tone as she described
the events at the Nicolson house as good an indicator of her exhaustion as falling asleep on the spot. Her voice was unvarying, even when
Jacoby interrupted.

"Now, when you fired from the yard at the deceased's back, you
knew him to be carrying a weapon because you could see it? That's
what happened?"

"Yeah, I knew him to be carrying a weapon because I could see it.
That's what happened."

Then she simply went on, not missing a beat, every detail neatly
wrapped. She'd come to New Jersey in the hope of persuading Joe
and Carla Norton to return to New York. No force had been applied
and none had been contemplated. When her efforts failed, she'd dispatched two of the detectives under her command to call in the local
police. It was only after they'd gone that she decided to make a last
effort which resulted in the attack on Peter Foley.

At that point Foley tuned out, though he knew Julia's statement
was meant as much for him as for her. Jacoby's task was to confirm
every point, to be sure there weren't any nasty discrepancies to catch
the attention of the press, or of the lawyers in case one of the suspects or Elizabeth Nicolson decided to sue. Thus, Foley didn't have to
pay close attention. If he made a mistake somewhere along the line,
Moe Jacoby would be sure to set him straight.

That was the good news. The bad news was that he, Peter Foley, had
fucked up, simple as that. He'd made a judgment and his judgment
was wrong and the price . . .

Sometimes, he told himself, the price of being wrong is so high
that you can't take the risk of being wrong, no matter how remote the
possibility. Too bad he didn't think of that first.

Then another possibility, this one rather more insidious, entered his thoughts. Maybe, he speculated, it was all as it seemed. Maybe Robert Reid had a heart attack and fell down the stairs. Maybe the impression on the comforter had been there for days. Hijuelos hadn't made a second impression, then measured the time it took for the down to return to its normal loft, if it returned at all. Maybe when you sat on a down comforter it stayed flat until you shook it out. And maybe Corry left the window in the kitchen unlocked. Maybe it was a lot of nothing, the memories he'd kept under lock and key for the past few years finally having their way.

When it came Foley's turn to report, he didn't falter. He confirmed Julia's version, as much as he'd witnessed, along with what he'd done on his own—which mostly amounted to getting shot. He hadn't discharged his weapon, much less killed anyone, and therefore wasn't all that important. At least not to Sergeant Jacoby, who listened to Foley's recital, then said, "What I'll do, if you don't mind, is I'll write up statements based on what you've told me, then send them over so you can review the details. Tell me, lieutenant, the one you captured, Nevin Gorovic, where does he stand in all this?"

"I don't know," Julia said. "I didn't speak to him."

Jacoby seemed nonplussed for the first time. "Sorry," he muttered.

"Gorovic turned," Foley said. "He'll say whatever you want him to say. Bottom line, though, I drove up and they started shooting."

An easy bottom line to draw, like the one he now drew: Within a day, he would confront the egomaniac who signed himself Destroyer and Destroyed, maybe demand an explanation. Either that, or. . . .

Another bottom line, the remote possibility of failure and the consequences naturally flowing from that failure. Take it back twelve hours, before they'd left for New Jersey, before the shooting began, he'd warn Julia Brennan, demand she take precautions, admit that he was an asshole whose own swollen ego amounted to a textbook example of narcissistic personality disorder.

But Julia was overwhelmed, with what she'd done as well as what she had yet to do. If he told her what he suspected, motivated by pride if nothing else, she would demand to come along. And she wasn't up to it. Nor could he afford to call in C Squad, the methods he would use to complete his task being well outside the parameters of standard police procedure. Still, he would have to leave a message for Julia in case he failed. He would have to leave her a route to follow as well as a warning, and he knew just how to do it. Nevertheless, he waited until they'd come through the Holland Tunnel, crossed the city from west to east and were on the Manhattan Bridge before leaning over to whisper in Julia Brennan's ear.

"Take me out of it," he told her. "When you ask yourself how he found the Mandrakes and Teddy Goodman. Take me out and it'll become obvious."

43

B Y T H E time Julia found Corry asleep in the small waiting room outside Woodhaven Hospital's Cardiac Care Unit, she'd more or less put Foley's little taunt behind her. At first she'd been angry, or as close to angry as her exhaustion permitted, pronouncing Foley's statement a challenge, which she didn't need, and his insensitivity almost a betrayal. At no time had she connected his demand to be taken out of the equation with the report given by Hector Hijuelos, not with so much intervening time between the two events. Nor, even while speaking to Hijuelos, had she connected the faint possibility of an intruder in her home with the serial killer who called himself Destroyer and Destroyed. Instead, she'd decided, after Hijuelos finished, that the question of what Robert Reid had been doing in Corry's bedroom, if he'd been there at all, was best put to Robert Reid.

"Corry?" Julia shook her daughter, very gently. "Wake up, honey."

"Mom, you're here." An instant later, Corry was in her mother's arms. "I was never so scared in my life," she said. "Uncle Bob was . . ."

"It's okay, baby, you did fine. I'm so proud of you."

Corry broke off the embrace, sat back on the couch and began to rub her eyes with the back of her hand. "How long have I been sleeping?" she asked.

"Don't know, but, c'mon, let's go see Uncle Bob, maybe have a heart-to-heart with his doctor. I want to get him out of here as soon as possible and we may have to arrange for a private nurse or a home health aide."

"We're bringing Uncle Bob to *our* house," Corry said.

Never having considered the possibility of her uncle returning alone to his apartment, Julia couldn't resist the urge to tease her daughter. "And how exactly," she asked, "do you know that, miss?"

For a moment, Corry looked bewildered, her eyes drooping slightly as she thought it over. Then the corners of her mouth widened into a sly smile, as if she'd successfully drawn to an inside straight. "Because," she declared, "we live right around the corner and Uncle Bob lives in Manhattan? Like on the west *side* of Manhattan? That's practically in New Jersey?"

WHEN THEY entered the CCU, arms around each other's shoulders, Julia couldn't repress a quick shiver that ran from the base of her neck into her scalp. It wasn't the first time she'd been exposed to the beeps, hisses, and whistles of the machinery, or the odor, a soupy blend of medication, disinfectant, and human waste; cops on patrol pass many hours in emergency rooms, detectives as well. No, her shiver was closer to a reflex. This was a place where people came to die.

But she needn't have worried. When she and Corry walked into Robert Reid's tiny cubicle they found him sitting up, his head swathed in bandages, his eyes open. As they approached, he turned slowly, peering through half-closed lids, his face expressing a zen-like serenity that Julia immediately associated with morphine.

Julia blew her uncle a kiss, received a smile in return, but didn't interfere with Corry's more effusive greeting. Somehow, Corry had wormed her way between the trailing wires of a heart monitor and a working IV pump to sit at the edge of the bed where she could hug her uncomplaining uncle.

Watching, smiling, Julia thought of Foley. Not of what he'd told her, but of what it must be like for him at this very moment, holed up in some little room, pecking away at his computer, the light from the monitor rendering his pale complexion ghostly. But that wasn't right. Foley was still in the Ford with Lawyer Jacoby. And what he'd do, when he got out of that car, is go on with his life. The man was always one step ahead of the pack.

Still, she couldn't convince herself. The thought of losing her uncle, even knowing that he was sick and had been for a long time, was beyond contemplation. How much worse for Foley, who'd lost everything? What must the pain be like? And what was the cost of keeping it below the radar screen? Of never showing it to anyone, even himself?

Julia sat by Robert Reid's bed for the better part of an hour, until Doctor Ryan, who introduced himself as the chief cardiology resident, strolled over to shoo them off. It was now after midnight. Uncle and daughter were both asleep.

"It'd be best," he said, "if you and Corry got some rest."

"Doctor's orders?" In truth, Julia was trying to gather enough energy to call a taxi.

"I'll write a prescription if you like."

In his mid-twenties, Ryan was a powerfully built man with a long narrow face and very small features. Julia found his smile engaging.

"The last thing my uncle remembers," she said, "is sitting in his car. He doesn't recall anything that happened inside the house."

"A common effect of concussions."

Julia nodded. As a cop, she'd dealt with skulls cracked by every manner of hard unyielding object, so her uncle's amnesia came as no surprise. Over time his memory would improve, but he would probably never revisit the moment when he'd tumbled down the stairs. "I know that," she said. "I've seen that before. But what about his last memory? Would his last memory likely be distorted? And also, is he on a high dose of morphine? Could that be affecting his judgment?"

Before he'd fallen asleep, Reid had told a story in bits and pieces, a story he'd needed to get out. Earlier in the day, he'd e-mailed Destroyer and Destroyed, asking if there were other victims and where they might be found. The reply, *Dig deeper*, had initially been deemed a taunt, but then, after he'd parked at the end of the block, he'd realized something of great significance. The problem was that he couldn't remember what it was, and he couldn't concentrate, either.

"Mr. Reid's doing very well," Ryan replied, "but you can't expect too much." He smiled again, that same homely smile, before adding, "But to answer your question, your uncle might be a bit confused about events immediately preceding his fall for any number of reasons. You give him a little time, wait a day or two until we withdraw his pain medication, I think his responses will become more consistent."

It wasn't until the good Doctor Ryan gently touched the back of her hand that Julia realized she was being hit upon. Annoyed with the inappropriate timing, as she'd been with Foley, she turned to shake Corry's shoulder. They would phone for a cab from the lobby, maybe even find a gypsy standing outside. Then she remembered that Dr. Ryan was six or seven years younger than she, and was properly flattered.

"Thanks for the time, doctor. I'll be back tomorrow morning."

Ryan pursed his lips. "Sad to say," he admitted, "I'll still be here. And the morning after that, too."

44

JULIA BRENNAN had a very good morning and a very bad afternoon. First, she awakened with the realization that she didn't have to go to work, and that she didn't want to go; the job's siren song was no longer alluring. All those little securities, the luxury of throwing herself into her work, of complete submersion, seemed unimportant as she stretched, then headed off to the bathroom. At least for now.

Before dressing, she called Woodhaven Medical Center and had Dr. Ryan paged. For someone who'd been working for at least fourteen hours, he was surprisingly chipper. "Mr. Reid is doing fine," he told her. "He's recovering well and we may transfer him out of the CCU as early as tomorrow."

"That's great. Then he'll have a telephone. In the meantime, if your paths cross, will you tell him I'll be there in a couple of hours?"

"Will do."

Julia dressed quickly, choosing a blue, man-tailored blouse, a red sweater, and a pair of faded jeans. She glanced into the mirror, fluffed her hair, pronounced herself appropriately casual before walking the length of the hallway to Corry's room. When her subsequent knock went unacknowledged, she entered to find her daughter still asleep.

"Corry?" Julia glanced across the bed to the window on the opposite wall. Immediately after arriving home on the prior night, before she'd even dealt with the blood on the stairs, she'd checked the house for any sign of an intruder, examining the windows in Corry's bedroom and the window in the kitchen. True, the tree in the back yard did come up close enough for someone to enter the house if the window was unlocked. But there were no jimmy marks on the lock, none she could find at least. The kitchen window was clean as well and the impression in the down comforter, still distinct, might have been made by an object as mundane as Corry's loaded backpack. More to the point, the household items that would have attracted the attention of a burglar, the computer, the stereo, the television, were undisturbed. No one had rifled through her jewelry box, and a purse containing eighty-seven dollars hanging from the knob on her bedroom closet still held its treasure.

"Mom?"

"I'm going downstairs to start breakfast. If you want to come to the hospital, you better get dressed."

"What about school?"

"I'm giving you the morning off. I need you with me."

When she came down to breakfast, Corry turned on the small TV in the kitchen, tuning it to NY1. The cable news station was running more or less continuous coverage of the unfolding events, employing four reporters, two working the NYPD end, the others the FBI. Though she didn't protest, Julia kept her back to the screen as she chopped onions for an omelette. If left to herself, she wouldn't, she believed, so much as glance at a newspaper headline. Nevertheless, she couldn't help but overhear.

Mycky Pancevski and Milan Markovic had been arrested in their respective homes at five in the morning. Because the media had been tipped, the coverage was intense, and each man had emerged from his home in handcuffs, bent forward like a scuttling monkey, coat draped over his head and shoulders. Meanwhile, the feds were parading their own suspects before an arraignment judge, in the process revealing the identities of these miscreants for the first time. As their number included a former deputy commissioner of the Human Resources Administration, two junior high school teachers, and a deputy mayor, the networks and the papers were paying close attention.

Julia pushed the onions from the cutting board block into a heated pan, then cracked four eggs into a bowl. When the toaster popped, Corry went to the refrigerator for a stick of butter without being asked.

The curious thing, Julia mused as she watched her daughter, was that a serial killer who'd already claimed six victims was being ignored. Nor had anyone realized that exposing the identities of the arrested pedophiles radically expanded the killer's choice of targets.

Well, it wasn't her problem. Nor was it her mission in life to right every wrong, collar every criminal. Foley was right. As long as there were human beings, there would be crime. It was the nature of the beast.

H AVING SUFFERED through the humiliation of a bed bath immediately before Corry's and Julia's arrival, Robert Reid was alert, though not altogether happy. "I feel fine," he insisted. "I can shower on my own."

Julia noted the oxygen canula in her uncle's nose, the IV line in his arm, the bandages capping his head, his greenish-gray complexion. "It's not up to me," she declared.

That point established, Julia asked her uncle if his memory had improved in the intervening hours. His reply, that the harder he tried to remember, the more mocking the injunction to *dig deeper* seemed.

"If he wrote that to drive me crazy," Reid explained, "he's succeeding. I feel like I'm trying to crack a nut with a toothpick."

Dr. Ryan strolled into the cubicle a few moments later, his engaging smile appearing a bit shopworn, to announce that Robert Reid would enjoy a lunch of Jell-O, beef broth, and tea. "You'll probably transfer out of the CCU tomorrow, or the day after. In the meantime, try to get some rest."

The good doctor reinforced his advice by ordering up a dose of

Demerol. Pain medication is what he called it. Dope is what Julia heard. Robert Reid didn't, in any event, protest when a nurse injected the opiate into a port in his intravenous line. His eyes fluttered once as the drug took effect, and he smiled a smile that by comparison made the Bhudda's seem dour.

"Why," he said after a moment, "I wasted my life on alcohol is beyond me."

Corry slapped him on the hand. "Don't talk like that. You're supposed to set an example."

He did, by promptly falling asleep.

SHORTLY AFTER lunch, Julia donned a well-worn set of sweats, found her running shoes at the back of the hall closet, and went for a jog in Forest Park. Although it was cold outside, not only was there was no wind, the sky above was a radiant blue and the January sun, despite a pronounced northern tilt, was bright enough to present the illusion of warmth.

Fifteen minutes later she was stretching out, one foot on the Jeep's front bumper, when her cell phone rang. Before she could frame a thought, she was seized by a fear that extended to within a millimeter of panic. She'd given this number to Woodhaven Hospital. Just in case.

"Hello?"

"Lieutenant." Harry Clark's voice boomed in Julia's ear. "How's your uncle doing?"

Julia felt instantly guilty; if she was up to a six-mile run, she was up to working. She pushed the guilt away, smiling to herself, thinking that the guilt was the problem. "He's doing okay, commander."

"Glad to hear it. I don't know what the job would do if it didn't have Robert Reid to kick around. He's been on our case for thirty years." Clark paused, then cleared his throat before resuming. "Confidentially, lieutenant, Pancevski spilled his guts. Six children have been recovered and we hope to have more by the end of the day. So we did a good thing here."

"We did," Julia agreed, affirming Clark's nonexistent contribution.

"The bad news is that the kids were being held in Chicago and Las Vegas, so we couldn't shut the feebs out."

"That's pretty much what we expected."

"True, but from what I hear, Morgenthau will turn the adoption case over to a federal prosecutor. He's settling for the Mandrake johns."

"It's the smart way to go," Julia said. The johns had been caught on videotape and would in all likelihood plead out their high-profile cases. An uncontested slam-dunk that wouldn't break the budget.

"Yes, but that's not why I called." Again, he cleared his throat. "Lieutenant, whatever difficulties we may have had, you've done outstanding work here. Outstanding. I'm going to recommend you for a medal of valor."

Julia smiled. First, Clark had claimed personal credit for an investigation he'd frustrated at every turn. Now he was claiming that the job's collective decision to reward her was his idea. Nice.

"That's very flattering," she said. "Thank you."

"Yes, well, in addition, you're going to be promoted to captain. It'll go down as a provisional appointment until you clear the list. Also, if you want, I'll transfer you to the DA's office on temporary assignment. Lily Han needs someone to command her investigators. Someone strong."

Julia straightened up, looked around. Traffic was heavy along the footpath, mostly women come to jog or roller skate or race-walk. The New York winters were long, and it only made sense, on a nice day, to allow the soul a bit of opportunistic feeding.

"I'm not ready to think about any of this," she said. "I need some time away from the job."

Apparently expecting Julia to kneel at his feet, Clark's voice expressed annoyance for the first time.

"I said, if you want, captain."

Julia held her ground. "Right now, I don't know what I want."

"Fine, you take all the time you need." He clucked once, a little popping sound that raised Julia's hackles. "But over the next few days, you need to consider talking to the press. Face it, captain, you're a hero, and the way the reporters are talking, if you don't go to them, they're definitely gonna come to you."

That being that, Julia dropped the cellular into her pack and began
to run. Somehow, the exchange with Clark had returned her to the
state of exhaustion she'd fallen into the night before and her feet
scuffed the path as she trudged along. The job simply would not let
her go, a situation so ironic she was sure it went to the heart of her
weariness. She'd broken every rule, deliberately choosing to distance
herself from her own ambition; now she was reaping the fruits of that
ambition. A captaincy? Commander of the Sex Crimes Unit? Could
Chief of Detectives be far behind?

Am I a *schmuck*, she asked herself, that I can't enjoy this moment?
Am I such a fool? As the words entered her consciousness she
smiled, a rueful smile to be sure, but still a smile. The recovery of
the children made the question even more compelling. After all, res-
cuing the kids was why she'd gone to New Jersey in the first place. So
then why, at this moment, could she not celebrate her victory? One
thing certain, her conscience was clear. The last thing she'd expected
when Foley crashed that rock through the Nortons' back window was
a promotion.

She thought of Foley then. Although he'd taken as many risks as
she, the silks downtown would be relieved if he left the job. And that
was only if they happened to notice. For Julia Brennan, on the other
hand, it was as if she'd passed some kind of test. Given the attendant
publicity, her promotion and transfer could not have been accomplished without the express approval of the commissioner.

Julia forced herself to complete her run, only walking the last hundred yards to her car. Duty first, then rest; that had been her way for
longer than she could remember. Leisure had to be earned. Dessert
always came last. If there was money for dessert.

She leaned against the Jeep for a moment, then began to stretch
the tendons in her legs. It had been a long time between runs and she
didn't want to stiffen up before she got into a hot bath. She worked
slowly, but methodically, from her heel up into her buttocks, gradually increasing the pressure until she reached her limits. Satisfied
then, she pulled herself into the Jeep and settled onto the seat. A
bath, she thought as she slid a key into the ignition lock. A bath and
a nap, just what the doctor . . .

Still in her pack, Julia's cellular began to trill, a six-note run that vaguely resembled the song of a bird. Even as she unzipped the pack, her eyes closed in protest. Whoever invented the cell phone, she thought, should be executed in a low-output electric chair. Once people know you have one, they expect you to be perpetually available.

"Hello."

"Julia," a familiar voice declared, "it's Bea Shepherd. How are you feeling?"

45

I DON'T know," Julia said for the second time that afternoon. "I don't know how I feel."

"That bad?"

As Julia reached over to adjust the Jeep's heater, she flashed back to the prior evening, when she'd turned to face Joe Norton. Neither his stunned look, nor the terror that rose into his eyes had deterred her in the slightest. And the funny part was that she couldn't recall being angry, or feeling much of anything. The same held true for the man she'd shot from the backyard and whose name she could not remember. She'd taken his life in the coldest of cold blood, heart and soul as frigid as the crusted snow in which she'd crouched.

"Well, you know, there's something about killing people that . . ."

That what? That left you convinced that you could return to that moment, with the power of life and death coiled on the index finger of your right hand, whenever you wanted? That you'd had it in you all along, a bloodthirsty little demon tucked behind your maternal instincts? She'd played Joe Norton like a violin, anticipating his moves and her responses, placing him quite deliberately in a setting where he could be killed with impunity.

"I never had the experience myself," Bea said. "I've never discharged my weapon."

"What it does is make you think, and that's basically what I'm doing. I've been promoted, by the way."

"I know all about it. That's why I called, to congratulate you." Bea's tone sharpened, the rebuke apparent. She'd been forced to reach out, a reversal of their proper roles.

"They want to transfer me to Lily Han's outfit, the Sex Crimes Unit. I'd run her investigators."

Bea sighed. "Yes, yes, yes. You'll take it, of course."

"I'm thinking it over." Julia's tone was adamant. She would not allow herself to bullied, or even manipulated. Not by Harry Clark *or* Bea Shepherd.

"Well, while you're at it, think about this, dear. The Sex Crimes Unit in the DA's office handles cases from every precinct in Manhattan, which means the networking possibilities are endless. Plus, as ranking officer, you get credit for whatever the unit accomplishes. You won't have to share the glory because in that setting you're on top of the food chain."

"What about Lily Han?" Julia covered her mouth to keep from laughing. The top of the food chain. It was idiotic, a babbling of infants to which she could not even pay lip service.

"At the press conferences, after the big arrest, you'll be standing right beside her. You know the reporter, Mike Murphy, on CBS? Well, he was a cop and he got his big break working the preppie murder case for the Sex Crimes Unit."

"That's good to know, but when I'm ready to come back to the job, I'll make a decision. Until then, I just want to be left to myself."

Bea Shepherd paused briefly, then said, "Credit where credit is due, Julia. You've become a formidable woman."

"Dangerous," Julia corrected. "A dangerous woman."

JULIA WENT home, had her bath, had her nap, and finally awakened to find herself still tired, but in a relatively good mood. Maybe there would come a day, she speculated as she ran an electric tooth-brush over her teeth, when all the things bothering her right now would become a source of pride. What was it David Lane had wanted to call her? Tiger Brennan? Killer Brennan would be more apt. Maybe some day she'd be Killer Brennan, a legend in her own time.

She paused only for a cup of coffee before driving over to Wood-haven Medical Center where she found her uncle asleep. A copy of the *New York Times* was lying on the chair and Julia transferred the paper to the foot of the bed without looking at it. A moment later, Dr. Ryan entered the cubicle. Though he spoke, initially, about Reid's condition, it was obvious to Julia that he'd come to flirt. Somehow, despite the sunken eyes, the smudged cheeks, the apparent exhaus-tion, his libido was running full-out.

As he went on, as she continued to respond, Julia thought of Foley, realizing for the first time that she didn't know how to find him, that Foley had again placed himself beyond the reach of the job. That was fine, his business to be sure. But why hadn't he called her, to ask how she was doing if for no other reason? Maybe he thought she'd demand that he reveal his new address to the job. She'd already done it once. Or maybe the sex wasn't as hot as she'd thought.

Julia turned her attention back to Dr. Ryan, to his homely, elon-gated face, his cheerful smile, his well-toned body. He was far too young, of course, to have mate potential. But Peter Foley didn't have mate potential either, and no terrible consequence had come from their union. As far as she could tell.

"What's your first name?" she asked, interrupting the doctor in mid-sentence.

Ryan blushed. "Timmy," he admitted.

A perfect name for a boy-toy, Julia mused. A doctor boy-toy offer-ing sex without obligation and his exalted company at dinner. Even her mother would be impressed.

Julia was suddenly horny, though not so aroused that she didn't know the man she wanted in her bed was named Peter Foley.

Corry chose that moment to make her appearance, whereupon Timmy Ryan, after a brief greeting, returned to his other patients.

Julia was still feeling positive. There had to be an end to her weariness, an accommodation, a healing. With the help of Robert Reid and Corry Brennan, she would get to it.

Mother and daughter chatted for an hour, until Reid's dinner was brought in: cream of celery soup, a slice of white bread, a pat of butter, an Italian ice.

"Uncle Bob?" Corry shook Reid's shoulder, very gently, before glancing back at her mother. "He really should eat."

"That's what I used to tell you," Julia responded, "when you were eight months old and spitting pureed carrots in my face."

They stayed until nine o'clock, then went out for a quick dinner in a small Italian restaurant on Queens Boulevard. Over a shared shrimp cocktail they spoke of Corry's school, of how all this was affecting her. At first, Corry insisted that her work was up to date, but under Julia's prodding finally admitted that she had a paper due at the end of the week and had yet to do the research.

"That's why you're not coming to the hospital tomorrow night. Uncle Bob will understand."

"What about you, mom?"

"What about me?"

"Puh-*leeeze*. Like you look as if you're ready to fall over? Like if I had a driver's license, I'd take your keys away?"

Julia glanced at the glass of wine set to the right of her plate. She'd barely sipped at it. "The difference here is that I don't have to go to work tomorrow. I don't have a paper due on Friday, either."

Corry raised a triumphant eyebrow. "That's what you said the last time you went on vacation."

JULIA'S SLEEP that night was fitful, images of Anja Dascalescu and Joe Norton and Peter Foley appearing from behind corners, from within closets, appearing suddenly beside her as she started the Jeep on a snowy morning. By six o'clock, she'd had enough, rising to take a quick shower, already planning her day, thinking that enough was enough. The whole business was self-indulgent. What she'd done, she'd done for good and sufficient reason. There was no doubt, not in her mind, that the men she'd killed deserved to die, had in fact gotten off easy.

Julia got the laundry going after breakfast, transferring the contents of Corry's hamper from the washer to the dryer before heading off to Woodhaven Hospital. Ryan was sitting at the nurses' station in the center of the suite when she entered. No longer chipper, or even alert, he barely glanced up.

Robert Reid, on the other hand, was ebullient. He'd been served a full breakfast, including, finally, a cup of coffee, whereupon the headache he'd been nursing for the past twenty-four hours had disappeared.

"Like magic," he declared. "I feel like a new man." He touched his chest. "A new man with an old ticker, but a new man nonetheless."

Timmy Ryan came in a few minutes later, accompanied by an older woman whose dark brown hair, elaborately arranged at the back of her head, glowed even under the room's fluorescent light. Her tan suit likewise glowed, the fabric obviously expensive, the fit, even across her broad hips and narrow shoulders, perfect.

"Dr. Wertz," Reid explained, "the bringer of bad news, not to mention inedible diets and libido-suppressing medications."

Wertz ignored him, turning instead to Julia. "Evelyn Wertz," she said, extending a hand, "your impossible uncle's cardiologist."

Introductions over, Wertz got down to business. "I'm not convinced," she told Reid, "that you had a heart attack. Your blood enzymes are near normal and you've demonstrated a normal sinus rhythm from the beginning. In fact, if you hadn't complained of chest pains, which may have been nothing more than angina, you would have been treated for a head injury and released." She pursed a set of full lips, then cast a disdainful glance at Timmy Ryan before turning back to Julia. Reid, she explained, would be transferred that evening to a mixed unit where his heart would be monitored for another twenty-four hours. After that, barring any problems, he would be discharged.

Dr. Ryan stood with his arms folded across his chest, his expression rigid. He was outgunned and knew it. Still, he refused to nod agreement as Wertz declared, rather flatly, that further tests to rule out the possibility of heart damage would best be done at her home base,

Mt. Sinai Medical Center in Manhattan which had a "state of the art" cardiac unit.

For the next hour, after Wertz and Ryan made their exits, Julia unburdened herself, describing her New Jersey adventure and its aftermath to her uncle for the first time. She really didn't have much choice. Once he left the CCU, he'd have access to a television and find out for himself anyway. Though clearly shocked, Reid listened carefully until she finished. Then he closed his eyes for a moment before asking, "Are you going to do the press conference?"

"I don't want to, but I don't want reporters coming to my door, either." She swept her long blond hair over her right ear, then failed to notice when she bent her head and it fell forward in a slow wave to again shield her eye. "I'm worried about Corry, that she's too much like me. I'm worried that if I don't slow down, I won't be able to slow down, ever. I'm worried that I care too much about work. I'm worried that . . ." She rose from the chair to sit at the edge of Reid's bed and take his hand. "Listen, Uncle Bob, I killed two men yesterday. But not only wasn't I frightened, I think I enjoyed it, at least while it was happening. Afterward, though, I couldn't stop shaking." She drew a sharp breath. "Then, when Corry told me that you'd been taken to the hospital, I was as scared as I've ever been in my life."

"What you're saying, it's perfectly normal. Time will most likely take care of it."

"I wish I believed that, but right now I'm too tired to make a competent judgment." She laughed. "Meanwhile, I'm bringing you home when you're discharged. I'm going to take care of you." She squeezed his hand. "No back talk, please. The last thing I need is to worry about you alone in Manhattan. I've got enough problems without that."

JULIA WAS thinking nap when she walked into her home, but duty called, one last chore to be finished up before she rewarded herself. The laundry awaited her in the basement, Corry's laundry which would have to be meticulously folded. It had gotten to the point, with Corry's mania for order, that Julia was half-hoping her daughter would advance to a sloppy adolescence, the sooner the better.

Working slowly, Julia filled a laundry basket to the top with T-shirts, trainer bras, panties, socks, jeans, sweat shirts, two pairs of pajamas, and a cotton nightgown. Then she trudged up to Corry's second-floor room and began to put the various items in a tall bureau, the task familiar and comforting. Pajamas and nightie went in the bottom drawer, then Corry's jeans, then her sweats and her T-shirts, finally bras and panties and socks. Julia smiled when she opened the top drawer to find Corry's socks, not rolled one into the other, but lying flat, as wrinkle-free as if they'd been ironed.

That's good, she thought, one neat-freak outdoing another. Now my daughter won't reject me, she'll compete instead. I wonder what I'll say when she informs me that she's taking the police exam instead of going on to college.

Julia gathered Corry's panties from the bottom of the laundry basket, cotton panties high enough in the rise to cover her navel. Well, they would go soon enough. These days, the best that moms could hope for was to avoid Brittney Spears syndrome. In the popular culture, virginity until marriage was virtually unknown, promiscuity a mere lifestyle choice, one possibility among many. Julia well remembered Corry, over dinner, casually remarking that a table in the rear of the lunchroom was occupied on a daily basis by a group of girls who'd chosen to call themselves The Sluts.

Sighing, Julia laid the stack of panties in her hand on the pile, started to close the drawer, then paused to look again as a little piece of her attention, still focused on the present, insisted that something was wrong. Nevertheless, it took Julia a long moment to realize what it was. Corry's panties, always laid waistband to waistband, crotch to crotch (so that looking down they might have been a single garment) were now pointing in every direction.

"No." Julia said the word aloud. Then she repeated, "No."

As if she could put her finger in the dike, hold back the ocean of certainty that quickly overpowered any trace of doubt.

46

WHEN THE wooden staircase pulled away from the wall, Foley dropped the six-battery flashlight he'd been using to light his way, but held onto his gun. The flashlight tumbled down the steps, producing a distinctive clang that echoed through the sub-basement even as the flashlight's beam traced an erratic arc, revealing gray floor, gray wall, gray ceiling. Then the flashlight struck the bottom step and broke into pieces, plunging the space into absolute darkness.

Figuring he'd do enough damage to himself without being smacked by several hundred pounds of oak and pine, Foley leaped away from the stairs. Nevertheless, his right leg collapsed beneath him as he hit bottom and the resultant snap, as the long bones in his thigh gave way, reminded him of a camping trip he and Kirstin had taken before Patti's birth. It reminded him, specifically, of cracking dry branches over his knee to make a fire, which now seemed to be burning in his leg.

Despite the pain, Foley rolled as he hit, shoulders hunched, chin tucked into his chest. Although he opened a narrow wound on the back of his head, he avoided a crushing blow to the skull and remained awake and aware as he skidded across the floor. The stairs crashed down behind him, raising a cloud of dust that fell over him like a blanket, coating his skin, clogging his nose, transforming the blood running over his neck into a gluey paste. When he tried to reach the handkerchief in his back pocket the pain in his thigh became unbearable, a lightning bolt ripping up into his back. After that, he decided to lay still, think it over.

But there wasn't all that much to consider. He was in the second—and lowest—of the sub-basements of the Empire Steel Warehouse, forty feet beneath the ground, lying in the dark. His flashlight was in pieces, some of those pieces more than likely covered, if not crushed, by the stairs. He still had his Glock, though, in his right hand; badly bruised shoulder or not, he'd held on, refusing to surrender his weapon, like any good cop.

That was what he'd been taught at the Academy—you never give up your gun or your badge. If a perp has a piece to the head of an innocent victim, even a kid, it's just tough shit on the vic.

Foley's instructor at the time, a hairbag three decades on the job, had begun every other sentence with the word, "Awright," and had never taken questions. That was Sgt. Borowski, who hit the toilet for a quick chug of scotch so often that some recruit had carved Borowski's name on the door of his favorite stall.

Stop, Foley told himself. Don't drift. Despite the darkness, this is not an isolation tank.

As if to prove the point, a light appeared in the doorway above. Foley turned far enough to bring his weapon from beneath his body, ready for the pain this time, ignoring it to point the Glock at the brightening rectangle.

"Show yourself," Foley whispered aloud. "Just for a second. Show yourself and let me kill you."

The light stopped advancing an instant later, as if Foley had been overheard. A voice, high-pitched and quavering, asked, "Hey, you still with us down there?"

"Unfortunately for you."

"Oh, I don't think so." A dramatic pause, then, "But I do admit to being disappointed. When I rigged the stairs, I hoped to snare a certain geriatric journalist. Instead, I've caught a cop."

"That's what happens when you're transparent. I missed you, by the way, at your apartment." After a moment, Foley added the man's name, "Hal Townsend."

"Ah, very clever. How'd you find me?"

"You don't know?"

"I could guess, but coming from you it'd be much more charming."

Foley took a breath as the pain in his thigh flared up, then slowly subsided. "The Clapham," he said, "where the Mandrakes lived, it has a new surveillance system. Very clear video, unusual in that setting. The task force went back to 10 A.M., twelve hours before the earliest time the Mandrakes could have been killed. Everybody coming in or going out was interviewed, even the delivery boys, and they didn't turn up a single suspect. I watched those tapes myself, Hal, and I read transcripts of the interviews. They were very thorough."

"Well, I hope they would be. Considering the gravity of the acts under investigation."

Foley ignored the interruption. The truth was that he, Peter Foley, had denied the gravity of those acts. He'd waited too long and now here he was, lying on his back in what could easily become his tomb. "The question that jumped out at me was how the murderer got into the building without passing one of those cameras. Did he, for example, land a helicopter on the roof? Or hang-glide through an open window? Or invent an invisibility potion? Or did he, perhaps, *live* in the Clapham?" Foley paused, but Townsend chose not to respond. "After mulling the various possibilities, I decided to begin with the last scenario. I approached a doorman at the Clapham, an Italian named Basilio Donatelli. 'Basilio,' I said, 'I'm looking for someone who resides in the building. He's in his thirties, white, single, living alone or with his mommy. A real fucking creep.'

"'Ah,' Basilio tells me, 'I'ma know this man right away. Hal Townsend. A cockroach in a coat. He's onna vacation.'

"Funny thing, Hal. That vacation began the day after the Mandrakes were killed."

"So you came out here."

"To your little cathedral of death. Hoping you'd returned to bask in the glory."

A long silence ensued. Foley fought to steady his breath, to relax his finger on the trigger. He would get only one chance and he had to make the most of it. The pain had returned with a fury. It was now threatening to overwhelm his defenses and he was afraid he'd pass out.

"You know I tried, right?" Townsend's voice echoed in the closed space around Foley. "I thought if I became an instrument of the Lord, I'd overcome my . . . propensities." He laughed, his tone rising to a true falsetto. "But it didn't work out and now . . . And now I have to serve a different master."

"A master who tells you to rape and kill little girls? Christ, Townsend, you're not only a creep, you're a bullshitter. You're making this move because grown men are too scary for you. In your heart of hearts, you're still that little kid bending over the kitchen table. Tell me, who got you first? Daddy? Uncle John? Mommy? You *are* a momma's boy, right? In fact, the story I heard, you've been living off your mother's fortune all your life."

"When my mother died," Townsend said, his voice now wistful, "it was the happiest day of my life."

"Couldn't wait to see her in the ground?"

"I jerked off on her grave."

"A liberating moment, I'm sure."

Though Foley's tone hovered between matter-of-fact and taunting, inwardly he berated himself for failing to anticipate the threat to Corry. He'd long known that serial killers are almost always sexually motivated and that Townsend was a heterosexual pedophile. He'd known, as well, that Townsend was under tremendous pressure, that he was breaking down. In the last analysis, Townsend's shift to a class of victims offering infinitely more pleasure was entirely predictable by all except the most arrogant of fucking fools. By all except Peter Foley.

"You don't know anything about it," Townsend insisted. "You don't know what it's like."

"That's right, Hal. I don't know what it's like because I'm not a player in that world. But I'm a player in *your* world. And I'm not going away."

A silence followed, a silence of perhaps ten seconds that seemed endless to Foley, who continued to pray that Townsend would show himself. This despite a severe trembling in his hands that left him barely able to keep the sights within the doorway.

"I knew you'd figure it out." Townsend's voice was louder now. "Bud and Sarah Mandrake, they were too close to me. I had to recover anything in that apartment with my name on it, and I had to shut them up permanently. You don't think my approach was too dramatic, do you?"

"More like desperate, Hal." Foley closed his eyes momentarily as he drew a breath. It was coming now. "You were too desperate."

"Well, this has all been very interesting, and I'd like to continue, if for no other reason than to see if your cop insights are more penetrating than those of my analyst. But I have miles to go and promises to keep . . ." Townsend laughed again, the same high-pitched trill. "Now, I think I'll just shut and padlock this door before I leave. To make certain your tranquility remains undisturbed."

"Clever, clever you," Foley said as he emptied the Glock's sixteen rounds into the rectangle of light above him.

The noise was near deafening, even to Foley who was prepared. The roar of exploding gunpowder, a sharp crack as each bullet ripped through the sound barrier, the eerie whine of multiple ricochets, overlapping, echoing, filling the air until there seemed to be nothing but sound. As if sound was a denser medium, like water, through which humans progressed as best they could.

Foley ejected the Glock's clip, then reached for the spare in his coat pocket. He had it in his hand, was about to slide it into place when a stream of bile cut a passage up through his throat into his mouth and nose. The pain in his leg, as he instinctively turned his head to the side, caught him completely unprepared. Barely aware of the diminishing light in the doorway above as Townsend beat a hasty retreat, Foley retched once, a stream of vomit that splattered in the dust, then he was gone.

FOLEY OPENED his eyes to a darkness so impenetrable he was unable at first to distinguish between awake and asleep. Then he moved slightly and the charcoal fire smoldering in his right thigh flared up to remind him that not only was he awake, he was alive as well. Hal Townsend, apparently unwilling to risk the possibility of being clipped by a ricochet, had deserted the field. Or maybe Townsend had actually been wounded, though not incapacitated. If he was incapacitated, or killed, there'd still be a light in the doorway.

Inch by inch, Foley rolled far enough to the right to free up the left-hand pocket of his coat where he'd put his cell phone. As he did, the jagged ends of the broken bones in his right thigh dug into the muscle, a carving fork jammed into a slab of beef. He was slippery with sweat by the time he admitted that the phone wasn't there and that he wasn't going to find it in the dark.

As Foley paused to collect himself, a series of questions ran through his mind. How long had he been out? Was it already too late? Where was Julia Brennan at this moment? Why hadn't he dragged an army of cops out to the Empire Steel Warehouse?

The last question grabbed his attention and he focused long enough to provide, if not an answer, at least a history. Time had been the problem, because Sergeant Jacoby hadn't dropped him off at his apartment but had taken him to One Police Plaza, where they worked on his statement until eleven o'clock.

"Let's just get it right," Jacoby had chided when Foley expressed a strong desire to leave, "before you disappear again."

Foley had run from Jacoby's little office to the Clapham, where the night doorman had refused to discuss the residents' private lives, despite the offer of a more than generous bribe. Then, his kidney aching, he'd gone home to grab a couple of hours of sleep.

At eight o'clock in the morning, his manner considerably more belligerent, Foley had cornered the day-shift doorman at the Clapham, Basilio Donatelli. Donatelli had considered all the potential outcomes after allowing Foley to describe the man he was looking for, a thirty-something who came and went at odd hours and who lived alone. Then the doorman had lifted his hat to run his fingers through his thinning hair before offering the name of Hal Townsend, who'd begun a vacation the day after the Mandrakes were killed and whose mail had yet to be collected.

Approaching the task force had been out of the question because Foley lacked the kind of hard evidence that would light a fire beneath the hierarchy running the show. It would take hours to convince them to act, if it could be done at all, hours Foley didn't have. That left him with a choice. Call Julia Brennan immediately or check out the Empire Steel warehouse on the slim chance that Townsend had returned to his killing field.

Foley had considered the possibilities while he purchased a container of coffee at a Third Avenue deli, as he tore away a triangular piece of the lid, as he sipped. Then he'd made his choice, the choice of a man who desperately needed to be a hero, a knight, to rescue that damsel in distress, to slay that bad, bad dragon.

Very gently, Foley eased his fingers along his right thigh, half-expecting to encounter the jagged ends of his broken bones. He didn't, though he felt a distinct bump halfway between his knee and his hip. Bad news because the bone was displaced. Good news because the bone, as long as it didn't protrude, could be splinted. If he tore his undershirt into strips, if he found a baluster to use for a splint, and a longer piece of wood to use for a cane, he could stand. And if he could stand . . .

If I can stand, Foley asked himself as he very slowly and very deliberately began to unbutton his coat, what will I do? Have a look around? I can't even read the hands on my watch. Could I climb up somehow? Townsend wanted to lock the door at the top of the stairs, which means he must have left a way out through that door when he rigged the stairway. A way out for a two-legged man, anyway. For me, right now, in my condition. . . .

But there was another possibility—remote, he instantly admitted—that couldn't be ignored. Maybe, if he covered every foot of the basement, he'd find another set of stairs, a hoist, a door, something. Of course, it might be too late; he might have been unconscious for hours. But at least he'd save his own sorry ass. Wouldn't that be great?

The irony was that he'd been carrying an irrational guilt for Patti's disappearance almost from the beginning and now he'd have something to be guilty about. In fact, if anything at all happened to Corry, he, Peter Foley, would finally have committed an act that precluded survival.

"Were talkin' motivation here," he said aloud as he began to pull his left arm from the sleeve of his coat. "Go, team, go."

47

JULIA BRENNAN was through the door, out of the drive, and on her way to downtown Manhattan within sixty seconds of shutting Corry's dresser drawer. A pair of red lights behind the Jeep's grill flashed alternately and the scream of the siren beneath the Jeep's hood rose and fell as she wove through and around the traffic on Woodhaven Boulevard. All the while, she frantically punched at her cellular's key pad with her thumb, missing the 411 sequence several times before she finally got to a human voice. Still, despite the physical ineptitude, her mind was clear and her thinking sharp, the veil having been lifted the instant she followed Peter Foley's advice. The instant she took him out of the equation.

"Ms. Sims speaking. How can I help you?"

After identifying herself as a New York City police officer, Julia demanded that she be put through to the principal's office at Stuyvesant High School. She expected a certain degree of resistance, but Ms. Sims merely grunted once before saying, "Give me a second to find the number and I'll connect you."

Three minutes later, as Julia tore up the ramp leading to the

city-bound Long Island Expressway, Stuyvesant High School's principal, Yolandi Powers, came on the phone.

"I have reason to believe," Julia told Powers after identifying herself for the second time, "that my daughter's life is in danger. I want
her brought to your office and kept there until I arrive."

"I'm afraid that's impossible."

"Why? It's only 2:30. She's still in class."

A pause, then, "How do I know you're who you say you are? You
could be anyone, anyone at all. I can't disrupt . . ."

"But I can," Julia responded. "I can put fifty cops in that school. I
can close it off and let nobody in or out. In fact, if it wasn't a half-
hour from the end of the school day, I'd be making arrangements to
do that right now."

The truth, Julia knew, was a bit less dramatic. Even if she was right
about everything, every factor in the equation, that didn't mean there
was someone at Stuyvesant High School waiting for Corry. Not when
Corry had gone to school on the prior day, then returned unmolested.
Briefly, Julia imagined herself calling Harry Clark, demanding that a
public high school be closed down because she'd found a stack of her
daughter's panties slightly askew. Yeah, that'd work.

"Principal Powers," Julia continued when Powers failed to reply,
"listen to this."

She rolled down the window, thrust the cell phone toward the
Jeep's hood and the wailing siren, then held it steady for a moment
before pulling it back. "As you can hear, I'm on my way. All I'm asking is that you keep my daughter safe until I arrive."

"This . . . *threat* to your daughter's safety, does it involve another
student? Or one of our staff?"

Julia choked back a laugh. Principal Powers was concerned with
her own ass, not with Corry Brennan's. Specifically, Powers wanted to
be assured that Corry's peril hadn't arisen from Stuyvesant High
School's neglect.

"The school's not involved in any way," Julia soothed. "And it
won't be as long as my daughter is protected."

That did the trick. Powers took down Julia's number and promised
to have Corry phone as soon as she came into the office. Julia mut-

tered a thank-you, then turned her attention to the road. Traffic wasn't particularly heavy, but the cars and trucks stubbornly refused to give way to a Jeep, siren and flashing lights be damned. Julia was forced to dodge and weave if she wanted to make any time at all, to run with the Jeep's left wheels on the median as she took the exit for the Brooklyn-Queens Expressway, and then again on the far side of the Kosciusko Bridge. She was heading for the Brooklyn Bridge and Chambers Street which led directly to Stuyvesant High School.

As Julia pressed on, ignoring a perfectly manicured middle finger extended through the window of a Mercedes sedan, she became aware of an idea that had been lingering at the back of her consciousness for some time. Just because Corry had made her way safely to school, then back to the hospital on the prior day, didn't mean that she wasn't being stalked. The wild card here was Foley who'd decided, for reasons of his own, to go after Destroyer and Destroyed by himself. His parting injunction, to factor him out of the equation, had been issued in case he failed. But had he failed? There was no way to know, not unless he, in all his majestic glory, chose to get in touch with her.

"You arrogant bastard," Julia muttered to herself. "If you've taken him out and haven't called me, I'll never forgive you. And if you're lying somewhere dead, I'll never forgive you either. In fact, no matter what happens, you're on my shit list for the fucking duration."

The outburst did nothing to mitigate her anger. Nor could it alter the simple truth that Foley had given her the key, that the key had been there all along, and if she wasn't a fixated jerk she'd have seen it long before. The only way, if Foley played no part, the Mandrakes and Teddy Goodman could have been targeted was if their killer already knew them, if their killer was himself a pedophile. And that held for all of his victims. He was able to control them, to lure them to their deaths because they trusted him, because he and they had pledged the same secret fraternity.

That's what the name was all about. Destroyer and Destroyed. He was the destroyer, not of pedophiles, but of human innocence, and he was destroyed by what he did. His motive was atonement, not revenge. Or at least, it used to be atonement. Now things had taken a

different turn and he'd shifted to a more satisfying brand of destruc-
tion. That was surely the way Foley had read it when she told him
about the open window discovered by Patrolman Hijuelos in her
kitchen, about Robert Reid found unconscious on the stairs.

Still, what hadn't made sense was a pedophile killing other pedophiles. Not even Sergeant Ross, the profiler, had suggested that the
man who slaughtered Teddy Goodman, the Mandrakes, and at least
three others was himself a pedophile. Foley had known, though. He'd
known all along and kept it to himself.

Julia eased into the right lane, avoiding the left-hand exit to the
Williamsburg Bridge, thinking that at least she knew where to find
her killer. C Squad had been all over the doorman at the Clapham, an
Italian whose name she couldn't remember, and they'd run the tape
from the video cameras trained on the lobby and on the service
entrance over and over. Every individual, entering or leaving, had
been identified and interviewed, and the Mandrakes' killer was not
among them. Which meant that Destroyer and Destroyed probably
lived in the Clapham.

Julia imagined the man learning of Anja Dascalescu's fate, then
coming down the stairs to knock at the Mandrakes' door. How many
had he already killed? At least the two unidentified victims found in
Queens, and if Sergeant Ross' profile was accurate, many more. He
would not have hesitated to rid himself of the Mandrakes and any
incriminating evidence, like a client list, in their apartment.

Julia exited the Expressway at Tillary Street, caught a piece of luck
when a traffic agent working the intersection of Tillary and Flatbush
Avenue waved her past the vehicles gathered at the light. She was just
about to acknowledge his professional attitude with a thumbs-up
when the cell phone on the passenger's seat began to trill.

"Corry?"

"It's Principal Powers. I'm afraid we're having a bit of trouble
locating your daughter. She was released from gym to prepare for the
school play, but she's not in the auditorium. But don't worry. We have
security posted at every door throughout the school day. She couldn't
have left the school."

"That doesn't mean somebody didn't get in."

"Outsiders cannot enter the school unless they have business in the school." When Julia failed to reply, she added, "The students are due to be released in ten minutes. I have no authority to detain them."

And there's no time, Julia thought, for me to find the cops to do it for you. Neat.

"Will you at least keep looking for Corry? Will you ask security to keep an eye out for strangers in the building?"

"Yes, I can do that."

Julia made a right on Adams Street and punched the Jeep's gas pedal, ripping through the long block, slowing just a bit for the sweeping left turn that led to the Brooklyn Bridge. Anybody, she reasoned as she ran up on the bumper of a green Toyota, could have made an appointment with any one of the counselors or administrative personnel in the school. And surely there'd been deliveries during the day, the arrival and departure of maintenance and kitchen staff, doors opening and shutting, security guards with their backs momentarily turned, grabbing a quick smoke, phoning a spouse or a lover. If you were patient and determined, and you had the experience, the low-level security presented by a New York City high school would not deter you.

The great mass of Lower Manhattan rose up as Julia crested the bridge, made all the more solid by the narrow twisting streets of the financial district. The day was overcast and the sun had long since dropped beneath the shoulders of the highest towers. In the twilight, the buildings, whether of glass or stone, presented uniform gray facades while the river beneath was a ribbon of black lit only by the running lights of a tugboat pushing a loaded petroleum barge north toward the Bronx.

Gotta think, Julia told herself. Can't panic. Goddamn that Foley. Goddamn him. If, if, if, if, if . . . Fuck!

48

A HUNDRED yards from the foot of the bridge, Julia pulled the Jeep to a halt behind a mass of vehicles extending to the traffic light controlling access to Centre Street. Much as she would have liked to, she could not force her way between them; the Jeep was too big for that. And neither could she hold the other drivers responsible. There was nowhere for them to go. The traffic light was at the corner of Centre and Chambers Streets, at the far end of a sharp curve, and the drivers stopped there could not see her. Nor could they use the Jeep's siren as a guide. The echoes generated by the stone canyons of lower Manhattan were too confusing, a reality driven home by a near-collision with an ambulance during Julia's first year on the job.

Julia took a breath, again ordered herself to calm down, to think. She was looking west, over City Hall toward the Hudson River less than a mile away, a mile that would take her twenty frustrating minutes to span, when the phone began to ring. Instinctively, as if at the hiss of snake, she cringed, for the briefest of moments glimpsing the person she would become if she'd failed to protect Corry Brennan. If while she'd been off protecting other people's children, her own daughter . . .

"Hello?"

"Mom, like what's going on?"

Julia began to cry at the sound of Corry's voice, silently, the tears running along her nose to spill over her lips. Reflexively, she tightened her mouth and wiped her eyes. First panic, she thought, then meltdown, a pretty sequence for a woman who's imagined herself running the Police Department of the City of New York.

"Corry, where are you?"

"I'm in Principal Powers' office?"

"I mean, where were you?"

"Like, I didn't do anything wrong?"

"You don't want to tell me?"

"Mom, could you puh-*leeze* give me a break? I was in the maintenance shop. We're making frames for the backdrops."

"The what?"

"For the *play*, if you happen to remember."

"Why didn't you tell somebody where you were going?"

"Because it's a school? Because it's not a prison? Because we're not *criminals*?"

"Alright, alright. I seem to be a bit overwrought. But I want you to stay in the office until I arrive. I think there was someone in the house when Uncle Bob fell down the stairs."

"And he's after *me*?"

Julia paused long enough to manage a narrow smile. Corry's voice expressed equal measures of disbelief and fear, with maybe a pinch of grand adventure tossed in for seasoning. "I don't know that for sure, but I'm not taking any chances. Don't be alone until I get there. No matter what."

"And, like, when will that be?"

"I'm not certain. A half-hour, an hour. I want to take a look around. Meanwhile, don't move."

INSTEAD OF taking the left onto Chambers when she finally cleared the light, Julia shut down the siren and headed north on Centre Street. She drove through Foley Square to Worth Street, where she turned west, finally making her way to Greenwich Street. Though she took her time, content to follow the herd, her mind was speeding along, various thoughts meshing like the gears of a fine watch. She did not make this transition from terrified mother to New York City detective through an act of will. Instead, with Corry safe, Captain Julia Brennan had simply glided onto the stage, already in costume, makeup perfect, not a hair out of place.

She thought of Foley again this particular Julia remembering that she'd already decided that she could trust him, and that the conclusions she'd drawn in the last hour had been known to him for at least two days. Without doubt, he'd already visited the Clapham, either unsuccessfully or with disastrous results. But he hadn't made an arrest, because there was no way to keep that sort of collar secret even if the job had a reason, which it didn't.

Might Foley have handled the problem extra judiciously? Yeah, he might have. But then why hadn't he called to tell her? If they'd reached the point where they trusted each other? What I can't do, she finally decided as she parked the Jeep a block from the intersection of Greenwich and Chambers Streets, as she dropped her parking permit on the dash, is let anything happen to dear Destroyer until I answer that question.

Then it was time to get to work, to answer a more immediate question. If I were stalking a thirteen-year-old student named Corry Brennan, she asked herself, and I knew (or at least hoped) that she'd be leaving school at a given time, where would I wait to intercept, then follow her until I got her alone?

Julia took a moment to visualize the buildings and roads surrounding the school, drawing on memory though she'd only visited Stuyvesant High two or three times. Set at the very northern end of Battery Park City, the school was designed to blend with neighboring apartment buildings. Thus its multihued brick, varying from cream to pale brown to buttery yellow, and its ten-story height which, she admitted, would make a thorough search extremely difficult. Whether that search was being conducted by a cop in pursuit of a suspect, or a killer stalking his prey.

But that wasn't necessarily bad news. Stuyvesant High was a magnet school, attracting applicants from all over New York City. Virtually none of its students lived within walking distance. Virtually all took one or another of the subway lines to the east. To do so they had to cross West Street which ran like a moat between the school and the nearest public transportation. The only place within blocks to make that crossing was at Chambers Street which fronted the school.

Julia could imagine the city's lawyers contemplating the prospect of defending the city if some drunk plowed into several hundred kids at sixty miles an hour. West Street was all that remained of the old West Side Highway. With traffic lights a half-mile apart, it was commonly driven as if it was the Indianapolis Speedway—especially by cabbies who combined excessive speed with quick unpredictable shifts from one lane to another on tires slick enough to polish the family silver.

The possibilities must have been too horrifying to contemplate because a trussed bridge, one end of which fed directly onto an entrance to the school, had been erected over West Street. The over-whelming majority of Stuyvesant High's students would cross the bridge when school let out.

Julia had observed the process about a month before, standing on the eastern side of Chambers Street at the bottom of a sweeping flight of concrete steps. A solid line of kids, walking four and five abreast, had poured across the bridge like migrating wildebeest fording a river, dispersing only slightly as they continued east on Chambers.

Opening the door, stepping out, checking the weapon tucked into her purse, Julia realized that she would have to search the entire route, every pizza parlor and coffee shop and fast-food joint on Chambers Street, and hope she got lucky. If she didn't, she would take Corry, bring her to Robert Reid's apartment with its twenty-four-hour doorman and state-of-the-art surveillance system. Then she'd call C Squad, put a bug in Carlos Serrano's ear that would send him back to the Clapham. He'd know where to go from there, Carlos Serrano whose only ambition was to make detective first grade.

Julia walked south on Greenwich, toward Chambers Street, until she reached an entrance to Washington Market Park. Half the size of a city block, the park fronted Chambers Street on its southern side, and had a convenient exit at Chambers and Greenwich, a block from the school, and a third exit, up a flight of steps to the Borough of Manhattan Community College and a small plaza. From the plaza, a broad concrete ramp led back down to Chambers Street. Julia would cross the rear of the park, climb the steps, then use that ramp to come upon the intersection of Chambers and West Streets unobserved. Along the way, she would check out the park.

Casually, her stride even, her expression neutral, Julia walked along a narrow path flanked to her right by trees and to her left by a children's playground. The playground was deserted, the mommies or nannies apparently intimidated by the cold. The swings were moving, though. Set into motion by a stiff breeze, they emitted a chorus of squeaks as they rocked to and fro that reminded Julia of newborn ducklings peeping at the approach of mother.

When the path emerged into the main body of the park, Julia pulled her collar up and her hat down as she quickly surveyed her surroundings. Except for three determined joggers, running in a bunch along a path that circled a lawn perhaps thirty yards in diameter, the park appeared to be empty. Julia was looking south toward Chambers Street, past a whimsical gazebo, Washington Market Park's sole distinctive feature. Six-sided, the white gazebo wore an elaborate wrought-iron skirt, also white, that complemented a second skirt above the eaves that, in turn, complemented a stepped aquamarine roof.

Past the gazebo and the high fence separating the park from Chambers Street, the first of a long line of Stuyvesant High students filled the sidewalk. In fifteen minutes the migration would be over. Julia hurried along to the steps leading to Manhattan Community College, then started to climb. She would begin at Chambers and West Streets, check the intersection, then the bridge, then walk back along Chambers toward the various subway lines. If she hurried, she'd complete a minimal survey before the last of the students passed by.

At the very top of the stairs, Julia paused long enough to look back over her shoulder, to make another careful pass. As she was about to turn away she glimpsed a movement behind the shrubbery lining the inside of the fence. The gazebo was between her and the shadow she thought she saw, the trunk of an oak as well.

Without slowing, Julia strode onto the plaza, continuing forward until she was out of sight. Then she doubled back to crouch behind a low concrete wall. The sun to the west had dropped almost to the horizon and it was nearly dark along the fence line. Nevertheless, after a moment, she was able to discern the shadow of a man among those cast by the trees and the gazebo. Perhaps driven by the cold, the man was moving slightly, rocking to and fro like the swings in the kids' playground. He wore an overcoat with the collar pulled up high, but no hat, and he was facing the sidewalk, apparently watching the kids walk past.

Julia retrieved the billfold that held her ID and her badge, slipping it into the breast pocket of her coat with the badge facing out. She reached into her purse, found her weapon, gripped it in her right hand. Though the exhaustion of a few hours before had vanished, she muttered two quick prayers before descending the steps. Please Lord, she begged, don't let me kill again. Please, Lord, let it be him.

49

JULIA KEPT her body turned slightly to the left as she retraced her steps across the northern edge of the park. She was hoping to conceal the badge she felt herself forced to display. The man she sought had killed five people with a pistol and there was every reason to believe he was armed at this moment. If she had to shoot him, if things got out of control, she could not risk the charge that she'd failed to identify herself as a police officer. Every cop had the absolute right to stop and detain a citizen, as long as those cops had the good sense to make their cop identities crystal clear.

Still, that didn't mean she had to show her badge if he happened to glance over his shoulder, not until the last minute when she had him trapped. With her badge invisible, from this distance she'd be just another pedestrian, maybe a teacher at the community college, or even a student, walking with her collar up and her head down, huddled against the cold and the wind.

Julia picked up the pace just a bit as the path curved south toward the exit at Chambers and Greenwich, evaluating the situation as she came. The wrought-iron picket fence where her suspect crouched rose to a height of seven feet, and the slender bars, only a few inches apart, were pointed at their tops. The fence wasn't insurmountable, but unless you were an athlete or you'd given it a lot of thought, you'd be as likely to find yourself hung up as you would on the other side, looking back.

Silently wishing for a radio, Julia removed her cell phone, thumbed 911 into the key pad, and hit the forward button. An operator answered on the third ring, demanding to know the nature of the emergency.

"This is Lieutenant Julia Brennan, shield number two-nine-seven-three. I'm in Washington Market Park, on the south side, approaching a homicide suspect. I need immediate back-up."

"And the color of the day is . . . ?"

Julia groaned. The color of the day was either green, yellow, pink, red, or purple. Chosen at random and revealed to cops before they went on patrol, the colors were used to weed out prank callers, or criminals in need of a diversion.

"I'm off-duty. I don't know."

"Well . . ."

"For Christ's sake," Julia hissed, struggling to keep her voice down, "I'm not asking for an army. I'm asking for the goddamned sector car."

"You're breaking up. I can't hear you."

"What?"

"You're breaking up."

"Just dispatch a unit, please."

In lieu of a reply, Julia listened to a soft humming as the phone went dead. It was the rush of blood, she realized, through her own ear, as if she was holding a seashell. She stared at the phone for a moment, then at the man by the fence. He'd moved back to the gazebo, perhaps to create a bit more distance between himself and curious Stuyvesant High students, and was casually leaning against one of the posts.

There was more light around the gazebo and Julia could see well enough to add a few details to the shadow he'd been a moment before. Hatless, he wore a full-length overcoat and a scarf, both of dark wool.

His hair was light and thinning, his scalp visible at the crown even in the dim yellow light cast by the art deco lamps scattered through the park. In his mid-thirties, he stood a couple of inches over six feet and weighed, Julia estimated, about a hundred and ninety pounds.

Too big to fight, though not too big to shoot. But Julia wasn't all that worried about hand-to-hand combat. The profiler, Ross, had told her that Destroyer was a coward, that he killed his victims before hanging or cutting them because he believed they were supremely powerful and he had to make them safe. Well, there was no way to make a cop with a gun safe. If faced with the ultimate choice, the man would flee, surrender, or start shooting.

As if to prove her point, he described a slow casual turn, scanning the park until his eyes came to rest on Julia. She was about halfway down the path now, and closer to the Greenwich Street exit. Marching steadily forward, willing herself not to hurry, she watched him out of the corner of her eye, hand again clutching the Glock within her purse.

His eyes grew wider as she came, the look on his face describing a gradual transformation from composed to astonished. He spun on his heel when Julia turned to walk directly at him, then took off across the lawn toward the steps leading to the college.

"Police," Julia shouted as she broke into a run, "stop right there."

He didn't stop, but she hadn't expected him to obey. Her command had been issued for the benefit of the three joggers. They were on the west side of the park and she didn't want them to cross the path of the man she chased. She could also use them as witnesses to the fact that she'd properly identified herself and that her suspect had continued to flee, a possibility not lost on her as she sprinted across the lawn, all those hours of running finally yielding a payoff.

She was within thirty feet when he went up the concrete steps, within twenty when he hit the top step, but then she lost ground as he careened down the ramp leading out onto Chambers Street, plunging into the line of students packing the sidewalk.

"Police," Julia yelled as the kids turned toward her, "get out of the way."

Miraculously, after only a single repetition, they parted to allow her passage. Good news—except for the cab parked a few feet from the curb. Though Julia did her best to control her momentum, she hit the rear passenger's door hard enough to yelp. She didn't pause, however, to evaluate her injuries. Instead, she looked west, then east, until she saw him standing at the southeast corner of West and Chambers. The traffic on West Street's eight lanes was light but steady, moving along at sixty miles an hour. Crossing against the light would be the ultimate test of a New Yorker's jaywalking talents.

"Hey, lady, what you think you do to my cab, eh? You got insurance?"

"I'm a cop," Julia said without so much as glancing in the cabbie's direction. "Shut the fuck up and get back inside your vehicle."

She began to walk diagonally across Chambers Street, taking her time, waiting patiently for a stretch Mercedes turning onto Chambers from West Street to pass in front of her. Two blocks further west, where Chambers Street gave way to the Hudson River, then to New Jersey, an impossibly bright sun hovered just above the horizon. She resolved, if the opportunity presented itself, to put herself between that sun and her suspect. Then she shuddered, realizing how easily she'd adopted the role of the hunter. How she'd progressed from exhausted Julia Brennan, to Detective Julia Brennan, to Killer Brennan looking for an advantage, any advantage.

"Police," she called as she reached the sidewalk on the opposite side of Chambers Street. "Stay right where you are."

He smiled at her, drawing his lips back over his teeth, his expression feral, the proverbial trapped rat. Then he turned to run directly across West Street, and Julia braced herself for the incredulous scream of tires and brakes. Instead, the three closest vehicles, all cabbies, swerved only far enough to avoid an inconvenient accident, then continued on their way.

Julia looked to her right, at a van traveling in the lane closest to her. When it passed, she decided, she would make her move. From across the street, an adolescent male, his voice jumping several octaves in the excitement, shouted, "Go for it, bitch. Go for it." But the van didn't pass. Instead it slowed as the light changed to red, then came to a halt, blocking the crosswalk.

Infinitely grateful, Julia looked up at a darkening blue sky as she

skirted the van, thanking whatever deity resided in the heavens for
her good fortune. For a moment she'd actually contemplated letting
the bastard get away.

No, she told herself, sprinting forward, not really. I was perfectly
willing to risk being reduced to roadkill. Right?

The man turned left at the first intersection, directly opposite the
main entrance to Stuyvesant High School. There were no students
using the stainless-steel doors, the bulk of the student body having
already left by a second-floor exit that led onto the bridge. There was,
however, a uniformed cop leaning against a black marble pillar, smoking a cigarette. His expression revealing only the mildest curiosity, he
watched the man run by, then glanced over at Julia.

"I'm on the job," she shouted without breaking stride. "I'm a lieutenant. Get your ass in gear."

"But I'm *assigned* to this post." At least forty pounds overweight,
the cop's gut swelled beneath his coat, a watermelon that echoed the
thrust of his buttocks. Without doubt, his supervisor had assigned
him to the school because he wasn't fit for any other duty.

Julia made the turn without further comment, knowing the cop
would be more likely to follow if she didn't acknowledge his protest.
She found herself on a newly paved road divided by an island planted
with a box hedge. Her suspect was standing on the island, behind the
hedge, looking back. Before he could turn away, Julia stopped in her
tracks and raised her left hand.

"Hey," she said, trying not to gasp for breath, to keep her tone natural, "why are you running away? I just want to talk to you. What's
your name?"

To her surprise, he answered without hesitation. "My name is Hal
Townsend. In case you didn't know." Behind him, a red brick apartment building, under construction and topped with a crane, rose
twenty-five floors.

"Well Mr. Townsend, I'm Lieutenant Julia Brennan." Julia took
several steps forward, then stopped once more. "Where do you live?"

Before Townsend could respond, the uniformed cop lumbered up.
Julia stayed him with a glance, noting his name tag. "Watch him
closely, Burke," she whispered. "Most likely, he's armed."

"I think," Townsend said, "that you already know where I live."

"The Clapham?"

Townsend drew his lips over his teeth, smiling again. Then he walked across the street, to the sidewalk, before strolling away as if he had all the time in the world. Julia followed on the other side of the street, hoping that maybe Townsend had come to his senses, maybe he'd finally realized that he could not escape.

They continued on that way for several short blocks, until Townsend stopped on the other side of the street, just a few yards from the North Cove Yacht Harbor where road and sidewalk abruptly ended.

Julia said nothing for a moment, merely watching as Townsend brushed the outside of his coat pocket with his right hand. Without doubt, she decided, he's got a gun in there, a gun he's afraid to use.

"Can we talk about this?" she finally asked. To her left, Officer Burke's labored breath steamed from his mouth and nostrils. He was shifting his weight from foot to foot, his fingers resting lightly on the butt of his .38.

"What do you want me to say? That I'm sorry? Because I'm telling you, lieutenant, I have no regrets. The men I killed, not unlike myself, deserved to die."

The casual admission reminded Julia that she'd neglected to inform Townsend that he had a right to remain silent. Nevertheless, having no wish to confront him with the inevitable, she said, "Ya know something? I was just gonna bring up that very topic. About not being sorry."

"Were you?"

"Sure. Most New Yorkers think you're a hero. They don't have a problem with what you did. You come in, you'll get a fair deal."

Townsend's eyes widened in mock astonishment and his smile, this time, was genuine. He was back in control. "If it goes to a jury, do you think I'll be acquitted? Do you think my admiring peers will render a verdict of not guilty?"

"Uh-uh." Julia shook her head without taking her eyes off Townsend. "That's not the way to play it out. You gotta give the jury an excuse. You ask them to let you walk away, they're not gonna do it, not after the way you offed the Mandrakes. On the other hand, you plead not guilty by reason of mental defect, they'll take the easy out, send you off to the shrinks instead of the penitentiary. It'll make 'em feel good about themselves."

Townsend continued to stare at Julia for a moment, his expression relaxed; then he turned and walked to the marina. Dubbed the North Cove Yacht Harbor, the sheltered marina was packed with wintering vessels, from twenty-foot sailboats to seventy-foot yachts. Townsend halted, briefly, a yard from the prow of one of these yachts, the *Royal Princess*. The yacht was tied to cleats along the sea wall, the wall itself part of a concrete pier jutting into the Hudson.

Julia's first thought was that Townsend would leap aboard the yacht, somehow commandeer the boat, that an action-movie sea chase would follow. Instead, Townsend strolled to the end of the pier, to a low rail, then turned to face Julia. Behind him, a narrow crescent of cold sun poked above the horizon, while the heaving black waters of the Hudson, flecked with ice, seemed as thick as oil.

"Endgame," Townsend said. "Nowhere to go."

"True enough," Julia admitted. "You've definitely trapped yourself." She jammed her left hand into her pocket, hunched her shoulders. The wind here, with no intervening skyscrapers to absorb the shock, drilled into the exposed skin on her face. "There's something else, though, something you might help me out with."

"And what's that?"

"Well . . ." Julia smiled. "This is a little embarrassing, but I seem to have misplaced one of the detectives under my command. His name's Foley. You haven't seen him, have you?"

"Tall, kinda skinny guy? Real good-looking?"

"That's the one."

"Haven't laid eyes on him."

Julia tried to imagine some wedge she could use to pry Foley's whereabouts from Hal Townsend, some bribe that would tempt the man. But there was nothing; Townsend was in complete control. Nevertheless, she gave it a try. "Look, if you help us out with Detective Foley. I'll personally guarantee that you'll be assigned to a protective custody unit. There'll be no mingling with the population at Rikers. You'll have access to an attorney as well, and not some underfunded

jerk from Legal Aid. With your money, you can have any lawyer in the
city. Plus, there'll be all kinds of publicity. You're an articulate guy,
Hal. You play your cards right, you could be a star."

"The rest of my life," Townsend said, his voice now tinged with
resignation. "In prison. Or in some hellhole asylum for the criminally
insane, pumped full of whatever drug catches the attention of the
psychiatrist in charge. You know what it's like to be so disoriented all
you can do is sit in a chair with your tongue protruding and a line of
drool running all the way to your collar?"

"I'm afraid I don't."

"Well, I do, lieutenant. I've been down that road."

Julia nodded eagerly. "Then you know you'll be released at some
point, right? We're not talking about a life sentence."

"Did you say we? Somehow, I don't think you're ready to join me
on my grand adventure."

"A figure of speech. Look, about Detective Foley. Was he alive the
last time you saw him?"

"I believe I said that I've never met the man."

"C'mon, Townsend, what's it mean to you? Foley's just another
cop. He's not a child molester, not a monster."

"He tried to kill me."

"What?"

"And all I ever wanted was to be his friend."

With that, Hal Townsend vaulted to the top of the low railing
between himself and the Hudson River. He paused to secure his foot-
ing, then looked back at Julia, the triumphant expression on his face
at once as greedy as that of a suckling infant and as filled with
depraved knowledge as that of the oldest demon in hell. "It's better
this way," he said. "Don't you think?"

Julia took a step forward, then stopped. She tried to think of something to say, but quickly admitted that they were beyond words. Her
hand tightened on the Glock in her purse. If she shot him, maybe
he'd fall forward, maybe he'd survive, maybe somewhere down the
line he'd tell her where to find Peter Foley. Then it was over. Then Hal
Townsend leapt backward, his eyes still riveted to Julia's, and crashed
through the ice, vanishing instantly and forever.

Next to her, his tone speculative, Patrolman Burke asked, "Lieutenant, you think it's our bounden duty to jump in after him?"

"You first," she responded, pulling her cell phone from her pocket. "I'll call in the cavalry."

"That's a joke, right?"

"Yeah, Burke, it's a fucking joke."

50

FOLEY DIDN'T become aware of the cold until he'd removed his T-shirt and begun to cut it into vertical strips with a small pocket knife, until he'd actually begun to shiver. Then he put the knife, which he carefully folded, and the T-shirt to one side before retrieving his shoulder rig and his outer garments. He could see nothing, not even the pullover rugby shirt as it slid across his face. There was no sense of dark, then darker. There was nothing at all.

It was enough, he decided as the pain in his thigh forced him to pause, to make a fella want to just give up.

In addition to everything else, Foley was very tired. He felt that if he closed his eyes, he would become instantly free of all discomfort, physical and psychological. But he did not close his eyes, and not for any reason he could name. There was something within him, a stranger he would not have acknowledged even an hour before, a stranger now running the show. This stranger had no interest in Foley's personal history. He just wanted to live.

It took Foley some time to work his way into his shirt and coat, and to stop shivering. He didn't know exactly how long because his sense of time was distorted by the absence of light and the need to rely solely on the sense of touch. He was lying on his back, staring at the flat black nothing in front of his eyes. Eventually, he knew, he'd have to crawl off in search of a splint. Eventually he'd have to sit up to secure the splint to his thigh. Eventually he'd have to rise to his feet, find a crutch, explore his new world.

As Foley felt for his knife and T-shirt, he resolved to not consider eventualities of any kind. He saw no reason to plan a next step which depended entirely on what he accomplished in the here and now. That message was driven home when he dropped his knife with the blade half open, nicking his finger, causing him to jerk away, causing the fire in his leg. . . .

He cried out, then was instantly angry. Just do this, he told himself: Find the knife, find the T-shirt, cut the strips. He repeated the message as he went about the task, a little mantra. Find the knife, find the T-shirt, cut the strips.

When Foley finished, he stuffed the strips into his pocket, then took a moment to plot the next step. What remained of the stairs lay in a heap directly behind him. In order to get to them he would have to turn onto his left side and pull himself along until he found a suitable length of wood to make a splint, perhaps one of the balusters. The important thing was to crawl in the right direction. He'd seen enough of the room before dropping his flashlight to know the space was enormous. If he lost his bearings, he'd be crawling for the better part of forever.

But he had it right. The stairs were only a few yards away and he covered the ground quickly, lying on his left side, pulling alternately with his arms and his hips. With his right thigh elevated, he barely felt the press of his bones, and he thought that a good sign until he finally rose to a sitting position, cut a slit in his pant leg, touched his own flesh. The skin was trampoline tight, the leg so swollen it was acting as its own splint.

He ran his fingers back and forth over his thigh, from his knee to his hip, wondering if the swelling had stopped or if his leg would stretch to the bursting point, then explode like a popped balloon. But that wasn't really the problem, though Foley didn't even suspect the truth. Foley thought his leg was filling with the sort of clear fluid common to sprained ankles and torn ligaments. In fact, his leg was filling with blood.

Loss of blood accounted for his exhaustion, and for an inability to focus that had him lying on his side, lazily running his hand over his thigh as if he hadn't a care in the world. Time passed, a minute, then another, then five, before he summoned the will to move on. Before he told himself that he would have to splint the leg, swelling or not, that the pressure of a splint would hold the swelling down, that even if the goddamned leg exploded the rest of him wanted to survive.

Foley located a length of wood, a baluster, as he'd hoped. He worked the baluster back and forth, each swing producing a pain sharp enough to keep him thoroughly awake, until it broke free of the railing. As he'd expected, the inch-thick plank of common pine was too long, and he rolled onto his back, raised his left knee into his chest, and settled the plank beneath his foot. He did all this by touch, and quite deliberately, so that when he pulled back hard, the board snapped in half on the first try while the anticipated explosion of pain was manageable, perhaps even, in the long run, bearable.

Wrong again. By the time Foley finished splinting his leg, any hope that his swollen thigh was shielding him from the worst of the pain had been thoroughly dispelled. He'd played it smart, tied small loops into one end of the cotton strips, then used the loops to pull the strips tight. It was a technique he'd learned moving furniture one summer in high school. You could draw a burlap strap tight enough, using that knot, to crush the box you were tying. You could crush human flesh as well, until your body was slick with sweat, until you realized that the scream echoing through the empty space was your own.

Finally, Peter Foley lay back and simply waited, not counting the seconds or minutes, while the pain gradually diminished. It was a peaceful time, actually, even as the sweat dried and the cold threatened to crawl into his bones, a time in which death presented itself to Foley as a distinct presence with a short, sharp message: You can die here and it will be all right.

Foley tried to move, to roll onto his side, but stopped when his thigh flared. The effort, he decided, to get over here, splint the leg, all wasted. Now what?

Another few minutes passed before Foley admitted that there was no contingency plan. There was only get up on your feet and find a way out. So he did it. Crawling as he had before, he located a broken section of the railing long enough to act as a cane, then used the cane and the rubble to pull himself to a kneeling position, with his weight resting entirely on his left leg. He tried to lever himself up from there using only his arms, but his grip on the cane, a two-inch pine board, was too uncertain. He was going to have to put weight on his right leg, there was no getting around it. And no getting around the likelihood that if he fell he might not be able to rise again.

So he absorbed the pain, realizing only after he was standing on his left foot that it was less than he expected. Encouraging news as he considered the immensity of the task before him. First, he would have to explore the area of the wall from which the stairway fell. More than likely, the stairs had been bolted to the wall. If Townsend had done nothing more than remove the nuts and slide the stairway out, if the bolts were still embedded in the wall, if they extended far enough to offer a purchase, he might use them to climb up. If not, he would have to trace a circuit of the room, perhaps with his right shoulder against the wall. He'd seen enough of the space before his flashlight went out to know it was smaller than the building. Maybe there was another room, maybe there was an intact set of stairs in that room, maybe there was a door into that room.

Maybe, maybe, maybe. If, if, if.

He found the bolts where he expected them to be, protruding a couple of inches from the wall, less than half the span of his hand. Even with both legs, he might not be able to make it all the way up. As it was, unwilling to risk a fall, he didn't dare begin. So it was off into unknown territory, the darkness beyond the darkness. Foley felt almost euphoric as he took that first hopping step, then the next, then the next. He was bracing himself against the wall with his right hand, holding the impromptu cane with his left, finding all this so much easier than he expected that he nearly burst out laughing.

Without sight, he couldn't really know how far or fast he was going.

But he was certain that he was making progress, moving right along, and that he wasn't about to give up. Not him, not Peter Foley, who was responsible for hundreds of arrests, who flew invisible through cyberspace in search of villains.

You've got a mission in life, he declared to himself as he hopped along, to warn Julia Brennan of the danger to her daughter. And by God you're gonna do it.

Of course, it might already be too late. It might be hours since Townsend disappeared. But that didn't get Foley off the hook. He was still obligated to go forward, hopping like a crippled rabbit, until he found a way out or collapsed.

That was how he saw it, find a way out or collapse, as if there were no other possibilities. But in fact there was another eventuality lurking in the shadows and Peter Foley found it a few minutes later when he braced himself against the wall with his right hand, took a little jump, and landed on a D-cell battery. Totally unprepared, his leg rolled up while he flailed away at the darkness with both hands, maintaining his equilibrium for the space of a few heartbeats. Then he fell over, straight back and down, managing to absorb only a bit of the force with his shoulders before the back of his head smashed into the concrete floor.

When he awakened, a minute or an hour or a day later, he found himself unable (or was that unwilling?) to rise. He wiggled the toes on his left foot. They seemed to behave, but how could he be certain without seeing them in action? Didn't paraplegics suffer phantom pain in limbs supposedly without sensation? Maybe the same thing was happening here.

Suddenly he realized that his right leg was transmitting a constant signal, sharp and fiery, that proved his spinal cord was very much intact. He reflected on this for a moment, wondering why it had taken him so long to recognize the obvious, then felt a little surge of pleasure, a faint, though definite relief. Because the pain was now far away, as if the Peter Foley who recognized the pain had divorced himself from the hapless, pitiful jerk who actually had to feel it.

No more pain, he said to himself without considering any of the implications, never again pain. Hurrah.

From there, his thoughts drifted to Julia Brennan and her daughter, then to his wife, Kirstin, and his own daughter, Patti. But they were gone as well, as irrelevant as his regrets. What could he do for them? What could they do for him? Bestow their forgiveness? That was no longer possible. If forgiveness was to be forthcoming at this point, he would have to forgive himself. There was no one else to do it.

Satisfied with this bottom line, he drifted for a while, aware of a consuming thirst and a penetrating cold that seemed no more real than the throbbing of his leg. Various thoughts and images flicked through his mind, but nothing stuck until he finally settled on one of those early memories that recur from time to time in the course of a life. Foley is seventeen, a junior at Holy Cross High School, and he and his dad are in the back yard of their Flushing home. They have gone out to play catch on a hot August evening, a ritual they perform whenever the weather and his father's policeman schedule permit.

At this stage in his life, Peter Foley, star pitcher for his high school and Police Athletic League teams, fancies himself quite the athlete. His father is also a fair athlete, a catcher by trade who still plays for an NYPD baseball team, though no longer behind the plate.

As Pete sets up on a makeshift pitching mound, he is acutely aware of his father's growing (though unexpressed) reluctance to handle Peter's best pitches. Peter has reached his full growth, standing two-and-a-half inches above six feet. He throws a two-seam rising fastball already clocked in the high eighties, and a four-seamer that crowds right-handed batters. Pete wants to learn to throw a curve and a slider, but his father believes that at seventeen Pete's joints are not strong enough to withstand the sharp twist necessary to get the proper rotation on the ball. So what Pete's done, without telling his father, is practice a split-finger fastball that dives for the dirt like a soldier at the whine of an incoming artillery shell.

Pete warms up slowly, allowing his arm to come through the pitching zone almost on its own, stretching the muscles in his neck and back. He is waiting for the point at which every muscle on his right side, from the tips of his fingers down into his legs, will lock into place, a single unit unfolding like the coils of a snake when he strides toward the plate.

"You up for a few hard ones, dad?" Pete asks when he's ready.

What can the poor man say? Dick Foley who put a baseball in Pete's hand fifteen years before, who demanded over the years that his son throw harder and harder and harder. "Yeah," he replies, setting up knee-high on the outside corner of the plate. "Fine."

The first few pitches crack into Dick Foley's glove, as loud and urgent as the report of the S&W .38 he routinely carries. He winces with each pitch and Pete notices this even through the bars of the catcher's mask. For reasons entirely unknown to him, reasons he refuses to consider, Pete enjoys his father's humiliation. His goal is complete dominance. His goal is to make his father quit.

Pete slows down as they continue, concentrating for a time on his four-seam fastball which for some reason has stopped breaking to the right. He works through the mechanics, varying release points in search of the problem, until his T-shirt and shorts are heavy with sweat and he has to go to the resin bag after every pitch. Then he kicks at the dirt in front of the rubber and says, "Wanna try one more?"

"Why not?"

Pete hides the ball in his glove before assuming the split-finger grip, but alters no other part of his delivery. The whole point of the split-finger is to fool the batter into thinking it's an ordinary fastball, to leave the batter unprepared for its sudden downward break. The catcher, on the other hand, having called for the pitch, is totally prepared. Ordinarily.

Dick Foley's glove is still knee-high, has in fact not moved an inch, when the ball catches the edge of the plate and ricochets into his crotch. He doubles over in pain, despite the cup he wears, then pulls off his mask and begins to vomit onto the grass. He and his son never return to the back yard.

Now, in the darkness, though Foley's lips move, his plea is soundless. "Forgive me." He tries again, this time managing a whisper. "Forgive me." Then, finally, he sleeps.

Foley's sleep is so peaceful that when he awakens to a light that seems to come from every place and no place, he does not open his eyes. He feels as if the light has nothing to do with his retina or his pupils, or the neurons deep in his brain. He cannot summon the will to move any part of his body, and he is no longer cold or in pain.

Again, he senses the presence of death, hovering over him, waiting. But not that spectral creature wielding his scythe, not the grim reaper. No, Foley senses the presence of a being infinitely more patient, infinitely more tender. He wants to go to this being, suddenly convinced that he has yearned all his life to rest within its embrace, that everything he's ever wanted or needed was no more than an expression of that yearning.

From a great distance, Foley hears a voice. He believes at first that he's been called, that he's been directed to those enfolding arms. But when the voice sounds again, he hears the words clearly and knows, without doubt, that he was not addressed by a patron saint or a guardian angel, and certainly not by the Creator of all the many worlds. No, there was something about heaven that precluded the insistent message expressed now for the third time.

"Yo, Goober, you still breathin' down there?"

51

THE FUNERAL mass was held at Holy Savior Church on a warm Tuesday in the middle of March. Julia sat in the first row of pews, Corry and Robert Reid to her left. Spread out behind her and on the other side of the aisle were Serrano, Lane, Turro, and Griffith, along with their families. Linus Flannery, Harry Clark, and a small entourage of ranking officers unknown to Julia filled the last two pews at the rear of the church.

The mass was conducted in Latin, as were all the masses at Holy Savior. Julia would have been lost, as she'd been on her prior visit, if not for Peter Foley, who'd supplied her with a missal that included a translation of the Latin chanted by Father Lucienne. Foley sat to Julia's right, his ankle-to-hip plaster cast thrust into the aisle. Though Foley's expression didn't change, from time to time he used both hands to adjust the position of his injured leg.

"Agnus Dei, qui tollis peccata mundi, dona eis requiem."

Lamb of God who takest away the sins of the world, give unto them rest.

Julia looked up at Anja Dascalescu's white coffin, thinking, Yes, please, give her rest. For the prior two months, Anja had been laying on a slab in the morgue while a fruitless effort was made to locate her family in Romania. The information in her INS file (as well as that in the business records of Pancevski and Markovic) was pure fiction, the address of the orphanage from which she'd supposedly been adopted an empty lot on the outskirts of Bucharest. The media in Romania had been no help, either. Though Anja's story had been covered in great detail almost from the day she'd been identified, for some inexplicable reason no one had come forward to admit that a child had been sold into slavery.

Julia watched Father Lucienne raise the Host, then glanced at Corry. She was watching the priest intently, her mouth slightly open, lips parted. It was the same expression she'd worn on the night Julia introduced her to Peter Foley. Foley was lying in a hospital bed at the time, his leg imprisoned in a steel cage that looked like an instrument of medieval torture. Despite the pain, the blood loss, and his thoroughly vulnerable position, the man had retained his confidence and his charisma, not to mention his good looks. "Awesome," was the way Corry had put it on the way home.

Julia did not take communion, though she helped Foley stand while he arranged his crutches beneath his arms. She was still on her feet when Linus Flannery and Harry Clark passed on their way to the communion rail. They wore similar disapproving expressions that reminded Julia of the nuns who'd ruled the classrooms of her childhood. Julia was a member of the Holy Name Society and there could be no good reason for her not to take communion.

A smile rose to Julia's lips as she sat down next to her daughter. More than likely Flannery and Clark believed that she'd finally been brought under control when she accepted an assignment to the Sex Crimes Unit. But the blessing of the high command hadn't played any part in her decision to join Lily Han in the DA's office. Her first impulse had been to not only refuse the assignment but her promotion to captain as well. As a captain her duties would become purely administrative when she wanted, more than anything else, to stay on the front lines. At some point between the discovery of Anja's body and the suicide of Hal Townsend, the joy of the hunt had invaded her very bones, as penetrating and persistent as a dose of radiation.

Too bad that joy hadn't overridden her ambition. A captain's bars, the extra twenty grand a year, the potential for a promotion down the line? In the end she'd decided to not only have her cake and eat it too, but also to bake the damn thing. The investigative arm of the Sex Crimes Unit included only fifteen detectives, small enough to allow her to remain personally involved in individual cases. Prior to Julia's appointment it had been supervised by a lieutenant named Roth-kovich, whose hands-off managerial style had resulted in chaos. Julia was being sent over, along with her captain's bars, in response to a series of blistering complaints from District Attorney Robert Morgen-thau, a man who tolerated no slackers and had the ear of the mayor.

"Anybody you want out," Harry Clark had told her, "you let me know and I'll see they're gone by the next morning. Same if you want somebody transferred in. Just let me know."

Six detectives were gone within the first week, another two by the end of the following week. The remaining seven had come to her office and promised eternal fidelity, not to mention their best efforts, if allowed to remain. In the meantime, the incoming replacements, including Bert Griffith, David Lane, and Carlos Serrano, had been told, on arrival, to produce or else.

Bottom line, the unit was her creation and she would be able to personally involve herself in any investigation. She would be the alpha wolf. She would run the pack.

PETER FOLEY stood to receive communion, bending forward as far as he could while the much shorter Father Lucienne rose up on his toes in order to place the Host on Foley's tongue. Afterward, as Father Lucienne turned to Frank Turro who was kneeling at the altar rail, Foley remained standing long enough to allow the Host to soften. He looked directly at Anja Dascalescu's coffin and felt, not sorrow, but an intense gratitude.

Foley was grateful for a number of things. He was grateful for being alive and for wanting to be alive. He was grateful to no longer be a cop. He was grateful for the assurance of his doctors that he would eventually walk without a limp. He was grateful most of all for Julia Brennan, for the simple fact that he loved her, for being able to love at all.

"You need a hand?"

Jolted out of his reverie, Foley turned to Frank Turro who stood to his left. "Just thinking," he said as he executed a clumsy U-turn, then headed back to his seat. As he eased himself into the pew, Julia looked up and smiled. "You okay?" she asked.

"Never better."

Julia reached over to squeeze his hand, propelling Foley back to that moment when he'd awakened after three blood transfusions and four hours of surgery to find her sitting alongside the bed. She'd been holding his hand, her eyes closed, her mouth open, her breath ragged in the back of her throat. Utterly beautiful.

Two days later they'd exchanged confidences, Julia admitting that his rescue had not come about through any sudden insight on her part. Instead, Robert Reid had finally recovered his last thoughts before leaving his car, then called Julia on her cell phone. She'd been in the principal's office at Stuyvesant High School, some three hours after Hal Townsend took the plunge, trying to explain things to Corry.

For his part, Foley had revealed the primary reason he could hand over his badge without hesitation. Shortly after Patti's disappearance, when the extent of the negligence at the Little Kitty Day Care Center came to light, he and his wife had begun a lawsuit that eventually resulted in a two-million-dollar settlement. Kirstin had insisted on filing the suit and Peter Foley had gone along because he knew his wife needed someone to blame, someone besides herself. The irony was that she'd committed suicide a week after the settlement check found its way to their mailbox.

Foley struggled through Father Lucienne's eulogy, adjusting the position of his leg every few minutes. When Doctor Goodwin predicted that his patient would recover fully, she'd quickly added a single qualification: "Provided you follow through with your rehab." Later, a physical therapist had elaborated, "A high threshold for pain," he'd flatly declared, "is a good predictor of results with injuries of this kind."

At times it felt as if his bones had re-separated and were boring multiple tunnels through his flesh, especially when he kept his leg in one position for an extended period. Like right now.

Foley rose as soon as the mass ended, before the coffin was removed. The pain was manageable when he was active, and he wanted to walk around outside before the trip to the cemetery. Thus, his mind was on other things when Julia opened the door and he stepped into a warm breeze that closed around his body as if staking a claim.

The seasons had rolled over, a turning of the dice that had come up seven for Peter Foley. His aims had not changed. He was still Goober in the chat rooms and he was in the process of opening a new website. The game, of course, was riskier now that he'd surrendered his law enforcement cover, but that was all right, too. And it was apparently all right with Julia Brennan who knew all and said nothing, who was satisfied even with the clumsy sex mandated by a cast that weighed thirty pounds.

Foley watched Linus Flannery, trailed by Harry Clark and the flunkies, come up to shake Julia's hand, then walk to their vehicles without so much as a glance in his direction. The slight left him grinning. He knew that he was nothing in their world, the only world they acknowledged, the world to which Julia Brennan aspired. By shaking her hand, they'd pronounced her worthy of those aspirations, the gesture as solemn as the ceremony of knighthood.

He wondered if they had any sense of Julia's other side, of her need to break free of restraint, to right the wrongs of the world. Maybe they thought her prior failures were a momentary aberration brought on by a misplaced sympathy for the victim, that in the long run she could be controlled. Or maybe they were simply cowed by her clear intelligence and her hero's status in the eyes of the public.

Carefully balancing his weight on the crutch beneath his left arm, Foley put his right arm around Julia's shoulders. He knew, because she'd told him, that her future, when she examined it, was as impenetrable as the dark in Empire Steel's sub-basement. There would be any number of "paths less taken" branching off from her career path in the years ahead, and any number of choices to make. With luck, he'd be there to watch her make them.

*   *   *

WHEN ANJA Dascalescu's coffin was lowered into the ground, Corry broke into tears. A moment later, Betty Turro and Irena Serrano joined her. The cops did not cry. The stood in a semicircle before the grave, separated from their families, shoulder to shoulder. They'd done all that a cop can do for Anja. They'd punished the men responsible for her death and they'd put a name on her tombstone. Nothing more could be asked of them.

They'd moved on, as well. David Lane had put away a pair of murderers in the two months since the discovery of Anja's body. Frank Turro had been transferred to Internal Affairs, a reward, perhaps, for being Commander Harry Clark's snitch. Julia herself had been up and running for the last three weeks. Along with detectives from Bronx Homicide, the Sex Crimes Unit was in pursuit of a serial rapist whose escalating violence had resulted in his last victim being tossed from the roof of a six-story tenement. There was no doubt in anybody's mind that if not stopped he would kill again.

Finally, Julia stepped back, away from her peers, to drape an arm around Corry's shoulder. "C'mon, honey," she said, "it's time to go."

Corry withdrew her hand from Robert Reid's and pointed to the open grave, to the dirt heaped beside it. "How can we leave her like that?"

What could Julia say? That Anja Dascalescu was up in heaven with God and the angels? Even if she believed that, and she wasn't sure she did, it would sound laughably trite. On the other hand, if she said what she did believe, that unlike a thief or even a rapist, a murderer takes everything, the future, the past, hope itself, Corry would be crying for the next two weeks.

What a cop does, Julia told herself as she steered Corry away from Anja Dascalescu's grave, is pick up one foot and move it forward, then pick up the other, then repeat the process, over and over. In that respect, policing had a lot in common with motherhood. When you gave birth, when you looked at your daughter for the first time, you had no idea how her life would play out. So you kept on going. You kept on going and you lived your life on the journey, wondering what would come next.